Chronicles of Charanthe #1

REBELLION

Rachel Cotterill

Published in the United Kingdom by Rachel Cotterill.

A CIP catalogue record for this book is available from the British Library.

ISBN 978-1-910331-00-2

4 6 8 10 9 7 5 3

Cover art by Jessica Soria Gázquez.
Typeset in Gentium.

Also by Rachel Cotterill:

<u>Chronicles of Charanthe</u>

Rebellion

Revolution

Reformation

<u>Novels of the Twelve Baronies</u>

The Golden Elixir

<u>Recipe Books</u>

Design Your Own Cookies

Visit Rachel's website at

http://www.rachelcotterill.com

for future release dates & offers

Prologue

His attention was caught by the snapping of a twig down in the valley. Laban held himself still, forcing even his breathing to silence, and turned his eyes to follow the sound. The disturbance came not a moment too soon; he'd been starting to doubt the quality of his informants.

It was a few moments before the girl emerged from the dense cover of the trees. She walked barefoot up the slope, a purposeful look on her face, and though she looked up she didn't seem to see him hidden between the branches. She was a thin child, short for her thirteen years, with stunning red hair which flowed down her back. She looked so like her mother.

She came blinking into the sunlight, paused for a moment, then seated herself cross-legged on the ground. Now she was closer, he could see she'd been crying.

He'd been thinking for so long about what he'd say when he met her but now she was here, tearful and intense and real, he felt everything he'd rehearsed slipping away from him. Nothing in his thirty-one years had really prepared him for this.

She pulled a slate from her pocket and began scratching something; Laban couldn't make out what she wrote but she'd fallen into an intense concentration, stylus moving rapidly across the slate as she worked.

He lowered himself from his perch, slipping silently to the ground, and took two small steps towards her. He knew he'd made very little sound – certainly nothing that couldn't have been attributed to the shuffling of a small creature or the gusting of a summer breeze – but she stopped writing and looked straight up at him, fixing him with the penetrating stare of those bright green eyes.

"Excuse me," he said, aiming a small bow in her direction. He watched the battle between fear and curiosity play across her face. He knew this was the most important moment, in a way, and it was out of his control – if she was too scared to be intrigued, there would be no sense in persisting. Yet he badly wanted her to pass this first test.

"Who are you?" she asked at last.

He breathed a silent sigh of relief, but he couldn't yet afford to relax. "My name's Laban. I'm sorry to disturb you, I was just going home." He took another couple of steps towards the rock face, tucked his fingers into familiar crevices, and started to climb.

Her incredulous voice interrupted him. "You live here?"

"Yes. Well, almost – just on the other side of the hill."

"You can't." The flat certainty of her tone amused him; she had a typical child's arrogance. "I've been up – it's just a cliff. You can't live there."

"Well, I do," he said, and continued to climb.

Once his fingers reached the sharp ridge of the summit he decided it was time to show off, so with one smooth movement he somersaulted over the ridge and dropped comfortably onto the rock ledge some ten feet below. He moved just far enough inside the cave to be sure that he was no longer visible from the hilltop and paused; waiting, listening. It was only a moment before his ears picked up the sounds he was hoping for – the echo of someone clambering up the rocks.

She was bold enough to follow him, then. That boded well.

PART I

Chapter 1

The hall fell silent at the headmistress's entrance, but all eyes were on the man who followed two steps behind her. The Imperial Assessors were the only men who ever visited Mersioc Regional School for Girls, and this one looked particularly austere in his formal grey tunic. He was carrying a large box of what could only be their assignments, and the girls craned their necks as if there was a chance they could glimpse the contents of the letters. The rivets on the Assessor's boots caused his footsteps to click, echoing into the rafters as Isabelle led him onto the stage at the front of the room.

"Good morning, girls," Isabelle said warmly. "And congratulations to you all on your Day of Assignment. You've been my charges for seventeen years, but today you become adults. I'm sure you're all looking forwards to learning what your future lives will hold."

"Are you excited yet?" Gisele whispered to Eleanor.

Eleanor shrugged, trying not to show any particular emotion for fear that the whole of what she was feeling would flood out.

"We'll see what happens," she said. The assignments had already been made, the letters already written; it was too late to change anything now. That knowledge didn't comfort her.

Annette leaned across, twirling one of her blonde ringlets idly in her fingers. "Oh, but we all know you're going to get something great. You've always been so good at all the physical stuff, *and* you're clever, you're bound to get something exciting."

Gisele nodded. "I know you don't want to let yourself think too much about the Specials," she said, "but there are loads of good opportunities for someone like you, even outside of the military."

"Well, we all know it'll be a mistake if they don't give me a place in the Special Corps," Eleanor said. But despite her confident words, her nerves made her feel sick to her stomach.

"There's a letter here for each of you," Isabelle continued from the front of the room, holding up one example. It was carefully folded and sealed with the Imperial crest. "And inside you will find details of your future career in the Imperial Service. But before we begin, I'm sure our honoured guest has a few words to say about the process."

"Indeed, indeed," the Assessor agreed. "In a moment I'll read out your names, and you may each come forwards in turn to receive your assignment. For some of you, there will be extra training at special academies; for others, any new skills you require will be learnt on the job. The details are all in your letter, along with your new address – which could, of course, be anywhere in Charanthe. It should all be self-explanatory, but I'll be here all day to represent the College of Assessors if you have questions."

Isabelle thanked him and turned back to the students. "As you must surely realise, over the past seventeen years a lot of effort has gone into matching each of you with your most productive future path, so I hope you will join me in extending heartfelt thanks to the Assessors for their work."

The girls all clapped politely.

"And now," she beamed, "our honoured guest will call for each of you in turn. When you hear your name, please come and collect your letter and leave the hall *quietly*. We have a lot to get through this morning."

The Assessor nodded, and picked up the first letter. The girls cast nervous glances at one other as they waited, but no-one dared speak as the Assessor read the names and identification numbers from each letter in turn.

Almost half of the girls had already gone by the time Eleanor was called. Feeling a little dazed, struggling to believe that this was really happening at last, she got to her feet and walked towards the front of the hall. The Assessor nodded as he handed her the letter, and she managed a weak smile back at him before turning to leave the room.

Pushing her way through the crowd who had thronged

around the corridor, who were swapping notes and giggling excitedly, Eleanor found her way outdoors at last. She wanted to be alone for this, and that left only one place she could go.

She stuffed the letter unopened into her pocket and slipped between the school buildings, making her way to the edge of the forest which bounded the school playing fields. There was no shortage of rumours about terrible things lurking in the darker reaches of the forest but Eleanor had taken refuge between the trees since she was about six years old, taking advantage of her classmates' fears to buy herself a little privacy. Even now they were older, most of the girls wouldn't venture beyond the first few trees.

Eleanor kicked off her shoes. Other than the occasional disturbance of a stone or beech-nut, the ground was comfortable underfoot; a thick mat of many years' fallen leaves covered the earth, slowly decaying into a soft mulch. She picked a familiar path between the trunks, winding her way up the steep hillside. She tried to make sure she varied her route from day to day, not wanting to create an obvious track, but her destination was always the same.

The walk felt longer than usual today, with the assignment letter weighing heavily on her mind, but eventually the trees began to thin and she came to the rocky outcrop – bare apart from a smattering of moss and lichen – which formed the top of the hill. The closest semblance of a walkable path from here was a long, winding route which would have taken far too long to negotiate, so Eleanor chose as she usually did: a direct climb was both more efficient and more fun.

As she scrambled up the rocks she remembered the first time she'd climbed this way as a girl; although she'd already been a moderately accomplished climber, she hadn't made that first ascent with the effortlessness she now managed. After four years of practice, her fingers knew every crevice.

Her mind was full of memories as she clambered over the peak of the rock, and down a slight slope on the other side until she was standing right at the edge of a deep, narrow gorge. It was barely five yards across, but the near-vertical rock ran much further down than that. A fast-flowing river filled all the floor of the gulley below.

With a quick glance behind her – it was a firmly ingrained habit to make sure she hadn't been followed before proceeding from here – she put her hands to the ground and lowered herself over the edge. Hanging by her fingertips, she allowed herself to drop, and landed smoothly a few feet below. Although the ledge was barely visible from above, she'd done this often enough now to feel comfortable with the routine. The platform on which she now stood extended back into the rock, forming a natural cave where she'd spent a great deal of her time over the past few years.

Whatever the weather outside, the cave was always cool and dark; even today's midsummer sun barely filtered inside. She kept a box of candles here and she lit one now, looking around in the flickering light. Everything was exactly as she'd left it. The target board on the wall to her left hung at its usual tilt, and there wasn't a single new crease in the pile of blankets and cushions which formed a makeshift bed against the opposite wall.

Today more than usual, she felt a deep disappointment that nothing had changed, that the cave was still abandoned, that he hadn't returned.

She pulled out the small throwing knife which she kept hidden beneath her clothes and flicked it towards the target, a familiar shot which she always executed perfectly. Today, however, the anxiety affected her aim and she missed the bullseye.

She knew it was irrational, but she'd hoped Laban might have come to wish her luck. She'd never stopped thinking of this as his cave, though he'd left eighteen months before, without so much as a note to explain. He'd taken all his possessions except for the knife, which she now carried everywhere.

She'd always wondered whether he'd return one day, but time was running out now.

She retrieved the knife, took a moment to focus her attention, and repeated the shot. This time, she hit the target perfectly – yes, she had talent, there was no doubt about that. Now it was time to find out where it was leading.

She sat on the edge of the pallet, pulled the letter from her pocket and slid her knife along to break the seal. She smoothed the paper carefully against her leg without allowing her eyes to focus on the words.

Only then, after a few deep breaths, did she pick up the candle and permit herself to read the first line of the letter.

Assignment: Police Officer, Level Three, Port Just.

Waves of bitter disappointment washed over her. She'd hoped against hope for the Military Special Corps – although, she admonished herself, it had been stupid to let herself get too attached to the idea, when she'd known all along that the odds were stacked against her. The recruitment for the Specials was only about fifty students per year from across the whole archipelago, and since she knew little of the hundreds of other schools across the Empire, she'd always known there was no guarantee of getting her dream. But this – a job in the local police force, not even a posting to the capital – was just insulting.

Eleanor longed for the bright lights of the city. Though she'd lived in the school all her life, the stories of Almont had an irresistible allure, and she'd just assumed that she'd be going there whatever the actual assignment had been. She'd also assumed that she'd get a Level One job, with further training and scope to progress over the years: she was undoubtedly the best in the school when it came to the physical arts. How could they overlook her talents like this?

She looked at the sheet of paper again, vainly hoping that it might have changed when she re-read it. But the words were still there in black and white: still the same; still depressing.

She flung her knife towards the target again and glowered at the quivering hilt; how could she possibly be expected to abandon all her skills and join the police? It wasn't as though Port Just was a hotbed of criminal activity, and they hadn't had a rebel disruption in years. She could almost see the lifetime of boredom stretching ahead of her. She was skilled to handle more than a little drunken rowdiness.

She settled back onto the bed and skimmed the remaining paragraphs of the assignment notice. Key phrases leapt out at her, each one feeling like a knife between the eyes. *A small role maintaining local order... No further training necessary... No need for the Assignee to encounter real responsibility... No opportunity for transfer to other locations...*

But the last line was arguably the worst of all, reading like the punchline to a horrible joke: *This assignment has been assessed to be the best fit for your known personality and skills.*

Eleanor wanted to scream. It was as though the letter had been written for someone else, or worse, as if it had been phrased specifically to annoy her every time she looked at it.

"And what about my unknown skills?" she yelled, shaking the sheet of paper as though it was to blame for the words so neatly inscribed there.

She flopped onto her back, watching the shadows flickering across the roof of the cave and wondering how long it would take before she could face her friends and pretend to be appropriately delighted by her assignment. No other emotion would be acceptable on a day like this, but she couldn't stop wondering how the Assessors could have got her assignment so wrong. The system was supposed to be perfect; it wasn't in anyone's interests to make mistakes. The whole functioning of the Empire was predicated on the assumption that everyone could be found a suitable job, and that people would work harder and be more productive if they were appropriately matched to their work. The lifelong testing and profiling measured every student's strengths and weaknesses to allow the Assessors to work out exactly what best suited a person. So why would they have given her something so very far from what she was capable of? Eleanor just couldn't believe that the best fit, for her, was to join the police force in a small provincial town.

She shuffled to try and get comfortable, but something hard was pressing painfully into the small of her back. Feeling behind her, she found a book half-buried in the blankets. She didn't remember leaving any books here, so she pulled it out and flipped curiously to the title page. *Stories of the Assassins: An Analysis of the Myths*, it said. It was marked as a school library book but she didn't remember taking it out; she certainly hadn't read it.

She flicked through the first few pages, hoping it might help to take her mind off her horrible assignment, but she just caught herself wishing she could have that kind of excitement in her life. Though the Empire had never quite denied the existence of an elite assassin cadre, facts were hard to come by. What survived was a mix of rumours and legends which were usually impossible, and often self-contradictory. A bit of diverting nonsense, nothing more. Yet, dredged up now from the back of her mind, the one story which really stood out in Eleanor's memory was that of the selection process. She remembered it just as Gisele had told it one night, up in the dormitory after lights-out, many years previously.

"Becoming an assassin is the hardest part of the job, you know," she had said in hushed, awed tones. "I heard one of the girls from our school tried, just one, just once, but she failed... ooh, it sounded awful! Blood everywhere. They took her eyes out first and then, once she couldn't see to fight her way out of trouble, they slit her throat. Left her like that in the fountain in the Grand Square in Almont for everyone to see. Can you believe it? But the stupid thing – the really crazy thing – is that she could have been a nurse. That's what her assignment said. But they say that's how it always is, they can't write *Assassin* on your letter, so they put something else, and you just have to know, somehow, if it's meant to be you..." Gisele had continued for quite some time, and they'd all talked well into the night about the trials and troubles of would-be assassins, swapping stories and trying to scare one another with tales of blood and gore.

Recalling the story now, Eleanor was mildly surprised to find herself wishing for there to be truth in the tale, wishing that it could apply to her, wishing that she could magically *know* that she was supposed to head off in search of some secret training academy instead of becoming a boring police officer. She shook her head gently, amazed that she'd let herself get so carried away by childhood stories. Being a mysterious assassin sounded much more appealing than some dull police job – but it was just a fairy tale. Nevertheless, she skipped to the relevant part of the book, where a very similar story was laid down. *Postulants are expected to reject their assignments in order to seek out the Academy.*

She dropped the book to the floor, annoyed at herself for getting distracted by such stupid things when she should be focusing on how to fix this mess. All that she really wanted was to hide away in the forest forever, but her friends would already be wondering where she was. She knew she'd have to face them eventually, so she snuffed out the candle and made her way back to the school.

As she passed by groups of younger girls playing carelessly on the lawns she wished – not for the first time – that she'd run away when she was younger. She'd thought about it often enough but just as she was growing old enough to act on those dreams, Laban had showed up in the forest and insisted she should stay and complete her schooling.

No-one ever left the Imperial Service – with the exception of the criminal fraternity, and a few who became desperate beggars, you did the job you were assigned to until you became too old to be useful to anyone. But perhaps she could've escaped from the Empire and found her way to some far-away land where people were free to do whatever they chose. Maybe that was still an option.

She'd never before stopped to wonder why Laban had been so insistent that she stay with the system, when living in a hilltop cave was clearly about as far from normal as it was possible to get. Could she do likewise, if she decided now was the moment to run away at last? So far as she knew, no-one else was aware of her cave... could she live out the rest of her days there, scavenging for food in the forest? But it wouldn't take long for that to become just as boring as being a police officer, without the comfort of a house and a wage.

Gisele, Annette and Sophie were already in the dorm when Eleanor arrived, sitting on their beds and waiting for her and Lucille to come and share their news. Eleanor had known she'd find them there; they'd grown up together in this room, and the dormitory group was the closest thing each girl had to a family unit, so when something of this magnitude was happening it was the natural place to congregate.

"And?" Gisele asked as soon as Eleanor walked through the door.

"Police," Eleanor said nonchalantly, hoping that no-one would read her true feelings on the matter.

"See, I told you! I knew you'd get something good!" Annette said, smiling broadly. "And I've got a teaching post *here*, which is perfect, and Gisele's off to the diplomatic corps like we always knew she would be – and Sophie's going to be a cook, if you can believe her luck!"

Eleanor felt relieved, really, that the system was so well trusted. No-one even stopped to consider the possibility that an assignment might not be the best possible thing that could happen to the person to whom it was given. Annette had instantly assumed that being assigned to the police force was brilliant news for Eleanor, and the others adopted the same view, so none of them actually asked her what she thought about it. Probably they assumed she was off to work on something exciting like fraud or smuggling or hunting out rebels.

A moment later Lucille burst through the door; she'd clearly come running up the stairs, gasping for breath and with her wavy brown hair strewn all across her face. "Assessor!" she cried happily as she kicked the door shut behind her. "I'm going to be an Assessor, it's a Level One, it's going to be *so* exciting!"

Another round of congratulations ensued. Eleanor wished she could feel happy for the other girls, wished she could set aside her own emotions for long enough to share in their celebrations, but though she put on a good act, all she felt was a cold, sick emptiness in the pit of her stomach.

She excused herself as soon as she thought she could get away with it, claiming she needed to visit the library, but in reality she marched back to the assembly hall, determined to sort this out once and for all. Just as he'd promised, the Assessor was sitting near the stage, looking rather bored as he pored over a folder of paperwork.

"Excuse me."

He looked up, surprised to have been disturbed. "How can I

help you?"

"Is this really my letter?" She pulled out the crumpled paper and offered it to him, but he didn't take it.

"Is it your identification number?"

"Yes."

"Your name?"

"Yes."

"Then it's your assignment."

"But I want you to check that it's right." She straightened the paper and pushed it in front of his face. "This doesn't sound like me at all, so I want you to check it."

He slammed his folder shut and looked up at her, still refusing to take the letter which she held an inch from his nose. "You must be Eleanor. No-one else at this school has ever had such a reputation."

"What reputation?"

"For being difficult."

"Difficult?" She stared at him. "I'm not difficult!"

He raised an eyebrow. "Do you have any idea how few complaints we receive? Every objection in the last five years has been from you. I suppose it was naïve to think you'd accept your assignment quietly."

"If you did your job properly, I wouldn't have to complain," she said. "If I hadn't had to fight so hard to even study the subjects I'm best at, then maybe some idiot wouldn't have put me in some dead-end police job now."

"Considering how much disruption you've managed to cause even while you're at school, I suspect it's best for everyone that you settle down somewhere quiet," he said, finally deigning to glance at the letter. "This sounds about right."

"It's not right at all! I want you to change it."

"Sorry, Eleanor, I can't do that."

"Well, who can?"

"The decision has been made; the College is in agreement. No changes will be made."

Eleanor snatched the letter back from him and tore it sharply down the middle. "Well that's what I think of your stupid assignment!" she said, continuing to rip the paper into jagged pieces which she then scattered into his lap. "And you can shove it wherever you please, because I'm not taking such a pathetic post, not now and not ever!"

He stared at her, stunned into silence, and she turned and stormed from the room before he recovered from his shock. It was only as she made her way to the dining hall, where the other girls were gathering for dinner, that she realised the magnitude of what she'd just done. It wasn't just a job she'd turned down; in a moment's fury she'd opted out of the whole Imperial system, and after they left school at the end of the month she wouldn't even have a place to live. Perhaps she'd be looking into those crazy assassin myths after all.

She toyed with the hilt of her knife and wished again that Laban would come back. Now more than ever, she needed someone she could trust.

She was just settling down to her meal when the headmistress came up behind her, the heels of her shoes clicking on the cold stone floor.

"Eleanor, a word, if I may."

Eleanor looked longingly at her plate, but decided that she'd better not argue. Ignoring the curious looks that her friends were shooting at her, she got up and followed Isabelle from the room without a word.

They walked through the corridors and up a flight of stairs Eleanor had never climbed before, into the headmistress's private office. The door closed behind them with a click that echoed through the room.

Isabelle indicated to Eleanor that she should sit down, and then pulled up another chair alongside.

"Now, Eleanor," she said, and though her voice was soft it lacked much of the warmth that was usually there. "I understand you've chosen to decline your assignment."

Eleanor nodded, a lump rising in her throat. She hadn't expected the consequences to come so quickly.

"I can't be seen to condone this," Isabelle continued. "This school has an impeccable record. We've had only one drop-out in our history – and her fate wasn't pleasant so we won't discuss that. I will allow you to stay here tonight, but unfortunately I'll

16

have to ask you to leave first thing in the morning."

Eleanor gasped involuntarily; she'd thought she'd have longer than this to plan her next move. "I thought we had the rest of the month," she said, a hint of a question in her voice.

"Usually. Usually, yes," Isabelle agreed. "But what you have done is not usual. You have to understand that you've put me in a rather difficult position. I cannot be seen to support your decision, and the girls must see that rebellion has consequences."

Eleanor nodded mutely.

A look of sadness flickered briefly across the headmistress's face and she looked as though she was about to say something, but then stopped herself. "I hope you know what you're doing, Eleanor," she said at last, and there was a slight tremor in her voice which made her sound almost worried. With that, she stood up and went to open the door.

Eleanor felt numb; she didn't even bother to go and check whether there was still food to be had in the dining hall. When she opened the door to the dormitory, she was surprised to find that all four of the room's other inhabitants were already there, looking expectantly at her.

"Well?" Gisele asked immediately.

Eleanor gave a mental shrug; they'd find out soon enough, so she might as well get this over with. "I rejected my assignment," she said flatly. "So I'm to leave the school tomorrow."

Four pairs of eyes stared at her in amazement.

"You did what?" Annette shrieked.

Gisele waved at the other girls to be quiet, and when she spoke it was with a calm, measured tone that befitted a future diplomat. "Eleanor," she said, "I think you'd better tell us what's going on."

Eleanor nodded. She wasn't sure what she had to tell them – but she'd grown up with these girls, they'd shared their childhoods, and she didn't want to lie to them. But she thought, in the circumstances, that it might be prudent to be economical with the truth. "The assignment I was given was dreadful," she said. That much was true. "I decided I'd prefer to go it alone."

There was a moment of stunned silence; even Gisele wasn't sure what to say to such a frank admission. Annette looked positively scandalized.

"So what are you going to do?" Lucille asked.

"I don't know." Giving simplistic but truthful answers was proving easier than Eleanor had anticipated. "I'd like to see Almont."

"Oh, well!" Gisele smiled, suddenly back on territory she could understand. "Lucille and I will both be there, you know. You'll be able to come round for tea."

"Excellent!" Lucille said happily, apparently satisfied that this was reason enough to forgive Eleanor's strange behaviour.

Annette and Sophie glanced at each other; Eleanor caught a glimpse of the look that flashed between them but chose not to take them up on it. She'd known they wouldn't approve, but she was happy with the minimum of discussion on the subject.

Deciding that the conversation was over – at least she hoped it was – Eleanor turned to gather her things together. She began to pull clothes at random from her wardrobe, throwing them haphazardly into her trunk – they'd each been provided with one the previous week so that they could start packing their possessions to move into their adult lives. She didn't feel it was important to be particularly neat about the process; a journey like the one she was about to embark on called for packing light, so she was fairly sure that she'd be leaving most of her things in the cave in the forest. She would only take essentials beyond the very first stage of her trip.

She was aware that the other girls watched her as she flung clothes and shoes carelessly into the case. She could picture their faces perfectly without looking round; there would be no shortage of surprise at the idea that Eleanor could possibly be doing anything in a less-than-meticulous manner. But she didn't really care what they thought any more, she just wanted to get the job over with.

Only when her hands reached her private bag of tricks, which she'd kept carefully hidden under a stack of trousers in the bottom of the wardrobe, did she begin to take care of what she was doing. The small canvas bag contained almost everything that mattered to her: a couple of knives she'd 'borrowed' from their hand-to-hand combat classes and conveniently forgotten to return, a number of crooked pieces of metal which came in very handy for opening doors, and an assortment of day-to-day useful objects like rope and candles. She knew that if she threw the bag too heavily into the trunk, the clattering of metal would generate unwanted interest from the other girls; she also knew that it would be noticed if she suddenly abandoned her casual manner to place the bag more carefully.

"I'm hungry," she pronounced suddenly, looking up at the others, who all immediately put all of their efforts into pretending they hadn't been watching her. She took advantage of the momentary diversion to slip the bag silently into a corner of the trunk, hastily flung in a handful of underwear to hide it, and stood up. As she did so, she realised that she really was hungry. "Let's go down to the kitchens and see if we can get a snack," she suggested, pushing down the lid of the trunk. It closed with a satisfying clunk.

"I'll come with you," Lucille volunteered.

Annette and Gisele both said "Me too," at the same time.

They all looked at Sophie, who nodded; she was the smallest of the five, thin in a feeble way contrasted with Eleanor's equally slender but well-toned frame. She'd always been a nervous girl, seeming young for her age, and not the sort of person to want to stay alone in the room at night, even though no-one had ever really questioned the safety of the school.

They walked down the stairs in silence, trying not to disturb any of the girls in the other dormitories along the way. When they reached the kitchen door, Eleanor slipped a couple of pins from her hair and proceeded to work on the lock; it was a simple design, and always opened easily. The only time she'd let anyone see any of her more unusual skills was when they had snuck down to the kitchen for midnight snacks, as they'd been doing off and on for years – none of the girls had ever asked her how she'd learnt, but they knew she was a practical person, so they probably just assumed she'd taught herself.

But when she turned to let them into the kitchens, Eleanor stopped short: Sophie was looking inexplicably terrified.

"You won't do that in the outside world, will you?" she asked, her voice wavering uncertainly. She looked like she might burst into tears at any moment.

"Of course she won't," Gisele said briskly. "Will you, Eleanor?"

"No, of course not," Eleanor agreed, although she was quite sure she was lying.

Sophie was visibly relieved. "Sorry," she mumbled, blushing a fierce shade of scarlet. "It's just, well, you know what they say about people who drop out..." She shuddered. "I don't want you to become a criminal, Eleanor. You'd be too good at it."

Chapter 2

It was only after breakfast the next day that Eleanor's thoughts
turned in earnest to wondering what she was going to do next.
She'd slipped as much bread as she could carry into her pockets
– that at least would buy her time to consider the options. She
would go first to the cave, of course, and she knew she could
stay there a night or two before she needed to venture out in
search of food. She wished she could borrow a horse from the
school stables, just for a couple of days, but she was in enough
trouble already – she didn't want to begin her adult life as a
fugitive.

She said goodbye to her friends without tears, though
Annette was sobbing uncontrollably, and she promised Gisele
and Lucille that she'd call on them if she ever found herself in
the vicinity of their new homes in Almont. She hugged them all
before she left, though Sophie still shrank away from her a
little, and then started to manoeuvre her trunk down the
staircase.

She'd decided she ought to leave the school by the front
gates; suspicions would be raised if she headed straight into the
forest, and she didn't want to be followed. She'd have to walk
an extra couple of miles, but it was worth it to avoid the risk –
the last thing she needed now was for anyone to discover her
hideout. So she dragged her trunk down the driveway, and went
a fair distance along the road towards Port Just before she
reached a convenient point to turn into the trees.

The going was tougher than usual, dragging a case which had
been designed not for carrying but for stacking on the back of a
cart, and she was confirmed in her view that she'd have to leave
most of her things behind if she was going to make reasonable
progress on the rest of her journey. Eventually she walked and
climbed her way to the summit of the hill.

It was then that she realised she didn't have a very good plan
for how to get a heavily-laden trunk down a sheer cliff-face and

into the cave.

She pulled some rope from her bag, but preliminary testing suggested it would snap if she tried to lower the trunk down full, so she sighed gently to herself and began to unpack. She heaped her possessions onto the rocks, and in time she had achieved an empty trunk which she could easily lower down onto the ledge at the mouth of the cave. Picking up an armful of clothes, she proceeded to lower herself using her other arm, dropping lightly beside the case and dragging it into the cave with her.

She scrambled back up the cliff to gather more of her clothes; several trips later she had managed to fill the trunk again, and there was no more to be done. She collapsed wearily on the bed, not even bothering to light a candle first, and closed her eyes to the world.

When she awoke, she lit a couple of candles and picked up *Stories of the Assassins* from where she'd left it on the floor. Time to do a little research. She could hardly believe she was letting herself consider something so ridiculous, but apparently she'd made her decision. Normal life was an option no longer open to her.

It was then she noticed the piece of paper tucked between the pages of the book. She was sure it hadn't been there before, and cursed herself for forgetting to check the cave for any sign of disturbance when she had come in. She'd been so busy moving her things, and so tired after an almost sleepless night, that she'd neglected to follow her usual routine. She unfolded the paper and read the short message. It just said: *Good luck, Eleanor*.

She would have recognised his writing anywhere; the very sight made her fume with anger. What was he doing? Laban must have heard what she'd done, that was the only explanation for the note, so why wouldn't he give her more guidance than this? And moreover, why had he come and gone so quickly, without waiting to see her, if he'd been so sure she'd come back here?

She glowered at the slip of paper for a while, then – deciding that was unhelpful – she screwed it up and threw it hard against the opposite wall. Feeling a little better, she opened the book and continued to read from where she'd left off.

She was about halfway through before it occurred to her to skip back to the point where he'd inserted the note, suddenly wondering whether the placement was significant. He'd chosen to hide it in the book, after all, despite several more obvious places.

It was the page she'd read so carefully yesterday, about students turning down their assignments.

Coincidence?

If not, he must have guessed what she was thinking, even before she thought of it herself. And his note, however short, could only be taken as encouragement.

She sat up with a jolt, feeling all the mysteries of her childhood suddenly falling into place. The seemingly chance encounter with a mysterious man who'd just happened to have a raft of skills she'd been desperate to learn – yes, it certainly made more sense in this new context.

She turned back to the book with renewed determination, and didn't stop reading this time until she reached the end of the final chapter. It was beginning to get dark outside, and Eleanor supposed she'd better start preparing for her journey – if she was going to get on with this new adventure, it would be best to set out early the following morning. She nibbled at a slice of bread, which was already starting to taste a little stale, and began to pull oddments of clothing from the trunk.

Before long, she'd assembled a small pile of things which she intended to take with her. The prim blouses and blue-hemmed skirts of the school uniform were thrown aside; useless. She would take nothing which could not be described as essential: she left even the library book in her trunk. She had picked out a couple of pairs of loose trousers – in addition to the ones she was wearing – and a small number of tunic tops. She had stuck to dark, neutral colours, suspecting that she was more likely to want to blend in than to stand out from the crowd. She somehow managed to squeeze them all into the canvas bag alongside her knives and other oddments, and decided she would also take a blanket, which could serve as a cloak if it was cold during the day – she knew she couldn't be anonymous if she wore her school coat.

Satisfied with her achievement, she settled down again to get a good night's sleep.

She was surprised to find she woke late the next day – the scarcity of natural light in the cave had thrown her body clock out of kilter. Annoyed at herself, she got up quickly and swallowed down another couple of slices of bread before wrapping an old green blanket around herself, hoisting her bag onto her shoulder, and scaling the cliff-face with a little more effort than it usually took her.

She walked briskly down the hillside and through the forest back to the road, all the time heading purposely in the direction of Port Just. It wasn't far, she told herself, so she hadn't lost much by oversleeping. She was much too hot, with the heavy woollen blanket draped around her shoulders, but she thought she might need it later, depending on how easy it was to find somewhere to stay in the town.

The track to Port Just was deserted, winding quietly between the trees, and aside from a few wild pigs Eleanor didn't see a soul until she came to the outskirts of the town. She was quite relieved, sure that she looked out of place in the summer heat, and she didn't really want to draw attention to herself any more than she had to. As soon as she saw the first houses along the road and knew she was coming into the town, she ducked off the path and searched the scrub until she found a hollowed out old tree-trunk in which she could conceal her possessions. Well, most of her possessions – she kept her favourite knife, as always, tucked away under her clothes.

Feeling a great deal more comfortable once she'd abandoned the blanket, she virtually skipped the rest of the way down to the harbour. It was starting to feel like an adventure. A few rows of shoddy market stalls were arrayed around a small square which faced out over the sea, and dozens of people were bustling around doing their weekly shopping. A few scrawny chickens scratched for scraps around the food stalls; Eleanor knew she'd have to pick up something to eat, eventually, but first she wanted to find somewhere to stay.

There was one small guesthouse, she knew, right by the sea

at the end of the road. She would try them first. She strode confidently through the crowds, occasionally being jostled against one or other of the shoppers, and had nearly reached the guesthouse when she spotted the bulge of a purse under a man's coat.

It wasn't something she'd ever tried before – she'd never had need to – but it seemed easy enough to slide her fingers between the drawstrings as she passed him. A scarily natural extension of her skills, she thought wryly, as she curled her fingers around a couple of large five-dollar coins and tucked them quickly into her own clothing. The girls had played games of stealth as children, trying to sneak up on one another without being noticed – Eleanor had been a natural, and this felt like the same game. She was a little ashamed of descending to petty criminality so quickly – Sophie's words the night before echoed through her mind – but she knew that she had little choice if she was to survive long enough to meet her destiny. Besides, she'd been careful not to take too much: she could have lifted the whole money-bag, but she felt it was fairer to take an amount that he wouldn't miss, though it would make all the difference in the world to her tonight.

The front door of the guesthouse was a faded green, its paint flaking away to reveal the gently decaying wood beneath. They didn't get many tourists here, and though the government paid a living wage to the landlady, the allowance wasn't enough to stretch to a fresh lick of paint. Eleanor reached for the heavy bronze knocker, which was refreshingly cold beneath her hand, and rapped it twice. When the landlady came to the door, Eleanor put on her best smile. "Excuse me, do you have a room for tonight?"

"Of course, dear," the woman gushed, beaming down at her and beckoning her inside. "Follow me."

Eleanor followed her up the narrow staircase and into a first-floor bedroom. It was only a tiny room, but had a large window looking out over the sea, and Eleanor thought it was beautiful.

It cost her half of what she had stolen just to pay for one night in the guesthouse, but it would be worth it: once she started out in earnest towards Almont, she knew she'd have to go days on end without a bed for the night. Once she had agreed the price and taken the key from the bedroom door, she headed back out into the street. She wanted food, and she needed to collect her belongings.

The friendly people of Port Just weren't wealthy enough, on average, to attract the kind of opportunist thieves who bothered the inhabitants of cities such as Almont, so their purses were easy targets for Eleanor. She didn't want to take too much from any one person, so she dipped her fingers casually in and out of pockets and purses as she made her way along the street to fetch her bag. By the time she returned to the guesthouse, she'd collected several dollars in change. It was almost ironic, she thought, how the town's first small crime wave was being perpetrated by a woman who was supposed to have joined its police force. Still, she hoped the amounts she had taken would be small enough to avoid detection, even amongst the most down-at-heel residents of the Port.

She treated herself to a substantial ham sandwich and a sticky fruit pie from one of the market stalls, and then settled herself happily by her bedroom window to watch the world go by as she ate. She spent an enjoyable afternoon just watching the sea and gently running over the varied assassin legends in her head, trying to decide where her fate should lead her next. *Stories of the Assassins* had said that the evidence for the location of the academy was inconclusive, mostly based on the places where young bodies had been found, presumed to be failed would-be assassins. Many legends pointed to Almont, but other sources suggested towns in much more remote parts of the country. But Eleanor had already made up her mind to start out for Almont the next day; she wanted to see the capital anyway. If she didn't find any leads there, she could worry more about other places to explore.

She woke cheerfully after a comfortable night's sleep – the old guesthouse bed wasn't a patch on the luxury of Mersioc Regional School for Girls, but it was certainly more welcoming than the cave where she'd spent the previous night. Looking out of the window she saw that a heavy summer storm was brewing, and although the day was warm, thick black clouds darkened the sky. Eleanor didn't have to work too hard to persuade herself that it would be better to wait out the storm in Port Just, so she rolled over and drifted back to sleep.

For the first time in her life, Eleanor allowed herself a proper lie-in. It was past midday when she woke again, and the rain was pounding on the window. She looked out. Most of the stallholders hadn't bothered to turn up at the market, or had already given up, but there was one bedraggled young man selling sausages. Deciding this was just what she needed to brighten up a dismal afternoon, Eleanor headed down the stairs and out into the street.

The young sausage-seller smiled cheerfully at her, said she was pretty, and gave her a discount, which made her blush but also left her feeling a lot better about the day. Since she was already soaked to the skin, she decided to take a walk in the rain as she ate. She wandered away from the market square, which was boring when it was so empty, and wove her way between the small houses into the domestic heart of the town.

When she spotted a man skulking in a doorway, trying to keep out of the rain, she couldn't resist the urge to practise her developing skills as a pickpocket; she would need to steal to survive in Almont, at least until she found her place, and it felt safer to practise in Port Just where the people weren't by nature suspicious. He was looking away from her, and she wandered up behind him and slipped her hand into his pocket as she continued past.

In an instant, his fingers closed tightly around her wrist, as he put his foot out in front of her and tripped her to the ground. Eleanor struggled to wrench her arm free but the man held fast, and he was much stronger than she was.

"Stupid little thief!" he said coldly, jerking her painfully to her feet so that they were standing face to face. She looked into his angry green eyes, glaring out at her from beneath waves of unruly dark hair. "Suppose you thought you'd make yourself a bit of extra pocket money, did you? You just wait until your school hears about this. One of Isabelle's, are you?"

Eleanor's heart skipped a beat. She couldn't be dragged back up to the school in disgrace, not like this, not so soon after she'd left with her head held high. He reached for her name bangle, and she reacted on instinct. "Let me go," she hissed, and in the same moment she had pulled out her knife with her free hand, and pointed the tip against his throat.

The instant she'd done it, she knew she'd made a mistake. Although the girls were all taught basic hand-to-hand combat up at the school, carrying a weapon in the streets was a long way from normal even in Almont: in a town the size of Port Just it was virtually unknown. Yet the expression on this man's face was not just surprise, there was also – she thought – a brief flicker of recognition.

She didn't have time to worry about what that might mean. In his shock the man loosened his grip on her arm just enough for her to free herself and she took the opportunity to run, her feet slipping on the stones as she sprinted madly away. She ducked between houses, taking as many random turns as she could to try and lose her pursuer.

She'd been running for nearly a mile when she found herself in a blind alley. In the moment it took her to think about retracing her steps, she heard his footsteps echoing towards her, and she knew there was no way she could escape a fight if she turned back. Without a second thought she hooked her fingers into the masonry in front of her and began hauling herself up the wall.

She'd tried to climb the walls of the school buildings before, when she'd been sure no-one was watching her, but had never found as much pleasure in it as in rock-climbing. Now, however, necessity ruled. Her fingertips scraped the cement uncomfortably, and jagged corners cut into her as she pushed herself upwards. She'd just reached the roof when the man rounded the corner and she pressed herself flat against the slates, holding her breath and willing him not to look up.

He glanced suspiciously around the alleyway and Eleanor watched in horror, her body frozen, sure he was going to look straight up at her. However, he simply glowered at the empty street and turned on his heel, stalking off into the rain.

Eleanor lay still for as long as she could bear, afraid he'd come back or else be waiting for her just around the corner.

Eventually the rain eased off, and she decided to risk clambering back down to the ground. She walked quickly and quietly back to the guesthouse, trying not to draw attention to herself, and nearly jumping out of her skin every time she saw someone in the street.

Only once she was back in her room did she breathe a sigh of relief, but even that was short-lived: she knew that word would spread quickly, and she didn't want to risk being in the town when people heard that a thieving, knife-wielding redhead was roving the streets. The chance of quietly finding a cart that would take her some or all of the way to Almont also seemed likely to have disappeared, so she'd have to walk. She bundled her possessions swiftly together and crept down the stairs, left a couple of coins on the hallway shelf to cover her debts, and let herself silently out of the back door.

Chapter 3

Eleanor walked until it began to get dark, and then she curled up under a thick hedgerow to try and sleep. The ground was sodden, and even wrapping herself thoroughly in her blanket only slightly slowed the rate at which water seeped into her clothes and hair. She lay as still as she could, listening to small animals rustling nearby and the birds chirping their evening songs, until she eventually drifted into sleep.

She was woken before sunrise by another downpour of rain, and although it was only a brief shower she was so thoroughly drenched that there seemed little point in trying to get back to sleep. Shivering and miserable, she pulled herself from the bushes and continued with her journey in the dim pre-dawn light.

For the next couple of days she walked determinedly along the coast-road towards Almont, ducking out of the way whenever she heard a cart rattling along the uneven track, and being sure to hide herself well away from the road each night when she settled down to sleep. In her hurry to leave Port Just she hadn't had chance to stock up on food so her diet consisted of increasingly stale bread, accompanied when she could find them by a few summer berries that the birds had not yet eaten.

Hunger, combined with near-constant drizzle and unseasonably cold temperatures, made Eleanor's walk more uncomfortable by the day. So it was with great relief that, three nights after leaving Port Just, she came to the outskirts of another small town. An old painted sign informed her, in slightly wobbly lettering, that she was entering Arche.

The first person Eleanor came upon in the rainy streets was a plump, middle-aged woman with greying blonde hair, clearly on her way home from the market, laden with her weekly shopping. Trying to suppress her coughs and sniffles, Eleanor asked the woman whether there was a guesthouse in the town where she would be able to rest for the night.

"I'm afraid there isn't, dear," the woman said, shaking her head. "I'm afraid there's not much call for that sort of thing round here. But you look sick, and you're absolutely soaked – you'd best come back with me and dry yourself out. My house is only just around the corner from here," she added hurriedly.

Eleanor was feeling too dazed and feverish to even consider rejecting the woman's kindness, and she allowed herself to be led through the narrow streets. A small part of her mind was alert enough to take note of the winding route they took between small, crowded houses. She'd never been this far from the school before, but something about Arche gave an immediate impression of poverty. Of course everyone had a roof over his head, but the houses were tiny and somewhat ramshackle – Eleanor sensed that in a town like this, only the most essential repairs were likely to get done. The woman took her arm and pulled her into an alleyway between two houses, then through a gate into a small, slightly overgrown courtyard, full of flowers. Even through the rain the pollen was overwhelming, and Eleanor started sneezing again. There were three houses facing out onto the courtyard and the woman pushed open the door to one of them, hurrying Eleanor inside ahead of her.

"Welcome to my home," she said, as Eleanor stood dripping in the hallway. "Now, come along, let's get you warmed up."

Her mind thick with fever, and feeling groggy in the sudden warmth of the house, Eleanor was only vaguely aware of herself as the woman encouraged her up the stairs, helped her to undress, and pointed her towards a bath-tub full of steaming hot water.

"I knew John'd have this ready for me," she said cheerfully, "which is just as well, really... I think you've already got a chill. That's right, lie back there, just try to relax and you'll warm through soon enough..."

The woman continued talking as she bustled around the house, wandering in and out of the bathroom, clearing Eleanor's wet clothes away and bringing a pile of freshly-laundered towels. The babbling voice washed over Eleanor as she lay in the hot water, half-asleep and hardly taking in a word.

Suddenly, a pattern of intonation followed by expectant silence told Eleanor that she had been asked a question and she sat up, startled.

"Oh, I'm sorry, dear!" the woman cried when she saw Eleanor's response. "I didn't know you were sleeping. I was just asking if you wanted any lunch, but maybe you should get some rest first?"

"Lunch would be good," Eleanor said weakly, her stomach now reminding her that she hadn't eaten properly in days.

The woman nodded, and passed her a towel. "You get yourself dried off, then, and there's a bed in the next room where you can settle yourself. I'll bring something up shortly."

The bed was warm and comfortable, and Eleanor was dozing again by the time that the woman came upstairs with a huge bowl of casserole and a mug of nettle tea. Eleanor ate quickly, glad of the hot food, and finished her drink in two mouthfuls.

She fell into a deep, feverish sleep almost as soon as her cheek touched the pillow. Though she woke many times over the following days, to eat or drink or use the chamber pot, she was sufficiently unwell that she paid little attention to the passage of time, or the comings and goings of the kindly woman and her husband who took turns at bringing food and water upstairs.

One day, however, she woke to find the sun streaming in through the bedroom window, and was suddenly aware that her fever had lifted. She sat up, wondering vaguely how many days she'd been ill, and for that matter what time of day it was now. Clutching a sheet about her for modesty, she made the short journey to the window in two wobbly steps. A glance outside told her that she hadn't missed the whole of summer – there were still flowers in bloom in the courtyard. The sun's position high overhead also suggested it was around midday, so Eleanor was optimistic that it might soon be lunch-time.

Her movements didn't go unnoticed, and she'd only just sat down on the bed again when her hostess came upstairs with a plate of sandwiches. "You're looking better today, dear," she smiled. "Do you think you might be getting up soon? I've washed your clothes."

"Thank you," Eleanor said. The woman's generosity was overwhelming. "I don't know what to say. You've been so kind – and I don't even know your name. I haven't been myself."

"Mary," the woman obliged.

"I'm Eleanor."

Mary pushed the sandwiches encouragingly in Eleanor's direction, and Eleanor was glad to take up the offer – although she had been well fed over the previous days, she still felt hungry.

"Now, if you're really sure you're better, then do get dressed – yes, your clothes are just here – and come downstairs. John would like to speak to you."

Eleanor nodded, and dressed herself quickly. She noticed immediately that her pockets were empty – even her name bangle was absent, and she felt naked and vulnerable without her knife. She forced herself not to panic. Mary would have had to turn out the pockets to do the washing – and if they'd had any reason for wanting to harm her, they could have done so very easily while she was lying in bed.

"Where are the rest of my things?" she asked, in what she hoped was a sufficiently casual voice. She didn't want to imply any criticism of the people who'd been so kind to her.

"Ah, John has everything downstairs," Mary replied. "Will you come down now?"

For the first time, as she followed Mary down the stairs, Eleanor really looked around at her surroundings. Compared to the outsides of the houses in Arche, the inside of this one was surprisingly smart and well-kept. Although the rooms were not large, there were little touches – a vase of flowers here, a silk curtain there – which suggested an elegance out of step with the rest of the town.

"The girl's called Eleanor," Mary said by way of introduction as they came into the kitchen.

John was sitting at a large, solid table, on which Eleanor's possessions were spread. He stood up as they entered. "Eleanor. Enchanted."

"Nice to meet you," Eleanor said, forcing herself to smile to conceal her irritation that they had laid out everything she owned for inspection. At Mary's indication, she pulled up a chair to the table; Mary stood stiffly by the door.

John paced gently alongside the table; a tall, stocky man with a chiselled jaw and thick, muscular arms. Eleanor was embarrassed to catch herself noticing how attractive he was, considering he was easily into his forties. "You're quite famous, Eleanor," he said at last. "Though no-one knows your name. The flame-haired assassin o' Port Just, they call you."

Seeing the look of panic which flitted across her face, he laughed. "Don't worry, we've not turned you in."

"Why not?" she asked, her voice icy. "If that's what you think." This wasn't what she'd expected to wake up to.

John laughed again; he had a hearty, cheerful laugh which would have been pleasant in any other circumstances. "I admit I've my doubts about the bit where a rogue assassin ends up picking pockets in a provincial town like the Port," he said, "but the harbour master's quite convinced that that's what you are."

Eleanor considered her options. She could run, of course, but she'd done that last time and she didn't really want to run into more sickness and malnourishment. From here, it'd be more than a week to get to Almont if she was walking all the way – and she couldn't risk asking anyone for a lift if there was a price on her head. Besides, this couple didn't seem to have any intention of hurting her, despite thinking her a criminal.

"Will you believe me if I say I'm not?" she asked, wondering how the harbour master, presumably the man who'd chased her, had possibly identified her as an assassin. It wasn't even true.

John nodded. "Aye, but I think you'd better tell us exactly what happened."

"I was hungry," Eleanor said; they would surely believe that given the state they'd found her in. Besides, it was true, and she knew from experience that if she had to lie then it was best to base her lies as close to the truth as possible. "I needed money to buy food, and I'm not a very good pickpocket, so I got caught."

"And the knife?"

"I panicked. I just wanted to get away."

John nodded slowly. "That all sounds very reasonable. I'm

sure a court would look kindly on you – probably only a year or two in jail, don't you think?"

Eleanor heard the thinly-veiled threat in his words and chose not to respond, waiting to see what alternative he would offer. If he'd just wanted to turn her over to the police he could have done it much earlier than this, so he must have a proposition.

"We've covered up for you this far," he continued, "but you can't stay here if you're going to be up and about. Can't have you wandering around Arche when everyone wants to know who you've come here to kill. However, I captain a fishing boat, and by all accounts you're practical enough to make yourself useful."

"Doesn't the government provide you with a full crew?" Eleanor asked in astonishment. Surely the assignment process would identify plenty of candidates who would make good fishermen; it didn't seem the hardest job in the Empire.

"For the fishing, they do," he said.

Eleanor's eyes widened a little; suddenly the small touches of wealth might make sense. She knew there was a lot of money to be made on the ocean wave, whether from piracy or smuggling, or from other things beyond her imagination.

"For my other operations," he continued with barely a pause, "we have to fend for ourselves, so to speak. And if I need a crew to operate outside the law, it's best to use people who're already there."

Eleanor wanted to ask why a fisherman would risk turning to a life of crime; did the government not ensure that everyone had sufficient to be comfortable? But she knew how hypocritical – and how very strange – the words would sound to someone who thought she was a common criminal, so she kept silent. It could be fatal to arouse any more suspicions.

"So?" John asked sharply. He'd clearly been expecting a response, but she wasn't sure he'd asked a question.

"Do I have a choice?" she asked, keeping her voice deliberately soft and submissive.

"Course you do. But I fear your story is bigger than you are, now... at least in these few towns. I'm not sure whether – without your knife – you could live up to what people think you're capable of." He twirled her favourite blade carelessly in his thick fingers.

Another threat. She tried to hold her reactions in check; she had few enough possessions, she couldn't let him think she had any sentimental attachment to the things she owned. He would recognise the superiority of the knife he held, of course – this house gave away its occupants' finer tastes, and a man with any kind of sideline in trade could hardly avoid noticing the relative value of things. Compared to the old school practice daggers she had appropriated, Laban's knife was a jewel; a beautifully constructed implement even without its emerald insets. An assassin's knife.

She wondered – but surely it couldn't be! If the harbour master had recognised the blade then he was more than just a harbour master, which seemed implausible. More likely he'd just come to wild assumptions from an overactive imagination, or else wanted to make the story more impressive so as not to be embarrassed by the fact that a woman, barely more than a girl, had outwitted and outfought him.

Eleanor's mind ran over her chances. She didn't want John to think she cared for the knife – let him think she'd light-fingered it from some more accomplished fighter! – but at the same time she was afraid that he might try to sell it.

"Will you let me arm myself in my own defence if I agree to sail with you?" she asked cautiously.

"You'll be safe aboard," John said, an edge of roughness entering his voice. "I won't let my men touch you, if that's what you're fearing."

It hadn't even crossed Eleanor's mind to worry about the crew, but the captain's words did little to cheer her. If he expected her to be afraid then there was something – however small – to be afraid of. She would have to tread with caution.

"I sleep easier at night with a knife in my hand," she confessed.

"Aye, well, you would on the streets, but life afloat's a bit different, and by all accounts you're a bit quick on the draw..." He left the sentence hanging for a moment, then added, "Besides, you've slept soundly enough the last few nights – and days."

Mary gave a gentle laugh, and Eleanor started slightly: she'd forgotten the woman was there. Irritated at herself, she swore not to be so careless in future – it wouldn't do to forget about an opponent just because he kept still and out of sight. But somehow, whatever games they were playing, these people had treated her too kindly to be enemies.

"I won't draw a knife against you or your men," she said. "You can have my word on that – and if we meet pirates, better we're all armed."

"Pirates won't touch us," he said.

Eleanor wished she could feel reassured by the certainty of his tone, but she worried she was heading into piracy herself and it didn't appeal. Though – she realised with some relief – if the captain didn't want her to carry a weapon then their main goal couldn't be anything as violent as proper piracy. She was beginning to get fed up with his dodging her at every turn. She decided to call his bluff; if the gambit failed, she would take her chances. "I'll join your crew if you let me defend myself," she said. "That's my final word."

"Aye, well, then," he sighed. "It's hard enough to get good people these days. I'll need at least six months out o' you before I give the knives back, though."

She nodded: it was good enough, and she didn't think she was going to do better. "What about my bangle?" She'd be unrecognised in the Empire without the gold bracelet which bore her name and identifier.

"The same – six months and you can have it back. We sail in twelve days, and you'll stay in the house till then," John said by way of a conclusion. He scooped all the weapons from the table, but pushed the rest of her possessions along the table towards her.

The deal was done. Secretly, Eleanor wondered what she'd just agreed to, but she preferred not to ask – she'd find out in time.

Mary broke the silence and the tension with a cheerful offer of tea and cake, which they all agreed was a lovely idea, and Eleanor wiped all thoughts of the sea from her mind. She had twelve more days here, with hearty cooking and amiable company, and she was determined to enjoy it while it lasted.

She threw herself wholeheartedly into this idea for a couple of days but although she was pleased to be well again, and happy to be warm and well-fed, she soon began to struggle with her confinement – and John was too busy, preparing for the voyage, to answer any of her myriad questions. He reluctantly agreed that she could go into the courtyard, but the small taste of freedom only made her even more frustrated.

She spent a day yanking angrily at weeds growing in the cracks in the courtyard paving, building up a sizeable pile of rubbish and gradually clearing the area of everything she didn't think was pretty or useful. As the sun began to dip, and the job was all but done, she allowed herself to sit on the step and rest for a moment. With her hands burning from the irritant sap of some unknown weed, she wished she'd paid more attention in her Herbal Remedies classes – maybe something here could ease the pain, if only she could identify it. She remembered being taught that antidotes often grew near their poisons, like nettles and dock-leaves, but with no idea what had caused her blistering fingers she knew she was unlikely to find any relief.

Annoyed and exasperated, she finished piling up the weeds in one corner of the yard, and went back inside. Mary had already made a pot of tea for her, but when Eleanor picked up her mug she gasped in pain as the heat seared her hands and aggravated the sores.

"What have you gone and done?" Mary asked, full of concern. She grabbed Eleanor's hands and examined them, then scuttled into the kitchen, returning moments later with a large glass jar. "Put some o' this on, dear," she said, unscrewing the top so that Eleanor could dip her fingers inside.

The jar was full of a cold, clear jelly. Eleanor rubbed it into her hands, glad of the soothing coolness. "What is it?" she asked.

"Oh, I don't know what they call it," Mary said. "It's foreign stuff, John brings it back from some o' the warmer countries. Not that you'll be needing anything like that once you've been at sea a couple o' weeks – you'll have calluses on your hands like he has, and there's no plants as'll hurt your fingers then."

Eleanor wasn't sure if she was expected to be alarmed or pleased at this idea. Certainly she couldn't imagine Mary ever getting callused hands – but then the woman was far too soft round the edges for any kind of physical work. "What's your job?" Eleanor asked, wondering for the first time.

"Me? Well, I man the fish stall, when we have fish." Mary hesitated, then went on, "Most o' the time John turns enough profit that we don't have to worry about that, really. I'll send him out if the town's short o' fish, mind you. But mostly my job's to stay here and keep the house while he's off on one o' these long runs."

"How long will we be at sea?" Eleanor asked. She knew John had said she had to work for half a year, but she had no idea how many trips that might involve.

"I don't know, love. Likely a few cycles of the moon, all told, with stops here and there. The boat carries over two months' water if you're careful – and you'll learn to be careful."

Eleanor gave a small gasp of surprise; even one month without setting foot on dry land sounded like a very long time. She'd never been on board a fishing boat before – despite growing up near the coast, and in spite of her natural curiosity about such things, Laban had strongly insisted that sailors were not appropriate companions for a young woman. Not wanting to risk upsetting her most valuable teacher, she'd stayed away, so her only experience of the sea was from the small rowing boats the school had supplied.

"It's not as bad as it sounds," Mary said.

"You've done it?" Eleanor asked in amazement.

"A few times, when I was younger."

"Can you tell me about it?"

Things improved after that – though the limitations on her movements still stung, Eleanor found that Mary could answer most of her questions about life at sea, and she had more than enough questions to fill the days. Mary drew numerous diagrams of the boat and its rigging, answered Eleanor's strangest queries with good grace, and even found time to share odd snippets of information that she was too ignorant to ask for.

Eventually the fortnight passed, and Eleanor was relieved to find that it was a clear, dry day when they were due to sail, with only a light breeze disturbing the air. Waking her at first light, John gave her a flat cap and one of his old cloaks to wear until they reached the boat. She pinned her hair in a tight knot on top of her head and put on the borrowed clothes; the disguise wasn't convincing at close range, but she hoped it would be enough to allow them to get to the sea without interruption. At least her distinctive hair was tucked out of sight. They said goodbye to Mary, who supplied them with enough sandwiches and cake to feed a small army, and walked swiftly to the coast.

Even before the sun had fully risen above the horizon, they walked down the rickety quay to where John's boat was moored. Compared to the others in the harbour it was a large vessel, a 48ft ketch needing a crew of ten – who would work in shifts, John explained, so they could sail through the nights, though he assured her she wouldn't need to work in the dark until she knew what she was doing. The name *CANNY ROSE* was painted in block capitals along the bow.

They stepped aboard, John with a seaman's easy confidence, Eleanor taking great care not to slip on the sea-sprayed deck boards.

At John's instruction she lowered herself through the hatch and climbed down the ladder into the dark cabin below. There were no portholes but dusty lanterns hung from some of the beams, just waiting for candles to bring them to life. Blinking as her eyes adjusted to the dimness, she took note of the room's layout. Hammocks were strung between the stanchions, and a small kitchen area occupied the stern. John came down the ladder behind her and beckoned her to follow him into the bow.

"You'll have this one," he said, indicating the end hammock. "We'll put this up to give you a bit o' privacy."

He was holding a blanket, which he then proceeded to nail to a beam that ran above their heads. It formed an effective curtain, and she nodded her approval.

"Thanks," she said, and placed her bag on a peg by the hammock. She was just loosing her hair from under the borrowed cap when the floor lurched beneath her. The motion was accompanied by the sound of footsteps echoing from above; Eleanor counted one, two, three, four men embarking... before the sounds of those already aboard were loud and chaotic enough to mask the noise of others arriving.

"Ah, that'll be the men," John said. "C'mon, let's introduce you."

Eleanor followed him up the ladder and back on deck, where they found seven men talking and joking. They all fell silent at their captain's approach, but their eyes were not on him but on the short, red-headed girl who came two steps behind.

They all spoke at once, but Eleanor managed to make out only one voice through the confusion of their mingled speech: "Can't have a woman aboard, Cap'n, it's bad luck." She guessed the others were making similar comments; the look of distaste was, at least, the same on all their faces.

"Silence, the lot o' you!" John called over the growing clamour of voices. "SILENCE!!"

Casting furtive glances one man to another, the men's shouts died down to hushed mutterings and shortly all fell quiet, their eyes expectantly turned on the captain.

"None o' you really believes that superstitious nonsense," John said once he had their attention. Eleanor could hear the same veiled threats, the same quiet authority in his tone, as he'd used the first time he spoke to her. "You don't want a woman in the crew because you don't think she'll do a good job. Well, either you trust my judgement or you get off my ship. We're a man short as it is, and this girl's as strong as you could hope for, just look at the muscles on her."

The man nearest to Eleanor, a blond-haired, muscular sailor who also happened to be the youngest of the men, took this as grounds to reach out and pinch at her arm; she pulled away sharply, but he just nodded his approval. "She'll do," he said, then turned back to Eleanor. "They call me Sandy. Welcome aboard."

The crew crowded in on her, and she struggled to pin names to faces as each spoke in turn. "Triangle." "Spice." "Mag." "Anvil." "Misty." "Jaws."

John watched their introductions, then turned to indicate Eleanor. "And this is..."

His hesitation was only momentary, but it was long enough for the balding, stocky man known as Anvil to interject: "We know who she is! She's the Assassin."

There was a general chorus of agreement from the crew, and Eleanor felt her spirits dip – was she going to have to fight to deny any link to the assassins at the same time as she struggled to find out about them? She had been hoping, if anything good was to come of this indenture, then at least the chance to visit distant shores might give her chance to seek out more stories and clues.

"Aye, alright then," John nodded ruefully. "You can't escape the rumours, lass, even if they're not true."

"And what do we call you?" she asked, suspecting it wasn't to be 'John' if none of these men went by the names their schools had given them, and seemingly she wasn't to be introduced by her name either.

"Captain," he said.

Chapter 4

Her first few days afloat passed quickly for Eleanor – she was kept very busy learning the ropes, trying to map Mary's diagrams on to her new reality and keeping as far as she could out of the way of the more experienced sailors. Their voyage took them north past the harbour of Port Just – borrowing Triangle's telescope to look inland, Eleanor was just able to make out the roof of her old school where it rose above the trees – and round a thickly-wooded promontory into the open sea. Up to that point they'd been able to see a dark strip of land on the horizon to the west, even as they sailed within a mile of the coast to their east – now, heading eastwards, the expanse of flat, grey ocean stretched unbroken into the distance until it blended into the northern skies. They'd been lucky with the weather except for one brief thunderstorm, and though Eleanor had wanted to find out how they kept the boat under control in bad weather, she'd been so seasick that she spent the whole time vomiting over the side and managed to completely avoid learning anything.

On the twelfth morning of their voyage, John suddenly announced that they would be stopping at Dashfort – the next major port along the coast – to restock their supplies; from there, they'd head out across the sea and on to foreign shores.

Eleanor was thrilled by the news. Having quickly grown bored with the diet of fish, biscuits and dried fruit she was looking forwards to fresh food again, and the chance to explore a new town – much larger than Port Just or Arche – appealed to her natural curiosity. Dashfort had even been mentioned in *Stories of the Assassins* – a couple of horrifically dismembered bodies, generally thought to be those of would-be assassins who had dramatically failed to join the academy, had turned up in one of the squares.

With growing excitement Eleanor leant over the bow of the boat, watching the buildings grow from dots on the horizon to take on a clearer shape. The city was built into a steep hillside, sloping away from the sea, half of the houses looking like they might fall into the water at any moment. A light mist shrouded the top of the hill and hid the full extent of the city. Eleanor tried to count the buildings – ten, twenty, forty... she lost count before she reached a hundred, but she still hadn't counted a tenth of what was visible. A thousand houses! If she wasn't going to be able to get to Almont any time soon, this was certainly the next best thing. The rest of the crew were obviously equally enthusiastic, and even those who might reasonably have been sleeping were on deck to watch their approach into the city.

"You not seeing this city before?" Spice asked her. He had sharp features and his skin was black-brown, a darker shade even than Gisele's. Combined with his strange manner of speaking, she wondered if he was from beyond the Empire, but none of the men wore their name bangles aboard and she hadn't dared ask him outright.

"I haven't been to any cities," she said. "I only just left school."

They were steering into the harbour when John came up behind her, interrupting her thoughts. "You'll be needing to get below deck now," he said.

She turned in surprise. "What?"

"You'll be needing to get below deck. Don't want anyone recognising you, now do we?"

Eleanor felt all her excitement drain away. "Can't I see the city?" she asked, her throat suddenly dry.

"We'll not risk it," John said. "You're a fugitive, and you'll stay out of sight till we're beyond the Empire."

"In a place this size they've got more to worry about than stupid stories coming out of Port Just, haven't they? And you're all criminals!" Eleanor felt indignation rising in her chest at the injustice of it all. "What's so special about me?"

"Better to be safe," he said flatly. "You've a higher profile than any of my men."

"But that's not fair!" she cried. A couple of heads turned towards her but she didn't care. She'd been forced into joining this band of criminals, and now she was being treated like she was worse than any of them.

John grasped her arm and pulled her forwards. "You made your own fate when you pulled out that knife, girl."

Though she struggled against him, gripping the nearest rope and digging her heels into the deck, he was stronger. He dragged her across to the hatch, which Sandy opened as they approached, and pushed her feet-first into the cabin below. As she fell heavily onto her knees she heard the wood slam down above her, and listened to the scraping sounds of some heavy object being manoeuvred above her until – she was sure without testing it – the weight held the hatch against her possible escape.

Hardly able to believe what he'd done, she banged her fists against the overhead and called for someone to let her out, but there was no response. Giving up in frustration she moved slowly across to her hammock – taking care not to trip in the darkness – and lay down, waiting. A short while later she was jolted to her senses as the boat thudded against the quay, and she heard the men moving around – felt the boat move as one and then another of the crew jumped ashore, then more gentle bumps as the mooring lines were secured, tying the *Rose* firmly into her berth.

Eleanor lay still in the dark for what felt like forever, just waiting for the commotion to die down, waiting long enough in the silence that she was sure all the men had gone ashore. She didn't want to try to get out if they were still standing guard; she wasn't looking for a fight.

Once she was sure she was alone she made her way back to the hatch, took a couple of steps up the ladder and pushed upwards as hard as she could. The wood creaked under the weight above, but moved barely an inch above its frame. Eleanor, however, saw her chance in the sliver of light. She spotted an old broom resting in the corner of the cabin; hopping lightly down she grabbed it, then scrambled back up the ladder and prepared to push again. With a hard shove she lifted the hatch just enough to let her slide the broom-handle into the space; now the inch was a permanent gain.

She pulled gently downwards, wondering if the handle would be strong enough to use as a lever, but it creaked worryingly under the strain. Frustrated, she looked around the kitchen for inspiration. She picked up a couple of flat, heavy pans and began to work one of them into the gap. With grim determination she slowly managed to insert them both, one on each side of the hatch.

Taking a deep breath, she heaved on both pan-handles. She felt something shift above the hatch and the broom clattered to the deck as the opening widened; it was working!

By the time she felt the pans beginning to slide it was too late to stop herself from falling and she landed painfully on her back – but as well as the sounds of her own fall, she also heard heavy movement above her. Had she succeeded? She pushed gently at the hatch, and to her delight it moved freely now.

Satisfied, she darted back across the cabin, seized the cloak and cap she'd borrowed from John for their walk down to the harbour in Arche, and hastily remade her disguise before scrambling up the ladder onto the deck. She swung the hatch closed again, but hard as she tried she couldn't drag the barrel back into place, so of course they'd realise as soon as they returned that she'd gone out. She wondered how long the men would spend in town – at least until nightfall, she guessed. They were probably as glad of the change as she was. She'd have to be careful, though – she didn't want to risk being stranded here, unarmed and alone.

Pushing her worries from her mind, Eleanor stepped ashore – though her legs wobbled uncomfortably beneath her, she was glad to be back on dry land. Her first priority was to find something hot and tasty to eat, and the smell of sizzling bacon called her towards a stall in the shadow of the city gates. There was a small queue but she didn't mind waiting, and when she reached the front of the line the woman behind the stall handed her a huge cone of flatbread overflowing with strips of bacon, sliced sausage, dry-fried beans and melting cheese. Distracted, Eleanor almost forgot to pay; she hadn't been out of school long enough for the idea of paying for meals to really take hold. Once she'd handed over a couple of small coins she wandered through the gates and began to make her way up the steep cobbled street, taking greedy mouthfuls as she walked.

She wandered at random between the houses, through narrow streets and covered alleyways. The city was built on too steep a slope for carts to be able to climb the hill, which had clearly shaped the growth of the town – she'd never seen anything so haphazard. While the harbour had been large and open, perfect for trading, the city within the gates was cramped and irregular. Eleanor had just swallowed her final mouthful when she emerged into a paved, hexagonal courtyard tucked between six large buildings. It was the first reasonably flat area she had come to, and she immediately realised where she was.

This was where the bodies had been found.

She shivered, and sternly told herself it was only because of the cold. More than ever, she wished John had given her knife back. She didn't know when she'd have another opportunity to investigate Dashfort's mysteries but she was reluctant to try anything risky when she was unarmed. Her eyes flickered from one corner to the next, looking for any kind of clues to what might be lurking here. It was quieter here than the rest of the town, but simple superstition would account for that – there had been deaths, that would be enough to keep away anyone who didn't need to come here. An occasional passer-by scuttled across one side or another of the hexagon but none stopped and none cast a second glance at Eleanor as she stood in the shadows.

The weather was becoming more autumnal, and a biting wind whistled through the streets as she huddled in a corner between two buildings, pulling the borrowed cloak more tightly round her shoulders as she took in the scene. She didn't want to think about how much trouble she would be in when she returned to the *Rose* but it was worth it just to be here, on her first step into the legends, her first tentative movement towards the life she hoped was to be her destiny. In this very place, someone had come close enough to success to find the most horrendous failure.

A single oak tree grew in the centre of the courtyard, its branches reaching up and spreading above the rooftops.

Domestic and commercial buildings seemed to have been scattered at random through the rest of the town, but Eleanor noted that none of the buildings around her here were houses. Dashfort's Fiscal Office announced itself with bold letters carved into the stone, and neatly-painted signs marked the police station, a small prison, the Dashfort Region branch of the Assessors' College, and the Administrative Hall. The sixth building had no words, just the Imperial insignia carved by its door; Eleanor could only begin to guess at what purpose the Empress's personal embassy might serve here.

An old man shuffled past and let himself into the Fiscal Office, the door swinging closed behind him.

Eleanor pulled her cap firmly down over her ears, tucking the last few strands of hair out of sight as she did so, and began to walk around the now-deserted square. On her first circuit she studied the ground under her feet, inspecting the slabs around the perimeter one-by-one, occasionally stopping when her feet found a wobbly stone but finding nothing of interest. On the second circuit she turned her attention to the walls of the buildings as she passed, but again nothing seemed out of place. It was only when she stopped, and found herself standing next to the huge carving of the Imperial crest, that she noticed a small gap between two overlapping elements of the insignia.

She pulled two of the pins from her hair and poked one through the crack; having confirmed there was indeed a lock concealed there she began to work at it, pushing at the levers until the drum finally rotated and a section of the wall swung open towards her. Just as she was peering into the dark opening, she heard voices approaching from behind; panicked, she ducked through the door and pulled it closed behind her. The latch clicked back into place as the door locked itself again; Eleanor ran her hands over the wall she had just come through, but there was nothing on this side to indicate an opening.

She cursed under her breath: no access to the lock from this side.

She turned and looked around her; as her eyes grew accustomed to the dark she could just make out a flight of narrow steps climbing away from her. She pushed half-heartedly against where she knew the door to be, not really expecting it to move. It didn't, so she began to make her way – very carefully – up the stairs. Instinctively she felt she was doing the right thing, but a small part of her worried that there was something not quite logical about trying to follow in the footsteps of some youths who'd suffered horrific deaths, particularly when she was without a weapon. She glowered into the shadows, annoyed at herself for having such thoughts – it wasn't as though there was much other evidence, in the assassin legends, apart from the bodies which turned up from time to time. And, she reminded herself, she was now trapped, so she had little choice apart from to get on with it, whatever 'it' was.

There were only a dozen steps before the space opened out into a small hexagonal chamber, about six feet across and lit by a shaft of light which fell from high above. Five of the walls were plain grey rock, but the sixth was made up of shiny black stone tiles.

Eleanor inspected the five plain walls first, tapping and prodding at every irregularity in the surface, but there was no movement – even judicious insertion of a hairpin between the stones found nothing this time. Her attention turned next to the floor; unlike outside, she had no concern about drawing attention to herself here, so she got down on her knees to examine the flagstones. She worked her way slowly around the room, spiralling inwards until she was sure she had checked every slab. Still nothing.

Almost disappointed by the lack of subtlety, she finally went over to the black mosaic.

The tiles were all different shapes, each about the size of Eleanor's palm; they fitted neatly together to form an apparently random pattern over a three-foot square. She started at the left-hand edge, gently trying to move each tile until one of them slid sideways by a fraction of an inch. Flushed by this apparent success, she tried the adjacent tiles, but none of them would budge. In her eagerness she pressed a little too hard; it was only by luck that she wasn't directly in the path of the blade which shot from the mosaic. The metal grazed her finger deeply as it passed, then clattered against the opposite wall.

Sucking her wound, she paced across the room and picked up the knife – a fine sliver of metal, far too flexible for hand-to-hand combat but strong enough to do a lot of damage if it came flying at an unsuspecting victim, particularly at the speed it had flown from the wall. And, she could tell from the acid pain searing through her hand, it was poisoned.

She sucked forcefully at her finger, hoping to draw out some of the poison. As she spat blood onto the floor, Eleanor realised the room would have to be reset every time someone came here – whether to remove a body or simply to put the mosaic back to its starting position. And the knives, of course, would have to be re-sprung. She shuddered as she recognised the scale of operation that was implied.

She tore a strip from the bottom of her tunic and wrapped it tightly around her finger, wincing with the pain but determined to stem the flow of blood – she couldn't afford to be distracted, she might not be so lucky if she sprung another trap. She returned to very gentle examination of the mosaic, her movements timid and slow now that she knew some of the dangers.

After a few moments' exploration she had worked out the game. The outer tiles would move, gradually, outwards – but only if she nudged them in the right order, which seemed to be random. The movement on each tile was almost imperceptible, but she soon found out that if she got one wrong then the pattern would lock until she went back and corrected it. Once she finished manoeuvring the outer ring, she hoped, she would be able to do something with the next layer of tiles.

Gradually she worked her way around the puzzle, sometimes finding that she had to move in towards the centre of the mosaic, sometimes outwards again, always with tiny movements so as to adjust the puzzle without causing it to lock up or fire blades at her. Despite her best efforts she occasionally applied too much pressure, and she'd been grazed by another four knives by the time that a small gap began to appear in the centre of the mosaic. She picked them all up, sure that even flimsy weapons were better than none.

Once the central gap was wide enough she reached her hand

cautiously in, extending one of the poison blades ahead of her fingers just in case there was another trap waiting for her. Beyond the edge of the two-inch thick mosaic tiles, she could feel nothing – there was an empty space. She managed to get her arm through the hole, all the way up to her shoulder, but still there was nothing within reach.

Frustrated, she resumed her work on the tiles, starting again at the outer edge. In her irritation she was careless and dislodged a couple more knives, one of which sank deep into her shoulder. She pulled the blade out and twisted her head to suck hard on the wound, only then wondering whether there was more to this poison than the acid burning sensation. She spat hard just in case.

After another few circuits of the mosaic, manoeuvring the pieces gradually further out, the gap in the middle finally looked big enough for a person to crawl into. Once Eleanor had established that all the tiles were now firmly locked in place, and nothing else seemed to be happening, she decided she'd have to go that way. She picked up the last of the knives from the floor, tucked most of them into her pockets, and climbed into the hole.

For a few feet the tunnel ran straight; Eleanor crawled into the darkness, fingers exploring ahead of her. After a short distance there was a sharp bend to the right, and then left again, cutting out the light from the room behind. She paused, waiting for her eyes to adjust, but there was very little to see.

She edged forwards again, following the tunnel through another three turns until at last a glimmer of light appeared at the end. After a few more yards of crawling she emerged into another, larger hexagonal chamber, blinking in the sudden brightness. She barely had time to look around before a clicking sound to her right drew her attention; she turned and flicked out one of the blades she was holding just in time to deflect the disc of metal which came flying towards her face.

She froze on the spot, wondering what she'd done to set off the trap – maybe it was just her weight on the floor, but she didn't want to risk any further movement until she had a plan. Her eyes wandered across the room; aside from going back the way she'd come, the only apparent way out of this room was a doorway set high into the opposite wall. The base of the opening was at least six feet above Eleanor's head – and she doubted it would be so easy as to just walk across and climb the wall, even if she could find adequate hand-holds between the smooth blocks of stone.

With a knife ready in each hand she took one cautious sidestep, listening for the giveaway click of a trap but nothing came. She relaxed a little, and bent down to pick up the metal disc from the floor, then cursed under her breath as the sharp edge sliced into her fingers and caused her to drop it again. Drying the blood on her tunic, she straightened carefully and looked around. At least these ones weren't edged with the acid which had burned on the earlier blades – she hoped no subtler poison was lurking.

She decided that only her weight on the flagstones could possibly have released the disc; with that in mind, she counted the shortest route to the far wall. If each stone would spring a trap then the number of stones she stepped on was more important than making her route a direct one; the best path curved to the left and seemed likely to set off six more.

Knives poised, she stretched out one foot and gradually shifted her weight onto the next slab. The click this time came from behind her; she spun around and narrowly dodged the flying disc which came at knee-height this time.

Wary in case there could be more than one trigger beneath a given stone, Eleanor edged onwards towards the next stone on her path. She wondered how she could have let herself get into a situation like this, unarmed apart from the flimsy knives she'd got from the mosaic, and only one false step away from being sliced in half. But there was no chance of leaving the way she'd come in so she had no choice but to go on, as stupid as it seemed. She gritted her teeth and prepared to step onto the next stone, moving as quietly as she could.

Three flagstones and three deflected discs later, she was beginning to feel a little more confident. True, the blades were sharp, but she'd only been harmed when she'd tried to pick one of them up. She stepped onto the next slab, listening for the now-familiar click – but this time two sounds disturbed her. She turned right and threw a knife to meet the spinning disc mid-air then twisted to her left with only moments to spare, managing to flatten herself to the ground as the second disc flew close over her head.

Heart racing, she got back to her feet, annoyed that she'd allowed herself to relax. There was only one more stone between her and the wall, now – but she couldn't let herself assume there wouldn't be any more surprises.

She slid herself gently forward onto the last flagstone, and again two clicks warned her of two blades slicing towards her. She deflected the first easily, but the second caught her elbow and she felt the warm flow of blood along her arm. She tore another strip from the bottom of her tunic and prepared a hasty tourniquet.

Reaching the wall at last, she tried to find suitable handholds for climbing, but the blocks of stone were neatly quarried and fitted together with barely perceptible cracks. Dismayed, she tried the only other thing she could think of, forcing one of the knives into the crack between two blocks. She tested it hopefully – maybe, just maybe it would hold her weight. She didn't want to risk snapping the metal before she was ready to climb, so she pushed a couple more knives into place higher up the wall. One more at around knee-height, and she felt she was ready to go.

A small voice at the back of her mind told her that she was being idiotic – that if she fell she'd almost undoubtedly set off a new trap, and would probably be too slow to fend off the resulting blades. But she had no alternative. Somehow, she had to manage this.

She swallowed back her fear, rested her left foot on the lowest knife-handle, then suddenly began to climb, as quickly as she could, up the metal ladder she had made for herself. She could feel the knives bending under her weight, threatening to break. She hooked her fingers over the edge of the opening, then tried to push herself upwards but the extra force snapped the blade she was standing on and she slipped down the wall, now clinging by her fingertips to the bottom of the doorway.

Her instincts took over and she scraped her toes against the stones, searching desperately for any irregularities which she could use to climb. Surely no mere wall could present a harder challenge than the overhangs and smooth cliff-faces she had practised on as a child. After what seemed like an eternity she managed to find one toe-hold. It was only just enough to take some of the pressure from her fingers, but she was relieved nonetheless. Encouraged, she lifted her other leg and began to search higher up the wall. It was a slow and awkward progress, but eventually she managed to find good enough footholds to haul her body up and into the opening.

After a brief rest she got to her feet again and pulled a couple more knives from her pocket – she didn't know what else she would be facing, but she wanted to be prepared. She looked around; she was in another small chamber, but this one had mosaic tiles on the floor, arranged to display the numerals 4 and 7. She wondered what that could possibly mean. Four and seven. Forty seven? It meant nothing to her. Bemused, she decided to concentrate on getting out. There was another doorway in the opposite wall, and she edged round the room towards it, avoiding stepping on any of the mosaic tiles.

She moved as quietly and carefully as she could, and for once nothing seemed to happen. By the time she reached the second doorway she wondered if something had broken – it was uncharacteristically easy. A flight of steps led down from here, and she began to make her way down, still afraid that there might be more traps. But nothing hindered her progress and she came to a door at the bottom of the stairs. She clicked open the latch, pushed the door and found herself in the same courtyard where she had begun. Of its own accord the door swung closed behind her, and she understood why she had not found this opening when she had been inspecting the walls – even now, knowing it was there, she couldn't find the outline of the door.

The sun was setting on the horizon, and Eleanor ran as fast as her feet could carry her down to the harbour and across to the *Rose*. She was relieved to find that she had got back before the others. Knowing she wouldn't be able to disguise the fact that she had been out, she settled herself in the bow to wait for the consequences; the sea air whipped across her face as she waited and made her wounds sting.

John, Mag and Anvil were the first to return, laden with rolls of brightly coloured silk and heavy woollen cloth. "These'll sell a treat in Taraska," John grinned as they loaded their purchases on to the boat. "You just can't beat a quality Charanthe cloth."

He stopped short as he caught sight of Eleanor; seeing his eyes upon her, she mumbled an apology and looked firmly at the floor. She knew how bad she must look, her wounds smarting and blistered, her hair tousled and her clothes torn. John glowered at her without speaking.

"Tol' you," Anvil said, breaking the silence. "Tol' you she'd get out, Cap'n. Can't trust 'em."

"No excuse to stop work," John said flatly, pulling open the hatch to the goods hold. "Come on, girl, you can at least help us load up."

Eleanor pulled herself painfully to her feet and clambered down into the hold, reaching up for the bundles which the men had brought and hoping her makeshift bandages were enough to stop blood from leaking onto the valuable cloths. As she stacked everything neatly into a corner, she wondered what John would have to say to her. She knew she'd let him down, and with hindsight she wasn't even sure it had been worth her while. What had she achieved, apart from a few injuries and some stupid, meaningless number? 47? It didn't feel like much.

Spice and Triangle had both returned from the town by the time she climbed back onto the deck, and as soon as he saw the state she was in Spice went to fetch a jar of ointment from his locker. Eleanor recognised it as the same kind of clear gel as Mary had given her back in Arche. He tore the bandages from the wounds she had patched, ripping away some of the scabs as he did so, and she tried not to flinch as he daubed her with liberal amounts of cold, sticky gel.

"What is that stuff?" Eleanor asked.

"Srakol – but the crew just calling it jelly. Keep it. We get more in Taraska, but you going to needing it before then." He looked disapprovingly at her wounds. "What you been doing, anyway?"

Eleanor saw John's attention pick up; she knew she had to watch her words. "I was exploring," she said.

"Explorin'?" Anvil snorted, voice full of disbelief. "Assassinin', more like."

"Think what you like," Eleanor said and forced herself to laugh, hoping that if she seemed sufficiently amused at the idea then the crew would eventually give up on it.

"I'm not going to ask you what you've been doing," John said at last. "I just hope you've been straight with me, girl. We can't afford to carry liabilities."

Chapter 5

"Pirates!"

Eleanor wasn't sure who shouted first, but soon the cry was echoing through all the crew.

"Pirates! Pirates!"

"Run the pennant up the mast!" John shouted at Eleanor. "Quickly, girl!"

She didn't need to be told twice; she ran across the deck to the locker, slid back the bolts and lifted the heavy wooden lid. Scattering flags and pennants everywhere, she eventually found the one she was after: green was for pirates. She stuffed the others back into their store, closed the lid and pushed the bolts home again before scrambling to hoist the small cloth triangle. Only once the pennant was fluttering atop the mast did she dare take time to indulge her curiosity.

Two weeks at sea hadn't stopped Eleanor being scared of meeting pirates, but now she knew they were in sight she was too intrigued to be properly afraid. She leaned over the side of the boat, squinting towards the horizon, convinced that she could just make out the speck of another vessel in the distance, silhouetted against the setting sun.

Triangle, his telescope clamped to his eye, stared across the bay without comment.

"Will they bother us?" she asked him as the boat came more clearly into view.

Keeping his attention focused through the lens, Triangle shook his head. "Shouldn't," he said. "Don't know what they're doing in Imperial waters, mind. They usually keep out the way."

"They're coming this way," Sandy said, somewhat unnecessarily since every man on deck was watching the approach.

They all stood in silence for a few tense moments as the other boat drew closer, until Triangle from behind his telescope said, "And they're well armed."

"Get Mag up here," John snapped urgently at Eleanor; wondering how that was going to help, she nevertheless ran and scrambled down through the hatch.

"What you want?" Mag asked once she had woken him.

"Captain wants you on deck. Pirates."

He cursed under his breath, but he didn't ask any more questions and he suddenly moved so fast that she had to hurry to keep up with him. The pirate ship was almost alongside their boat by the time she got her head above deck again, and once Mag saw them he ran across the deck, shouting as he went. "Ghiida!" he called out across the waves. "Ghiida!" And then he launched into a rapid series of sounds that Eleanor couldn't even split into words.

"What's he saying?" she asked John.

"It's Magrad," he answered. "Course all the men speak it a bit, it's the main language o' trade beyond the Empire, but Mag's a native – they'll listen to him."

Eleanor thought about this for a moment. "So... Mag's short for...?"

"Magra. Haven't you asked the men where they got their names?"

"So he's a pirate?" she asked, wondering vaguely why she'd never thought to ask any of the men about the origins of their nicknames. It explained the accent, at least.

"Not all the Nomadic Seafaring People of Magra have piracy in their veins," John said sternly, but she saw a twinkle in his eye as he added, "But in Mag's case, yes."

"And what about Spice?" His was the strangest accent of all the men.

"He's from Taraska, where all the food is–"

They were interrupted by a voice booming from the pirate ship, but the man spoke Charanthe not Magrad. "You're under arrest! Don't try to fight. I repeat, in the name of our mighty Empress, do not try to fight."

"Vaarhu!" Mag cried, slamming his fist against the gunwale, and Eleanor knew from intonation alone that if she'd understood the word it wouldn't have been a polite one.

"Accursed Imperial seaslugs!" John muttered. "Right – everyone ready for this?" He looked expectantly round at his crew, who were already drawing their weapons.

Eleanor added her voice to the chorus from the men: "Ready!"

She wondered how long the Imperial forces had been appropriating pirate ships for, with grudging admiration for the strategy: it had allowed them to get close enough for a fight this time and – assuming they escaped – John's crew would certainly be slower to trust Magra vessels in future. "Divide and conquer," she murmured under her breath. Very clever.

She pulled out the handful of knives she'd picked up in Dashfort. Flimsy, yes, but they'd be okay for throwing. She hid one inside her trousers just in case she needed it, poised a second in her right hand ready for throwing, and held the others loosely in her left.

Taking a moment to look around at the rest of the crew, she realised she was the only one whose weapons had range – the others had daggers, and Sandy had also picked up a short sword, but there was nothing that would help until their attackers tried to board. Eleanor took a deep breath, then loosed the first knife. It was supposed to be a warning – she aimed at the ear of the man who had spoken – but the pitching of the boats defeated her and the blade clattered harmlessly onto the deck of the Magra boat. She cursed quietly; this was going to be harder than she'd thought.

Before she could aim a second shot, Eleanor was almost knocked off her feet as the two boats bumped together. As the pirate vessel scraped and rocked away from the *Canny Rose*, one of the Imperial officers swung his leg over the gunwale and thudded onto the deck of the ketch.

Eleanor flung her next blade in his direction, and it caught the top of his arm before ricocheting down and lodging in the deck a finger's width from Mag's bare foot. She was glad that Mag didn't have time to look around for the source of the knife – he was too busy defending himself against their uninvited guest.

A couple of the Imperial officers were attempting to tie the two boats together, having apparently got hold of one of the *Rose*'s mooring ropes. Eleanor sent three knives in their direction, but again the way the boats pitched and rolled caused her aim to fail again such that even her best shot caused only a graze. She was running out of blades and a few more of the Imperial force had now made their way aboard the *Rose*; the sound of dagger ringing on dagger, along with the occasional curse and cry, filled her ears and she wished that John hadn't stripped her of her weapons. With only a couple of flimsy strips of metal to protect herself she felt vulnerable and defenceless in a way she'd never experienced before.

Above the noise of the fight, she didn't hear the man who stepped up behind her and grabbed both her arms above the elbows. His grip was strong but she stamped hard on his toes, distracting him just long enough for her to wrench her left arm free.

She swung around to face her assailant, feeling something tear in her right shoulder as she did so. Her fist connected clumsily with his jaw and she knew she'd lost; she'd really only had one chance. She brought her knee up into his groin but it was too late; he pushed her down onto the deck, angered rather than incapacitated by the pain, and rolled her forcefully onto her stomach before binding her hands and feet with rough mooring lines.

He leaned in over her, and she could feel the point of his sword against the back of her neck. "I've half a mind to slit you open for that," he growled. "Except they'd have my neck for it." He stood up, and aimed a hard kick at her head before returning to the fray.

She struggled against her bonds for a while, but she was too tightly bound to free the dagger from her trousers. Thinking it better to conserve her energy in case one of the others managed to cut her free, she lay still, just listening to the sounds of the fight continuing around her.

A moment later a couple of Imperial guards threw Spice down beside her, and she caught one of them muttering "Bloody foreigners!" as they stomped back to what remained of the fight. There was less noise now; fewer blades remained in their owners' hands.

"We're losing," Spice said once he'd recovered his breath. "We'll all be hanged before we know it."

Eleanor didn't know what to say to such fatalism; she could only hope he was wrong. She hadn't thought the death penalty was used for such minor offences; come to that, she wasn't sure they'd actually done anything illegal. At least, not before they'd started to resist this supposed arrest.

Eventually all sounds of fighting subsided; looking round as best she could, she could tell it hadn't gone in their favour. The *Rose*'s crew, injured to varying degrees, were all heavily bound and laid out on the deck.

"That's her."

Eleanor recognised the familiar Port accent, and looked up to find she also recognised the face. She froze in surprise. What kind of business could have brought the harbour master of Port Just out here?

"Did you follow me?" she asked, sensing there was little point in pretending not to recognise him.

"Oh, all the smuggling ships out of Arche come via Dashfort," he said. "You were easy to find."

"But why? Why me?"

He didn't answer, but turned to a couple of the other officials and said, "Secure them all for the night; we'll anchor here till morning."

"Why?" she repeated crossly, but still no answer was forthcoming.

The men picked up Eleanor and the rest of the crew like sacks of potatoes, hauled them over to the pirate vessel, and piled them into a prison cage which filled half the hold.

Once the guards had left them alone, John turned on Eleanor. "I trusted you, lass," he said harshly. "I'll not be making that mistake again."

"I didn't do anything!"

"You lied."

"Don' say we never tol' you, Cap'n," Anvil muttered. Eleanor looked round at him, and he glared at her with a venom she'd never seen before.

61

"I didn't," Eleanor objected. "You knew that harbour master's got some delusions in his head. I didn't know he'd come after me!"

"If you'd kept your head below deck in Dashfort like I told you, you'd've never been seen, and they'd've never come after my boat."

"Maybe." Her shoulder hurt, and she was too tired to be bothered with arguments. "But none of this is helping – we need to find a way out of here, preferably while they're sleeping."

Anvil snickered. "What're we goin' to do, genius? We're all tied up an' they took all our weapons."

"Not mine," Eleanor said. "I've still got a knife, if someone can help me get to it."

John looked across at her. "Thought I took all your knives away."

"I picked up another in Dashfort," she said. "It's not very good, but better than nothing. Anyone's hands free enough to help?"

"They tied my hands in front o' me," Triangle said, shuffling across the cell to her side. "So I prob'ly can."

"Can you reach my belt?" She turned her left hip awkwardly towards him as he reached her. "If you can hook your fingers underneath, you should be able to find the handle. Careful now!"

He managed to pull the blade out without cutting her, and held it firmly in his fist. "Now what?"

Eleanor turned her back to him and held out her bound wrists. "If you can cut the rope, we can both work on freeing everyone."

Anvil shook his head. "You wanna get us all killed?" he asked sullenly. "If you hadn't noticed, we'll still be in this cage even if we cut all our bonds. No good jus' causing trouble."

"I'll take my chances," Eleanor muttered. Her hair was fastened in a tight bun at the back of her neck; she was confident she could spring the lock with a couple of hairpins. "Tri?"

He ran the flimsy knife back and forth along the knotted

rope, slicing each fibre in turn. It was much harder work than it would've been with a decent blade, but it was working. His hands slipped once and the blade grazed Eleanor's skin; he started to apologise but she just urged him to continue working at the rope, and before too long her hands were free.

She flexed her wrists, glad to feel the blood coming back to her fingers, then took the knife from Triangle to return the favour.

"Is Anvil right?" he asked before she'd cut through more than a quarter of the thickness, pulling his wrists away from the blade. "Is this rebellin' just goin' to get us killed?"

"I don't think so," she said. "But if you want, I'll get the door open first."

She was aware that everyone was staring at her and she realised that in the fight to persuade them she wasn't an assassin, she'd just taken a huge step backwards. Still, their current plight seemed more pressing. She sighed, abandoned Triangle's bonds and began to work on freeing her own feet. If they weren't going to trust her, she'd just have to prove her point.

She stood up and moved across to the door of the cage, pulling pins from her bun as she went and feeling the waves of hair falling down onto her back. This sort of prison-cage was never supposed to be opened from the inside so she had to reach around to get to the lock; she was going to have to work at a very awkward angle. She stowed her knife back under her belt and reached her hands through the bars to get at the keyhole.

With her fingers curled around the lock she began to explore the mechanism with her hairpins, pushing at each lever in turn until she felt the cylinder move and click into its new position. She heard murmurs from the crew behind her, but she couldn't afford to spare them any of her attention – the lock was stiff and the job was fiddly, demanding all of her attention.

A couple of times the boat lurched beneath her, causing her fingers to slip and lose the progress she'd made, but eventually a final click brought the cylinder into its open position, and she pushed the gate open.

She turned in triumph. "See?"

Suddenly everyone wanted their bonds cutting – even Anvil. She resolved to leave his till last for his attitude.

"You'll all be free in a moment," she said as she began to work on Triangle's wrists first. "But once you step out of this cage, you're on your own. Those Imperial halfwits are only sleeping, and if you wake them, don't think they can't overpower us again. Okay?"

Most of the men just nodded, but Jaws spoke up: "We should kill them in their beds. Slit their throats while they're sleeping – then they can't follow us."

Eleanor looked to John. "Can the *Rose* outrun this ship?" she asked. He nodded, as she'd expected. "Then we should just go, as fast as we can, or we'll be in more trouble than we are now."

"Quite right," John agreed. "If any of us ever wants to set foot in the Empire again, we'll leave them alive."

"If we kill them, no-one knows who did it," Jaws countered. "Leave them alive, and they can run back with any tales they like."

"I'm not caring about the Empire anyway," Spice added, a vicious glint in his eyes.

"No." John's voice was hard now, and Eleanor wondered if he was the only one with a wife back home. "When the girl cuts you free, you'll leave this boat and get back to the *Rose* as quickly and silently as you can. No detours. That's an order."

His pronouncement seemed to be enough to silence the dissent, and Eleanor went back to slicing the men's bonds as fast as she could. Once they were all free, John led the way up the ladder and across the deck to where the *Rose* was still lashed in place.

The nine sets of footsteps echoing on the deck worried Eleanor; she was sure they'd be heard, and she held her knife in readiness. She didn't want to make herself more of a fugitive than she already was, but if it was a choice between imprisonment and freedom then she knew what she'd choose.

Somehow they made it aboard the *Rose* without incident, and while John collected up the assorted weapons which were still scattered across the deck his crew hurried to untie the mooring lines, haul the anchor, and rig the sails for a quick getaway.

Eleanor turned to John as they left the other boat disappearing into the distance: "Now, can I have my real knives back?"

He eyed her suspiciously for a moment, then nodded. "Aye, girl, I suppose we owe you something now."

He went over to the safe and brought out the two school daggers first, then her throwing knife and name bangle.

"Whenever you're ready to tell me the truth," he said as he handed them over, "I'm all ears."

Chapter 6

They were at sea for another month and a half before they
sighted land again; a dark strip appeared along the horizon and
by borrowing Triangle's telescope Eleanor was able to identify
the outlines of many tall spires silhouetted against the sky as
they drew closer.

They sailed into Taraska La'on early the next morning, a
light breeze carrying them smoothly into the harbour. Eleanor
was the first to jump onto the quay, mooring rope in hand,
looking around in amazement. Even the harbour was like
nothing she'd ever seen, many of the huge four- and five-masted
ships wouldn't even have been able to sail into the shallower
waters back at Port Just. And beyond the harbour the city
sloped gently into the distance, its rooftops sparkling in the
autumn sun – so many tiny pinnacles, pointed spires, and
towers topped with bulbous domes of a kind she'd never seen
back home. She hurried to loop her rope through one of the
heavy iron rings, passed the end back to Sandy aboard the *Rose*,
and waited impatiently for the others to finish.

Spice somersaulted from the boat, obviously as delighted as
anyone to have reached dry land, and jogged over to a small
fruit cart parked in the shade of the city wall.

All Eleanor could remember being told in school was that
Taraska was a tiny nation, barely more than a city-state,
inhabited by barbaric foreigners who couldn't comprehend
Imperial civilisation. No-one had thought to mention just what
a city it was! She'd expected to see a poverty-stricken,
unsophisticated settlement – not this vast, beautiful metropolis.

Once the boat was securely moored, John called out to the
nearest quayside official and paid for three nights' berth in
advance – though what he handed over looked like a couple of
glittering gemstones rather than any coin known in the Empire.

Then he took Eleanor to one side before he went back to the
boat. "We'll make all our sales this morning, then restock just

66

before we sail," he said. "You'll help us take the goods up to the market, then we won't need you until we're ready to leave – though you're welcome to sleep on the *Rose* if you want."

"Thanks," Eleanor said, thinking she didn't really have any alternative to sleeping on the boat. She had only a few Charanthe dollars – and she didn't know if her money would be accepted in this strange town, outside of the Empire, even if she had wanted to spend it all on a night or two of accommodation.

They were interrupted when Spice returned, carrying an armful of large, bright orange spheres. He handed them round, and when Eleanor looked at hers in puzzlement he said, "Eat it. It's keeping you healthy after so long sailing."

She tried to bite into the fruit's waxy skin, and found it not only tough but bitter. The men laughed at her, and she saw that they were all peeling the thick skin away with their fingers, dropping it to the ground and eating the juicy segments inside. She spat out her bitter mouthful and copied them.

"What are these?" she asked Spice.

"Blashka," he said. "But men from Charanthe are just calling them orange."

Mag and Jaws had already disappeared into a nearby tavern, but once they finished their fruit the others were all enlisted to take cloth to the market. John gave Eleanor two rolls of silk to carry, which she hoisted onto her shoulders. Though the weight wasn't much the shape made for an unwieldy burden and she walked awkwardly under the load, struggling to keep her balance as she followed the men into the city.

The city wall ran parallel to the coastline, and a grand castellated gateway marked the entrance to the city. The crew had to stop in the gate house to have their wares assessed by the smartly uniformed – and very well armed – guards. After exchanging a few stilted words in Magrad, John reached into his pocket for more gems, which he handed over to the officials.

"What were you paying them for?" Eleanor whispered as they were waved through. Hadn't they already paid for their mooring rights?

"Taxes," John said. "You can buy and sell anything in

Taraska, but the city takes her cut." Seeing Eleanor's troubled expression, he added, "It's worth it though, no doubting that. You can turn a very healthy profit here."

The broad earth track running into the heart of the city was rutted from the heavy cart traffic it had borne over the years, and Eleanor watched in fascination as a small puff of sandy dust rose into the air beside her feet each time she took another step along the road. The air and the ground were dry – when they moved aside to let an old cart rattle past, clouds of dust filled Eleanor's mouth and lungs, making her cough and choke.

They followed the road until the market opened up to their right – an area where, instead of stone buildings towering above them, small wooden shacks with brightly coloured canvas canopies stood in crowded and uneven rows.

"This way," John said, leading the way into the first narrow alley between two rows of market stalls. They walked quickly, taking numerous turns and – Eleanor was sure – doubling back on themselves more than once before John eventually stopped at an empty stand.

"This'll do," he said, placing down the bundles that he'd been carrying. The men all went to add their loads to the table, and Eleanor followed them.

"Busy day," Anvil said, glancing around. "Thought we weren't going to find a spot."

"Busy is good for trade," John said. "Now get out of the way, all of you – we can't make a decent profit if the customers can't get to the stall."

Eleanor took this as her signal that she was free to explore, and turned back the way they had come. She wandered through the market with no particular plan, just soaking up the strangeness. Voices babbled in a hundred incomprehensible tongues as deals were made and goods exchanged. She'd been too busy concentrating on keeping her footing, while she carried John's cloth, to really look at the other stalls – now, the colourful variety overwhelmed her. In one booth, stacked cages teetered in unstable piles, filled with iguanas and tortoises, sloths and tiny monkeys – creatures Eleanor had only ever seen sketched in books, suddenly alive and caged before her eyes.

On the next stall, hundreds of brightly coloured birds fluttered in agitation around a small aviary, and as she watched the stallholder opened a small gate in the side, seized a tiny green bird, and knotted a string around one of its legs before handing it over to a bored shopper.

She rounded a corner, past heaped crates of colourful fruits and strangely-shaped vegetables – and came upon a sight which stopped her in her tracks. At the next stall were tethered not exotic creatures, but children.

Eleanor gasped in horror, unable to tear her eyes away. These children were nothing like those who filled the schools back in the Empire; they were ragged and bony, barely recognisable as human, dressed only in scraps of cloth and held from escape by heavy iron manacles. Their wide eyes stared back at her, some filled with terror, others pleading.

The stallholder, noticing Eleanor's attention, leaned towards her. "Ghor liid? Lam skanda vramasda? You want to buying?"

"No thank you," she mumbled quickly and hurried on, trying to ignore the eyes which followed her, trying desperately to forget what she'd just seen. How could they possibly allow the sale of children? Yet she couldn't think of any way she could have misinterpreted the man's question. John had said many times that anything could be bought and sold in Taraska, but somehow she just hadn't considered such a horrendous possibility.

She shook her head sadly and walked on, trying to regain the sense of marvel she'd felt only moments earlier, but she found it hard to concentrate on what she was seeing when her head was filled with the unshakable image of half-starved children.

After a little more aimless wandering she came upon a stall filled with jars of creams and bottles of strangely-coloured liquids, with bunches of dried herbs hanging from the top of the booth. Some were familiar to Eleanor from school but most were not, and she wondered what they were all for. She spent a few moments examining the various containers – their labels written in a script she didn't recognise – before she decided that she'd managed to find a medic. She wondered whether he would accept her Imperial coins in exchange for a jar of the magic jelly which she'd found so useful for her wounds.

Once the stallholder had finished transacting with another customer, Eleanor edged along the front of the stall towards him.

"Excuse me," she said, wondering whether the man understood any Charanthe.

He turned to face her; he had a surprisingly youthful face under his shock of white-grey hair. "Ghor liid?" he asked, gesturing towards the table.

"Sarakol?" Eleanor asked, hoping she'd remembered the word correctly. There were so many new words.

"Ahhh, srakol!" He picked up a jar and handed it to her.

After making a quick inspection of the contents Eleanor nodded, and fished out her purse. "Do you take Charanthe money?" she asked cautiously, holding up one dollar by way of an example, unsure whether the man understood anything she said.

"Gharanded? Davh, davh." The man nodded, beaming broadly, and reached out to take the coin. He examined it closely, then reached into his pocket for a handful of smaller golden coins. He counted out eight, and dropped the rest back into his pocket. "Bagh iina Gharanded" – he paused mid-sentence and held up Eleanor's dollar again, pocketed it, then began counting the small coins back into Eleanor's hand – "iina, miiz, dagh, ved, maad, ghaad, deg, biila Magrad."

Before Eleanor had chance to respond, the man then took the jar from her hand and held it up. "Bagh iina," he continued, "dagh Magrad. Dagh." He held up three fingers, then pointed at the small gold coins in Eleanor's hand.

It suddenly dawned on Eleanor what had just happened. She'd assumed she was getting change from her dollar, but in fact it seemed the man had just exchanged the dollar for an equivalent amount of Magrad coins, and was now expecting her to pay. She picked out three of the small coins and handed them to him, and he passed the jar of jelly back to her with a smile.

"Davh daan," he said, giving her a half-bow.

She smiled back at him, hoping to acknowledge whatever he'd just said – she guessed it had to be goodbye or thankyou –

then turned and continued her stroll through the market. *Iina, miiz, dagh*, she repeated to herself as she walked, which was as much of the counting as she'd managed to remember. It was good that she'd met someone so helpful, she thought, for her first attempt at buying something in a foreign country. It was only after she'd walked on past a few more stalls that she realised she had no way of knowing, yet, whether she'd actually been given a fair rate of exchange – her fingers went to the hilt of her knife: he might have been friendly, but if she found out he'd robbed her she'd find her way back.

With her mind dwelling on violence her attention was drawn to a weaponsmith's stall, which spanned two booths. Alongside the kind of daggers and small swords Eleanor had practised with in her hand-to-hand combat classes at school, hung elegantly curved blades and huge, two-handed longswords. She longed to try one of the longswords for weight, just to see whether she could learn to wield that kind of weapon efficiently, though she wondered vaguely when anyone could ever have use for such an implement beyond the field of battle.

It was the display of smaller items, though, which really caught her eye. Although throwing stars hadn't been taught at her school, she recognised the principle behind the various sharp-edged discs and stars. She fingered one with caution, noting how much heavier – and, in fact, less sharp – these weapons were compared to the discs she'd fought against in Dashfort.

Her fingers wandered next to a pair of iron batons, linked at their ends by a heavy metal chain. She ran her hand along the chain, wondering just how this was to be used as a weapon – there was no doubt that was its purpose, given the nature of the stall.

Moving along the table a little she picked up one of a matched pair of throwing knives and examined the intricately carved handle, assessing the balance as she weighed the knife in the palm of her hand – it was a solid, well-crafted blade, much closer in quality to the knife Laban had given her than those the school had supplied for practice. Tiny blue and white sapphires inlaid in the handle sparkled in the sun.

"Vramasda vrat olskanda?" the stallholder asked, noticing her attention. His face was dark and pointed like Spice's, and Eleanor guessed he was another native of Taraska.

"How much?" she asked, thinking it couldn't hurt to at least find out the price.

"Ahh, Charanthe!" The man nodded his understanding. "I little speaking. Not you Magrana speaking?"

She shook her head. "Sorry."

"You will learning," he said, a very certain tone to his voice. "Easier Magrana than Tarasanka. Tarasanka hard for you. It being nice knife, yes?"

"Very nice," Eleanor agreed, hefting it from one hand to the other. "How much?"

"For you..." He thought for a moment. "Four of Charanthe coin."

"Four?" She held up her fingers just to check, and he nodded. She was sorely tempted, but it was almost all the money she had, so she shook her head. "Not today," she said. "Thank you."

"But it being nice," he insisted.

"They're lovely," she agreed, placing the knife down carefully alongside its twin. "But not today. Sorry."

He reached out and clamped her wrist firmly in his hand. "You must being careful," he said, a sudden coldness in his voice. "No place in this city for wasting time."

He released her arm as suddenly as he had caught it and Eleanor turned sharply away, not wanting to get herself into trouble – particularly when he had such a display of weaponry at his command.

As she walked on, she realised she was hungry – and, in the dry heat of the city, growing desperately thirsty. She hadn't seen any stalls selling hot food since the edge of the market where they'd first arrived so she headed in the direction of the main road, hoping she'd be able to find her way back without passing the enslaved children again. She was having enough difficulty pushing the image from her mind without needing to see their pleading faces again.

After negotiating a couple of dead-ends, and being forced by the market's layout to make a couple of turns which went against her instinctive sense of direction, she eventually found herself back on the road.

Ignoring the tempting aromas drifting from the various food stalls, she went first to a cart selling freshly pressed juice – she didn't recognise the fruit, but it looked a little like an over-large apple, and she was sure it would do the job. It turned out to be more sugary than she would have chosen, but watery enough to satisfy her basic need.

Her thirst quenched, she picked out a food stall by the length of its queue – she recognised little enough of what any of them were selling, but if this one was busiest then she reasoned it was probably good quality.

"Tras'o skanda?" the chef asked her as she reached the front of the line.

Eleanor realised she had three choices – each of which looked like a chaotic medley of vegetables in a different thick sauce. "What's the difference?" she asked, but the chef's blank and impatient look told her that she would get no further speaking Charanthe. Obviously not all the Tarasanka natives had bothered to learn any of the Imperial language.

Feeling she had no basis for an informed decision, she pointed at the centre pot, which had the most reddish sauce. The chef picked up a sheet of a strange-looking flatbread, rolled it into a cone, and scooped a helping of her selection into the middle. "Bel magrana," he said, holding up two fingers.

She reached into her purse for the Magrad coins the herbalist had given her and offered two of them to the chef, hoping she'd understood him correctly. He pocketed the money without any further words and handed her the food, moving on to the next customer before she could even attempt to thank him.

She stepped away from the stall and made her way into the shade of a nearby building before taking a cautious mouthful of whatever it was she'd just bought. The bread had an unusual sponge-like texture, and stretched under Eleanor's teeth as she tried to bite through it; when she did manage to tear a corner away, she found that in addition to the spongy texture the bread also had a sour flavour to it. Though she was grateful to have a change from the limited diet available on the boat, Eleanor really hoped that for her next meal she could find some food which was more familiar to her. Still, she munched her way hungrily through the whole pocket of bread, which turned out to be filled with vegetables and strips of something which tasted quite like chicken, all smothered in a tangy sauce which left a bitter aftertaste in her mouth. The unusual flavours, combined with the mouthful of sand she got each time a cart trundled past, made the experience an unpleasant one and she was glad she had a little juice left to wash out her mouth once she'd finished.

She headed back into the shade of the market; the day was growing more uncomfortably hot, and at least the canvas canopies offered some protection from the glaring sun. She walked aimlessly and curiously, deliberately slowing her pace to give herself time to glance at the stalls without seeming to look too hard at any one thing – she was mindful of the way the weaponsmith's attitude towards her had suddenly changed the moment she'd tried to leave without buying anything, and she didn't want to attract attention to herself.

After a short while she passed the stall where she had bought the jelly; the herbalist gave her a friendly nod of recognition as she passed and she smiled back, feeling a little self-conscious. At the next opportunity she took a sharp right turn, determined to avoid passing by the starving children again, and found herself walking along a row of jewellery stalls. The whole area sparkled with gold, silver, and coloured jewels; there were rings and earrings, pendants and brooches, bracelets and hair ornaments... Eleanor found it hard to imagine just how much wealth was amassed on these few tables. Unlike the stand John had taken to sell his cloth, or for that matter most of the traders she'd passed so far, these stalls had an air of refinement to them – silk tablecloths provided a backdrop for the shimmering wares, and brightly painted signs hung from the canopies.

One particular pendant, a gold oval set with a large black onyx, caught Eleanor's eye but she forced herself to walk on, afraid to even think of how much it would cost. She briefly considered going back and trying to slip it quietly into her pocket, but the thought didn't last long – stealing money for food was one thing, but taking something just because it was pretty would make her feel like an outright criminal. Besides, she wasn't a skilled thief, and she was sure that getting caught would prove more dangerous here than it had been back home.

She emerged a moment later onto an open road, not quite as wide as the one by which they'd come in to the city, but clearly still an edge of the market. Deciding that this was as good a time as any to explore the rest of the city, Eleanor stepped into the road, and was almost run down by a passing cart as she crossed. She cursed under her breath, and took the next opportunity to turn into a narrower side-street where she felt safer and less exposed.

She walked for some time between the towering buildings, meandering through the streets and alleyways, climbing the gentle slope of the city. Almost all the walls were built from a stone which looked like it was made out of solid sand – when Eleanor scraped the fingernails of one hand along one of the surfaces, coarse grains came loose under her nails. She kept looking upwards, trying to spot any of the towers which had been visible from the harbour, but from the ground it was hard to get her bearings.

She tried to be systematic in her wanderings, though she had no particular goals – she thought she'd see more of the city if she tried to walk up and down the streets in some kind of order, but the roads were laid out in irregular patterns, and more than once she found herself for a second time in a square or street which she'd already visited. As she continued to walk, the sun dipped out of sight and the temperature dropped rapidly, a cold breeze ruffling Eleanor's shirt – it had been so hot earlier that she hadn't even thought about wearing a coat.

She was beginning to shiver, and thinking about turning back to the harbour, when an open door caught her attention. The door itself was wooden, carved with an image of a gigantic coiled snake and set with iron studs. It was the round, high tower into which the door opened, however, which really drew Eleanor's curiosity: she'd found one of the bulbous domes that she'd noticed from the boat.

She glanced around to make sure there was no-one else in

sight, then gave the door a tentative push. It swung silently on its hinges, allowing Eleanor to step inside the tower. A stone staircase spiralled upwards to her left, and to her right was another door, of a similar design to the one she'd just come through. She could see a crack of light around the door, and knelt to peer through the keyhole into the hall beyond. The room was lit by many flaming torches, but there didn't look to be anyone inside. A balcony ran around the hall's perimeter – guessing that the stairs would take her up there, Eleanor turned away from the keyhole and began to climb to a better viewpoint.

She'd counted eighty-eight steps by the time she came to a door which opened off the stairwell – and still the stairs continued upwards, spiralling above her head. She'd never seen anything like it. Part of her wanted to climb to the top of the tower just to see what the city looked like from such a height, but she thought it might be more sensible to look inside the hall first, while she was sure it was empty, so she opened the door and let herself onto the balcony.

Looking down over the ornate wooden balustrade – this, too, was carved with intertwined snakes – she took in the room below. The hall was even larger than the Great Hall at Mersioc, and she knew that the school's two thousand inhabitants had all been able to fit in there when they'd needed to. Two rows of carved benches ran around the walls, facing inwards, directly beneath the balcony where she was standing; the balcony itself also made a complete circuit of the hall. She saw other doors at each corner, and wondered if each one led to a similar spiral tower. She'd just begun edging along the balcony to check when she heard bells ringing somewhere out of sight, quickly followed by footsteps echoing from the hall below: people were beginning to fill the benches.

Instinctively, Eleanor fell to her knees and flattened herself to the floor. She was above the level of the torches, here, so she hoped she could blend into the shadows. Once she was comfortably arranged on her stomach, she edged forwards and peered down between two snake-heads.

The people filing silently into the hall were dressed in long

76

green robes which reached to the floor, and they had matching green hoods which covered their faces. One, whose green robes were edged with a yellow trim, was carrying a small drum; while the others sat on the benches around the edge of the room he went to the very centre of the hall, drumming as he walked, and sat cross-legged on the floor. Once the benches were full of green-robed people, two others in yellow robes walked down the centre of the room, stepping in time to the rhythm of the drum. They came to a halt by the drummer, and stood facing one another over his head.

"Ngavra!" pronounced the taller of the two, raising his arms above his head. His voice boomed out, and echoed clearly back again from the rafters, allowing Eleanor to pick out every syllable although she could make no sense of the sounds. "Ngavra srapakastsa skantsa!"

The second replied, her voice revealing her to be a woman. She mirrored the man's gesture as she spoke.

The green-robed congregation rose as one to their feet, and sang out in unison. As the drummer continued to beat out his simple rhythm, the yellow-robed woman began to play on a small, high-pitched pipe. Her companion moved across to a large basket which sat beside the drummer, and removed the cloth which was covering it. The anticipation in the room was palpable as he reached into the basket and lifted out a large, live snake.

Eleanor held her breath, wondering what she was witnessing. She could only guess that it might be a religious ritual; the girls had been warned about the dangerous allure of religion from their earliest days at school.

The man draped the snake around his neck like a scarf, then began to walk around the perimeter of the room, stroking the snake as he carried it. As he passed, each green-robed individual reached out to touch the head of the snake, murmuring as they did so.

The man returned to the centre of the room, and the drummer and piper suddenly fell silent. He lowered the snake back into its basket, where it slithered calmly back into a still coil.

The yellow-robed couple made another series of

pronouncements, and the drummer started beating his rhythm again as everyone in the room began to chant in time: "Ngavra, ngavra, ngavra!"

The chanting reached a natural crest and then subsided; a few moments of silence followed. The congregation began to move after that, but while a few of them left the hall immediately, many gathered in small bunches for whispered conversations.

Eleanor waited for as long as she could bear, hoping the room would clear, but some of the little groups showed no sign of breaking apart. Eventually she shuffled on her belly back to the door, and – relieved to have got out unnoticed – continued her climb of the spiral stairs.

The steps levelled off into a stone floor, creating a round tower-room well above the city. A tall, narrow window let in a shaft of moonlight by which she could see that the room was bare apart from a couple of dangling ropes in the middle and a series of iron bars set into the wall to form a ladder. She moved over to the window and looked out at the peaks of the rooftops below. It was clear from this vantage point that the city's towers were more spread out than she'd imagined from the boat; she wondered, as she admired the view, what the builders had done to make the tops of the spires and cupolas sparkle in the day's last light. Surely it couldn't really be gold.

She looked up, trying to work out where the ladder would lead, but the tower was too dark. She set one foot cautiously on the bottom bar and tested it for strength; there was no give in the metal so she began to climb, pulling herself up into the darkness. At last she reached the top and stepped off the ladder onto a small wooden platform, whereupon her shoulder collided with something cold and hard. The ringing which followed told her she'd walked into a bell.

She cursed under her breath, hoping no-one had heard. She was just about to lower herself back down the ladder when she heard voices drifting up from the bottom of the tower; they sounded to be coming closer. She ran her hands along the walls and eventually found a small door; without thinking, she opened it and stepped outside. Luckily there was a narrow ledge running around the edge of the tower, and she found herself just beneath the cupola. She pulled the door closed behind her and flattened herself up against the curved wall at her back, glad that the growing darkness would give her cover from anyone looking up from the street. She began to inch carefully along the ledge, moving around the tower away from the door, not stopping until she thought she'd reached the opposite side.

Whoever had climbed the stairs to investigate managed to avoid knocking into the bell, but Eleanor heard the door open and froze. If anyone came onto the ledge, her only escape was downwards.

She heard the door close a moment later, and after waiting a while to be sure no-one was coming Eleanor edged back round to the doorway. She turned the handle, but the door wouldn't open. There was no keyhole – presumably there were some bolts on the other side that she'd simply failed to notice, and she was furious at herself for the elementary mistake.

Since there seemed to be no other options, she sat down and began to lower herself over the edge, searching for any plausible footholds. With a little difficulty she managed to make her way down from the tower onto the steeply pitched roof of the hall, which she slid down faster than she would have chosen, alarmed at how much noise the slates made as they rattled under her movement. She reached the edge of the roof without stopping and tumbled down into the street, much to the surprise of a beggar who was crouched in a nearby doorway.

As she dusted herself off and checked for broken bones, he hissed and spat at her from his doorstep. Still feeling generally annoyed, Eleanor spat back before running as quickly as she could back to the boat for the night.

Her second day in Taraska passed as quickly as the first, in a blur of dry heat and colourful stalls. She tried a different shop for lunch and managed to find herself something a little more palatable, but she still longed for a hearty Charanthe meal. Everything here seemed to come smothered in a thick sauce which made it hard to know what you were getting and less pleasant once you got it.

As she walked back through the darkened streets that evening, her attention was drawn by strains of music coming from a small tavern. Intrigued by the unfamiliar sounds – it was nothing like the music she'd learnt at school – she pushed the door open. The room was packed, and she found herself unable to move more than two steps inside. A group of four musicians played from a gallery above the throng; the drummer beat out an energetic, erratic rhythm while the others provided the melody on two pipes and a large stringed instrument.

In the centre of the floor a small space had opened up around a dark-skinned woman with long black hair which whipped behind her as she moved. Eleanor had to stand on tip-toes to see what was happening, and she still only caught glimpses of the woman's movements. From what she could see, the dance was a mixture of fluid swaying movements and occasional acrobatic leaps; as the music sped up, so did the dancer.

A few moments later, a second woman cartwheeled into the circle. She was shorter than the first and more voluptuous, with short blonde hair spiked up into peaks.

The onlookers stepped back to make more space for the dance, and Eleanor found herself pushed backwards, crushed up against the people behind her. She strained to see what was going on as the two dancers slowly circled.

"Vashta! Vashta! Vashta!" the crowd chanted, clapping furiously.

The blonde woman did an impressive backflip then launched into a series of stamping movements, using her feet to play out a rhythm to rival the drummer.

The black-haired woman just watched, swaying gently where she stood, until the stamping subsided – then she in turn began to move furiously, tapping with her feet and swirling her arms in a complex pattern.

Eleanor began to work her way around the edge of the room, trying to get a better view. Another sudden surge of excitement in the crowd pushed her into a young man.

"Sorry!" she said quickly.

He looked curiously at her. "Ven Magrad," he muttered, as much to himself as to her, shaking his head. "Ven Darasgad. Valisgad? Gharanded?"

She guessed he must be wondering about her nationality, so

she said, "I'm from the Charanthe Empire." She had to raise her voice to be heard over the frenzied music.

"See not vashta before," he said. It was barely a question.

Eleanor shook her head. "What's happening?" she asked.

"Vashta. Is woman-fight here in Darasga."

"A fight?" Eleanor asked. It didn't look like any kind of fighting she'd ever seen; the two women weren't even touching.

"Fight," he confirmed. "Winner take everything."

Another surge of the crowd separated them again, and Eleanor turned her attention back to the dance. The women took turns at dancing a short sequence each, getting more and more complex turn by turn, until suddenly the crowd stopped chanting and cheering, and began hissing as the blonde woman danced. She redoubled her efforts with extra acrobatics, but the onlookers were unimpressed and eventually she stopped, threw a handful of coins at the floor, and made her way out of the bar.

The black-haired woman stood smugly with her hands on her hips, still swaying to the music, until another challenger stepped forwards and the whole cycle began again.

About twenty women had danced by the time the contest came to an end, leaving the final victor to gather up her winnings from the tavern floor – with plenty of help from admiring men in the crowd.

Eleanor left the tavern in a daze, still humming under her breath, and turned back towards the harbour. She wanted to dance like the women in the circle; every muscle in her body wanted to react to the music. Before she and her classmates had been old enough to begin combat training, dance had been Eleanor's strongest subject and she'd once hoped to work in the theatres. Her childhood joy rekindled by the display she'd just witnessed, she skipped a little as she walked down the street.

She was just about to emerge from the alley onto the seafront when a heavy object connected with the back of her head and the world faded into blackness.

Chapter 7

Eleanor regained consciousness to the sound of hushed voices talking a harsh, guttural language that she recognised as Magrad, though she couldn't understand what they were saying. There was an unbearable pain somewhere behind her left ear – unable to remember what had happened to bring her here, she turned her concentration to working out what was going on around her. She could feel the rough stone floor under her body, her back was pressed uncomfortably against a wall, and her left leg was folded painfully under her.

She opened her eyes and glanced around; in the flickering torchlight she could make out five figures – the two familiar shapes of Anvil and Misty, and three dark-skinned strangers. Though she couldn't make sense of what they were saying, they were clearly engaged in very urgent discussions with little attention to spare for her; she hoped her friends were negotiating her release. One muscle at a time, she tested her movements – though she still felt groggy and sick with concussion, and her whole body ached with fresh bruises, nothing seemed to be seriously damaged. And, she noted with a moment's relief, whoever had brought her here hadn't even bothered to tie her hands.

She didn't have time to investigate further before a cry came from one of the foreign men; suddenly he was on his feet, pointing at her and shouting in alarm. Before she could react Misty and Anvil were beside her, hauling her to her feet and pinning her to the wall in one movement. They lifted her clean off her feet, banging her head on the base of one of the torches as they held her up against the wall.

"What's going on?" she asked, realising then that something was very wrong.

"You're worth ten thousan' Magrad dollars," Anvil said, his voice coloured with half-hearted apology. "Nothin' personal."

"What?!" Eleanor struggled against the two men, trying to

break free, but the arms gripping her shoulders were strong and unforgiving.

"Nothin' pers'nal," Misty repeated, leering stupidly at her. "You're gonna make us rich, assassin-girl."

"How?" Eleanor demanded, her mind unwittingly going back to the pathetic, shackled creatures at the market. As she spoke, she found a foothold in the wall; a crack between two stones where she could safely lodge her heel. They held too tightly for her to make much movement, but she launched herself upwards – the direction, she suspected, that they were least expecting – and there was a sickening thud as her head connected with the base of the torch.

The pain was nothing compared to the blow which had knocked her out, but she knew she'd succeeded; the force was enough to dislodge the torch from its bracket. A moment's pause to see which way the flames fell, then she took full advantage of Anvil's horror and surprise as the burning torch dropped towards his face – he loosed his grip on her arm, and without hesitation she seized her knife from her belt and plunged it deep into his chest.

Misty fled the room at once, not waiting to see what would happen, not even for the chance of ten thousand dollars. Warm blood flowed over Eleanor's hand as she shook the dead weight from her blade, and her concussion sickness was overwhelmed by a different kind of nausea as she realised what she'd done. She hesitated a moment too long; before she had chance to run the three foreign men were upon her, knocking her to the ground and taking the knife from her hand. Taking no chances this time, they bound her thoroughly with strong hessian rope to hold her hands behind her back, her arms to her sides and her legs together. One of the men tore the name bangle from her wrist and pocketed it.

Eleanor lay still, trying not to react as one of the men patted her down, his hands roaming roughly across her body as he searched for weapons – he pulled the two school daggers from her belt and tucked them under his own clothes, and scattered the other contents of her pockets on the floor. She silently willed him to ignore the pins in her hair but she was not so lucky and even those were confiscated. Once he'd finished searching her the man kicked Eleanor halfheartedly in the back before going to join his two companions, who were talking in angry whispers.

Eleanor's fingers were resting against something hard; after a moment's fumbling she identified the jar of jelly which she'd bought at the market. Deciding that it might come in useful, she struggled to work it under her clothes and out of sight at her waist.

Eventually the men seemed to reach an agreement and one of them came over to Eleanor, picked her up by the ropes that now bound her, and hauled her from the room. He carried her up a long flight of stairs – she counted a hundred and sixteen steps – and then dropped her to the floor again outside a heavily-bolted door.

The man pulled back the bolts then took a key from a chain around his neck and unlocked the door. He took out a knife, slashed carelessly at Eleanor's bonds, and pushed her hard into the cell. She stumbled and fell, managing to look round just in time to see the door shut heavily behind her. She heard the key turn in the lock, and the sound of thick bolts sliding home.

She stretched her arms and legs, glad that she could move again, and looked around the room. It was a cold, stone-walled cell, with only one tiny window set high in one corner. Enough to let in a faint glimmer of moonlight, but too small to offer any chance of escape. There was no furniture.

The sound of ragged, uneven breathing drew her attention to a small shape huddled in one corner. She didn't think she would have noticed him if she hadn't heard him. "Ghiida," she said in what she hoped was passable Magrad. That seemed to be the language everyone understood.

"Don't... speak..." the boy said, his voice strained as if he was struggling for every word.

"Me neither," Eleanor said, moving closer. Now she could see that his face was gashed, and swollen with bruising. "Are you from the Empire too, then?"

He gave a small nod.

"I'm Eleanor."

"Raf."

They sat for a moment in silence; Eleanor's mind wandered back to Misty, who would surely be back at the boat by now. She could imagine how much his story would have changed by the time he told them what had happened – and she found herself hoping against the odds that John wouldn't believe the lies. She hated the idea that, after he and Mary had been so kind to her, he could possibly think she might have killed one of his crew out of malice.

"What school are you from?" she asked Raf, more to distract herself than out of any real desire to know the answer.

"Venncastle," he said. "You?"

"Mersioc Regional School for Girls – it's near Port Just. But you shouldn't try to talk," Eleanor said hurriedly, feeling guilty that she'd even tried to make conversation when every word caused his face to contract with pain. Suddenly, she remembered the jelly which she'd managed to lodge under her belt. "Don't move," she said, struggling to pull out the jar. "I'll try not to hurt you."

He looked curiously at her but didn't speak. She scooped out a little cold jelly and reached out to him, gently smoothing the gel into one of the cuts on his cheek. He flinched beneath her fingers, but still said nothing so she continued to tend his wounds, working her way around his face and neck, pushing his scruffy black hair out of the way to reach the gashes on his forehead.

"Thank you," he said as she finished and pushed the lid back onto the jar. She shrugged, embarrassed by his gratitude, and tucked the jar out of sight beneath her clothes again.

They sat in silence for some time, until their captors brought some water and a little dry bread to the cell. Eleanor insisted that Raf should eat it all – he was worryingly thin, and it had clearly been much longer since he'd had a proper meal. Though he tried to refuse, she was stronger. Eleanor allowed herself only a couple of sips of water to ease her thirst.

Once the food was gone Raf fell asleep quickly, curled on the floor, and Eleanor pulled the ragged blanket over him. She didn't think she'd be able to sleep while her head was still throbbing from the earlier blow but she stretched out on the cold stones anyway, and eventually pain faded into sleep.

She was woken the next morning by bright sunlight streaming through the high window. She stood up, intending to climb the wall and look out – but the moment she got to her feet she was overcome with nausea and sank back to her knees almost immediately.

"Are you okay?" Raf asked her, rubbing the sleep from his eyes. He winced as his fingernail caught one of the cuts on his cheek.

"A bit faint," she admitted. "But much better than you. Don't try to talk."

"Me? I'm fine." He gave her a brave smile. "I'm getting used to all this."

Another wave of nausea washed over her and she retched.

"If you're going to be sick, try over there," Raf suggested, pointing towards the corner of the cell.

She crawled in the direction he'd indicated and found a small hole between two stone slabs where a narrow shaft ran straight down through the floor. The stench of urine overwhelmed her as she leaned over the opening and vomited into the darkness.

"So how long have you been here?" she asked once she was sure she'd finished throwing up.

"Oh, aeons. I'm not sure exactly – it was twelve days past the solstice when they caught me. How long are we from the equinox?"

Eleanor counted on her fingers, working through the time she'd spent aboard John's boat. "About a month away," she concluded, though it was hard to be certain when she'd spent so much time at sea. The boat had seemed a harsh enough prison, but her rough calculations suggested that Raf had spent as much time locked up here as she'd spent sailing.

They were interrupted by the door being unbolted and unlocked. Two guards waited stiffly by the door as a third came in to the cell, lifted Raf by his collar and hauled him to his feet. Eleanor stood up as well, but Raf shot her a warning glance that she could only understand to mean that he didn't want her to get involved. Seeing how heavily armed the three men were, she thought he was probably right – even if both of them were up to fighting, they couldn't overpower three armed guards with their bare hands.

The guards took Raf from the room and locked Eleanor alone inside, leaving her only a small cup of water for breakfast. Still feeling somewhat nauseous, she decided to take advantage of her solitude to examine the cell. She pressed her eye to the keyhole and peered out into the corridor beyond, watching as Raf was led round a corner and out of sight. They were going in a different direction to the way that she'd been carried up the stairs the previous night, but apart from gathering that small snippet of information, she saw nothing of interest.

Turning her attention to the lock itself, Eleanor wished again that the guards hadn't thought to take her hair pins from her. Without anything more delicate than her smallest finger to poke inside the lock she could tell only that the iron mechanism was very solidly built, and that it would probably take more force than a hair pin to spring open the lock in any case. Besides, she reminded herself, the bolts on the other side of the door were more than enough to keep her imprisoned.

If she was going to get out of here, it was going to take a lot of planning.

She moved on next to examine the walls of the cell. Unlike the crumbly, sandy stone she'd seen outside, the walls around her were built of large blocks of a glossy grey rock which was cold and hard to the touch. The blocks fitted together almost seamlessly, reminding her of the wall she'd had to climb in Dashfort – only this time she didn't have any knives to force between the blocks. She made a futile attempt at getting up to the window, but the lack of footholds combined with Eleanor's residual nausea to make any progress impossible. She resolved to try again once she was fully recovered, and sat down to have a sip of water.

As soon as the first drop of liquid passed her lips she realised just how thirsty she was, and gulped down two large mouthfuls before it occurred to her that she should probably save some for Raf, who hadn't had chance to drink anything before he'd been taken from the cell. She set the cup down on the floor – which was made from identical stones to those in the wall – feeling rather forlorn. She had no idea why she was here, except that two people she'd thought were her friends had spotted some opportunity to make a quick profit. Why anyone had wanted to buy her, she had no idea.

She couldn't stop wondering about the children she'd seen in the market – was she fated to end up in shackles on a market stall? They'd been younger than she was, but maybe there was also a market for older girls. John had said that anything could be bought and sold in Taraska, but she wondered just how she'd managed to become a commodity.

Her train of thought was interrupted by the door opening again. One guard deposited Raf on the floor, and another placed down a cup of water and a lump of bread. As he stood up again he caught sight of the water which Eleanor had saved, and aimed a kick at the cup. The pottery broke when his foot connected and the water spread across the stones, disappearing into the cracks.

Eleanor glared at him, but said nothing. There seemed little point causing trouble.

"Ellie," Raf began once the guards had left.

She bridled to hear the diminutive form of her name: it made her feel like a baby again. She looked across at Raf, intending to point out how much she hated it, but she froze when she saw his face. A fresh, bloody cut stretched across his cheek from nose to ear, but the pain in his expression was even worse.

"What happened?"

"Have you got any more of that gel?" he asked weakly.

Eleanor fished the jar from her pocket. "Stay still, then," she said, and moved across to apply the jelly to his face. She pulled back once she'd finished. "There, that should do."

"I'm afraid that's not all." He shuffled slowly round till he had his back to her, and then carefully lifted his top to show her his back. The skin of his lower back was marked at irregular intervals with blistering red blotches.

Eleanor gasped involuntarily. "What did they do to you?"

"I can do it myself if you like," he offered, dropping his shirt and turning to take the jar from her hand.

"It's okay. But it'd be easier if you took your shirt off," she said awkwardly, feeling a hot flush rising to her cheeks. "If you don't mind."

He pulled the shirt off, grimacing as the fabric caught his blistered skin, and Eleanor leant over to dab jelly onto the wounds. She wished she could afford to be more liberal in her application but they wouldn't be able to get more once this jar ran out so she rationed herself carefully, allowing only a small coating for each blister.

Once she'd finished and returned the jar to her pocket, she repeated her earlier question: "Raf, what happened?"

"I couldn't see," he said. "They had me face down."

"But why? Why do they want to hurt you?"

He didn't answer, but reached across to the bread and water which had been left for them. He broke the bread in two and handed Eleanor the larger piece.

"It was kind of you to try and save me a drink," he said, motioning towards the patch of floor which was still slightly damp from the spillage. "But the guards here don't like kindness. They'll be worse if they think we're friends, they always are."

"There've been others here?"

He nodded, and made a muffled affirmative noise through his mouthful of bread.

"What happened to them?"

"All dead, I think."

Eleanor chewed thoughtfully on a corner of crust. He wasn't sure. Suddenly, she launched into a hurried account of what she'd seen in the market, the stall with young children for sale, and her theory that she seemed to have become a tradable commodity. It didn't fit, though, with the fact that Raf seemed to have spent the last couple of months being tortured.

By the time she finished, Raf was nodding slowly. "You're right," he said. "It doesn't add up."

"But unless they're going to sell us on, what could they want us for? We're only just past school age – we're not worth anything!" She wondered whether she should mention the price that Anvil had put on her, but she didn't really want to have to explain.

Again Raf just shrugged, giving no response except to take another mouthful of bread; Eleanor wondered what he was hiding from her, and why. He must know why they were torturing him – after all, what was the use of torture except to make someone talk?

She was frustrated with his reticence but it seemed unfair to pressure him while he was so badly hurt. She just wished he'd trust her. She turned back to her meagre lunch in silence – if he wasn't willing to talk about the important things, then she wasn't prepared to make small-talk.

Later in the day, Eleanor was summoned from the cell by one of the men who'd been talking with Misty and Anvil. He was a short, balding man with a wiry beard – all the Tarasanka men seemed to have beards – and apparently he was the one who spoke a little Charanthe. A couple of lackeys accompanied him, whose only job seemed to be to hold Eleanor tightly by the arms, and they half-carried her into an unoccupied cell nearby. The short man barked something incomprehensible, and they thrust her forward so he could speak to her.

"You will to talking?" he asked.

"What about?" Eleanor asked, thinking she would really be happy to say anything that would get her out of this ghastly place sooner.

"You know," the man said. "You will to telling?"

"I don't know what you want."

The man shook his head, looking disappointed. "We being nice at you now, no? You want we being nasty?"

"Like what you did to Raf?" The words slipped out of Eleanor's mouth before she had time to think about whether she was making a mistake.

"Your friend not talking enough," the man said. "But he will – as you will."

The threat behind his words was obvious. Eleanor felt a sudden pang of guilt for assuming Raf had not trusted her enough to talk about why they were hurting him – there was another possibility. It was looking more and more likely that

90

their captors were just stupid.

"What do you want me to say?" she demanded in exasperation. The concept of being tortured was bad enough in any circumstances, but this was a threat of torture without any end in sight unless she could work out what they wanted.

The man sighed and took a step away from her. "We have time," he said. "You will to talking eventually."

He sat down on a low bench by the wall, and looked expectantly at Eleanor. She met his gaze as steadily as she could, though the two men holding her twisted her arms and made her wince with pain. They held her there for quite some time, apparently waiting for her to do or say something.

Eventually, the short man stood up again and pulled out Eleanor's throwing knife. "This is yours?" he asked, holding it up for her to see. Dried blood was still encrusted on the blade.

She nodded, her throat suddenly dry.

"What it does?"

"It's a knife." She couldn't help herself, though she knew it might be unwise to take a sarcastic tone with her captors. "It cuts."

"What also?" He was holding the point to her neck now, right against the artery, and she knew he could kill her with a flick of his wrist. She could only hope that he believed, whatever he wanted from her, that she was more valuable alive.

"I don't know what you mean," she said, trying to keep her voice level. "It's just my knife."

"You will to talking," he repeated, turning away from her and replacing the knife in his pocket. "Now or later."

It was dark by the time the guards deposited Eleanor back in the cell; there was no more food or water that night. Raf was already sleeping and she didn't want to wake him so she curled up in a corner and tried to get some rest. She slept only fitfully; it was very cold, and she couldn't relax while visions of the short man – and Laban's knife – swam in her head. She wondered what on earth they could want from her.

They came again the next day, early, rousing Eleanor from her broken sleep – this time the short man didn't come as far as the cell but three guards collected her, leaving a morsel of bread behind for Raf. The guards carried Eleanor roughly through the corridors, taking her to a different room this time.

Her heart skipped a beat when she saw where they'd brought her. The previous day's questioning had been in a simple cell, bare apart from the wooden bench where the short man had sat – but this was quite different. This room had one clear purpose.

Eleanor had never thought about possible designs for a torture chamber but she was sure that if she had, she wouldn't have been able to come up with anything more fitting than this. She swallowed hard as the guards fastened manacles around her wrists, suspending her in mid-air from a heavy iron cage in the centre of the room, and then secured her ankles with chains to the bottom edges of the cage. The walls were hung with various contraptions, mostly forged from iron and mostly beyond Eleanor's powers to identify. There were knives, hammers, saws, and other small tools that could be put to painful uses – but the things she couldn't even name were all the more terrifying.

The short man who had questioned her the day before stood in one corner, poking casually at a small furnace. He turned to face Eleanor. "So, you will to talking today?"

"What do you want me to talk about?"

"Shatrokda!" the man barked, and Eleanor heard a guard step up behind her.

She craned her neck, trying to look round, when something hit her lower back and caused her to cry out in pain. Again and again the object slammed into her back, until she was long past caring what it actually was that was hitting her. Then, just as suddenly as it had started, the assault stopped.

"Now you talking?" the short man asked.

Eleanor drew herself up as straight as she could in the shackles, and glared straight at him. "If you don't tell me what you want," she spat furiously, "then I can't help you. *Whatever* you do to me!"

"Ngavra kalgsa!" he cursed, and swung his fist straight towards her face.

Unable to duck out of the way, Eleanor just closed her eyes and braced herself for the impact. There was a sickening crack as his knuckles smashed into her nose, and she screamed.

The guards removed her from her iron bonds and threw her back into her cell without a word, slamming the door behind her. She fell to the floor, sobbing uncontrollably, blood flooding from her nose.

Raf edged across the floor towards her and tried to put his arm around her waist, but her bruises were too fresh and she gasped with pain when he touched her. She stretched her arm out to him instead – her other hand clamped to her face – and he held her hand as she cried until she ran out of tears. Eventually she fell asleep, her hand in his, curled on the cold stone floor.

Chapter 8

The next morning Eleanor awoke to find Raf sitting by her side, a serious expression on his face. "What is it?" she asked once she'd returned to full consciousness.

"I was wondering what they want from you," he said.

"I don't know."

He studied her face. "What do you know that they don't?"

"Um, well..." She thought for a moment, and decided that she really only knew one thing worth knowing. "There's a secret room in Dashfort," she said hesitantly, uncertain whether she should really be telling anyone about it.

His eyes brightened, and a smile spread across his lips. "The puzzle chamber – of course! So you're trying for the academy as well."

"You too?" Eleanor asked, feeling a thrill of excitement at the idea. If he was on the same path as she was then there was some reality behind all the legends – and that meant she'd made the right decision back at the school, for all that it felt like a lifetime ago. And, however strongly she felt that everything had gone wrong, if she'd ended up in the same place as another postulant then she knew that she couldn't have steered too far from her intended course.

"I was, until I fell into the trap at the code tower. Is that where they got you?"

"No, I was... Well, it's a bit complicated. Some smugglers tried to sell me. It's a long story."

He raised an eyebrow but to Eleanor's relief he didn't ask for more details; she didn't want to talk about it more than she had to. Anvil's death still weighed heavily on her mind.

Instead, Raf asked, "So do you know which country we're in?"

"Taraska. I guess we're still in Taraska La'on, I don't think there was time for them to move me out of the city while I was knocked out."

He nodded. "Thought it might be. Bastards. This is just the sort of thing they'd do."

"Why?"

"They've always wanted to break the Association – they see the Empire as a threat to their trade routes, but we always find their spies."

She almost laughed. "You know everything!"

"I didn't know they'd started taking girls into the academy – otherwise I would've guessed sooner that you were one of us."

Eleanor stared at him in surprise. Weren't all jobs available to anyone with the right abilities? Wasn't that the whole point of the assessment system?

"The Association was around long before the Empire with its current laws was formed," he explained when he saw the confusion on her face. "It can be a bit old-fashioned."

"Oh." She didn't really know what to say. "Do you know a lot about it?"

"A bit."

"So what was your assignment?"

"I don't know," he admitted. "I didn't even read the letter."

She couldn't help feeling impressed with his confidence. "I'd have been happier if I hadn't – some stupid local police job. I thought this would be better, but I'm almost wishing for a quiet life now."

"It won't all be like this," he said. "We were caught by surprise. And we haven't been trained."

"Do you think..." She hesitated, wondering if what she was about to say would sound too stupid. "Do you think this is part of the induction?"

"No." Though his voice was firm he didn't seem to be mocking her for wondering, which came as a relief. "One of the others who was here, when he tried to escape..." Raf illustrated his point by drawing his hand across his throat, a chilling gesture which said everything more succinctly than words could have done. "I had wondered, but I think this is real."

"Then we have to get out of here."

"Yes," he said slowly. "But not just yet."

"Well, we'll need a plan, but–"

He cut across her: "We have to wait. The academy doors open on the equinox – we have to keep them busy till then, or this might all be for nothing."

"Why?" Eleanor fought to keep emotion from her voice, but the idea of deliberately staying here for any longer than they had to seemed ridiculous. She already had a broken nose, and she didn't want to think about how many bones in her body remained to be broken.

"They know they're close to getting everything they need, but I don't think they know when the doors open. If we can keep them busy till after then, then we've got a whole year to get back and deal with their men back home. Otherwise..." he shrugged. "There's no point getting back sooner if we destroy the Association in the process."

"But if they kill us–" Eleanor began.

"So what? It'll be more than just us who get killed if they break the Association."

She stared at him in disbelief. "Would you really rather die than tell them what you know?"

"Don't you think it's worth it? Isn't it more important to protect the Empire from them – from people who do this?" He indicated his most recent wounds. "Besides, what makes you think they wouldn't kill us as soon as we told them anything?"

Once he said it, it was obvious: the only thing keeping them alive was the value of the information in their heads. If they gave in and talked, they would undoubtedly be disposed of.

"How do you think I've survived so long?" he continued. "They know I'm not telling them everything. The others either tried to escape, or just told everything they knew about the code tower – and they never came back. I don't cause them any trouble but they know I'm keeping things from them, however much they hurt me."

Eleanor's fingers went to her nose, which had swollen hugely overnight. "You might have to teach me how to do that," she said. "I don't know how much of this I can take." This felt like a significant gap in her education – even Laban's extra tuition had given her no training in how to resist interrogation under torture.

"We can get through this," Raf said softly, taking her hand in both of his. "All we have to do is survive. One day at a time, okay?"

She nodded. One day at a time. If they couldn't even plan to break out before the equinox, then they didn't have much choice.

"Let's play a game," he suggested. "Take your mind off the pain."

"Okay," she agreed, though she found it hard to believe that anything would really take her mind off it.

"Do you know the guessing game?" he asked. "You think of an object, and I have to ask you questions to guess what it is."

"I know it."

"Good. Can you think of something?"

She nodded, and he began the guessing. Was it alive? No. Was it smaller than a person? Yes. Was there one in the room? No – she laughed at the very idea, they had so few things. Was it made of metal? Yes.

"Is it a weapon?" he asked.

"How did you know?"

He smiled, and pressed on with his questioning without answering her. "Is it a dagger?"

"Not quite."

He paused for a moment then asked, "A sword?"

"Yes!"

"Any specific sword, or just generally?"

"General will do – I was thinking about some longswords I saw at the market. Is it my turn to guess now?"

He nodded, and she smiled. Maybe the distraction was helping a little.

For a few days after that they were only disturbed by guards bringing water and food – often dry bread but sometimes a bowl of boiled grain, and occasionally a few scraps of meat. They occupied themselves with various games and riddles, trying not to dwell on the torture chamber which waited just around the corner.

"They're giving you time to think about it," Raf explained.

"They want the threat to really sink in."

"It sank in when he smashed my nose," Eleanor said bitterly. The break was still causing her a lot of pain, and though she would never have admitted it at the back of her mind she was scared of seeing her own face again if she ever escaped to somewhere with a mirror.

"They want you to have time to imagine much worse than that," he said. "Luckily, it gives us time to work out how to keep you alive. You have to think what you can tell them without giving them the number. Or the way into the puzzle chamber, if you can help it."

"I don't know," she said for what felt like the hundredth time. She knew it was important – her life might depend on it – but she just couldn't think of anything that could work.

"Think harder. Ellie, you have to do this."

Suddenly, it came to her. "My knife," she said, remembering with a shudder the way the man had held the point to her neck. "He was asking about my knife."

"Go on."

"Maybe I can think of something about that."

"What's special about the knife?" he asked. "Is it school issue?"

She shook her head. "No, I was given it. But if I can come up with something interesting..."

"It has to be true," he warned. "When they've got you under pressure, the last thing you'll be able to do is lie. So tell me about this knife."

"It's silver, I think. It has emeralds set into the handle, and it's perfectly weighted for throwing–"

"They know all that!" He sounded impatient as he cut her off. "They have it right there. Tell me the history."

"It was given to me by my mentor – well, he left it for me when he disappeared. I was only fifteen. I think he wanted me to have something better than the school knives to practise with."

"Excellent! That's a very promising start – just let slip that this man gave you the knife, then let them beat you up a bit more, but they won't want to kill you until they find out who he was. So that should get you through at least a couple of days."

Eleanor found it hard to reconcile the look of excitement on Raf's face with the fact that she was about to be tortured, but at least his strategy seemed to be keeping him alive. Just survive, she reminded herself. Concepts like comfort belonged to a different world.

Two more days passed before the guards came and hauled her back to the torture chamber. They locked her back into the manacles and left her alone to wait for her questioner, while she rehearsed in her head what Raf had told her to do. They'd agreed what she would say, but she knew that to be convincing she had to endure as much as she could before she seemed to give in.

They left her hanging until her arms were aching before the short man came in. "Today you talking?" he asked her.

She bit her lip. She had to wait for him to ask her about the knife again; she couldn't just start volunteering information, however much pain she was about to cause herself by keeping silent.

He beckoned a guard from across the room, and Eleanor braced herself for what was about to come. Today it was a five-tailed whip, with iron beads threaded onto the end of each strand; the guard today made sure she got a good look at it before he took his first swing. After a few lashes her shirt ripped, and then the beads tore into the flesh of her back until she could feel the blood beginning to dribble down.

Eventually the short man motioned to the guard and – after another crack for good measure – the whipping stopped.

"What do you want to know?" Eleanor asked again, gasping through the pain.

She was relieved that he brought out the knife; she didn't have a reserve plan. "Where you getting this?" he asked, holding it up to her face so that the flat of the blade pressed against her swollen nose, causing her to wince in agony.

"I was given it," she said. She knew she was breaking too soon, but she couldn't help it. At least he was asking the right questions.

"Who giving?"

She pressed her lips together and ignored him, concentrating on the way the cold iron of the manacles cut into her wrists, trying not to think of what was bound to follow if she didn't answer. He pressed the knife harder against her nose, the point pricking between her eyebrows, and she squeezed her eyes shut in a feeble attempt to protect her vision. Even if he wanted her alive, he probably wouldn't care about blinding her.

Suddenly he moved the blade down and left in one sharp movement, slicing into her cheek. It was all she could do not to scream. As he stepped away from her she felt the blood well up, and then a hot trickle down her cheek.

"Talk," he said flatly.

She kept her eyes closed and her mouth shut, and prepared herself for the next inevitable assault. She heard the whip moving through the air before it reached her, and she flinched even before the iron balls gouged her back. She counted five lashes, ten, twenty. The pain was more intense this time as the new wounds fell on already bruised and broken flesh.

"Who giving knife?" the short man asked once the whipping had stopped again.

Eleanor forced her head up to look at him, blinking tears from her eyes. His face was impassive; unreadable. "My teacher gave it to me," she said. "It's just a knife."

He growled and motioned for the guard to inflict a couple more lashes of the whip, but seeing how close she was to fainting he ordered her to be taken back to the cell almost immediately afterwards.

Raf hurried to her side as soon as the guards had left, the pot of jelly ready in his hand. He spread a little across the cut on her cheek and she couldn't even stop herself from yelping at the pain, tears streaming down her face.

"Be careful," she said, when she opened her eyes again and saw how much of the jelly he'd scooped out. "We can't get any more."

"Shhh. Don't worry about it now." He moved around to reach her back, and she braced herself for the fresh assault on her nerves. "How much did you have to tell them?"

"Not much." She hoped he wouldn't be disappointed in her –

for breaking so soon, or for taking such a beating, or for feeling so faint now. "Only what we agreed."

"You need to rest," he said once he'd finished rubbing the jelly into her back. He handed her the tattered blanket. "Sorry there's nothing better."

Another five days passed before the guards came for Eleanor again – although they took Raf one day in the meantime, bringing him back bruised and shaken though he insisted he wasn't really hurt.

The next time they took her to the torture chamber the guards fastened her into the manacles as usual, and left her hanging while they conferred in hushed voices. The short man was nowhere to be seen, and the other guards had showed no sign of being able to speak Charanthe – she wondered what they were going to do with her if they couldn't even understand a word she said.

After a prolonged discussion with his colleague, one of the men – she recognised him as the one who'd wielded the whip with such enthusiasm a few days earlier – came across and grabbed roughly at her hair, forcing her face up towards his until he was peering straight into her eyes. The wiry hairs of his beard tickled her face; she could feel his breath warm against her cheek and could smell the stale remnants of his last meal. She stared blankly past him, determined not to react, focusing instead on the strange iron contraption the other guard was fiddling with.

The bearded man prodded at her face with bony, long-nailed fingers, paying particular attention to the broken line of her nose, and the cut that snaked across her cheek. She closed her eyes, hoping not to betray the pain she felt with every touch, and trying not to think about what might come next.

Eventually he stepped away from her, and a grating metal sound made her look up. He was turning a wheel above her right shoulder, gradually winding in the chain which attached her right arm to the metal cage. It didn't take long before her joints were stretched beyond her comfortable reach, and she cried out in pain as her shoulder gave way again where she'd pulled it aboard the *Rose*. The guard smiled unpleasantly, and moved around to a similar wheel on her other side.

Once both of her arms were painfully extended, the guards left her alone in the room. On his way out, the one who'd turned the wheel picked up a silky green robe from a hook near the door. She hadn't noticed it hanging there earlier, but now she was sure it was the same distinctive green as she'd seen inside the strange building with all the snakes. She wondered if he was part of that religion – if that was indeed what it was.

She didn't know how long they left her hanging there, with no windows to monitor the changing light, but she guessed it was going on for half a day before the short man came in to see her. A cruel smile curled his lip when he saw her discomfort.

"You feeling tired?" he asked. "You wanting rest? You just need to talking."

She put as much energy as she could muster into glaring at him, and he laughed.

"You will to telling me about your knife-teacher?"

She shook her head. She and Raf had agreed that she could go into a little more detail on the training Laban had given her, but she was afraid there wasn't really enough to say to keep her interrogators interested. Why would they care?

The man stepped towards her, and aimed a careful kick towards the bottom corner of the cage; it was then Eleanor realised that the chains from her legs could also be shortened by winding them onto a small wheel. She gasped as her left hip was jerked downwards.

"Talk," he said. "Teacher was at your school?"

"No."

"Where?"

She shook her head.

"What he teaching you?"

She would have refused to answer, but he leant casually against the side of the cage and rested his foot on the wheel again.

"Knife-throwing," she said quickly, though she knew she was only delaying the inevitable. "More advanced than the school classes. And close-combat, with weapons and without."

"Why he teaching you this?"

Eleanor swallowed hard. The conversation was turning the wrong way, this was beyond what she was supposed to be saying today – while she still had plenty more she could bring out on *what* Laban had taught her. Besides, she wasn't even confident that she knew the answers.

She delayed too long, and the short man kicked the wheel by her left foot again. "You want we bringing your friend in? Maybe he making you talk."

She shook her head again. If she was going to be pained and humiliated, she at least preferred to be alone; she couldn't help fearing that Raf's support might evaporate if he saw how badly she was handling herself. He wouldn't take her side if he thought she was a risk to 'the Association', as he called the assassin organization, or to the Empire.

"Tomorrow, then." the short man said. "Tomorrow we bringing you both together." Then he called out to summon the other guards.

They unlocked Eleanor's manacles and she felt the relief in her muscles even as they carried her back to the cell and deposited her unceremoniously on the floor.

Raf looked her over before handing her the blanket. "It's working," he said. "You've got them convinced that they need you alive. However much pain they cause you now, they'll be careful not to risk killing you."

She didn't know what to say, so she said nothing. In a way he was right – she'd escaped from today's interrogation with a minimum of physical damage, but though there were no marks left on her skin the pain had still been unbearable. At least when she'd been thinking about broken bones, her imagination had been limited by the number of bones she knew about; with more subtle forms of torture, they could start all over again every day.

"All we have to do is survive," Raf said gently. "You're still alive; that means you're winning."

She closed her eyes, unable to feel any truth in his words. She didn't want to argue so she curled up beneath the blanket and lay in silence, too shaken even to cry, until she eventually drifted into nightmare-filled sleep.

She woke a little later, some time after darkness had fallen, to find Raf still awake at her side. "They brought some meat," he said. "I think it's chicken. You should eat."

She began to protest that she didn't want anything, but he pushed the bowl into her hands. Once she started eating she realised how hungry she was, and then the food ran out sooner than she would have liked.

"He said they were going to bring us both together, tomorrow," she said once she'd finished.

Raf didn't look surprised. "More stupid games," he said. "We should've expected this sooner."

"Why?"

"They know we're helping each other; they don't like that. They want to turn us against each other by making me responsible for your suffering, and you responsible for mine. *Talk or his arm gets broken*, that sort of thing. We should've expected it."

Eleanor didn't want to explain how she was feeling so she said nothing. He was undoubtedly right about their captors' intentions, but even armed with that knowledge she couldn't promise she wouldn't react exactly that way. If he had the power to stop them hurting her, and he didn't do it, she didn't know how she could avoid hating him for it – no matter how kind he'd been to her so far. She looked away, ashamed of herself.

"We need a code word," he continued. "A signal – then if things are getting too much for you to cope with, you can let me know and I can throw them something to make them ease up."

"Okay," she agreed. "Any suggestions?"

He thought for a moment. "We don't want them to know we're doing it, so it can't be too obvious. It has to sound like something you might actually say – or scream."

"Like... 'help'?" It sounded silly even as she said it, but it was the best she could think of.

He looked hard at her. "Can you promise me you won't say it unless you mean it?"

She nodded, then had to squeeze her eyes closed to stop a

couple of tears which were threatening to escape her. This was going to be one of the hardest trials yet.

"Besides, it's a gift to us if they start interrogating us together," he said thoughtfully.

She was about to object but he put a finger on her lips to silence her.

"I know it'll be hard," he said. "But think about it this way: both of us, out of this cell, in a room full of weapons. They're giving us a way out, if we can work out how to take it."

She nodded. He had a point – if they could only find a way to take advantage of it. "Any bright ideas?"

"Not really. Those manacles are a problem, so we'd have to break away at the beginning or the end, while they're moving us."

"Beginning," she said firmly. "We'd be too tired... afterwards." She didn't need to say after what.

They fell into silence, both trying to think of a plan, although Eleanor found herself distracted by the horrors lurking in her imagination – as bad as the actual torture was, it was made many times worse by the way her mind constantly tried to anticipate their captors' next innovations in cruelty.

The next morning one of the guards woke them before it was even fully light outside, gave them each a drink of water, and left them alone again. Eleanor wondered if they'd have a day's reprieve but they weren't that lucky, although it must have been past midday by the time that four guards came to the cell and, as promised, took both of them back to the torture chamber.

The room had been rearranged since the previous day, with two cages now set so that once Raf and Eleanor were manacled in place they were facing one another, their bodies barely a foot apart.

The short man arrived quickly today, a strange smile twisting at the corners of his lips. "Now, who will to talking first?" he asked, looking between them.

"Neither of us want to talk to you," Eleanor said flatly, finding her confidence increased now Raf was with her. She smiled at him despite the aches in her joints – she hadn't recovered from the previous day's ordeal, and her shoulders felt dangerously close to dislocating today before the real trials had even begun.

"Vras shatrokda," the short man said, waving his hand in Eleanor's direction.

She heard a couple of the guards step up behind her, and one of them pulled the back of her shirt up before touching something red-hot to her skin. She screamed before she could help herself; of course she'd been expecting pain, but the sudden burning heat had caught her off guard. She could feel the first blister forming even as the guard moved his brand to another area of her back.

"Who will to talking?" the short man asked, then turning to Raf: "You want to saving your girlfriend from hurt?"

The assaults came at irregular intervals, sometimes giving Eleanor time to catch her breath and wonder whether they'd stopped, but always there was another burning touch to plunge her into agony again. *Help.* She turned the word over and over in her mind, all of her efforts focused on not saying it. She had to hold out. A few times she caught herself wondering why Raf didn't make them stop when he could so obviously see her pain, but she scolded herself for letting such thoughts cross her mind – the whole point of having an agreed word was so that they didn't have to second-guess one another's tolerances. But still she couldn't help wishing he'd bail her out sooner.

Eventually the short man motioned to the guards, and they turned their attention to Raf. Eleanor couldn't bear to watch as they brought a fresh poker from the furnace, glowing white with heat, and touched it to his arm; she squeezed her eyes closed, bit her lip, and tried to block out the sound of his agonised breathing. She wanted to make it stop, but she knew Raf would be more angry than relieved if she intervened.

They went through three cycles before both were too exhausted to even scream any more, and the short man gave the order for them to be taken back to their cell. They were given a small bowl of meat scraps, a lump of stale bread and a cup of water, and they shared out the last of the jelly to soothe their burns.

It was a struggle to find any sleeping position which didn't exacerbate the pain of the blisters. Yet as she lay unable to sleep, listening to Raf's light snores, Eleanor felt a small sense of triumph – somehow, they had survived another day, and they'd even managed it without giving anything away. Now they just needed to find a way out.

Chapter 9

Eleanor was woken by the first shaft of early-morning light which fell through the high window, and found Raf already wide awake. "Morning," she said, sitting up and then wincing as one of her blisters caught on her shirt.

He turned to look at her. "You sound a bit happier this morning."

"I'm thinking how to get out of here. We'll need to work on getting our strength up." She knew that she was beginning to weaken through poor nutrition and lack of exercise, and Raf was in a much worse state. "We need to start using our time in here properly. No more sitting around feeling sorry for ourselves."

He grinned. "That's the spirit! What are you thinking?"

"We've still got about two weeks to the equinox, so we've got time to start with the basics – push-ups, stretches, a bit of jogging." She'd been thinking it through before she'd fallen asleep, and it still seemed reasonable in the morning light. "We can't do this without some serious training."

They started slowly, finding that even simple stretches were hard on their tired and underfed bodies, and there was constant pain from their wounds. After only a few short exercises they were interrupted by the sound of bolts sliding open on the other side of the door, and both sat down quickly to hide the fact that they'd been doing anything.

The guards gave them water and a bowl of cold grain for breakfast, then left them to their own devices again.

For the next few days they devoted themselves to their new training schedule, taking breaks only to sleep, eat, and recover from the now-daily sessions in the torture chamber. They became experts at listening for the slightest sound at the door, and at slowing their breathing so as not to arouse the suspicions of the guards. If anyone noticed they were sweating more than usual or breathing a little heavily, they hoped it would only be attributed to fever – an illusion they tried to reinforce by coughing and snuffling whenever they were under observation, and which seemed to be convincing because they started to be supplied with bowls of hot stew instead of the usual cold fare. Even the intensity of the torture sessions decreased for a couple of days; apparently someone really did want to keep them alive.

Eleanor quickly felt her muscles relearning old patterns of movement; Raf was having more difficulty, but then he'd been longer without regular exercise and a proper diet. He forced himself to keep going almost to the point of collapse most days, trying to make up for his weakness by pushing his body beyond its natural limits and insisting – whenever Eleanor suggested he should take it easy for a day or even a morning – that it was his own fault for letting himself get out of shape while he'd been alone in the cell.

Over the same period they discussed and rehearsed their plan, going over it again and again, constantly suggesting refinements. There could only be one attempt; they had to get it right first time.

Eventually, once their calculations suggested that the equinox had been and gone, both agreed that they were about as well prepared as they'd ever be able to get in the circumstances.

"Today, then?" Eleanor checked after the guards had left them alone with their breakfast.

"Yes. Are you ready?"

She nodded. The time had come. "Yes, but..." She took a deep breath, trying to gather the courage to say what needed to be said, painfully aware of the way he was watching her. "Have you ever killed anyone?" she asked.

"No." There was a faint question in his voice.

"It stunned me," she said. "The first time. I only ended up in here because... because I hesitated. I think I'm ready now – I'm expecting it this time – but I wanted to warn you because we can't afford to get this wrong. We won't get a second chance."

"Thank you." He reached out to touch her hand, and she breathed a silent sigh of relief; she hadn't known how he would take it, afraid it would sound like a criticism although she meant it only as a practical warning. The last thing she wanted was to alienate him when, now more than ever, they were going to have to work together to survive.

It was getting late before the guards finally came for them that day, and they were relieved that it was just four men to the two of them – that was what they'd planned on. The guards half-dragged them to the torture chamber as usual, and they both tried to act naturally, feigning their typical combination of resistance and resignation.

As the guard on Eleanor's right reached up to fasten her wrist into the manacle, she lurched sharply down and to the left, freeing her wrist and aiming a kick sharply up towards the groin of the guard on her right. She could hear that Raf had also made his move, as they'd agreed, but she didn't have time to turn and see how things were going for him.

She rolled as she hit the floor and tore herself free of the second guard's grip, just in time to see the first one take a glowing poker from the furnace and turn back towards her. She looked around desperately for a weapon, but from her position on the floor the only thing she could reach was a length of iron chain. It would have to do.

She wrapped the ends of the chain around her hands as she scrambled to her feet, and as the poker came down towards her head she held up her hands to defend herself. Sparks flew as metal hit red-hot metal and she pulled the chain taut to create a block, forcing the guard to step backwards to avoid being burnt by his own weapon.

She heard the other guard moving up behind her; unable to turn without losing control of the poker situation, she waited until she was sure he'd come within striking distance and kicked backwards towards where his stomach should have been.

Her foot hit only air and she was left struggling for balance; the guard with the poker took advantage of her instability and pushed forward as hard as he could, knocking her to the ground.

Flat on her back on the floor, she knew she didn't have time to move out of the way; both men were almost upon her. She released one end of the chain and began to spin it, faster and faster until it was whipping through the air fast enough to do serious damage. Wishing she'd thought to try this earlier, she tilted her wrist to change the angle and the chain cracked into the temple of the poker-wielding guard, causing him to drop his weapon as he fell to the floor.

She got to her feet, still spinning the chain to keep the other man at a safe distance. She flicked her wrist and the chain cracked downwards, knocking the dagger from his hand. He cried out as the metal smashed his fingers, and finding himself suddenly disarmed with the chain still whirling towards him, he backed quickly from the room.

Eleanor glanced back at her first assailant to reassure herself that he definitely wasn't getting up, then turned to where Raf was still fighting. He'd managed to take a short sword from one of the guards, but it was two against one and he was barely holding his own. Eleanor reached for the nearest sharp object, a crooked metal spike from the bench to her left, and sent it flying across the room; it sank deep into the neck of one of the guards, piercing his windpipe and leaving Raf free to devote his attention to the other – and after that the fight was over in two sharp blows.

"Time to get out of here," Raf said, taking the dagger from the hand of the guard he'd just killed.

Eleanor put down the chain and joined him in collecting weapons, wanting to be as well prepared as possible for what was still to come. "I don't think it's over yet," she said. "One of them got out alive – he'll bring reinforcements to look for us."

"All the more reason to get moving – come on."

She followed him into the corridor, and instinctively they both turned away from the cell that had been their prison. Their plan hadn't covered anything beyond fighting their way out of the torture chamber; Eleanor realised she hadn't truly believed they'd even get this far, and besides, she'd assumed the way out would be obvious. It wasn't.

After only a few paces the corridor forked; looking both ways gave them no indication of the right direction but a slight noise echoing from the right-hand branch was enough to persuade them to go left.

They made their way carefully along the corridor, passing several doors and tensing with fear every time they heard movement from any of the rooms, trying not to make any sound that might disturb the castle's occupants. Most of the doors were closed, but one rested ajar and made them doubly nervous as they edged past.

They rounded the corner at the end of the corridor and came upon a flight of spiral stairs. Eleanor remembered being hauled up stairs when she'd been captured, and there had been light at the bottom of the latrine shaft so their cell couldn't have been underground – they must need to go down to ground level. She hesitated with her foot on the first step and glanced at Raf for confirmation; he nodded and moved past her.

They started their descent at speed, but they'd gone down only about twenty steps when they heard someone – no, several people – coming up the stairs below them.

They both instinctively froze, then: "Run!" Raf yelled, grabbing her elbow as he turned and sprinted past her, pulling her back up the way they'd come. She tried to keep pace with him, her injured shoulder threatening to tear again as he raced ahead of her taking two steps at a time. She struggled to keep up but he had a firm grip on her arm and didn't stop hurrying her until they reached the top of the flight where the stairs opened out onto a circular stone platform under a domed ceiling.

"Stand there," he said, pointing her towards one side of the stairwell; he took the other side and fell into a fighting stance with a scavenged knife in each hand. "If they're following us they'll have to come up this way – we've got the advantage."

They waited, ready to launch themselves at anyone emerging from the stairwell, but the expected pursuit didn't materialise. No footsteps followed them up the stairs.

"How long do we wait?" Eleanor asked, only daring to speak once she was quite sure no-one was coming.

"Stay there," he said, and moved away to examine the room. "There's a door over here – not locked. Come on."

He held the door open and she followed him out onto a small ledge which formed a path around the tower.

"We did it!" She cried, finally willing to let herself believe it. They'd actually escaped; the fresh air blowing her hair across her face confirmed it. She threw her arms around him in a celebratory hug, but let go quickly when she felt him flinch; in her excitement she'd forgotten his wounds. "Now what?"

"Over to you – you know this town better than I do."

They were at the top of a high, round tower, on a stone ledge about two foot wide. The side of the golden cupola bulged out just above their heads, and beneath them the walls were met by the next-lowest section of the roof about two storeys below. Eleanor looked over the edge. "Well, I suppose first we'd better think about getting down."

The tower wasn't that different to the bell-tower she'd fallen from on her first exploration of the city – but on a larger scale. A fall from this height would do serious damage even if they weren't already injured. She flattened herself on the ledge and extended her arm as far down as she could reach, sweeping her fingers across the wall. The stones were worryingly smooth, blocks of hard rock like those which had enclosed their cell rather than the crumbly stone most of the city was built from; it was going to be hard to find a good grip.

She prodded at the wall with one of the knives she'd picked up, trying to insert the blade between two stones. When her first attempts failed she tried to chip at the crack, but to no avail – the knife would break before these stones splintered. She shuffled along on her belly and tried other cracks; she'd travelled half the circumference of the tower by the time she found a gap which she thought might be wide enough to accommodate her fingers.

She lowered herself over the edge, toes questing lower down the wall for a foot-hold. This was going to be the hardest climb of her life; the smooth quarried blocks offered few options. She'd worked her way a few feet further down the wall before it occurred to her to wonder where Raf had got to – she didn't know if he could climb the way she could, and if she was going to have to help him then she needed to get his attention sooner rather than later. She wedged her fingers and toes more tightly into place and craned her neck upwards to look for him.

As her lips were forming his name to call for him, he stepped into view; she stopped herself shouting out just in time as she realised he wasn't alone on the ledge. He was backing away from a uniformed guard, and a moment later another guard came round from the other side of the tower.

Eleanor could only watch in horror as they fought, Raf with his back flattened against the wall of the tower, one attacker on either side. There was no way she could get up there in time to help so she pressed her body against the stones and held herself motionless, watching.

Raf had a blade in each hand, fighting in both directions at once, arms and legs whipping out in attack any time an opportunity presented itself. She could only imagine how much it must be hurting him but he showed no sign of it, suddenly fighting with twice the vigour he'd shown inside. Another kick, a quick slice down with his right arm, and one of the guards fell from the ledge; Eleanor felt a gust of air as the body dropped past her, and clung even more tightly to the wall. The guard clattered heavily on to the tiles of the roof below, and bounced down into the street. If he hadn't been dead when he fell, he certainly would be by now.

Eleanor didn't have time to look up again before the second man also dropped, flailing and screaming as he passed her although his screams were silenced before his head smashed into the ground below.

"Raf!" she called out once she was sure the fight had subsided.

"Ellie!" He looked down, a broad grin spreading across his face. "I thought you were dead!" He vaulted over the edge towards her, and she had to drop downwards in a hurry to free up a foot-hold for him. Her shoulder wrenched with the sudden weight, and she cursed as she nearly lost her grip.

"How well can you climb?" she asked once she'd stabilized herself. "It's a tough one if you don't want to go down the way they did."

"Don't worry. I'll follow you."

They made slow progress, having to take a complex route around the tower to find enough useful gaps between the stones, but they reached the lower roof without mishap and rested for a moment on the ridge tiles to catch their breath. The lower section was an easier climb with plentiful foot-holds, and they were on the ground in no time.

In the half-darkness they almost stepped on the body of one of the guards Raf had knocked from the tower. Though dusty and bloodied from the fall, his clothes were still in better shape than the rags Eleanor and Raf were wearing, so they quickly stripped him to his underwear. Raf took the guard's trousers to replace his own and Eleanor pulled on the tunic, which reached to her knees, and belted it at her waist. In the nearly-new clothes she felt almost human again, and even ran a hand through her knotted hair before fastening a taut ponytail at the nape of her neck.

After glancing around to check her bearings, she led Raf down towards the sea. She picked out a complicated route, choosing narrow and deserted alleys whenever possible, but in time they came to the gate where the main thoroughfare passed through the city wall. She didn't want to go through – it was too soon to risk drawing the attention of the guards – but she was pleased to see a few traders' stalls were pitched on this side of the wall.

Motioning for Raf to wait for her, she sidled up alongside a grocer's cart and slipped two large, pear-shaped fruits into her pockets while his attention was occupied by another customer. Then she returned to Raf, took his arm and pulled him back into the maze of narrow lanes from which they'd just emerged.

"Where are we going?" he asked as they hurried along.

She ducked into the darkened arch of a nearby doorway, tugging him behind her. "Here, eat." She handed him one of the fruits she'd stolen, then took a hungry bite out of her own. The flesh was grainy, and too sweet to be properly refreshing, but at least it was food. Once they'd both finished, Raf repeated his question.

"We need money," she said. "Food. Clothes. Weapons. Luckily, I know how we can get some."

Even through the gloom she could see him raise a questioning eyebrow as he waited for an explanation.

"Vashta," she said, enjoying the blank expression on his face. She'd been willing to let him take the lead inside the castle, and he'd got them through it, but she was happy to be back in control again. "It's a dance contest – they call it a fight between the women. I saw it the evening before I was captured and the winnings were huge – and I'm sure I can win."

"Won't that draw a lot of attention to us?"

She laughed. "Look at me! I'm already about the most distinctive fugitive there could be. But money can buy anything in this city – that must include some black-market freedom. Besides, no-one has to see you, you'll blend into the crowd."

She led the way through the streets until they came to the tavern where she'd seen the contest previously. The critical gap in her knowledge was how often the Vashta happened, but it had looked spontaneous and she hoped she could start it herself if necessary.

Raf hesitated on the threshold, looking concerned. "What if you lose?"

"I won't lose." He didn't look satisfied, so she made up the simplest Plan B she could think of. "Okay, if I lose, you'll just have to steal the prize money from whoever wins – and get out of here before anyone gets a good look at you. In which case I'll meet you down by the harbour just before daybreak tomorrow. Now, time for you to blend in." She winked at him and then slipped ahead of him between two groups of drinkers, leaving him alone by the door.

There was no music being played yet, but up in the gallery the string player was adjusting the tuning of his instrument. It was still early, and although the bar was already getting crowded the crowd was mostly quiet; just a gentle hum of conversation filled the air.

Eleanor made her way to the edge of the room, as far as she could get from the bar – she didn't want to be challenged when she had no money to buy anything. She lurked in the shadows, waiting for the musicians to strike up, painfully aware of how strange she must look with her ill-fitting clothes and very foreign colouring. The last thing she wanted was to attract attention to herself before she even started dancing. She wondered how long it would take for word to spread that two fugitives were on the loose – and how tempting a price would

116

have been placed on their heads. By all accounts Taraska was a more liberal, and more lawless, state than anywhere in the Empire – unlike back home, people here didn't depend on the authorities for their livelihoods, so why would the average person care if she was on the run? Money was the only reason these drinkers might take an interest in her.

She was still pondering this when the whine of instruments being tuned transitioned into the distinctive sounds of Tarasanka music over a strong drum beat. She started tapping her foot even without thinking, adapting her body to the rhythms of the music even as those rhythms changed every few bars. The tempo was slow to start with, almost too slow to dance to, but it wasn't long before the musicians picked up speed.

Eleanor waited to see if someone else would start the dance, but although the music grew louder and more lively there was no sign that the crowd was paying any attention to it. Then, just as she was about to see if she could start the contest herself, a woman climbed up onto one of the tables and began to dance.

The musicians responded to every tap of the dancer's foot on the table, as if she were pushing them to play faster and faster. She was a well-built girl with black skin and wide hips, her hair tied in half a dozen plaits which flicked across her face as she stamped and swayed on the table-top, and a long blue skirt which swirled around her ankles.

The crowd pulled back a little to leave space around the table, and a few of the spectators began to clap in time to the music, but no-one stepped forward to make the challenge. Eleanor took a deep breath, wondered for the last time whether she was making a mistake, then launched herself forwards through the crowd. There was no chance to turn back; hands grasped her and lifted her, carrying her forwards until she found herself deposited on another table facing the first dancer.

Spying her competition the dancer slowed until she was moving at a quarter-time, watching Eleanor with wide, suspicious eyes. Eleanor's muscles froze against her will; she hadn't planned beyond this moment and her heart pounded in her chest. She'd been a good dancer at school but Charanthe dances had regular rhythms, repeating patterns, and a sequence of steps to execute in turn. Here she had nothing but her instincts to guide her, and the threat of the price on her head lurked in the back of her mind.

Sensing the growing anticipation and impatience in the crowd she started to move her hips in time to the music, swaying and twisting her arms above her head as she brought herself back into tune with the constantly-changing beat of the drum. It didn't matter that she wouldn't be following a standard Charanthe dance, she could still use the same steps to get herself started. Knowing her nerves wouldn't fully dissipate until she was simply too exhausted to care, she tapped out a series of steps on the table top, spinning and hopping as she got into her stride. It was a very limited platform, too small for what she really wanted to do, so she somersaulted down to the floor when the first opportunity presented itself – and the crowd erupted in cheers and shouts.

The woman on the table made a half-hearted attempt to continue her dance, but hands pulled her back into the crowd and another girl was pushed forwards in her place. This time the competitor was a narrow-waisted blonde, wearing short trousers and with her generous bosom barely restrained by a strip of red cloth tied around her chest. Eleanor couldn't help staring, and clearly the audience was similarly captivated.

The girl began a stamping, swirling dance, playing to the crowd who cheered and chanted as she shimmied close to them, breasts constantly threatening to escape from under the band of cloth. Eleanor was conscious of the relative inadequacy of her own figure, with what little curves she had well-hidden beneath the folds of the stolen tunic, and her determination steeled. This was a dance contest, and she could dance better than this immodest hussy. She didn't wait for the blonde girl to finish, but cut in with a few steps of her own, challenging for the crowd's attention and suddenly understanding why they called this a fight. All the same feelings gripped her, and her heart pounded with the same urgency as when she'd been fighting for her life.

The two girls fell into a natural rhythm, alternating short

sequences, each responding in turn with quicker steps, higher kicks, faster twirls. Eleanor's muscles ached with every movement but she pushed herself harder and harder, determined to match the pace of her opponent. The knotted mass of her hair whipped against her back as she threw herself more vigorously into the dance. Coins and gems were starting to accumulate on the floor, hard against her bare feet, providing a sharp reminder of why she needed to emerge victorious.

Remembering the crowd's reaction to her somersault, she decided to risk a move from pure dance into acrobatics. She hadn't seen any of the other dancers do anything like it – tonight or previously – but maybe in this environment being different would work in her favour. She danced her way to the edge of the crowd, freeing up space behind her, then performed a series of back-flips to take herself across the room.

Even as she landed and spun back to the dance, an incongruous movement in the crowd caught Eleanor's eye; someone striding across the room, pushing his way through the audience and destroying the atmosphere. The crowd pressed around him and slowed his progress, trying to prevent the interruption, but it was too late. The blonde dropped to her knees and started scooping up money and jewels from the floor; Eleanor followed suit, pocketed as much as she could, and made her way quickly to the side of the room.

"I think now would be a good time to disappear," she murmured beneath her breath as she reached Raf at the door.

They ran through the streets back towards the now-deserted market, where they ducked between stalls until they were thoroughly lost.

"That should do it," Eleanor said, smiling broadly. She might not have managed an outright victory but her pockets were heavy with what she'd collected and it felt like enough; surely they could buy themselves some secrecy with this much wealth.

"And now what?" he asked.

"We wait. In the morning, we'll see what the winnings will buy us." She dropped to her knees and crawled under the nearest stall. "We can sleep here."

Chapter 10

Eleanor woke at dawn, disturbed by the sounds of the first stallholders setting up their wares for a new day of trading. She shook Raf by the shoulders, determined that they should move on before they were spotted hiding beneath the table.

"Breakfast soon," she said as she caught the scent of sausages wafting from a nearby stall and realised just how hungry she was for a good hot meal. "But first, we have some business to conduct."

Raf followed her without question, and after a little wandering she managed to locate the weaponsmith's stall which she'd seen on her previous visit to the market. He recognised her as they approached so she reached quickly for four Charanthe dollars from her winnings, plus an extra half-dollar for good will, and laid the coins on the table. She picked up the pair of throwing knives she'd admired earlier and sheathed them at her hips. The smith nodded as he took up her money, and she knew she'd redeemed herself in his eyes.

"Pick what you want," she told Raf, then turned to consider her own options.

Once they were both well armed, Eleanor leaned in and spoke in hushed tones to the weaponsmith. "Now, we need one more thing. We need to disappear."

He looked at her in puzzlement. "You wanting leave the city?"

Raf began to nod but Eleanor said, "No, not yet. I want to be invisible."

"Invisible is hard," the man said.

"Invisible is expensive," Eleanor corrected, spreading out a handful of jewels on the table-top and hoping it was enough to prove her point. "You sell all the best weapons – I'm just asking for a more subtle blade."

He beckoned them to join him behind the counter; Eleanor gathered up the jewels before following. The smith then dropped to his knees and began tracing in the sand with his own pocket-knife. Eleanor and Raf followed his example and knelt to see the map he had drawn. "This is market," he said, pointing to a square. "You can be here – is tavern, with bedrooms. They not asking you questions."

"Good start," Eleanor said. "And to move around the city without being seen?"

His brow furrowed. "Wait," he said, standing up to serve a customer. Eleanor and Raf shuffled under the table out of sight and waited.

"What are we doing?" Raf asked in a barely-audible whisper.

"Surviving," Eleanor replied, keeping her voice just as quiet. "I'll explain later."

The smith bent down to their level again, and continued: "There is ways, but you not speaking Tarasanka, and not Magrana. Is difficult. Best I think is silent monks."

"Silent monks?"

"They wearing red clothes, and on they heads..." He waved his hands around to indicate a hood over the face. "Impossible to tell one from another, and they silent, so no problem that you not speaking. People seeing you, but seeing only a monk."

Eleanor thought back to the green silk robes hanging in the corner of the torture chamber, and the ritual she had witnessed before she was captured. "What about the group with the green robes?" she asked. "And the snakes?"

"Cult of Ngavra," he answered. "Is harder for you. They not silent."

"But if I wanted to..."

"Clothes is easy, but you will to struggling without language. Is not so good for you."

Eleanor ploughed on, ignoring Raf's puzzled expression. "Can we get both sets of robes?"

"Yes, yes," the smith agreed. "Two days. Meanwhile, you is going to there–" he plunged his knife into the sandy map again "–and waiting. Say Branav is sending you."

Once she was sure the sketchy map was lodged well enough in her brain, Eleanor stood up and kicked it into the dust. "Thanks," she said quickly, then grabbed Raf's arm and pulled him into the morning's growing crowd.

They slipped quietly towards the edge of the market, following the route that the smith had indicated, stopping only briefly to buy a few essential items of clothing. They passed through the jewellery section, and Eleanor noted that the pendant she'd liked was still there – she told herself that if they had money left after everything they needed to do, she'd go back and ask how much it cost. After making a few unnecessary turns just in case anyone was trying to follow them, they eventually arrived at the shoddy little tavern. The door stood open wide, its red paint beginning to flake, and a curtain of beads hung inside the doorway.

A voice called out as soon as they parted the beads and stepped over the threshold, questioning in Tarasanka.

"Branav sent us," Eleanor said boldly, hoping the man would understand. "He said we could stay here."

"You is Charanthe woman?" The landlord shuffled into the room, looking curiously at his two guests. He was a dark-skinned, broad-shouldered man with a round, cheery face. "And one boy. Ftar'o kel... You being friends of Branav?"

"Yes," Eleanor agreed. "He said you had rooms here."

"You will paying?"

She nodded, and the man's smile broadened. He beckoned them to follow him through a low door behind the bar, which led into his cramped living quarters at the back.

"Rooms is up," he said, waving towards a wooden ladder which disappeared up through a hole in the ceiling. "But you needing food first?"

"Yes please."

She and Raf sat down at the table, and the man filled two bowls from a pot which was bubbling over the stove. The stew was made mostly of fish, and had the same bitter aftertaste that Eleanor had found so strange about her first meal in the city, but they were both so hungry that they wolfed it down without complaint and gladly accepted second helpings.

When they'd eaten as much as they could manage, the man climbed up the ladder to show them their attic room. There were four narrow beds tucked under the eaves, and a small table in the middle of the room.

"There always being food for you, down there," the man said. "And toilet also down, and outside. Okay?"

"Is anyone else staying here?" Eleanor asked, suspicious of the extra beds.

"No, no. You paying, so all is for you."

She smiled and nodded her approval, and then he disappeared back down the ladder.

"Now, are you going to tell me what we're doing?" Raf asked once they were alone. "What were you talking about with green robes and snakes?"

"I had a bit of time to look round the city before I was captured," she began, not really sure where best to start. "One of the things I saw was – well, some kind of religious ceremony, I think. Very odd. But they all wore identical green robes, and I saw the same kind of robe when we were... in there."

He stared at her. "Revenge?" he asked. "Do you think that's a good idea, when there are only two of us against all their men?"

"Not exactly revenge. But at the very least we have to go back for our bangles." *And my knife*, she added silently; she'd mention that bit once they were back inside the castle.

"We can get new ones. Let's just get ourselves back to the Empire, and worry about it later."

"And leave my identity with those bastards? No thank you. You don't have to come with me, but I'm—"

He cut her off. "I'll come."

"You don't have to."

"I wouldn't leave you to face them on your own. We've been in this together from the moment they threw you into that cell."

"So, I think with the green robes we can find a way in, or at least a way to get at one of the guards. We can go and check it out once we've got the silent monk disguises – in the meantime, there's food here, and we've got time to train with our new blades."

She brought her purchases out from her pockets and laid them on the table – the pair of throwing knives, a stiletto, a short dagger, and a handful of stars which she'd picked up on impulse. Raf matched her with two curved daggers, a double-bladed knife, and one small throwing spike.

"So you've got the range," he said, indicating her selections.

"We can share." She held out a couple of stars, but he shook his head.

"I'm a bit useless over distance. Give me a straight hand-to-hand any day."

"Well, that should be all we need – I only picked these up because they looked fun." She twirled one of the stars in her fingers, then gave an experimental flick of the wrist and sent it soaring up to the rafters. It lodged in a thick cross-beam. "Love it! Can you reach that?"

"You need to grow a few inches." He winked at her and reached up; even with his extra height he could only just pull it out of the wood. Once he had it in his hand he turned it over, examining it. "Hey, these things are barely sharp."

"It'd feel sharp if it came at you fast."

"Oh, I know." He tried to mimic Eleanor's technique, but his hand wasn't steady enough so the star wobbled through the air and bounced harmlessly off the beam before clattering to the floor. "You'll have to teach me how to do it properly."

"It's easy!" She flicked another one into the air. "You just have to get it straight."

He glanced up to where the second star had lodged itself in almost exactly the same spot as the first. "Show-off. You can get it yourself this time."

Laughing, she walked across to where the rafters sloped down towards the floor, low enough that she could hook her hands and feet around to climb. She edged her way up until she reached the appropriate cross-beam, then swung herself on top of it and walked along to where the star was embedded.

Just as she was about to lean over for it, Raf reached up and pulled it away from her. "You'll have to come and get it!" he said, stepping back beyond her reach.

She swung down from the beam, landed heavily on the rickety floorboards, and was about to chase him across the room when she realised she was standing right by the table with a much greater choice of weapons than the one single star he'd taken.

She picked up his double-bladed dagger and turned it between her fingers. "Want a fight, do you?" she asked. "Maybe it's time we got in some sparring practice."

He held out his hand and she sent the knife spiralling through the air towards him; he caught it deftly by the handle and took three long strides so that he was almost upon her by the time she'd picked up her stiletto in her right hand and her dagger in her left. She turned just in time to ensure she was positioned between him and the remainder of the weapons, and blocked his first attack with her dagger. As the blades slid noisily along one another, she was glad she'd chosen a design with a robust guard.

Raf attacked relentlessly, keeping her on the defensive and never seeming to give her chance to respond with a counter-attack of her own. She knew she was at a disadvantage – her preference was for throwing-knives but she couldn't use her best skills in a friendly fight. At least when the knife was in your hand you could stop it a hair's breadth from your opponent's throat; there was no way to pull back a flying blade once you'd released it.

He moved the knife effortlessly from hand to hand, always coming in with a different angle or surprising her with a feint, and it was taking all her efforts to fend him off. Suddenly she ducked and rolled under the table, coming up on the other side a moment later; it gave him chance to pick up a second weapon but at least she felt she'd regained the initiative, and a little breathing space.

She moved around the table and out into the room, trying to give herself space to move. Raf came at her again but this time she dodged under his arm, came around behind him and grabbed his elbows before using a leg sweep to unbalance him. He managed to roll as he fell, turned on her and pinned her to the ground with his dagger under her chin.

She beamed up at him. "You're right, you're good at this."

"That was close, though, and you'll get better with proper training – we both will." He got to his feet and offered a hand to pull her up.

"I wonder what our landlord made of all that noise!"

"Shall we go and find out? I could really do with a drink after all that."

They climbed down the ladder, but there was no sign of anyone so they helped themselves to water and, since it was still on the stove, extra helpings of stew; the landlord returned just as they were finishing.

"You hungering much!" he said, laughing a little. "More?"

They refused, slightly embarrassed and wondering what he must think of his strange, half-starved guests. Especially if he'd overheard their sparring – though, even if he hadn't heard them this time, there'd have to be more of the same before they went back to the castle. They needed to be in the best possible shape to attempt that.

Suddenly Eleanor had an idea. "If I give you money, can you buy something for us?" she asked him.

"What you wanting?"

"Shrakol." She was fairly confident that she remembered the word now.

"Srakol? Is sauce for hurting skin, yes?" he checked, and she nodded – that sounded close enough.

"What's that?" Raf asked.

"I'm asking him to get us some more of that jelly stuff."

"I going market now – is good?" the landlord asked.

"Great. Thank you."

"Thank you, thank you," he repeated, smiling. "You needing anything else?"

"No – thanks. Branav's getting some things for us too."

The landlord picked up an empty wicker basket for his shopping, and let himself out without another word.

"What do you want to do?" Raf asked once they were alone again.

"Sleep? I'm exhausted!"

"Well, you get some rest, then – I might go and have a look outside."

She wanted to tell him to be careful, to make sure that he wasn't seen, but she was afraid of offending him so she kept silent. He wasn't stupid. She climbed back into the attic and flopped down on the nearest bed, where she slept soundly until

Raf's footsteps on the ladder disturbed her.

"I've got the gel," he said, putting it on the table. "Oh, sorry, did I wake you?"

"No, it's fine." She sat up, rubbing her eyes. "How late is it? How long have I been sleeping?"

"Don't worry. It's barely mid-day – besides, you should get as much rest as you need. We're safe here."

She nodded. "Okay. Pass me the jelly." Srakol, she mouthed silently. Srakol. She struggled to mould her lips around the foreign sound combinations. "What did you see outside?"

"I only went to look round the back. There's a good sized yard, out by the toilet. A good place to practise if we don't want to risk going through the floorboards – out of sight of the road."

"Great." She looked up from applying the jelly to her wounds. "We can have a rematch later."

"Whenever you've recovered," he said.

There was nothing critical in his tone but she felt the latent challenge behind his words. "Now?"

"If you like." He picked up his knives and lowered himself onto the ladder. "See you downstairs, then?"

Eleanor grabbed her dagger and stiletto and followed him, not wanting to give him time to find an advantageous position. She had enough trouble matching his skills as it was.

She smiled at the landlord, who was unpacking the groceries he'd bought at the market, and stepped outside. She couldn't see Raf but her confusion lasted only a moment – then she heard him move behind her, and realised he must have been lurking behind the door. She turned and parried his attack, and tried to slip her stiletto beneath his arm for a counter-blow but he stepped easily out of her way.

They circled the courtyard, feinting and dodging, until Raf spotted an opportunity to make his second attack; he caught hold of her with one hand and had his knife against her throat before she could defend herself.

"Sorry," he said as he released her. "I know I'm not playing fair."

"How so?"

"In a real fight you'd never let me get that close – not the way you handled those stars! We need a way to account for that."

She shrugged. "I'm learning from you."

"Fine – but it's better if we both learn something. What else could you throw?"

"Anything that's got enough weight to it." She picked up a fairly straight stick from the ground at her feet, and aimed it at him. It wasn't heavy enough to fly properly but it spun towards him and he met it with his dagger, knocking it to the ground.

"Too easy," he said.

She corrected him: "Too light."

"What else could we use?"

"Forget it – I'll just teach you to throw properly. Here." She handed him one of the stars from her pocket. "You just need to make it go flat – like a wheel." She turned it in his fingers to demonstrate, then pulled out another and sent it spinning across the courtyard. It sank into the wood of the toilet-shed door.

Raf did a few practice flicks of his wrist before he released the star, trying to mirror her movements, and he threw it much straighter this time. One point cut into the wood, and the star hung precariously for a moment before falling to the ground.

"So close," he sighed.

"No need to sound so disappointed – that was a huge improvement! If you keep going like that you'll be better than me by tomorrow." She was sure that wasn't true, but she wanted to encourage him – he'd fight better if he was confident.

They spent the rest of the afternoon throwing things at the shed – stars, knives, and the spike which Raf had bought. Raf found the spike easiest – the dual points gave him a good chance of making it stick, but without needing the precision of the stars – and Eleanor understood now why he'd bought it. She remembered the trouble she'd had on the *Rose* – she was good with her knives, but in that environment she'd have been better off with something less precise. By the time they went inside for the night the shed door was splintering in several places, and they agreed they'd have to find a more suitable target tomorrow.

The landlord gave them bowls of a different stew for dinner, along with some of the flat, stretchy bread that Eleanor had first tried at the market. The sauce was almost painfully spicy, leaving them both gasping for water to soothe their throats, but the lumps of meat were tasty and succulent, and they managed second helpings despite the way it burned their mouths.

After dinner they took turns in the small wash-room, scrubbing the accumulated dirt from their skin and, in Eleanor's case, trying to work the knots out of her hair. Raf simply shaved the matted hair from his head at the same time as removing the beard and moustache which had grown while he was imprisoned.

"You should cut your hair, too," he said, offering her his knife. "It can't be practical like that."

But Eleanor wasn't willing to be persuaded.

They fell into bed exhausted and slept late the next morning, warm and comfortable for the first night in much too long. The following day they kept themselves busy practising hand-to-hand techniques, still in constant pain and with their muscles still struggling to complete some of the more demanding exercises.

As Branav had predicted, it took two days for their robes to arrive; a young lad arrived with a package mid-morning after their second night in the tavern. By the time Eleanor had fished out enough jewels to pay him – even after negotiating as hard as she could over the price – she realised their money wasn't going to go as far as she'd hoped. They'd have to find more from somewhere before they could pay their landlord for his hospitality.

Once the delivery boy had left, she tore open the parcel and held one of the red robes up against her body. Raf picked up the other one, but they quickly realised the robes were different sizes and they had them the wrong way round; once they'd swapped them over both fitted moderately well, although Eleanor's trailed slightly on the floor. When they pulled their hoods up, their faces disappeared into the shadows.

"It suits you," Raf said from beneath his hood.

"You can't tell it's me under all this! At least, I hope you can't, that's the whole point."

"No," he agreed. "But the shape works for your figure."

She blushed, thankful that her face was hidden by the hood. "You make a fairly dashing monk yourself."

"Shall we go out, then?"

"Let's have lunch here first," she said, pulling the robe off over her head. "Buying food out there is hard work!"

There was no sign of the landlord so they helped themselves to slices of bread and cold meat from the kitchen and ate quickly, impatient to get out into the city under their new disguises. They'd had a pleasant couple of days sparring and resting, but Raf was itching to see more of the city and Eleanor wanted to go back to the Ngavra building and investigate the possibilities there.

They made sure they were well armed beneath their robes – insurance in case their cover was somehow blown – then started to walk back towards the city centre.

"Where first?" Eleanor asked.

"Shhh. We're supposed to be silent, remember? You know this place better than I do – just lead and I'll follow you."

She steered them back to the market first, where the comings and goings of daily life would give him a good impression of how Taraska operated. She was also aware that the bustle of the market-place held possibilities for stealing the money they so desperately needed. Being a fugitive was distinctly expensive.

They passed by Branav's stall, and Raf tugged at Eleanor's sleeve to keep her moving: monks wouldn't be stopping to shop for weapons. She was cross at herself for falling so easily into patterns of behaviour which could give them away, but it was hard trying to emulate something of which she had no knowledge. Monks, indeed! All the warnings against religion that they'd grown up with – and now they were pretending to be monks.

She scanned the various stalls as they passed, hoping to spy an easy opportunity, but the stall-holders all guarded their takings carefully. Likewise the shoppers didn't wear their purses openly in the way of those back in Port Just; this was a suspicious city. She hadn't dared mention to Raf that they were running out of money, uncertain how he'd take to the idea of stealing to survive, but she was starting to think she might have

130

to involve him – if one of them could create enough of a distraction, maybe they could get away with it. But planning required discussion, and they couldn't talk while they were hidden by their silence.

She led him deliberately and slowly through the opulent jewellery market, then up towards the Ngavra tower but today the snake-carved door was locked, and they made their way back to their inn feeling slightly dejected.

"Maybe it'll be open tomorrow," Eleanor said uncertainly as they both stripped off their red robes. "We just have to be patient."

"Maybe." Raf didn't sound convinced. He folded his robe and placed it neatly on one of the spare beds. "Here, I got you something. Shut your eyes."

"Why?" He was reaching into his pocket and she was suspicious, not willing to give him the advantage if he was after another sparring match.

"Don't you trust me? No tricks, I promise."

Still feeling a little wary, she closed her eyes, listening as he moved towards her. She felt his hands brush the sides of her neck, then something cold against her skin. He stepped back.

"You can look now."

She opened her eyes. He was holding up a small, slightly cracked mirror. Her reflection dismayed her – she still looked like she'd been dragged through a hedge – but her eyes were drawn to the sparkling ornament he'd hung around her neck. It was a wrought silver star, set with tiny emeralds which twinkled in the lamp-light, hanging from a thin silver chain.

"It might not be all that practical with the running around we'll be doing, and I know it's not the one that caught your eye," he said before she had chance to speak. "But the green really matches your eyes."

She took the mirror from him to study it more carefully. "It's beautiful," she said, twisting it in the light to make the gems sparkle.

"You're beautiful."

She shook her head in disbelief. "Have you even looked at me? My hair's a nightmare, my nose is smashed, I'm getting an amazing scar..." She ran one finger along her cheek where Laban's knife had sliced the flesh; it still ached. "And I was hardly a beauty to start with."

He shrugged and took the mirror from her. "You don't have to believe me. Just take care of the necklace, it was hard to pick that up without anyone noticing – especially you!"

Chapter 11

There was fish stew again for breakfast – it seemed that most Tarasanka meals involved stew, whether it was served with stretchy flatbread or, like this morning, over a bowl of grain. Apparently they made no distinction here between breakfast, lunch, and dinner.

Eleanor fiddled with the emerald pendant as she ate. She'd slept with it around her neck, one hand clasped protectively around the chain.

"So you just picked this up as we walked through the market?" she checked.

He nodded. "Sorry if that seems crazy, but I wasn't sure our money would stretch that far and I really wanted you to have it. I hope you don't mind too much."

"It makes one thing easier," she said, "because we're nearly broke."

"No way, I'm not letting you sell it – I got it for you to keep, and besides, it's too risky. Someone might recognise it."

Her fingers tightened on the pendant. Maybe it was worth enough to clear their debts at the tavern, but somehow she didn't want to give it up. "I wasn't thinking of selling it, but you've proved you've got a useful skill there."

"I'm not a thief," he said quickly. "I never stole a thing in the Empire."

"I'm sorry," she mumbled into her stew, feeling the blood rush to her cheeks. "I didn't mean to offend you, I just meant, well, just..."

"Don't panic. I'm not offended. I just don't want you relying on my skills as a master thief. I think I was lucky."

The nervous tightness in her chest was gone as quickly as it had arisen, and she smiled back at him. "Then I'm sure you can be lucky again."

"What's your plan?"

"Well I was thinking about the market, and how everyone's

very careful, but maybe if one of us created enough of a distraction, we might make ourselves an opportunity. But that was before you demonstrated what you're capable of – maybe we should just take another gentle stroll."

"I told you, I've never done that before. But we must have the same sorts of skills, or you wouldn't be going for the academy – so I bet you'd be just as good as me."

"No." He looked expectantly at her, so she tried to explain. "When I tried, I got caught. This was back home... just a few dollars here and there, picking the odd pocket... only so I had enough to live on..."

He heard the frantic tone creeping into her voice and reached out to rest his hand on her arm. "It's okay."

"How is that okay? How is any of this okay? We're turning into criminals." Sophie's words still haunted her – not usually the brightest girl, but for once she'd been worryingly perceptive. Eleanor didn't know how many laws she'd broken, now, but the descent into criminality was certainly a slippery one.

Raf interrupted her thoughts: "You did what you needed to do, right?"

Eleanor nodded, and scraped up the last spoonful of her breakfast.

"Then that's fine. That's the best anyone can hope for. And you've identified we need more money now, so come on, what's the rest of this plan of yours?"

She shrugged uncertainly. "I didn't get much further, but there's no hurry – unless we need the money sooner, there's no point taking risks until we're ready to leave the city."

"The sooner the better, though. We need to get back to warn the Association."

"About the trap?" She was too ashamed to admit that it had completely slipped her mind. "I'm not sure why they need us to warn them – surely they'll have noticed by now that they've got no students this year."

"They'll know something's wrong, but if those Tarasanka bastards are half as sneaky as they seem they'll have disappeared without trace in the hope they can pull the same trick next year. We can't let that happen."

"Okay," she agreed, though she still felt he was rushing for no reason – next year's students wouldn't be graduating until the summer solstice, and they'd be home well before then. "So we need to get our bangles back, get some money, and get out of here. Time for another walk?"

Hidden beneath the red robes once more they walked again to the Ngavra building, skirting the edge of the market this time. Raf tried the door: still locked. They exchanged frustrated glances but ducked round the corner and made sure they were alone before either of them dared to speak.

"Maybe we should try the roof," Eleanor suggested. "I came out that way – we'd just have to be careful of the bell."

"That's it!" He struggled to keep his voice low. "The roof. Ellie, you're a genius."

"What?"

"How did we get out of the tower? The roof. Forget all this faffing around with disguises and snakes, let's just go in the way we came out."

"That's not an easy climb." She remembered their struggle to get down the slick walls of the tower; going up would be harder, though at least they'd be prepared this time.

"I thought you liked a challenge?"

"I do." She smiled in spite of herself. Yes, it would be hard – but it was the sort of challenge she relished. "What about you?"

"Looking forward to it already. Plus, it means we can use those green robes as cover for our grand heist at the market tomorrow." Raf wasn't bothering to disguise the excitement in his voice; now he was getting back to peak physical form, he was in his element. "Come on, let's get back."

His enthusiasm was infectious, and they spent the rest of the day sparring in the courtyard, laughing and joking in the lulls between bouts of energetic fighting. They completely forgot to get lunch and came inside only when darkness began to fall, to the evident amusement of their landlord. After another hearty dinner they went to bed, still buzzing with adrenaline but physically tired enough to fall easily into a deep sleep.

Raf shook Eleanor awake the next morning – caught by surprise, she lashed out and was trying to wrestle him to the ground before she woke up sufficiently to realise what was actually happening.

"Sorry!" she cried, releasing her grip. "I'm so jumpy. And I was always first to wake up at school, I'm not used to people touching me while I'm asleep..."

"You shouldn't waste your energy," he said, smiling, and threw her green robe onto her bed. "We've got a busy day."

She rubbed the sleep from her eyes. "Did we make a plan?"

"Enough of one, don't you think? Today, money. Tomorrow, back to the tower. And then – run. Easy."

"Easy," she repeated. Easy was the one thing it was unlikely to be. "Don't we need to think it through in a bit more detail, though?"

"Ellie." His voice was firm. "You're obsessed with details. We need to get this done, so let's just do it. Trust yourself, okay?"

"Okay." She turned to pull on her robe, hoping he wouldn't sense her continued uncertainty.

The green robes were cut to a different style than the red, and fitted slightly less well but it would have to do. It was only for one day – for one theft – and then they could return to the relative safety of the red disguise. Pretending to be a religious adherent of any kind was hard enough – Branav had been right, silence was a big advantage for them.

Eleanor's mind filled with worries as they made their way towards the market. They had no plan, and though Raf had obtained her pendant by taking advantage of some unpredictable chance she wasn't sure they'd be so lucky twice. Besides, to work together they both needed to spot the same opportunity.

They turned between two rows of crowded market stalls, pressing amongst the throng and quickly noticing that today they were not jostled in the same way as the other shoppers. Indeed, space opened up around them as they moved deeper into the market, and many people even averted their eyes. Something about this uniform made them objects to be avoided.

As they turned the next corner Raf lurched sideways and fell to his knees, clutching first at the sleeve of Eleanor's robe and then, as he collapsed to the ground, seizing the corner of tablecloth which trailed from a nearby grocery cart. Eleanor's stunned reaction was genuine – but as the cascade of fruits began to tumble and roll towards the next stall, she suddenly understood what he was doing. A grocery cart wouldn't have much money, but the clothes stall beyond it looked expensive and – suddenly – abandoned. She stepped quickly across and dipped her hand into the cash box, intent on scooping as much money as she could into the purse she wore beneath her robe.

She turned back to Raf, ready to run, but his was no longer the only green-robed body in sight. In addition to his prone form on the ground, two others knelt beside him. As she watched they lifted him, muttering incomprehensibly to one another. One of them cast a glance in her direction, motioned sharply for her to follow, and then they were off – striding quickly through the streets, the crowds parting ahead of them. She hurried to keep a pace behind them as they walked swiftly to the same building where she'd previously seen the snake ritual.

The door was still locked, but one of the men had a key and ushered them inside. The other man took Raf's limp body and laid him in the middle of the room, then barked a command at Eleanor and indicated a door which led from the back of the hall.

She didn't know what was expected of her – she'd worried about her ignorance in trying to imitate these people, but this was beyond the worst scenario she'd envisioned. She didn't dare hesitate, but strode across the room and let herself through the door. She breathed a sigh of relief when it clicked closed behind her; at least this gave her a moment to think.

Her relief was short lived, though, when she realised she was standing at the edge of a small pit full of snakes. She swallowed hard, and wondered whether they were dangerous. On the plus side, there was now very little question as to what she was supposed to do: the room contained only the snake pit, and to her left a large wicker basket.

Simple, she told herself. Snake into basket, basket through to where Raf was – she hoped – still pretending to be dead. After that, they'd just have to take things as they came. She reached down towards the nearest snake, which rose up and hissed into her face; when she tried to touch it, it hissed more loudly then turned and slithered out of reach.

She tried a couple of different ones but none of them seemed to want picking up, and they slipped all too easily from her grasp. Maybe they knew she wanted to put them in the basket.

She picked up the basket and laid it on its side at the edge of the pit; as one slithering mass, the snakes retreated. Eleanor stepped warily into the pit, convinced now that the snakes were more scared of her than she was of them, and pushed the basket further towards them. She kept inching forwards, then picked up a handful of sand and threw it, scattering it over their heads and sending them into a panic as they tried to avoid the falling grains. She felt the basket move beneath her hand and scooped it up as fast as she could. It was heavy; her plan had worked.

With the snake still writhing inside the basket, she clambered out of the pit and let herself back into the hall. The two men had vanished, leaving Raf lying in the middle of the floor, and Eleanor put the basket down and rushed to his side.

"It's me," she whispered. "Don't move, I don't know if they're watching us."

In spite of her warning he sat bolt upright. "I don't care, we can run faster than them. Come on!" He jumped to his feet, grabbed her arm and pulled her towards the door; they heard footsteps on the stairs as they left but it was too late for caution.

They sprinted through the streets until they were close enough to the tavern to worry about being followed, then pressed themselves into the recess of an abandoned doorway and waited for nightfall before creeping back.

"That was close," Raf said once they were safely back in their room. But there was a glint of excitement in his eyes.

"Too close."

He shrugged. "We did it, didn't we? We didn't even have to fight."

"I had to fight those stupid snakes! And I don't even know why I bothered – how soon did they leave you?"

"It went quiet just before you came in. I couldn't see

anything, they pulled that blasted hood right over my eyes – I wasn't sure they'd gone until you said."

They fell into silence for a moment, then Eleanor brought out the purse she'd filled. "I think this should be enough," she said. "At least – I really hope so."

Raf lay back on his bed and flicked a throwing star casually towards the ceiling; he'd borrowed it to practise with and he was slowly improving. This time it caught the wood, but didn't sink in deeply enough and he had to roll out of the way as it fell again.

"We should go at night," he said, flicking the star upwards again. "They won't be expecting us, anyway – they'll assume we've done the sensible thing and already left the city – but we don't want to be seen."

"Tomorrow night, then? Not tonight."

"No, not tonight." He reached up for the star, which had lodged properly this time. "We'll rest tonight, sleep as late as we can, make sure we eat well... all that."

"Sleep sounds good." Eleanor yawned. "I'm tired. Don't you ever wish you'd just accepted your assignment?"

"No." He thought for a moment. "I mean, I'd never have accepted the assignment they actually gave me, whatever it was – that's the point, isn't it? I'd never settle for that and they know it."

"You're so certain about everything. So confident." She wondered what he'd make of the envy in her tone. "I nearly settled for what they gave me, even though I knew it wasn't right. I didn't know whether to believe all this. I didn't really believe it till I met you, and even then, sometimes..."

"Sometimes what?"

"Sometimes I wonder if I did the right thing. If I'm supposed to be doing this."

He sat up to face her. "Ellie, you're being daft. You're doing fine, and the day after tomorrow we're going to go home and get back on track properly. It's time you stopped worrying."

"Okay." She blew out the lamp and curled under her blanket. It was easy for him to say 'stop worrying'; nothing seemed to worry him. But she was somewhat reassured by his confidence in her. "Good night."

The next day, after wasting as much daylight as they could, they started getting ready to go out. They both arranged their weapons about their persons before pulling the red robes over their heads, and Eleanor tucked her pendant safely inside her sock.

Once they were ready they explained to the landlord – whose name they'd never learnt – that they were leaving. If everything went according to plan they'd find a boat ready to sail from the city as soon as they were done, and it would waste valuable time if they had to come back for anything. They settled their debts easily, and Eleanor stashed the remaining money in a pouch out of sight at her waist.

The night was pitch black and navigation was difficult in the dark; although they'd been out and about in the city a little, they hadn't been back as far as the castle and it took them a couple of attempts before they were sure they were looking up at the right tower.

"Certain?" Raf checked. "We don't want to end up doing this more than once."

"Pretty certain," Eleanor said. But they couldn't even see the top of the tower through the darkness.

They took off their disguises and strapped the folded robes to their backs – if they were caught creeping around inside the castle then pretending to be monks probably wouldn't help, and it would certainly make the climb a lot harder.

The lower section was as easy to climb up as it had been to come down, apart from negotiating the overhang of the roof. The roof-tiles were cold and a little slippery, but presented no major obstacle, and before long they'd crawled along the ridge of the roof until they could touch the smooth stones of the tower itself.

Slowly and carefully, feeling for hand-holds in the dark, they began the climb. It was just as tricky as they'd anticipated, made more so by the darkness and the cold of the night. But eventually, with no damage more serious than scraped fingers and aching arm muscles, they reached the ledge beneath the cupola.

After a moment's rest, sitting with their legs dangling over the edge, Eleanor got up to try the door. It was locked, but a little investigation proved it was a simple lock, and a moment later they were inside.

With every step they tried to move in silence, glad that their leather-soled boots weren't riveted, every ounce of concentration focused on making as little noise as possible. They crept down the stairs, and smiled awkwardly at each other by the flickering lamplight as they emerged into the corridor they recognised all too well – relieved to be in the right place, but unable to quite block out the horrors they'd faced here. Raf reached across and squeezed Eleanor's hand, and she squeezed back, fighting against the tears which threatened to escape her eyes.

Each door they opened was a risk, they were afraid they'd end up in some guard-room or someone's bedroom, but it seemed that this part of the castle was genuinely deserted at night and they relaxed a little as they progressed. It took them a couple of attempts before they found the right room – a small office, with a pile of golden bangles at one corner of the desk.

Eleanor picked them up, sorted through for her own and clipped it firmly into place, fastening it above her elbow so that it wouldn't be visible, then started looking through the others for Raf's name.

"V-N-five-nine-F-six-two-E-Y-G... is this you?" she checked, reading from one of the bracelets. He nodded, and she handed it across to him. "What do you think we should do with the others?"

He held out his hand. "We'll take them back with us. The Association needs to know what's happened here."

She passed them across and he tucked them into his pocket, as she picked up everything that looked like it could be valuable.

"Okay, let's get out of here."

"Wait... while we're here... I'd quite like to get my knife back." She'd been hoping their captors would have stored everything in the same place – that would have made it much easier.

"I know it's special to you, Ellie, but finding one knife in a building this size is going to be tricky. And what if someone's using it?"

"Oh, I know." She tried to force a casual tone onto her voice. "I wasn't going to search every guard, but it might still be in the torture chamber. I just want to have a look."

Finding the torture chamber was easy; they'd been taken there enough times. Eleanor hesitated briefly as her hand reached the door handle, the fingers of her other hand tightening on the hilt of her dagger. She could rationalise, tell herself repeatedly that there was no more danger in this room than any of the others, but her heart still thumped in her chest and she knew that part of her would never believe it was safe.

She took a deep breath and pushed the door. The room was deserted and dark, just the furnace in the corner glowing with a faint red light. Raf unhooked one of the lanterns from its bracket in the corridor and followed her, the swaying lamp casting distorted shadows across the room.

"I can hold this for you," he said. "Just tell me where you want to look first."

She felt guilty for keeping him here, sure that the memories this room evoked were no more pleasant for him than they were for her, but she couldn't leave without her knife. What would Laban say? And besides, the beauty of that knife was the only reason she'd even stepped onto this path – if she hadn't held that perfectly balanced blade, if she hadn't possessed the skill to throw it with such accuracy, she'd be bored out of her mind in the Port's police force right now. Again she wondered if that would have been better; boredom was seldom fatal. But oh, how dull it would have been.

Raf had started scouting the room as she stood distracted by her thoughts.

She scanned the top of the shelf from which, she was sure, she'd once seen the short man retrieve her knife. A few rusty nails, some thumbscrews... a work of art like her knife would have stood out in such company, and it didn't. Her heart sank. Maybe one of the guards was indeed using it as his own, though the thought angered her – none of them deserved it.

As she turned to examine the next surface, however, a sparkle of green caught her eye and she cleared aside a small pile of iron tools to reveal the bejewelled hilt of the blade she knew so well. She pulled it out and held it aloft in delight: "Got it!"

"Great!" He sounded genuinely pleased, though she suspected that was mostly because she'd now be willing to leave.

They went out the way they'd come in, and though the climb down the slick tower wall was no easier they were growing more confident as they learned where the best holds were to be found. They stopped atop the peaked roof to put their disguises back on before sliding down the last easy stretch of wall into the street.

"To the harbour, then?" Eleanor asked, excitement bubbling at the idea of getting home and pushing on with their quest. It had been a lengthy and painful diversion, but it would all be worthwhile once they were back in the Empire.

"Shh," Raf hushed her, a little half-heartedly. There was no-one around to worry about whether silent monks were speaking.

She tucked a few stray hairs safely out of sight beneath her hood, and started down the steep alley which sloped towards the sea. They'd taken only about a dozen steps when an unexpected noise made them both freeze.

Raf reached for his knife but they were upon him before he could wrench the dagger from its sheath – two broad-shouldered giants who dwarfed his skinny frame. One of them lifted him easily two feet into the air and shook him, shouting something in Tarasanka. Eleanor flattened herself against the nearest wall and felt beneath her robe for her throwing stars, hoping they wouldn't notice her until it was too late.

Her first star sliced across the throat of the guard who was holding Raf, causing him to drop his prisoner as he collapsed onto the cobblestones. Raf stumbled to his feet, dagger in hand now, and lunged towards the remaining guard but the gigantic man deflected the blow all too easily and lodged his own blade between Raf's ribs.

"Raf!" The scream ripped from Eleanor's throat against her will as she watched him fall, the anguish of everything they'd suffered together filling her voice. She wanted to run to him, but the guard was turning his attention away from the fallen bodies and she knew with grim certainty where his focus would fall next.

She fumbled with another star, shaking with nervous energy, feeling sick with fear for herself and for Raf. She couldn't let the guard get close to her; she'd stand no chance hand-to-hand against a man of this size, and he was clearly pulling no punches. This time, no-one cared to keep them alive.

She flicked the star from between her fingers; it was a good shot, but not quite good enough, ripping into his shoulder without slowing him. He grabbed her by the throat and lifted her, his other hand ready with the dagger. She kicked at his arm, twisted desperately so that his blade glanced away from her, and somehow managed to plunge her stiletto into the side of his neck.

He died quickly and noisily, not releasing his grip on her until his last living moment, and his corpse fell heavily across her, knocking her to the ground. She pushed his body away and he rolled a few feet down the hill as she got up. Finally she was free to run to where Raf lay on the ground and dropped to her knees beside him, relieved to find he was still breathing in ragged gasps. A dark stain had spread across the front of his robe, black-on-black in the gloom though she knew exactly what it was.

"Come on," she said, slipping her arm beneath his shoulders to pull him into a sitting position. "We have to get to the harbour. Who knows how many more of them are coming?"

"You go," he rasped. "I can't travel like this."

She shook her head. "I can't leave you here. We're in this together, remember?"

"You have to. You have to get back and warn them. Can't let something like this happen again."

"Don't be stupid. I'm not leaving you here where they can find you. Let's get you back to the room and then we can talk."

She ignored his protests, hauled him to his feet and half-carried him through the streets and back to the tavern; there was no sign of the landlord so she had to help him up the ladder on her own, and he collapsed on the bed.

"You shouldn't have done that," he said weakly. "Now you've got further to go."

"Don't worry about me. We'll hide out here till it dies down."

"No, you need to go now, you need–"

She cut him off. "We're in this together. That means I'm not leaving without you."

"Stop being so stubborn. I'll be right behind you, just as soon as this all heals up. But you need to get back, you need to get a message to the Association as quickly as possible. Do you know someone you can contact?"

She shook her head: she knew only Laban, and she had no way to get in touch with him if he didn't want to be found.

"Then the easiest thing is for you to go to Venncastle – just go to the guards at the gate and tell them that the Provost needs to contact the Association. Tell them there was a trap at the code tower. They'll understand, and it'll be passed on as quickly as you could hope."

She was bemused but it seemed easier not to argue. "So where is Venncastle?" she asked.

"Flying Rock Island – do you know it?"

"No, I grew up on the mainland."

"It's easy to get a boat from Dashfort or Almont – or wherever you end up. And once you get there, the school's pretty obvious. Big, black building – looks a bit like a castle, mostly because it is."

"Okay."

"And you know how to get to the code tower and the maze, do you?" Her blank expression must have given her away, because he sighed a little and said, "Right, go to Venncastle first. From Flying Rock Island you can borrow a boat and row across to the White Isle, which is where the code tower is – it looks like a lighthouse. You might want to leave it a week or two to give the Association time to clear up any stray Tarasanka, but Flying Rock's not a bad place to be. Then back to the mainland. Dashfort you've done before so that's easy, you just need to do it again for the new number, and then head inland, south east about a hundred miles – the maze is well inside the Silver Forest. Are you going to remember all that?"

"I'll remember. Thank you."

"Now get moving," he said urgently. "Before word gets round."

She pulled off her red robe and handed it to him. "You'll need this," she said. "Yours is ruined, but we can use it to patch up that wound." She used her knife to slice away the bottom of his robe and tied a makeshift bandage across his chest. "And you'll need money." She reached beneath the folds of her clothes, and placed the purse with all their remaining coins and jewels on the bed beside him.

"What about you?"

"Oh, I'm a commodity in my own right! Once I find a ship, I can work my way back across the sea."

Raf pulled the spare name bangles from his pocket. "You'd better take these – give them back to the academy."

She took them from him and linked them together to form a loose chain, which she then threaded onto a strip of cloth and tied tightly about her waist, out of sight beneath her clothes.

"Now go!"

She nodded, fighting back tears. "I'll see you at the academy, then?"

"I hope so." He reached out and squeezed her hand. She flung her arms around his neck, hugged him quickly then turned and fled the room, determined not to let him see her cry. She ran towards the harbour and somehow – she didn't know how – she managed to stop herself looking back.

Dawn was breaking as she reached the shore. She had no idea how she was going to find a ship heading in the right direction, but she knew she had to do it quickly now she'd abandoned her disguise. She assumed there would be more smugglers bound for the Empire, if she could only find them, who'd be grateful for an extra pair of hands. She avoided the rows of heavily-armed Tarasanka military vessels, pausing only briefly to wonder how such a small country managed to find enough sailors to maintain such a large navy, and headed towards the merchant ships berthed where the *Rose* had been all those weeks earlier.

She started off by asking everyone she met whether they spoke Charanthe, but she got only blank looks; before long, she resorted to just repeating "Charanthe? Dashfort? Almont?" to anyone whose attention she could catch.

Eventually, one man – at the end of a human chain loading crates onto a large ship – responded. "You Gharanded?" he asked, passing the last of his crates along to his colleague. "What you want?"

"I need to get back to the Empire. I need to take a boat." She pointed at the ship, not quite sure how well he understood her. "Where are you going?"

"Going? Going now."

"Where?"

The next sailor from the chain came over to join in as soon as he'd handed on the crate. "You not Magrad," he said. "You want Magrad man? Not able!"

"No!" She shook her head vigorously. "I don't want a man. I want to work."

"You? Work?" They both looked incredulous.

"Yes! If you're going to the Empire. Charanthe? Yes?"

"Dazzford, in Gharand... yes?" the first man checked.

"Yes." His pronunciation left a lot to be desired but the words were just about recognizable.

"You wait here." He beckoned his colleague to follow, and climbed up onto the ship.

Eleanor waited, conscious of the passage of time as the sun rose into the sky. She wondered whether she should give up and try to find a boat which had actually come from the Empire, whose crew spoke Charanthe with native fluency, and who could be guaranteed to take her home. But it had taken so long to find someone who understood her even partially, so she pushed those thoughts from her mind and concentrated on her surroundings, alert for any sign she might have been recognised. A small crowd had begun to gather at the bow of the Magra ship – men, women and children all stared down at her, waiting to see what would happen.

Eventually the first sailor returned, accompanied by another man. "Here is captain," he said, indicating his companion. "He not speak Gharanded. You speak, I tell him what, yes?"

"Tell him I want to work on the ship, to get home."

He turned to the captain, and they exchanged a few short sentences in Magrad. The captain kept glancing at Eleanor and shaking his head.

"He say, you is woman."

"So?"

"Woman not work."

"But I can work! I know how to sail." She wasn't sure how much he understood, so she walked across to one of the mooring ropes and picked up the spare length at the end of the line. "Look, I know all the knots." She tied a figure of eight, then loosed it and demonstrated a bowline, and then a sheet bend.

The captain said something in Magrad, and the other man translated: "You come ship, and show."

He set off towards the ship and she followed him, wondering what she was supposed to be showing. He stopped by the smallest of the ship's four masts. "Show," he repeated.

The sails were rigged ready for the boat to sail out of the harbour and she wasn't sure what they wanted her to demonstrate so she simply folded down the smallest sail, hauled it up again, and turned back to the captain to see if she could work out whether she'd satisfied him of her usefulness. Most of the crew seemed to have gathered around, and the women and children watched in fascination from a little further back.

"Davh," the captain said, nodding.

"He say yes," her translator said. "You come. I show you bed; come now."

The hammock she was assigned was in the women's quarters, and she was alarmed to find that this also meant sharing a room with all the prepubescent children the ship was carrying. The other women had all followed them down from the deck – some watching and chatting amongst themselves with evident suspicion, while others were simply curious. There were eleven women in total, and about twenty children of varying ages;

none of them spoke a word of Charanthe but one woman provided Eleanor with a pillow, blanket and towel, which seemed about the warmest welcome she was going to get.

Relieved to have found a suitable ship, and in the interests of trying to keep below deck and out of sight until they left the harbour, Eleanor made a big show of rearranging her few belongings and hanging her bag on the peg by her hammock.

"You work night," the sailor said. "You sleep now."

"Okay," Eleanor agreed, though she was far from happy with the idea of working the night shift. Still, it was a good excuse to stay out of the way for a while, so she climbed into her hammock without further comment.

The other women stayed staring at her for some time, though she closed her eyes and tried to pretend they weren't there, fingers clasped around the ropes of the hammock. Tears welled behind her eyelids as she thought of Raf, alone now in a hostile city. She wondered if she should have argued, stayed to keep him company, tried to nurse him back to health. But at least this way she could take the message to Venncastle as he'd suggested, and she'd see him again at the academy. *Assuming he survives.* She tried to push such painful thoughts from her mind, focusing instead on the gentle rocking of the ship and the breathing of the women who were still watching her. She pressed one foot against the other, feeling the hard metal of her pendant digging in to the sole, comforted and distracted by the almost-pain.

After a long moment the boat started moving; she heard footsteps as the women went up onto the deck and then silence. Finally alone, she managed to fall asleep.

She was woken by a middle-aged woman, who shook her harshly and then pointed upwards as soon as her eyes flickered open. Once she got out of the hammock, the woman pushed a smoked fish into one of her hands and a beaker of weak ale into the other.

"Thank you," Eleanor said, and took a mouthful of fish.

"Dhang oo?" the woman repeated, puzzled.

"Thank you, yes. It means... oh, never mind!" Eleanor gulped down her drink and ate as quickly as she could, collecting fish bones in her empty beaker, then followed the woman up on to the deck. Time to learn how the night shift worked.

Chapter 12

Eleanor marked the passage of time by carving little tally marks into the wood at the side of her hammock and tried not to be impatient as days turned into weeks at sea, for all that she longed to be back in the familiar waters of the Empire. It would presumably take about as long to get home as it had taken the *Rose* to reach Taraska, but she wished the time would pass more quickly – once she was home she'd have things to do that might take her mind off Raf and the state she'd left him in. She had little time to dwell on it during her shifts – working by moonlight required extra concentration – but during daylight, as she struggled to sleep with the sounds of the ship's normal life going on about her, she often wondered how he was faring.

She found it strange to be on a ship with women and children who did nothing to pull their weight so far as the sailing was concerned – although the women did cook, which made for a somewhat more varied diet than aboard the *Rose*. It felt very old-fashioned to have such a strong divide between gender roles, and Eleanor could only imagine how odd they must find it to have her insisting on working alongside the men.

The women eyed her with curiosity and no shortage of suspicion, and the intensity of their stares didn't diminish as the days passed. Eleanor found herself glad to be working at night, once she got used to the poor visibility, since that meant the women and children were mostly sleeping while she worked and working while she slept. It reduced the intrusion, and gave her space to herself when she was in her hammock.

They'd been at sea for eighteen nights when, suddenly, the command was given to drop the anchors.

"What's happening?" Eleanor asked Bhal, the man who spoke the most Charanthe, as they worked together to heave a large iron anchor over the side.

"Stop," he said. "Get money."

She was puzzled, but there was no time for asking more

questions. Even the men who usually worked the day shift were on deck, and they set about lowering three small rowing boats into the water. Eleanor simply joined in where she could see an extra pair of hands would come in useful – she didn't need to know what she was doing. The men had rope ladders, and began climbing down into the rowing boats; Eleanor went to follow, but Bhal stopped her.

"Captain say not," he said.

"Not what?"

"You not come. Woman not come."

She shook her head. "It was 'women not work', a couple of weeks ago, but everyone still seems to be alive."

"Woman not come," he repeated firmly.

"Okay." It was pointless trying to have a discussion when they had so little language in common. She sat on one of the lockers and watched as the little rowing boats started out into the sea.

It was only when the moon came out from behind a cloud that she could see what they were heading for. Another ship. All of a sudden she understood: piracy. Of course, this was what the Magra were famous for. She felt rising indignation that they'd thought she wouldn't be any good at this, before realising they'd never seen her fight. Besides, she told herself, she had no desire to be a pirate. But she still felt left out.

She wandered across the deck to where the scout's telescope was mounted and swung it round, hoping to get a better look at the raid, although it was hard to make out any details through the darkness. After only a short while, though, she saw the rowing boats begin to move back towards her.

Once the day shift were back in bed, Eleanor approached Bhal again. "What were you doing?" she asked. Surely an act of proper piracy would have taken longer.

"Tax," he said. "In Tarask, tax at port. Here, tax for Magra."

"Tax." She repeated it softly and wondered if that was the reality behind the legends of piracy. Were they simply levying a tax on traffic across 'their' seas? Things weren't always as they seemed.

The next time the ship anchored was in daylight. One of the

women woke Eleanor and led her up onto the deck, where Bhal assured her that they were now "very near" to the Empire.

"How near?" she asked, unable to see any land as she squinted towards the horizon.

"Yes, yes – very near. Five days, or ten. Very near."

"Days? Then why are we stopping?" She was aware of a small group of women and children watching her intently.

"Stop, yes."

"Why?" She couldn't keep the exasperation out of her voice. If they were close, now was not the time for stopping. She wondered why they'd woken her up to tell her this.

"You need bag," he said. "You need leave."

"My bag?"

"Yes, bag." He pointed vigorously down towards the sleeping quarters.

She shrugged and went to get her things together, collecting her bag from its peg by her hammock, wondering what was going on. They surely weren't expecting her to take one of the rowing boats. But his meaning had been clear enough: she needed her bag because she was leaving.

A short while after she'd made her way back on deck, a small Imperial fishing craft moved alongside them and threw a rope across; Bhal caught it and tied it loosely in place. As men from both sides set about moving crates between the vessels, Bhal exchanged a few words of Magrad with the captain of the smuggling boat.

He turned to look at Eleanor, who was looking on with interest.

"You want a lift home?"

"Yes please."

"And they say you can sail."

"Fairly well, yes."

"Dashfort's okay for you?"

She nodded, though anywhere in the Empire would have been fine at this stage.

"Alright, climb aboard – and don't be long about it, the wind's in our favour. We want to get underway as soon as we can."

Eleanor picked up her bag and scrambled over the gunwale, rolling as she hit the deck of the smuggler craft.

"What's a nice Imperial girl like you doin' out here, anyway?" he asked as she picked herself up.

Eleanor rolled her eyes. "It's a long story – maybe later."

"My name's Jack," he said, extending his hand.

She shook it. "Eleanor."

She breathed a sigh of relief as she helped the smugglers turn their ship to head back towards Imperial waters. She wasn't quite home yet, but it was starting to feel closer.

The smugglers were a jolly crew which made for pleasant company, but she was relieved when they finally came in sight of Dashfort; the weeks in cramped conditions were beginning to take their toll. Jack insisted she take a small allowance out of the boat's profits – "just by way of thanking you for your help, lass" – and gave her a hearty clap on the back by way of goodbye. She disembarked unsteadily and headed straight for the line of food stalls by the city gates.

She walked around the harbour to get used to the feel of solid ground beneath her feet again, before making her way up the hill and back to the puzzle chamber. Knowing exactly what she was doing this time made the whole experience rather more pleasant. There was no-one in the square when she arrived, and she quickly unlocked the concealed door and let herself in. She managed to rearrange the mosaic while tripping only two acid-laced blades, and knowing when to expect the spinning discs – coupled with the fact that she was properly armed to defend herself – meant she escaped with a minimum of cuts.

And a new number which, she realised, she still didn't understand.

She wished she'd thought to ask Raf about it, but she hadn't had enough time to work through the consequences when he'd told her she had to go on alone. Ever since she'd found out that they had the same goal she'd assumed he'd be there to guide her through, or at least to work everything out alongside her. She was suddenly overcome with grief, and guilt at the idea that she might have left him to die there; she collapsed to the ground in the square and all the tears she'd been holding back streamed silently down her cheeks.

Eventually she dried her eyes and got to her feet, feeling a little better for it, and started walking slowly back to the harbour. She wasn't looking forward to yet another boat journey, but at least Flying Rock Island was within the Imperial archipelago.

The harbour was almost deserted – it was good sailing weather, and all the fishing boats were out at sea. The first man Eleanor saw down by the sea-front was a weathered old sailor busy repainting his hull; he glanced up as she approached.

"How can I help you, miss?"

"Do you know of any boats going to Flying Rock Island?" she asked. He looked like the sort of person who should know all the comings and goings.

"Day after tomorrow," he said. "That's the regular supplies boat."

"Oh. Thank you." Eleanor tried to keep the disappointment out of her voice, but she'd been hoping to start her journey sooner than that. Still, she reminded herself, a day or two was unlikely to make much difference.

"You might find someone else headed in that sort of direction, but I'd say it's unlikely at this time of year. She's called the *Arabella*. She should be berthing tomorrow evening, so you'll want to come back then. I'll still be here painting," he added. "So I can point her out if you have any difficulty."

Eleanor thanked him again and turned back towards the city. She needed to find somewhere to stay – it was too far into winter to risk sleeping on the streets – and unless that was going to be the puzzle chamber, she needed to get some more money first. Unfortunately, the streets were all but deserted, and the few people she did pass were well wrapped in their cloaks and walking far too briskly to provide an easy target.

She stopped in a doorway and counted the money Jack had given her. It was enough for a few meals, and she could hardly complain about the rate of pay when she'd only been after a way to get home, but a guesthouse in the city would be expensive.

She reached the harbour again and realised she'd walked in a big loop. Her eyes settled on the boat where the old sailor had been, its fresh paint gleaming in the last of the day's sun. He'd said he was going to be painting again tomorrow – there was no way that boat was going anywhere in the next couple of days. Glancing around to make sure she wasn't seen, she scrambled up the ladder and let herself into the boat's small cabin. This was only a tiny craft, the sort that would take one or two men to sea for one day's fishing at a time, but while it wasn't set up for sleeping it would surely be much warmer than outside.

She slept with one hand on her knife, eyes flickering open at the slightest sound, but morning dawned without incident. As soon as she saw daylight she got up, not wanting to be caught out by the boat's owner when he came back to resume his painting, and made herself scarce in the city streets, determined to take full advantage of this chance to stretch her legs.

As the sun began to dip lower in the sky again she made her way back to the harbour. As the old sailor had predicted, the *Arabella* was already moored; she nodded hello as she passed him, and approached the *Arabella* wondering what they would think of her request – and whether it would cost her.

A young sailor was sitting in the bow with a large tankard gripped in both hands.

"Excuse me!" Eleanor called out, stepping along the plank towards him. "Excuse me, is this the supplies boat for Flying Rock Island?"

"Aye," he said. "An' the other islands that side o' the reef."

"Could I get a lift?"

"To Flyin' Rock? Well sure, I don' see why not. We'll be leavin' around daybreak, so don' you be holdin' us up, though – we won' wait."

"Actually..." She took a couple more steps and dropped lightly onto the deck. "I was wondering if I could spend the night on the boat."

"Oh." He looked a bit taken aback, but quickly recovered himself. "Uh, sure you can. Want a drink?"

He held his tankard aloft but Eleanor shook her head. "Thanks, but I'm tired. Where should I...?"

"Oh, grab any bunk." He waved languidly at the hatch. "Most o' the crew won' be back tonight – I drew the short straw to watch over her."

Eleanor made herself comfortable in one of the hammocks, and she woke only once the boat was already moving out to sea: as the youth had predicted, no-one came in to disturb her sleep in the night.

It was eight days before they reached their first port, and Eleanor was disappointed to be told that this wasn't the island she wanted. The next day, however, Flying Rock Island came into view.

She could see a castellated building looming at the top of the island's highest cliff. "Is that Venncastle?"

"Aye."

She was speechless. As schools went, this was surely the most impressive. Raf had said it was a castle – and it really was. The vast structure was built out of black rock and looked like it rose straight out of the cliff, built to withstand an attack from lower ground on the island while looking out to sea for enemy ships. It was an uncompromisingly military structure, clearly designed back in the days before the Empire brought its peace across the archipelago. There could be no need for such a building now.

"You headed up there?" the sailor asked. "Because you can get a lift on the supply cart, if you're prepared to help us unload first."

So Eleanor helped unpack the crates of fruit and vegetables, wheat and barley, leather and paper – all things that an island this small and this rocky couldn't produce in feasible quantities. They loaded three carts – one bound for each of the two small towns on the island, and the third solely for the school. Eleanor climbed up alongside the driver, and they started to make their way up the hill.

"What you want with the school, anyway?" the driver asked as they drove up the winding lane. "You don't look pregnant – and even then, it's usually the fathers as bring children up to Venncastle."

"I just need to pass on a message," she said.

"What kind o' message?" he asked, but she stared out to sea and ignored him, and thankfully he didn't push the question.

Eventually they reached the school's vast gate-house, and the driver brought the cart to a halt parallel to the gates. "They'll come out to fetch their goods," he said. "They always do. If you need to go further, you're on your own – but they won't let me past the gate, and I've been doin' this delivery for twenty-odd years."

"That's great," she said, jumping down from the cart. "Thanks."

She turned and came face to face with a dozen black-uniformed youths – students approaching the end of their time at the school, she guessed – who began lifting crates from the cart. Eleanor's eyes were drawn to the stylized 'V's embroidered at the collars in striking green thread. A couple of the students cast suspicious glances at her, but most of them ignored her just as they ignored the cart's driver, focused only on their duties. Once they'd emptied the cart they turned and filed neatly back into the school.

Eleanor made her way across to the gate-house, where two guards flanked the gate with crossbows in their hands. Armed guards felt excessive for a school, particularly in such a remote spot, but it was in keeping with the imposing military feel. They were wearing similar uniforms to the students, but edged with green piping. One of them lifted his bow, somewhat half-heartedly, and aimed an arrow at her as she approached.

"You can't come in," he said as she continued undeterred.

"I don't want to come in. I've just got a message for the Provost." She wondered whether a Provost was something like a headmaster. She walked up to the point of the guard's arrow, and looked him straight in the eye. "You don't have to let me past. You certainly don't have to shoot me. All you have to do is pass a message on to the Provost so that he can send word to the Association."

"You're nothing to do with the Association," the guard said with flat certainty. "You're a girl."

Eleanor felt anger rising in her chest. "Do you want to bet the safety of the Empire on that?" she asked, inspired by Raf's melodramatic style – if it was good enough for him to claim that defeat of the Association would eventually lead to the destruction of the Empire, then she could certainly borrow a little of his rhetoric. She wished he were here to back her up, particularly as the guard met her gaze impassively and silently. They'd listen to him. "There's a trap at the code tower," she continued. "Most of this year's aspirants are dead... I need this to get through to the right people."

The guard continued to stare at her along the shaft of his arrow. She wondered what he was waiting for. Was there something she could say which would persuade him to take her seriously? Nothing obvious came to mind; it took her an uncomfortably long moment to think of an angle to try.

"Listen, I was locked up with an ex-student of this school – he said I should come here. His name's Raf, his ID number is V-N-five-nine-F-six-three..." She paused for a moment to double-check her memory. "No, six-two. V-N-five-nine-F-six-two-E-Y-G."

Still the guard made no response.

"How can I make you listen to me?" she asked, frustrated.

"I've been listening," he said, a hint of irritation creeping into his tone. "You do go on. Have you finished?"

"Well, are you going to pass on the message?"

"In the proper time."

"Why not now?"

He shook his head. "I'm on duty."

"But–"

"Oh, be quiet! I've heard what you said, and it's not so urgent that it can't wait for the end of my shift. Now, are you going to leave so I can stop waving this blasted bow around?"

"Okay." She could tell she wasn't going to get any further by arguing. "Thank you."

She walked down the hill feeling wholly dispirited. It hadn't gone at all the way she'd hoped, and though she'd followed Raf's instructions she didn't feel confident that their message was going to reach the right ears. Why did a school need an armed guard anyway? And what was the special link between Venncastle and the Association that meant this had been the right thing to do? She suspected the two questions were related.

It was getting late by the time she reached the town again. She enquired about local guesthouses only to be told that the island didn't get enough visitors to warrant one, but that one of the taverns might find a corner where she could sleep for a reasonable rate.

The rate she managed to negotiate did indeed seem reasonable, though the attic cot was hard and she could hear rats scuffling under the eaves as she tried to get to sleep. The tavern wasn't in the habit of providing overnight hospitality – the sheets smelled musty, and for breakfast the landlord managed only a few morsels of bread and cheese, meaning Eleanor was still hungry when she went out again.

If, as Raf had suggested, she was going to leave it a few days before going to the code tower, then she had time to kill. Not sure what she was hoping to accomplish, she made her way back up to the school. Today's guards were different youths but the uniforms, the crossbows, and the unflinching stares were the same; after an abortive conversation, she walked on to see if she could see the code tower from the cliffs here.

After her fourth pointless conversation with Venncastle's impassive guards, who would still give her no information about whether her message had been acted upon, Eleanor decided she was going to have to take a more direct approach. Her daily walks were giving her a fair impression of the castle's layout; the guards could survey all approaches to the main gate from their station, but although the school clearly took its security seriously they seemed not to bother with patrols on the ramparts looking out to sea. That would be the only way to get in without detection – and once she was within the walls, she hoped there might be further clues to help her find the Provost himself.

She asked the landlord at the tavern that afternoon whether he knew anyone with a boat she could borrow.

"What for?" he asked.

She was sure it was an innocent question, but an honest answer would've aroused his suspicions so she simply said, "I was hoping to visit the White Isle – a friend of mine said it was easy to row from here."

He pushed the door open. "That's the White Isle, just down there," he said, pointing across the water. "It's uninhabited – they say it's haunted – but you're welcome to borrow my boat to row across if you're really interested."

"If you don't mind," Eleanor said. Tales of a haunting didn't bother her; she knew all about using superstition to keep people away, she'd played often enough to her schoolfriends' fears.

"Of course. The tide's in your favour at the moment – if you leave now, you should just about be able to make it before dark. Tomorrow morning's probably your best bet for getting back."

"Do you need the boat back tomorrow? I was hoping to have a couple of days to look around."

He shrugged. "There's not that much to see – but do what you like, I don't use the boat much out of season."

He took her down to the beach, turned over his small blue rowing boat and pulled it into the sea for her.

"Take as long as you like," he reiterated as she settled herself on the seat of the boat and slotted the oars into place.

"Thanks." She knew it'd take her more than a day, if she had to break into Venncastle before she could even think about going across to the code tower. She started rowing towards the White Isle until the landlord disappeared back into the tavern, then turned the boat to steer her way around the coast.

The cliffs rose sharply to her left; not an easy climb but at least it was a natural surface, nowhere near as difficult as the smooth rock of the Tarasanka buildings. The walls of the castle would be a different matter but she couldn't predict that from here.

She found a small inlet towards the northernmost tip of the island, and moored the boat against a jagged column of rock; it bobbed gently in the waves as she scrambled up onto the rocks.

As she'd guessed from water-level, the climbing was mostly easy, with only a couple of challenging sections. She paused to catch her breath after negotiating a particularly difficult overhang, then turned to look up for her next handhold and found herself face-to-face with a dark-haired young man.

"No-one has much time for people who poke their noses where they don't belong," he said. He was hanging from a rope which looked to go all the way up to the castle's battlements, with his feet planted firmly against the rock.

"What do you mean?" Eleanor asked. The young man's uniform appeared to be of the student design, without the green piping of the guards, so she wondered what she could get away with.

"Who'd notice if you didn't return?" he asked, pulling a knife from his belt.

She considered his question. The landlord would miss his boat, eventually, but it wouldn't be that hard to find it. Other than Raf, no-one knew where she was; the threat was real. Assessing the situation, though, she knew she had no choice but to talk herself out of it. He had too many advantages over her as she clung by her fingertips to the rock face. Even reaching for a weapon of her own carried too many risks.

"Raf would notice," she said boldly. "He asked me to come here."

"Raf?"

She struggled to keep the smile from her lips; she could tell she'd got him. His voice was loaded with familiarity and expectation. "He was a student here until last year," she said. "Did you know him?"

The young man nodded but said nothing, still waiting – for what, Eleanor could only wish she knew.

"Raf got hurt," she said. Easier not to mention that he was in a different country at the time, or she'd lose what little protection she'd gained by saying he knew she was here. "He wanted me to bring a message to the Provost – can you help?"

"Why'd he send you?"

"I just happened to be there," she said. It wasn't far from the truth. "He was injured too badly to come himself."

He eyed her suspiciously. "Why not just walk up to the gate?"

"I tried." She allowed herself a pained sigh, partially for dramatic effect but also to let out a little of her frustration; her arms were aching from holding herself in place, and her injured

162

shoulder was beginning to twinge again. "Any sane person would try that first, but the guards here don't listen. Well, not to me." She looked him straight in the eye and batted her eyelashes. "Will you help me?"

He sheathed his knife and extended his arm towards her. "Give me your hand."

She reached up and gripped his wrist; he pulled himself upwards on the rope, tugging her after him. The extra lift made it easy for her to scramble up the rock behind him, and in no time they were scaling the wall of the school.

"I have no idea how much trouble this is going to cause me," he said as he helped her over the battlements. "But Raf was a good bloke, even to those of us who'll never make the grade."

"What grade?"

"Never mind." He blushed slightly. "I'd hoped catching you might count in my favour, you know. I could do with a bit of extra credit. But if Raf sent you, well, you're virtually one of us. Come on."

He led her along the battlements, winding the rope around his arm as they walked, and into a small tower.

"My room's not far," he said as they started down the steps. "You can wait while I fetch the Provost for you."

His room turned out to be set into the side of the tower, a tiny space which must once have been a guard room and now contained a low bed, a small wardrobe, and a rack of practice weapons. A couple of arrow-slits gave views over the sea, and she understood now how he'd happened to spot her as she tied up her boat.

"Make yourself comfortable," he said, waving her into the room. There was barely space for both of them beside the bed. "I'll be back soon."

Eleanor perched awkwardly on the edge of the bed and studied the room with interest. How very different to her own school, where bedrooms had been shared and all weapons held in a central repository. These weapons were of a much higher quality than the cheap practice knives they'd had at Mersioc; she wondered if the difference was some kind of throwback to times before the Empire, when men had formed all the armies and women had stayed home to raise children, or whether this school just had better kit because it was in an old castle. Whichever it was, she felt just a little envious.

She was still deep in thought when the young man returned. "The Provost will see you in his office," he said. "I'll take you across."

They went down to the bottom of the tower, across a cobbled yard to the keep, and into another tower. The Provost's office was high up in the tower, a semi-circular room with green velvet curtains covering what must have been a very large window looking out over the school.

"Thank you, James, you can wait outside."

The Provost was a grey-haired, sharp-featured man with a stern expression; he didn't get up from his desk to greet them, and Eleanor hesitated before taking a seat across from him.

"So you're the girl who's been bothering my guards, are you?" he said once she'd settled herself.

She swallowed, wondering if he had more to say, but he seemed to be waiting for something. She sucked her lip nervously and wondered if this had been a bad idea. "One of your ex-students sent me," she said. "Raf. He wanted me to bring you a message."

"About the code tower?"

She nodded. Obviously some part of her message had got through to him already.

"Why did you think you needed to break in to my school? Young James would've been perfectly within his rights to kill you – but he's got a soft heart, that one. A little too soft."

Eleanor wondered how anyone could be considered 'within his rights' to kill her for a little rock climbing, but she didn't voice her thoughts. The Provost wasn't obviously armed but his manner carried more than a little menace and she was sure he had a few tricks up his sleeve. She didn't want to have to fight her way out of the school.

"Did it occur to you that we might already know?" he continued. "Did you think that, just maybe, such a clumsy trick might have been noticed?"

"Raf thought we should share what we learned in Taraska,"

she said. "So they can't try the same thing next year."

"*They* won't be trying anything else, next year or ever," the Provost said. "Not that it's any concern of yours. For someone so determined to meddle in things which don't concern you, I'd say you've been lucky to last this long. Now, please ask young James to escort you from the castle, and expect my guards to shoot you on sight if you try to come back."

Eleanor kept her eyes fixed on the floor as she made her exit, feeling a total failure.

"Success?" James asked as she pulled the door closed behind her.

"Sort of." At least she knew the message had got through. She felt cross at Raf for sending her here to be so humiliated, and then angry at herself for blaming him. He'd only been trying to help – as had she. "You're to show me out," she added.

"The way you came in?" he asked. "Or would you prefer a more conventional route this time?"

"I'd better go the same way," she said. "I need to get the boat back, and I don't fancy swimming round."

It was pitch black outside, and although James held the rope for her to abseil down the cliff she still had to take care of her footing in the darkness. She held the end of the rope until she reached the boat and then released it, watching the end snake upwards as he reeled it in. Then, because it was too dark to risk anything else, she curled up in the bottom of the boat and wrapped her cloak tightly around herself. It was going to be a very cold night.

She woke at first light the next morning, muscles stiff and aching from the cold, and started rowing as much to warm herself up as to go anywhere – the tide was against her, it would be quicker to simply wait, but she was shivering and knew the exercise would warm her. She realised she'd forgotten to bring any food, and hoped she'd find enough winter plants to provide some sustenance.

She took a momentary break from rowing and looked over her shoulder towards the White Isle. The tower stood alone, isolated at one end of the islet. It looked for all the world like an abandoned lighthouse, with an equally-abandoned cottage at its base where the lighthouse-keeper would have lived. A small sandy bay looked like the ideal spot to land, and she turned the boat slightly to aim for the strip of sand.

Eventually she reached waters shallow enough that she could see the bottom, and stepped into the ice-cold water to haul the boat up onto the beach. She dragged it across the sand and up onto the pebbles beyond the tide line, safely out of harm's way, and turned her attention to the code tower which was just a few paces further up the hill.

The only obvious door went in to the cottage; a low, wide door with faded red paint. She tried the handle, not expecting it to open, and was taken by surprise when the door swung easily inwards on well-greased hinges. Was she really in the right place, or was this – as it appeared – simply a deserted lighthouse?

She drew her dagger as she stepped inside; the Provost had implied that the trap had already been dealt with, but she wasn't prepared to take any risks where the Tarasanka were concerned.

Quite out of keeping with the run-down appearance of the building's exterior, she found herself in a well-presented farmhouse kitchen. The iron stove was cold, but a stack of dry logs waited by the fireplace. Curious. Again she wondered if she'd come to the wrong place, but Raf's directions had been perfectly clear. The code tower was on the White Isle – and here she was.

There were two doors at the back of the kitchen and a ladder leading up into the attic. Still holding her knife in readiness, she climbed a few rungs up the ladder and peered around – there was a neatly made-up bed under the eaves, but other than that the space was empty.

Deciding there was nothing of interest up there, and assuming the heart of the code tower was likely to be the actual tower, she next tried the door to the left of the kitchen. The door lead not to the tower but rather into a pantry – she was only half-surprised to see that the shelves were stocked with pickled vegetables, smoked meats and dry biscuits. There was something very strange here, a house just sitting ready for someone to move in. Someone had prepared this place.

Aware of her rumbling stomach, she reached for a biscuit before she went to open the final door, so it was with a mouth full of crumbs that she finally understood why they called it the code tower.

The tower itself was circular, only about eight feet in diameter, and the internal walls were whitewashed then painted with a seemingly endless stream of numerals which ran together but formed no recognisable sequence. A series of pegs protruded from the walls forming a kind of sparse staircase spiralling upwards, a ladder which would have to be climbed to read all of the numbers. The eponymous code, Eleanor assumed. Overwhelmed by the enormity of the task, she decided to satisfy her hunger first – the wall wasn't going anywhere, and she was starting to understand why the pantry was full. This was likely to take some time.

Once she'd eaten her fill, and got a small fire going in the grate, she returned to the tower. It didn't look any better the second time – one long string of numbers which, so far as she could tell, ran unbroken from floor level up to the roof of the tower. She climbed to the top of the ladder, but the code didn't make any more sense from her new perspective.

Sixty-one... that was the number she'd got from her second visit to the puzzle chamber at Dashfort, and she wondered if it would help her here. She tried counting sixty-one digits from the end of the string, and sixty-one lines up and down, but it meant nothing to her. Besides, Raf would surely have told her if she'd needed to do these things in a particular order.

She wished again that he were here to help her. He'd known so much about everything in this process, surely he would've known what to do with all these numbers. If only she'd thought to ask him.

Frustrated, she sat on the floor and started looking at the first few numbers, hoping to force some sense out of the sequence. Add seven, subtract two, add one, subtract four... it was easy to imagine any number of ways that the digits could be related but she could see no repeating patterns, no obvious links. She didn't even know what she was trying to find.

She spent the rest of the day manipulating digits at the

beginning of the string – adding and subtracting, dividing and multiplying, but learning nothing. As darkness fell she picked out some more food from the pantry and sat watching the flames dance in the hearth, wishing for inspiration. When no ideas were forthcoming, she went to bed, annoyed at herself over a wasted day.

The following morning she tried mapping numbers on to letters, trying to force the sequence to speak to her, but every attempt yielded only more gibberish.

Over the next couple of days she really came to appreciate the comfortable bed, the well-stocked pantry, and the firewood chopped and stacked neatly by the door. It was clear to see why the Tarasanka had thought to lay a trap here; it would be easy to relax in this place. All too easy to let your guard down while trying to solve the riddle of the numbers. She wondered again if that wasn't part of the point, still a part of her unable to shake the feeling that the Tarasanka trap could also be part of this strange quest, set up by the Association to further test its postulants. It would explain why no-one at Venncastle had seemed very interested in what she'd had to say.

Yet the torture they'd endured had been more than real, and Raf had been really injured when she'd left him, and the others hadn't made it out of the castle. If it was a test, not many would pass.

There seemed only one way to find out, and that was to wait – if being captured here was a normal part of the process, it would happen again. She was making little enough progress with the numbers that the idea of taking her time certainly appealed; she'd always disliked arithmetic, and it was even harder without instructions.

She tried starting at both ends of the sequence, and at arbitrary points in the middle, trying to find any pattern that linked the digits. Whenever she thought she'd hit on something, looking a little further on would reveal a point where the pattern broke down, however devious she thought she'd been.

Growing frustrated and bored with the task at hand she took to practising acrobatics in the tower, scrambling some way up the wooden ladder and somersaulting back to the ground, trying to land steadily on her feet with a knife in each hand as she leapt from greater and greater heights. The spinning numbers as she recovered her balance each time seemed to make no more or less sense than before.

The time passed slowly, and she lost count of the passing days amid the numbers swirling in her head. There seemed to be no logic to it all. Believing she was looking for another two-digit number, she tried to convince herself that the paint on this digit or that one was of a subtly different shade, but tricks of the light meant that her choice of 'different' digits was continuously changing throughout the day.

As she rested at the top of the tower one afternoon, she started to count the threes for no other reason than that her nose rested near to one. Once she'd counted up all those she could see from where she was, she started climbing down again, adding to her mental tally as she went.

Her heart skipped a beat when she realised what total she'd reached at the end. One hundred and three threes. That couldn't be a coincidence, could it? She climbed back to the top of the tower and counted them again, just to be sure. Again she got a hundred and three.

Suddenly excited, she scrambled up the ladder again, counting the ones as she climbed. One hundred and one. It was too neat to be chance.

The twos, fours, and fives fitted the same pattern but the sixes, when she reached them, seemed not to. One hundred and nine sixes. Wrong by three. She counted again to make sure, but found the same result.

The sevens were back to what she expected, but the eights were wrong at a hundred and fifteen.

Could it really be so simple?

She counted the nines and the zeros to check her theory; the totals were as she'd expected. Just two wrong digits. Sixes and eights. Out by three and seven respectively.

Did that mean the number she was looking for was sixty-eight, thirty-seven, or something altogether more clever? She wasn't sure, but she was fairly confident that she didn't need to be in the tower to mull it over.

Chapter 13

She dragged the rowing boat into the sea as soon as the tide was favourable. As she waded out, she thought back to her conversation with the boat's owner and wondered if he'd been joking when he'd suggested she might be back the next day. Surely, living in a spot like that on Flying Rock Island, he must often lend his boat to the Association's postulants – especially boys from Venncastle itself. She struggled to believe that anyone could have started and finished at the code tower in only one day, unless they already knew what they were looking for. Perhaps he simply hadn't realised that was why she was going; perhaps, like Raf at the beginning, he'd discounted her for being female. That idea still rankled; it was hard to believe there were people in the Empire who still thought in such old-fashioned ways.

She rowed back across to Flying Rock Island, beached the boat, and went to tell the landlord that she'd returned it. He made no comment on the length of time she'd been away, but agreed that she could sleep for the same rate in the attic cot until the supplies boat made its next rounds from Dashfort.

The traders on the supplies boat recognised her, of course, and she had to fend off awkward questions about how she'd spent her time since they'd dropped her off. The sailors assumed she'd spent the whole period in the school, and though part of her yearned to correct them she knew she was better off keeping her mouth shut – even when their implications, joking or not, made her feel sick.

When they finally made it back to Dashfort it was raining hard, and night was beginning to fall as they moored. Eleanor bought herself half a dozen fried sausages from the one stall which was still open, and sheltered by the city wall to eat. Once the sailors from the supplies boat had gone to their homes, the harbour was left deserted. On a day like this there was no chance of finding a cart bound for the right direction; anyone with any sense would wait for calmer weather, and she'd have to wait for them if she didn't want to walk through the storm.

She was about to start munching her way through the final sausage when a broad-shouldered, hooded figure stepped out of the darkness towards her. A dagger glinted in his hand.

"Did you miss the day at Assassin School when they taught you not to be seen?" asked a sullen voice from beneath the hood. "You draw far too much attention to yourself."

She stared at him. That Port accent sparked her memory as though their encounter had been only yesterday. She recognised the voice, but surely it couldn't be him. How could he have known where to find her... or when?

"I'm amazed you dared to show your face in the Empire again, after what you did to our ship."

"What I did to your ship," she said carefully, "was to leave it safely anchored so you could sail back home the next morning. You should think yourselves lucky for that."

"Oh?"

"The others would've killed the lot of you as you slept."

He snorted. "So now you're claiming to be an assassin with morals?"

"I'm not claiming to be any kind of assassin," she said, resisting the urge to reach for her own knives. If she had to fight her way out of this one she'd never escape the stories he'd tell. "What do you want with me?"

"I'm getting bored of your games."

"I'm getting bored of you showing up," Eleanor retorted. "This is quite a grudge to bear for one failed attempt to pick your pocket."

"You're no common thief, girl. A woman with reflexes like that... carrying that knife?"

She'd been right, then: he'd recognised it from somewhere. She wondered what it meant. If she was ever going to find out, this was probably the time. "Beautiful blade, wasn't it? The man I stole it from was–"

"Bullshit!" The word exploded from him and he stepped closer to her, his knife held awkwardly across her chest now. "That was Laban's knife, and he'd never let no half-wit thief get a hand on it."

"Lah-ban?" She tried to pronounce the name as if she'd never heard it before.

"Laban." He turned and spat as though the word had a bad taste to it. "Didn't he tell you his name? Well, Laban always was better than anyone, even at school. Even when the Assessors gave him a Level Three – oh no, not for him. He was much too special to take up his assignment. Off to become a bloody assassin."

"You're obsessed with assassins. They're not even real, are they?"

"Don't play stupid, girl. Your kind are just a particularly nasty kind of rebel, if you ask me. So where is he?"

He pushed her back towards the wall with the flat of his knife and she allowed herself to be moved, not threatened by the dagger; she'd seen enough now to be confident that she could overpower him if she had to. He was clumsy even when he wasn't moving.

"I'm sick of chasing bloody shadows," he continued. "I'm not playing your bloody games any more. Tell me where he is."

"Or else what?" She met his gaze defiantly. "I don't even know anyone called Laban."

"You know the man who gave you that knife," the harbour master said. "Where've you hidden it? Why aren't you trying to kill me?"

"Why would I want to kill you? You're the one who's been following me!"

With his spare hand he reached towards her, presumably to search for her knife but she wasn't going to wait to find out. She deflected his arm and then pushed him hard, causing him to lose his balance and fall, sprawling hard on the wet cobblestones.

"Don't touch me," she warned as he got to his feet again. She wondered if she should run while she had the chance, but he'd proved his tenacity – he'd dedicated himself to tracking her down, and she'd no reason to think he wouldn't do it again. Somehow, she needed to persuade him that she wasn't worth the effort.

"I'll haul you all the way to jail if I have to," he said. "I know this city's police quite well. So if you want me to forget that little incident at sea, you'd better tell me where I can find your assassin friends."

"I don't know the bloke I got the knife from," she insisted. "I've no more idea than you of where to find him... probably less, since you're clearly so good at following people."

"Why should I believe you?"

He held the point of his dagger near her waist now. She wondered where he'd even obtained a weapon he was so ill-qualified to use.

"Is there somewhere we can go to talk?" she asked, as another burst of heavy rain swept across them. She was already soaked to the skin, and this was shaping up to be a lengthy stand-off.

He shook his head. "There's nothing to talk about. Tell me where I can find Laban, or you can dry out in jail."

She took a deep breath. The truth – that she didn't know – was apparently not enough to put him off. After her experiences in Taraska of being tortured for information she didn't possess, she was in no mood for putting up with his threats.

"If you're looking for an assassin, I think you need to go to Almont," she said, thinking back to what she'd read in *Stories of the Assassins*. If it was good enough for the book's author, it would do for this infuriating harbour master – and hopefully if she could suggest something else for him to chase, he'd leave her alone. "There's a huge marble fountain, that's apparently some kind of secret gateway."

"You think I haven't tried that?" he asked, leaning in until his face was a finger's breadth from hers. "I don't want regurgitated legends from you. I want you to tell me, right now, exactly where he is."

"I don't know." She tried to sound calm and reasonable. "Listen, I doubt I'd know that even if I was an assassin. Would you let a group of assassins know where all their colleagues were, all the time?"

"Laban wouldn't give his knife to just anyone. If you don't know where he is now, you know when you're next going to see him."

Eleanor could only wish that was true. If she'd had any idea how to find Laban again, she'd have felt a little bit more secure – as it happened, she knew only some meaningless numbers and that she next had to find a maze in a forest. Assuming, of course, that she could get out of this without going to jail as a smuggler.

"So?" the harbour master prompted when she failed to respond.

"No plans," she said. "I'm afraid I just can't help you."

The harbour master grabbed her shoulder and pulled her away from the wall. "We'll go over to the night watch tower, then," he said. "I've some crimes to report."

His fingers dug into her injured muscle, but he still held his dagger in an awkward fashion and she knew this was the moment where her choices ran out – now, she simply had to escape.

She turned sharply, pulling herself free of his grip and moving his knife arm safely aside, then throwing a swift kick back so that her heel planted itself in his abdomen.

He reacted more quickly than she'd anticipated, grabbing her ankle so that she crashed to the ground as she tried to run, and he swung his dagger down towards her. She pulled out a knife of her own just in time to block him, metal screeching on metal as the blades ran along each other, and as he moved to pin her more firmly against the ground his movement gave her chance to ram the knife into his stomach.

She acted on pure instinct, and then went cold with terror as she realised what she'd done. Killing strangers in Taraska was one thing – now she was in the heart of the Empire with blood on her hands and a body to dispose of. Who would believe her when she said she was only defending herself?

She pushed the body away from her, got to her feet, and glanced around to check no-one was watching; she couldn't see anybody through the rain, anyway, and that ought to mean they couldn't see her. She rinsed her knife in a puddle then sheathed it, wondering what Laban would say if he could see her now. The murder of minor Imperial officials probably wasn't what he'd had in mind when he'd trained her.

It was the first time she'd had to worry about disposing of a body – not the sort of thing they covered in the school curriculum, even for would-be military students such as she had been. The only thing she could think of was to dump him into the sea. She grasped his arms and started to drag him down towards the water, struggling as his clothes seemed to catch on every other cobblestone till she reached the steeper descent into the harbour.

She waded a few feet out into the water, and stopped short. He was floating beside her. Floating. That wasn't going to do any good at all.

Cursing to herself, she pulled him back to the shallows and started loading rocks into his pockets and inside his clothes until he eventually began to sink below the surface. Once she'd weighed him down sufficiently she swam a little way out to sea, towing the now-leaden body behind her, and made her way round to a small cove out of sight of the harbour. It wouldn't do for anyone to see him staring up at them from beneath the waves as they took their boats out to fish.

Satisfied that she'd gone far enough, she allowed him to sink. She could only hope the rocks would be enough to keep his body below the water until he decayed beyond recognition.

She swam back to the harbour and, with no way to dry herself, huddled shivering beneath an upturned rowing boat for the night.

She slept fitfully and woke, startled, at the first sounds of life the next morning. The events of the previous night came back to her in a sudden, terrifying flash which made her feel sick to her stomach. At first she wondered if she'd simply had an awful dream, but she could remember every movement, every sound, every horrible instant in far more detail than any dream she'd ever had – and her clothes were still uncomfortably damp.

She made her way nervously across to where it had happened, staring at the ground, searching for any trace of blood on the cobbles. To her relief she saw nothing out of the ordinary; the heavy rain had been her ally for once. Still, it would be best to make her way out of the city as soon as she could. She was glad it was still raining, though the downpour had slowed to a drizzle – at least her bedraggled appearance didn't look too much out of place.

Chapter 14

After a quick stop at the market to stock up on food, Eleanor made her way towards the main road southbound out of the city. There was a continuous stream of traffic between Dashfort and Almont, and surely someone would offer her a lift sooner or later. She spent the first half of the morning standing by the side of the road, just beyond the city gate, trying to attract the attention of a driver. After the twentieth cart drove straight past her she grew impatient and started walking.

Eventually, as the sun was beginning to dip behind the trees, a small convoy rattled past.

"You alright?" a young man shouted out, slowing his horses and leaning over towards her.

"I could do with a lift," she said. "If you didn't mind."

He reached out a hand to her and she managed to scramble up onto the cart as it continued onwards.

"We'll be stopping soon, for the night," he said as he urged his horses back to a faster pace to keep up with the rest of his party. "Do you want a ride all the way to Almont?"

"Just about half way, I think," she said. "I'm trying to get to the Silver Forest."

"It's a big con," the young man said. "It's not silver at all – just green, like normal trees. You should come on to Almont with us, we'll be just in time for the carnival."

"Carnival?"

"Yeah, it all starts on the equinox – we should get there by the second or third day, if we don't slack off. And we won't, with the carnival ahead of us! Dancing in the streets, all night long... much better than that lousy forest."

She couldn't deny she was tempted, and a short detour probably wouldn't ruin her plans. But she wanted to get the maze out of the way as soon as possible – there would be plenty of time for carnivals later. "I wish I could," she said. "But I'm, uh, meeting someone. When's the next one?"

"Next year – it runs for a few days from the spring equinox every year. Have you really never been? You mustn't miss next year."

She travelled with the convoy for two more days before her companion dropped her off at the side of the road and pointed her down a track which branched off between the trees.

"Just don't blame me when you're disappointed," he said with a wink. "And promise you'll dance with me at the carnival next year!"

"I'll try," she said, though she had no idea what she'd be doing this time next year. It felt so far away – she had a whole life to create before then.

She started along the road wondering what she was looking for. If the Silver Forest was in no way silver, she wasn't sure she'd know when she'd reached it – or where she'd find the maze within.

After a further two days' walking, she was beginning to get seriously worried. She'd passed no signs and no settlements. Had the young trader's directions been wrong?

The track was getting smaller and more overgrown by the day, winding between tree trunks into woodland so thick that only a little light filtered down between the branches. If there'd been any forks in the trail she would've turned back to try another direction, but however insignificant this track appeared it was the only one she'd seen.

A couple of days later, however, the track disappeared completely.

After an almost-sleepless night in the undergrowth, she decided it was time for a rethink. She was following Raf's directions to look for the maze – the third piece of the Association's jigsaw puzzle. Logically, that meant that some number of students must make this journey every year, and even if it had been months since the last person had passed this way there should still be some signs of their passage.

She dropped to her knees and began to study the ground, working gradually outwards in small circles from the spot where she'd spent the night. Her own careless passage the previous evening had disturbed a large strip of ground, but eventually she found the sign she'd been looking for – a faint heel-impression in the soil, the remains of the mark left by a foot too large to be her own.

Following in the direction pointed by the footprint, she worked her way forward on hands and knees, encouraged each time she found another imprint. And a couple of strands of blue thread, caught on a bramble a few yards further into the forest, lifted her spirits even as the thorns snagged her skin.

As she inched along, something hard beneath her knee caused her to yelp in pain and she reached down to move what she assumed was a stone. It was cold to the touch, though, and embedded deeply in the ground. She turned to study the object, using her knife to scrape back soil from what, it turned out, was a metal ring.

With a triumphant feeling rising in her chest she got to her feet and hauled on the ring, moving out of the way as a section of ground swung upwards. A trapdoor – of course! She was a little embarrassed that she hadn't predicted it. Below ground was the most obvious place to hide something in a place like this, at least if you had the vast resources that the Association seemed to have at its disposal.

The trapdoor opened only part-way, making an opening just wide enough for her to slip inside. She lowered herself into the hole, the trapdoor pressing down on her back as she slid further, searching with her feet for any kind of steps but finding only a tunnel of earth. Unable to reach any further without allowing the trapdoor to close, she dug her toes into the soil and took hold of a handful of roots, testing to make sure it would hold her weight.

In the darkness she scrabbled for reasonable hand- and foot-holds to lower herself down the tunnel, and she thought she was being careful but somehow she missed her footing and fell. She wasn't sure how far she dropped but she crashed painfully to the ground, thankful that the landing was on earth rather than rock.

She reached out for the walls, but found nothing within reach of where she'd fallen; she seemed to be in some sort of cavern but with no light it was hard to judge the size of the space.

Wary of the uneven ground, she crawled forwards until she

reached the wall, then stuck one of her Tarasanka throwing knives into the ground to mark her place and began a slow circuit of the space in which she'd found herself. By the time she finally returned to her starting point and sheathed the knife again, she'd identified three passages leading outwards, approximately evenly spaced, and a small rivulet of slightly acrid water from which she refilled her flask.

Unable to identify any way to choose between the different passages, she simply continued round until she reached the first opening again. She had only a couple of day's worth of food left; there was no time to waste on excessive thinking.

The ceiling in the passage was just high enough that she could stand without needing to bend, and with one hand on each earthy wall she began taking careful steps into the maze.

She moved as quickly as she dared, conscious that time was of the essence but wary of potentially deadly surprises lurking in the darkness.

Out of sight of daylight there was no way to track the passage of time, so she slept when she was tired, ate (a couple of mouthfuls at a time) when she felt hungry, and for the rest of the time pursued her walk of the maze.

It wasn't a huge surprise when she eventually found herself back in what she believed to be the same open area where she had started; if the passages didn't connect, she'd had only a one-in-three chance of getting it right first time.

When it happened for a second time, she even felt a little bolstered by the fact that there was only one route left. Whatever she was looking for, it couldn't be far away now, and she hadn't even come across any unpleasant traps or tricks.

The third time she found herself back in the cavern, however, she was becoming desperate. She'd run out of food, she was feeling constantly tired, and now she'd exhausted the entire labyrinth of tunnels.

She sank to her knees to rest, and contemplated climbing back out of the maze to look for something to eat. But she didn't know what distance she'd fallen or how easy the climb would be, and she was sure she must be overlooking something obvious. She'd been around the whole maze – or had she?

Feeling around in the dark was time consuming, so she certainly hadn't fully explored the walls as she'd walked. Maybe there was another hidden passage somewhere in the darkness.

She checked the floor of the cavern first, searching for another trapdoor, but found nothing. Then she entered the nearest passageway, running her hands up and down the walls this time as she progressed.

Before long she needed to stop and rest; the 'days', as she counted according to when she slept, seemed to be passing more quickly and she wondered if her need for sleep was increasing as she grew more hungry. Maybe this was how it happened – one day she'd simply drift into sleep and never wake up.

As she was dozing off she was disturbed by something crawling over her leg; she reached out and snatched up what turned out to be a rather large beetle. It writhed in her fingers and she was about to throw it out of the way when a vague memory from her schooldays stopped her – all the Empire's native beetles were supposed to be edible. She had no way of cooking, but she was too hungry to be squeamish about that. After snapping off the legs, head, and casing, she was left with a small, chewy morsel that she washed down with a gulp of water.

Scrabbling around in the dirt turned up another half-dozen bugs. Hardly a gourmet meal, but it was better than nothing and she finally slept with slightly less rumbling in her stomach.

She continued her examination of the tunnel walls as soon as she awoke, now assessing every grub that she uncovered in hope of finding a few bites to eat.

She was about to stop for another rest when she was disturbed by what felt like a light breeze ruffling her hair. That was odd: she was quite a distance into the system of tunnels.

She paused, holding herself totally still – and there it was again.

Cautiously, she extended one arm above her head. Even when her arm was fully straightened, her fingers had touched nothing; she was beneath an opening in the roof of the tunnel.

Her optimism revived, she pulled herself up into the second

layer of the maze. The floor and walls here were wooden, and the tunnel was high enough only for crawling.

She was careful not to neglect the roof as she made her way through the next set of tunnels, checking regularly for any gaps above her head. Up was the right direction, after all; she'd need to make her way back to ground level eventually. It took her two 'days' to find the next opening between levels, a trapdoor which opened – worryingly – downwards and guided her into a set of wood-lined passages which, she guessed, must be in some way interleaved with the earthen maze where she'd begun.

After another day or so she found a vertical shaft and pulled herself up into the third layer of the maze. She had to pull herself along on her belly in this set of even narrower wooden tunnels, shuffling forwards until she put her weight on a wobbly plank.

The floor spun beneath her; she grasped at the walls but to no avail, and she landed hard a few feet below. The earth beneath her fingertips told her she was back somewhere in the bottom layer of the maze. She got to her feet and pushed at the roof of the tunnel, but there was no sign of the opening she'd fallen through.

By the time she worked her way back to the narrowest tunnels she was exhausted, and determined not to make the same mistake again. She pulled herself along slowly, with weakening muscles, wary of every tiny imperfection in the boards beneath her.

When she reached the point where she'd fallen, she pressed her hands and feet against the walls to carry herself across the wobbly section without touching the floor. Applying the same technique every time she came to an unstable area, she eventually came to another gap in the ceiling.

She clambered up, expecting yet more tunnels, but found herself emerging into a large, rocky cave. She blinked as her eyes adjusted to the relative brightness; the number she'd been looking for was painted in large white digits on the ground: 23.

A metal turnstile at the end of the cave let through a crack of light, and she pushed her way out into the daylight again.

She found a small spring only a few feet away; this had been planned with the impeccable attention to detail she was coming to expect from the Association's efforts. She leant across the stream, dipped her face to the water and drank until she could drink no more, then sank back to the grass, dripping but refreshed.

But there was none of the triumph she'd expected to feel. If anything, she was a little disappointed. She'd hoped that, once she had all three answers, a pattern would emerge to help her work out what to do next. But nothing was apparent, whichever number she picked from the code tower's possibilities.

Disoriented by her experiences in the darkness, she had to work out which way was north from the gradual motion of the sun. After a brief rest, and having found a few leaf-buds to nibble, she settled on a direction and began to make her way through the forest.

It was a six-day trek before she reached the main road again, and another half-day walking towards Almont before she heard the first cart rattling along behind her. She turned and waved hopefully at the driver, a round-faced woman whose black hair was scraped into a tight knot.

"Are you okay?" the driver asked as she reined her horses to a standstill. "Need a lift?"

"Yes please. How far are you going towards Almont?"

"All the way. Jump up, then." She patted the bench beside her. "Going to the Marble Quarter, will that do you?"

"Perfect," Eleanor said, though she had no idea what that meant. It sounded suitably grand that it had to be central. And with no other clues, the only thing to do was to follow the legends once more, to the fountain she'd read about in *Stories of the Assassins*.

Chapter 15

It was not called the Marble Quarter for nothing. The cart pulled up in a broad, tree-lined avenue with pure white colonnades running down both sides. Eleanor thanked her driver, passed her a couple of small coins to show that she meant it, and jumped down into the road. Carefully dodging the traffic, she couldn't take time to look around until she reached the colonnaded walkway. When she did, it took her breath away.

She was standing on vast slabs of grey-veined marble which made up the pavement and – more impressively – the entire road surface. She could hardly begin to imagine how many people must be employed just to keep the place clean, yet the stones gleamed in spite of the seemingly endless horse-and-cart traffic trundling past.

At one end of the avenue, she could see the sparkling water spraying from the fountain in the Grand Square; looking the other way, the palatial façade of the central government offices filled the horizon with yet more marble glistening in the evening sunshine.

Once she managed to tear her eyes away from the amazing architecture, Eleanor began to take note of the people. No beggars or hawkers here, no street stalls to clutter this perfect district. The patrol of blue-uniformed guards was a subtle presence, in contrast to the ostentatious display of the buildings, but it carried the same message: here lay the heart of power.

She was tempted to walk straight to the fountain to see if she could identify the place she'd be looking for once the equinox rolled around, but something stopped her. She needed to be a little more subtle than that, and she didn't want to risk whatever traps may have been laid for people trying to get in at the wrong time.

She thought back to what Gisele and Lucille had said when she'd left the school, and hoped the offer to visit was still good.

She'd memorized the address Gisele had given her but it meant nothing, and in a city of this size it was highly unlikely she'd find the right area by chance.

A quick enquiry with one of the Imperial guards, however, and she was on her way – to a road, as it turned out, only a few streets away from this administrative centre. Gisele had always seemed destined to do 'something important' in government, and her new address reflected the nature of the post she'd been assigned: a large building in a district of broad avenues which, while nowhere near so impressive as the Marble Quarter's colonnades, would still have dwarfed any street in Port Just. There were even a few ornamental trees planted at the junctions.

Eleanor rapped her knuckles loudly on the door, hoping Gisele would be back from her office by this time of day, but the door was answered by a petite, immaculately-presented blonde girl of around Eleanor's age.

"Can I help you?" she asked, studying Eleanor with an expression of thinly-veiled distaste.

Eleanor tried not to laugh as she realised how dishevelled she must appear; it had been weeks since she'd bathed, her clothes were tattered and her hair knotted.

"My name's Eleanor," she said, extending her hand and enjoying the look of horror which creased the other girl's features as she reconciled herself to the only polite response. The handshake was as brief as it could have been while still satisfying the social necessities, and the blonde girl wiped her hand discretely on her skirt as she stepped back.

"Sayah," she introduced herself, her face now composed again into perfectly polite neutrality. "How can I help you?"

"I was hoping to find my friend Gisele – she invited me to stay with her here."

"Oh. Come in."

Eleanor guessed that Sayah must be training for the same diplomatic career as Gisele; certainly she did an admirable job of hiding her disappointment that this strange, messy creature intended to enter her neat and respectable home.

"Gisele's still at school," Sayah continued as Eleanor

followed her into the large sitting room which comprised the ground floor of the house. "She shouldn't be long. Would you care to take a bath while you're waiting?"

Eleanor toyed with the idea of refusing, just to see whether she'd even be permitted to sit down in this house without cleaning up first, but she sensed it would be unwise to push Sayah's limits any further. The girl was already nervous of her unexpected visitor. Instead, she mustered what she hoped was a gracious smile, and simply said "Thank you."

Sayah led her up one flight of stairs, pausing briefly to tug on a bell-pull by the bathroom door, and moments later a middle-aged maidservant appeared to fill the bath.

"Anna will wash your clothes," Sayah said, indicating the maid. "I'm sure Gisele won't mind if you wear her robe."

Alone in the bathroom, Eleanor smiled as she lowered herself into the perfumed water. It had been mildly entertaining to tease the pristine Sayah, but the hot water against her skin was a welcome treat and she looked forward to being properly clean again.

After a lengthy soak, and having teased the worst knots out of her hair, Eleanor dried herself and wrapped Gisele's blue bathrobe around her body; her own clothes had already been efficiently swept away for washing, though she wondered if they'd really look any better for it considering the number of snags and tears in the fabric.

Her weapons were left in a neat pile without comment – so the maid had also been selected for her tact. Eleanor tucked the blades out of sight behind the washstand, not wanting to have to explain her circumstances to Gisele straight away.

When she went back down to the sitting room, Gisele and Sayah were both waiting, along with an equally well-manicured young man.

"Eleanor!" Gisele exclaimed, getting to her feet and moving to embrace her schoolfriend.

"You said I was welcome to visit," Eleanor said as they parted after a brief hug.

Sayah and the young man looked on and exchanged amused glances; Eleanor wondered if Sayah had told the others what a complete mess she'd been when she'd arrived. Or was the young diplomat-in-training too diplomatic for that?

"Of course," Gisele agreed. "You've met Sayah, and this is Ron. We're all on the same diplomatic track, and I must say you've made it just in time – we'll be leaving Almont in a couple of months for our first postings."

"Is it going well?" Eleanor cast her eyes across the room to include all three in the question; Ron and Sayah nodded with restrained smiles.

"It's been a great year," Gisele said, then dropped her eyes to the floor before asking quietly: "What about you?"

"Great," Eleanor echoed. "I've had a fascinating time." That at least was true.

"Well, I'll have to get Lucille to drop in and you can tell us all about your adventures," Gisele said crisply. "It'll be just like the old days."

"That sounds lovely," Eleanor said, though she had no wish to talk about any of the past year's 'adventures'.

"Anyway, it's nearly time for dinner," Gisele continued. "You can't stay in that silly robe – come upstairs and I'll lend you some proper clothes."

As Gisele hunted in her wardrobe for "something that won't drown you," Eleanor wondered how long it would be – now they were out of earshot of the others – before the serious questions started.

"Try this for size," Gisele said, proffering a summer frock of lilac cotton.

The dress would have been knee-length on Gisele, but fell to the middle of Eleanor's calves. "Perfect," she declared, twirling to make the flowing skirt fill out with air.

Gisele nodded her approval. "It'll do until you can buy yourself something that fits. So where have you been for the last year?"

"I thought you were going to wait for Lucille to come round."

"It's not that she won't want to see you," Gisele said. "Really. She'll be as delighted as I am. But your behaviour did worry all of us, you know, and especially with Lucille going on to be an

188

Assessor. If you've been doing crazy things, we need to work out what you can tell her. I mean, look at your face... those scars tell a story all on their own!"

Eleanor rolled her eyes, and sat down on the edge of the bed. It had always been Gisele's place to try to lead their little group, and always Eleanor's role to be the rebel loner, but she'd done too much fighting recently. Resistance now would be a pointless waste of energy. So her conversation with Lucille would be doubly filtered – she'd reduce the past year's events to what she could safely tell Gisele, and Gisele would decide what was suitable for Lucille to hear.

"Do you want to do this right now?" she asked, hoping for a little extra time to think of a coherent story. "What about dinner?"

"Okay, after dinner," Gisele agreed. "You'll have to sleep in here anyway, we don't have a guest room."

Dinner was a sober affair, a mostly silent procedure punctuated with brief pockets of polite conversation. Eleanor concentrated on the food – which was simple but tasty, delivered to the table by the maid Anna – and tried to ignore the way Sayah and Ron were watching her every movement. Gisele, for her part, tried to start several threads of conversation but found her attempts doomed to failure in the stilted atmosphere.

As soon as they'd finished their dessert – whole baked pears with a sweet cream filling – Eleanor announced that she was exhausted, and excused herself for the night. Gisele accompanied her upstairs.

"Your colleagues don't think much of me," Eleanor said as she settled into the makeshift bed Gisele had arranged by the window.

Gisele shrugged. "You surprised them. They've met Lucille, of course, but you're a bit different."

Eleanor smiled despite herself; Gisele had a natural talent for understatement.

Gisele snuffed out the room's main lantern, leaving only a small night-light to illuminate their faces, and climbed into bed herself. "So, are you ready to tell me your story?" she asked.

189

"Stories by candlelight? This really is like the old days."

"Stop stalling. We're going to do this tonight, so you might as well get on with it."

"Okay." Eleanor had been thinking hard throughout the meal, searching desperately for enough details that she could stitch together to make a convincing whole. In the end she was almost truthful about the way she'd fallen ill in Arche, told the story of her smuggling adventures without mentioning the trouble with Port Just's harbour master, and glossed over the time she'd spent in Taraska as though it'd been a pleasant holiday. There were some things she wasn't ready to talk about.

"But what about your face?" Gisele asked when she'd finished describing her route back to the Empire aboard the Magrad ship.

"Just got into a bit of a fight over in Taraska," Eleanor said. "People aren't very civilized outside of the Empire."

"Incredible." Gisele seemed almost lost for words, and it was a long moment before she spoke again. "Well, I don't know what we can tell Lucille, really. She'd never forgive you for running off with pirates, would she?"

"She might."

"No, we'll have to change it a bit – say you were kidnapped by those smugglers, that sounds better. Do you think you can sound convincing?"

Eleanor stifled a laugh; she was already lying by omission, but it amused her to hear the ever-proper Gisele giving such advice. "How about I was drugged? To explain why I couldn't fight back."

"Excellent." Gisele blew out the night-light. "Good night."

The next morning Eleanor woke early as usual but resisted the urge to get up until Gisele was already dressed.

"I'm off to school soon," Gisele said. "Anna will make you breakfast, if you like. We usually get ours there."

"Thanks."

"You'll be okay on your own today, won't you? I'll send a message to Lucille's office to see whether she's free this evening."

Eleanor waited until she was sure Sayah and Ron had gone with Gisele to school before she ventured downstairs.

Anna was busy polishing the fire surround, but turned when Eleanor came into the room. "Breakfast, ma'am?"

"If it's no trouble," Eleanor said.

"No trouble, no. It's my job to look after the young diplomats and their friends." She disappeared down a small flight of steps at the back of the house, and returned a little while later with a platter of fruit and cheese.

Eleanor thanked her and helped herself.

"How long might you be staying, if you don't mind my asking?" Anna asked.

"I don't know."

"It's only..." She hesitated. "It's only that the house is usually empty while the young diplomats are studying, and it would make my days quite long to be looking after your needs all day and theirs in the evenings."

"Oh, that's okay, I don't need much looking after."

But something wasn't quite right; the housekeeper looked awkwardly at her.

She tried again: "I can arrange to be out during the day if that helps."

"That would be a great help, ma'am."

Eleanor wondered what that was really about. Either Anna desperately valued the time by herself in the house or – more likely? – someone had indicated that Eleanor wasn't trusted to be left alone here. She only hoped it hadn't been Gisele who'd given that instruction.

So Eleanor let herself out after breakfast and spent the day wandering the city, returning to the house at dusk.

"It really is you, then?" Lucille had been in relaxed conversation with Sayah, but interrupted herself mid-sentence when Eleanor appeared. "I'd like to say you haven't changed, but honestly Eleanor, you look like you've been to war and back."

"Sort of," Eleanor said. "I'll tell you about it later. How's life at the Assessors' College?"

"Still training," Lucille replied. "But it's truly fascinating.

You see things you'd never guess... it throws everything into a new perspective."

When Eleanor was finally called upon to tell her "great adventure story" over dinner, she launched herself into it with abandon. She entertained herself by embellishing details, half-daring Gisele to challenge the more blatant fabrications. Lucille, Sayah, and Ron lapped up her story with interest; Gisele listened with increasing perturbation but said nothing until she was alone with Eleanor at the end of the night.

"What was that all about?" she demanded.

"What?"

"You know what. Lying."

"You told me to lie." Eleanor slipped out of her borrowed dress and clambered into bed. "I was just trying to be convincing."

Gisele gave a heavy sigh, but didn't argue.

Eleanor spent the next couple of weeks exploring Almont's central districts, with frequent visits to the Marble Quarter where she still hoped to find some clue to her next steps. But however many times she went back to walk by the fountain or study the surrounding buildings, nothing leapt out at her. No secret entrances, no concealed mechanisms that she could detect as she ran her hands along the damp stones of the fountain's edge. And with the blue-uniformed guards quietly patrolling the streets, she had to be careful not to draw attention to herself, keeping her reconnaissance trips brief and irregularly timed.

As the equinox approached, she caught herself feeling sick with nerves more and more often. She'd been careful not to mention anything about the Association to Gisele, and soon she'd have to make her excuses and leave with nothing more than a hope that, on the right day, something would suddenly be obvious.

She struggled to get to sleep on the night before the equinox, and woke again well before daybreak. Unable to fall asleep again she got up, hoping she could creep out while it was still dark without attracting Gisele's attention – that would avoid any awkward goodbyes. If everything went according to plan she could come back and explain later, and otherwise... she hated to let herself think about the other possibility, but if by some chance everything didn't magically fall into place then she might want to come back here, and it would be a lot less embarrassing if she hadn't announced her intention to leave. Particularly when it came to Sayah and Ron, who were still treating her like some kind of fascinating insect to be studied from a safe distance.

She gathered her things quietly, thankful to find that her weapons were still stashed behind the washstand. She left Gisele's dresses behind, dressing in her own tattered clothes again, and let herself out of the house in silence. She headed straight for the fountain and perched on the edge, feeling the occasional splashes of water against her back. It was the equinox, she was sure something should be different but in the pre-dawn light nothing looked to have changed.

Hungry and irritated, she headed to the market district for breakfast; it was on the other side of the city, but she had nothing better to do with her time and she knew from her previous explorations that she'd find better food there.

She thought nothing of the young man who bumped into her in the street until later, when she was preparing to return to the Marble Quarter again – at which point she did a quick check of her weapons, and found her favourite knife gone.

She cursed loudly, and glared at the people who turned to look at her for it. It was her own fault for favouring that blade and keeping it the most accessible. Somehow that didn't make her feel any better – and since that knife was her only link to the 'something' she was searching for today, there was no way she was willing to rely on getting through without it.

She was fortunate that the thief was greedy; she spent much of the afternoon stalking the market, and caught him with his hand on another lady's purse strings.

"Police," she reassured the woman as she marched the youth away at knifepoint. It could have been true, though she knew she didn't look the part. Fortunately the woman was shaken, and in no mood to argue with her rescuer.

She steered the youth into a deserted side-street and pushed him roughly against the wall, dagger still against his throat. "Recognise me?" she asked, using her spare hand to pat him down for weapons.

He nodded mutely. This could have been the last thing he expected when he chose to 'accidentally' brush against her in the crowd.

"Where's my knife?"

He shook his head, and she pushed the flat of her blade more firmly against his neck.

"Where is it?"

"I don't have it." He gulped nervously and avoided her eyes. "Sold it."

"Already? Well, I'm sure you know who you sold it to – you must have some regular buyers."

"On the market," he said. "It'll have gone by now, sorry. I can pay you back."

"You could never afford it. Now, this is what we're going to do. You're going to turn around *very* slowly, and I'm going to put my arm around your waist." She pulled back just enough to give him space to move. "Get close and pretend you like me, or this knife goes into your back. Understand?"

He nodded, and turned as she'd instructed.

"Now, we're going to visit whoever you sold my knife to, and you're going to buy it back. And if we can't, it's going to be very, very unlucky for you."

She kept the point of her dagger pressed into his lower back as they walked together back into the market, but allowed him to lead the way. They came to a small table crowded with trinkets; Eleanor found herself irrationally disappointed that her knife could have been sold on to such a collector of junk rather than fetching its proper price with a real weaponsmith.

The man behind the table clearly recognised his supplier, and piped up with a friendly "'Ello, mate – this your girl, then? She's a stunner!"

Eleanor looked expectantly up at the thief, then jabbed him in the back to prompt him to speak.

"Listen, mate," he started awkwardly. "Any chance of getting back that knife I sold you this morning? Turns out it's kind of special."

"Nah." The seller shook his head. "No way, I like that one. Reckon I can get a good price from the smuggling crowd."

"He'll pay you back double," Eleanor said sweetly, daring the thief to contradict her.

"Oh, well. Must be really special then? Make it three times, and we're talking."

The thief paled, but Eleanor gave him a sharp reminder of her blade against his skin, and he nodded. "Three times. That's fine. Should never have sold it, mate, that's all."

The thief emptied almost the entire contents of his purse onto the table, and the stallholder reached beneath the table for the knife.

Eleanor took it, sheathed the blade under her clothes then turned and ran, disappearing into the crowds before the thief or any of his friends could come after her.

Feeling the pressure of time, she jogged back to the Marble Quarter and sat heavily on the edge of the fountain again.

She was only just in time.

In the last of the evening's light, a thin shaft of sunlight fell between two carved statues on the roof of the building behind her, drawing an arrow in shadows on the wall. The door to which it pointed could easily have been mistaken for a side-door to the palace; no-one would think twice about any comings and goings... she could have kicked herself for missing something so obvious. A doorway disguised, not as a fountain or a wall, but as a door, highlighted by the precise alignment of the light as it fell between innocent carvings, an alignment which presumably only worked as the equinox sun fell towards the horizon. No wonder that nothing had been apparent earlier.

She was about to get up to try the door when a couple of young men rounded the corner, and she ducked out of sight behind the fountain. When she peered round a moment later, they were gone.

She ran across and rattled the handle, not really expecting the door to open and it didn't. Somehow she still had to find a use for the numbers she'd collected.

But something had moved beneath her fingers as she'd

tugged at the handle. She inspected it closely. There were three fine gold dials set concentrically around the circular door-handle, well disguised within the intricate mouldings of the handle. The first ran from zero up to twenty-five, the second from zero to fifty, and the third from zero all the way to seventy-five.

In that case, it was easy.

She turned the first dial to twenty-three, the second to thirty-seven, and the third to sixty-one, and confidently turned the handle. She felt the dials moving mechanically back to their zero positions as the door swung open before her.

She slipped through the opening and pushed the door closed behind her, breathing a sigh of relief. She'd arrived. Whatever was to come, surely nothing could be as bad as the trials she'd experienced over her year of searching for this place.

PART II

Chapter 16

In the darkness Eleanor could only just see the flight of stairs leading down to her left, and she ran her hands along the walls for stability as she began to make her way down, taking each step carefully in case of hidden traps. The stairs were alarmingly steep and she almost fell a couple of times, but she finally made it to the bottom without mishap. The passageway then led straight onwards, in pitch blackness, for a considerable distance – she guessed it must have been at least a mile, and she wondered whether she'd still be within the city limits once she emerged. Her natural sense of direction was useless underground.

After a time the floor began to slope upwards, gradually at first, and the passage began to wind back and forth as it worked its way back up to ground level. In the darkness at the end of the passage her hands found a door; she pushed it open, and stepped out into an oak-panelled, stone-floored hall.

A number of grand candelabras flooded the room with flickering light, and she blinked as her eyes adjusted to the brightness. There were a few young men in the room already, standing in small groups and speaking in hushed tones. No-one seemed to have noticed her enter so she closed the door quietly and stood with her back against the wall, looking from face to face. Presumably these were the other students. She was the only girl – but if Raf was right that they'd only recently started allowing women to enroll, it was hardly surprising.

But Raf wasn't there.

She shuddered as she wondered what had become of him. Had he even managed to escape from Taraska? She couldn't bear to think what they would've done to him if they'd found him again.

Pushing the thought from her mind, she edged towards the

nearest youth, the only one of the group not to be in conversation already. He was tall – standing head and shoulders above Eleanor – with a slim, toned frame. A mop of blond hair fell across his eyes and he held himself stiffly.

"My name's Eleanor," she said once she was close enough. "Who're you?"

"Daniel," he replied, hardly bothering to glance down at her.

She waited, and when nothing more was forthcoming from him, she asked, "Which school did you go to?"

She didn't expect the answer to mean anything to her, and it didn't. She wasn't even sure she could have reproduced the lengthy, foreign-sounding word.

He must have registered her blank expression because he added: "You have heard of us, if not by name. We are on a ship."

Hearing him speak more than one word, Eleanor noticed that his accent was slightly foreign, too. He enunciated every word carefully and quietly in a soft tenor, but the sounds weren't quite right: his 'V's morphed into 'F's, and there was a breathy quality to his voice. Even through the gentle lilting tones, which fell strangely on her ears, she could sense an absolute confidence – bordering on arrogance – in his words.

It took her slightly longer to absorb the meaning of what he'd said. Of course she'd heard rumours of the ship-board school. Everyone had. And everyone at Mersioc Regional School for Girls had dismissed it as pure fiction. Eleanor could hear her friends' words clearly in her mind: *A school on a ship, honestly, it's just stupid. Who would start a story like that?"*

Eleanor herself, who had always held a secret longing for the sea, had reserved judgement. She hoped this had been enough to protect her from showing any surprise; she doubted the young man would be happy to find out that no-one actually believed in his school.

"So what was that like?" she asked.

"It was just a school. I am glad to have left."

While she was still trying to think of an intelligent response, he turned away. Glad to be saved from having to think of any more small-talk, Eleanor settled to studying the other students again. Aside from all being male, they had other things in common, like the obviously toned physiques, the practical clothing, and the weapons hidden – and in some cases not so hidden – about their persons. There could be no question she'd found the place she was looking for.

By the time she'd made her brief assessment, Daniel had moved across to the edge of the room and settled himself on the floor, leaning back against the wall. Eventually others also started to sit, or even to lie down, and some seemed to settle into sleep. Eleanor sat cross-legged on the floor and allowed herself to doze, but with her hand clasped tightly around the hilt of her dagger.

They were disturbed some time later by the opening of a door – a door which, until that moment, Eleanor hadn't realised was there. She watched carefully as it swung closed again and then examined the wall, determined to find some subtle sign that she had missed, something which showed that those particular panels in fact concealed an entranceway. It was, she was sure, the kind of thing it would be useful to notice. After a moment's study she identified a very slight bow to the wood along the edge of a couple of the panels, giving away the hinges. And on the other side of the door, her eyes settled on a small knot in the wood – she was too far away to be sure, even with her keen vision, but she suspected that the apparent defect in fact concealed access to the mechanism.

Satisfied, she turned her attention to the man who had entered. He was short and slightly stocky, and completely bald though Eleanor thought from his face that he looked only a year or two older than she was.

His footsteps made no sound as he moved into the room, and Eleanor noted with envy that silence seemed to come naturally to him; she had to work hard when she wanted to move quietly. She suspected everyone was thinking along the same lines as they watched him: this was their first glimpse into what their futures held, and it was impressive. She only hoped the baldness wasn't compulsory; she was unreasonably fond of her long, flame-red hair.

"Welcome to the academy," the man said as the students

gathered in front of him. "And thank you all for coming.

"Three of the council's intended recruits did not choose to join us; they will have taken up their Level Three postings by now."

He looked around at the assembled students, and his eyes fixed on Eleanor; she met his gaze steadily, assuming he'd picked her out for her gender and not wishing to give him the satisfaction of seeming self-conscious about it.

When he next spoke, however, his voice had changed and his words shook her to the core. "But who are you?" he asked.

Eleanor felt eight pairs of eyes turn on her. Maybe it was yet another test of her courage.

"My name's Eleanor," she replied, drawing back her shoulders and straightening to her full height. She watched the man's face carefully as she spoke, trying to measure his reactions, but he didn't leave her in doubt for long.

"You," he indicated sharply to Daniel. "Guard her. I shan't be long."

Daniel gave a small nod, but otherwise remained still at her side.

The man turned and left by the door he had come in through, and Eleanor was slightly mollified to find that she'd been right about the position of the mechanism.

As soon as the man had gone, one of the boys turned to Eleanor. He was a tallish, heavy-set youth with short, light-brown hair and an unsmiling face.

"You not supposed to be here?" he asked, reaching for a dagger which he kept sheathed at his hip. His voice was just as miserable as his face.

"How would she know?" Daniel asked before she could respond, positioning himself slightly between Eleanor and the other boy.

"Well, the school... My headmaster told me what to do, not much space to get it wrong – didn't yours?"

Eleanor thought back to her conversation with Isabelle just before she'd left school. The headmistress had seemed like she was holding something back – should there have been more information?

200

"You must be of Venncastle," Daniel said. "Famed only for such transgressions."

Venncastle! Eleanor's ears pricked up at the familiar name. But she was bemused by their exchange; clearly they shared some understanding which she lacked. She held herself silent, doubting she'd do herself any favours by asking questions at this stage.

"And with that accent, and stupid ideals like that – you must be one of the fantasists from the ship," a skinny, gaunt-faced lad sneered at Daniel. "But why protect the girl? You her boyfriend?"

"She is here," Daniel said. "That is what matters."

"If the girl was meant to be here, she'd be sure," said the surly youth. He looked hard at Eleanor. "Are you?"

"I'm here," Eleanor said, drawing a little confidence from Daniel's words. Maybe it didn't even matter whether she'd been expected: maybe just getting here would be enough to prove her worth.

"Leave it, Jorge," the skinny one muttered. "They'll get the council to sort it."

The group fell into an uneasy silence. It seemed to be forever that they stood there, held in a kind of stalemate. The thick-set youth – Jorge – stood with his dagger held loosely in his hand, glaring at Eleanor but not daring to step past Daniel to reach her; his skinny friend hovered just behind. Daniel had his back firmly to Eleanor, standing stock-still and keeping his eyes on the knife.

For her part, Eleanor was determinedly studying the floor, managing to find great interest in a corner of the cracked grey slab. She assumed the eight young men surrounding her were all equipped with similar skills to her own; superior, possibly, if they were supposed to be here and she was not – if she had indeed come all this way following a trail which hadn't been intended for her. So having quickly discounted the idea of trying to run or fight, she simply resigned herself to waiting. Daniel seemed to have interpreted the instruction to guard her as meaning to protect her from the others as well as to stop her from leaving, so she felt safe enough, particularly as her fingers also touched lightly against the hilt of her own favourite knife.

Eventually, the bald man returned. He swept back across the room and addressed himself directly to Eleanor in the first instance.

"You have arrived," he said. "So the council have deemed you will stay."

Eleanor saw Daniel's muscles relax, and he finally allowed his eyes to move away from the knife blade. Jorge shoved the dagger roughly back into its sheath, but he still watched Eleanor with a look of deep suspicion.

The bald man turned back to the room at large, continuing where he'd left off: "Three have chosen not to come. Two who made the attempt have sadly not survived the journey. And Eleanor has, uhmm, surprised us."

It was the last time he mentioned her by name, and he now continued with what seemed to be a standard patter.

"You're all here because you were smart enough to look for the truth behind the legends," he went on. "You will have been expecting Level One posts, and you had the sense to turn down assignments which were so obviously beneath you. Your reward is Level Zero training."

There were gasps and murmurs; no-one had ever heard of Level Zero. Any interest the boys might have had in Eleanor's fate was wiped from their minds, at least for now.

"There will be time for questions later," the man said. "You will all have heard, of course, some tales of mythical assassins. All of you will have encountered different stories, but it's time for a grain of truth. The Association does not only – or mainly – deal in assassination."

Eleanor was sure she saw a look of disappointment flash across Jorge's face, although he quickly hid it.

The man continued, "Wherever a job needs doing in secrecy and in silence, the Association is called upon. We do some work for the Imperial Throne, but we are not ruled directly by the Empress or her Parliament; we have our own council and follow our own laws, which you will learn."

"What, so we're rebels?" asked one of the youths.

"Not rebels, no," Andreas said. "Just not entirely a part of the

Imperial Service. You'll understand in time. For the next two years you will live in the academy. Your training will be a mixture of classroom instruction, supervised practice, and competitive test missions. You will train in order to acquire the necessary skills for your job, and you will compete for a seat on the council. Only one of you will be awarded that honour."

Eleanor looked around the room, wondering whether the others felt the same mixture of excitement and relief and nerves. Finally, after the previous year's ordeals, she really felt she'd arrived. Finally she was being given a glimpse into this strange new world.

"My name is Andreas," the bald man said. "I graduated this summer. I am here to answer your questions, so far as I'm permitted."

He made a small bow and looked around for questions.

"When do we start?" asked a small, sinewy lad. His voice was pitched high with thinly-disguised excitement, and he had a broad, slightly cheeky grin.

"Soon enough," Andreas replied with a faint smile. "Though I think we'll have lunch first."

They all laughed nervously; it felt dangerous not to laugh at the joke of a trained killer. Eleanor suspected it wouldn't take long for them to lose that sense of unease. Already she felt a certainty that the staff of the academy wouldn't harm them deliberately, even her, even if she hadn't been expected. Accidents could happen, of course, in practical training. That was inevitable. But this small band of students was clearly too valuable a commodity to waste indiscriminately.

"We will get a schedule soon?" Daniel asked.

"Tomorrow, yes. Your classes will start in two days time."

"And when do we get our new weapons?" asked the skinny, sneering youth.

"You'll meet with our weaponsmiths tomorrow, and the tailor will be available to take your measurements for clothing," Andreas said. He looked around expectantly. "Anything else?"

"Shouldn't we all introduce ourselves?" Eleanor suggested. Though she was sure Andreas already had them all identified, she wanted for herself to know who the others were. "I'm

Eleanor, but then you all knew that. I've come from Mersioc Regional School, near Port Just."

Daniel nodded slowly. "Daniel," he said. "Of Hessekolenisshe."

Eleanor repeated the word silently to herself, trying to drum the strange sounds into her head: hess-heck-oh-lay-nee-shay. She still wasn't sure she'd remember it.

"Mikhail," said the sinewy boy. "From Almont City 7."

"Charles, Dashfort City 3."

"Jorge. Venncastle."

"Sebastien, from the Forest School near Bastion."

"Mack, also from the Forest."

"Paul, Almont City 18."

"Frederick, Venncastle." That was the skinny one who'd mocked Daniel's accent.

"Good," Andreas nodded. "And now, lunch. Then I'll show you to your rooms. Leave your belongings here for now."

Eleanor fell into step with Daniel as they followed the others from the room. "So... what's it like being at school on a boat?" she asked.

"I have known no other kind," he said, and she blushed a little; of course he had nothing to compare it to. Even if the school prided itself on its most unusual feature, it was merely normal for the students.

"I learnt to sail on a fishing boat last year," she said, trying to recover the conversation as they walked along the broad, wood-panelled corridor. Framed portraits of young men posing with a variety of weapons were hung at irregular intervals along the walls. "But it was only a small boat. And then I sailed with a Magrad ship for a couple of months."

"It was strange to come to the land," Daniel said. "It still is hard to sleep."

They were saved from further conversation by their arrival at the dining hall. A heavy oak table ran down the middle of the room, surrounded by about thirty chairs – only two of which were occupied. Andreas stopped abruptly and indicated the two young men who were already seated: "Our second year students."

"Jorge!" one of the second years called out, raising a hand in greeting.

Jorge nodded to them. "Jon; Victor."

"Come, sit!" the other youth – Victor – said. "And you, Freddie. Food here's even better than school."

"So they are both Venncastle also," Daniel muttered under his breath, as Jorge and Frederick crossed the room to join the older boys. The rest of the group followed slowly, and Eleanor found herself sitting between Daniel and Sebastien.

"Only two of them left," Sebastien said, glancing nervously towards the second years. "That's a lot of accidents, if their group started out the same size as ours."

Eleanor shook her head. "I don't think so. Some strange things happened last year... the Tarasanka killed a lot of us before the year even started..." Her voice trailed off as her thoughts came back to Raf, and she blinked back tears.

"What do you know about that?" Victor asked, looking intently at her from beneath a fringe of thick black hair. She was caught by surprise that he'd been listening to her, when he'd appeared to be engaged with his old schoolfriends.

"I was in Taraska last autumn," she said quietly, uncomfortably aware that she'd become the centre of attention again. Her fingers played on the broken ridge of her nose, and she almost gasped with remembered pain. "I know they set a trap at the code tower, and we... I mean, me and Raf... I mean..."

She bit her lip and screwed her eyes closed, determined not to let herself cry – not while everyone was watching. Taking a deep breath, she addressed herself directly to Victor.

"You must have known Raf," she said. "You will have been in the same year at Venncastle."

He nodded his confirmation but said nothing, though his intense brown eyes asked a thousand questions.

"Well, the two of us had to keep the Tarasanka security service busy last year," Eleanor said, almost relieved to have the chance to talk about it at last, to people who knew Raf even though they didn't know her. "Past the equinox, to stop them coming here. They were torturing people for the clues. Killing them."

Subconsciously, her hand went to the unusual belt she'd fastened around her waist. She wondered when would be the best time to show it.

"Raf's dead, then?" asked Jon.

Eleanor looked away. "I don't know," she murmured. Suddenly she was very aware of the decision she'd made in leaving him. Had she condemned him? What would they think of her, these boys who had been his classmates? But he'd been so insistent, and it had made sense at the time. "We escaped, but he was injured, too weak to travel. Last time I saw him was in Taraska La'on, nearly a year ago."

"And he's not here," Victor said.

"No." Eleanor felt herself on the verge of tears again. *Why isn't he here?* It seemed reasonable to assume that he was dead. "How did you avoid the trap?" she asked, hoping she could change the subject for long enough to recover her composure.

"The school are very good," Jon said.

Daniel muttered something under his breath but Eleanor ignored him, more interested in finding out what had happened.

"Someone kept his ear to the ground. We were still at school when the first reports came in, and they encouraged us to go to the maze and the puzzle chamber first, while they cleared it up."

"They must have been too late for Raf, though," Victor added. "I never understood why he was in such a rush."

It all made sense, though Eleanor still found it incredible that all but two of the previous year's students had fallen into the trap before it had been discovered. It was some coincidence that they were both Venncastle students, though of course Venncastle was very close to the code tower. She continued with her lunch in silence and a hush had fallen over the rest of the students, too, so that for a while the only sounds were made by their cutlery scraping on the plates.

Once she'd eaten her fill, Eleanor reached under her shirt to untie the belt she'd been secretly wearing for so long. She couldn't have explained why she'd kept wearing it even after her return to the Empire – it would have been safer to tuck it into a corner of her bag, and safer still to just dispose of it altogether, but she'd promised Raf that she would bring the name-bangles to the Association. She pulled the belt out from under her clothes, and laid it on the table in front of her; the links jangled against one another as she removed the strip of cloth to leave only the chain of interlocked bangles.

"These are the name-bangles of the students who were killed," she began. "We didn't really know what to do with them... Raf thought we should bring them back here." Her voice trailed off as she caught sight of Andreas' face. Her fellow students looked curious, but his stare was cold and accusatory.

He stood up, walked around the table and reached over her shoulder for the bangles. "I cannot deal with this myself," he said, the chain clinking loudly as he snatched it up. "You must account for yourself to the council."

Eleanor swallowed, her throat feeling suddenly very dry. She asked herself again why she hadn't simply dropped them into the sea; it would've been so much easier.

"Victor," Andreas continued. "Please run ahead and warn the council that their attention will be needed again. This must be dealt with at once. Jon, please show the others to their rooms."

Jon nodded his agreement; Victor had already left. Andreas steered Eleanor from the room and they walked in silence through the empty corridors, until Andreas stopped her outside a heavily-riveted door. A moment later, Victor emerged from the room.

"All assembled," he said, then turned to give Eleanor a reassuring smile before sprinting away.

She followed Andreas into the council chamber, to be faced with a room full of men sitting around a large, heavy table. Eleanor guessed that their ages ranged between twenty and seventy years; all looked displeased. Andreas moved around the room and whispered in the ear of a thin, silver-haired man, leaving Eleanor alone by the door.

Her eyes quickly came to focus on the one familiar face amongst all the strangers: Laban. In spite of everything, she breathed a sigh of relief. If he was here then she knew she was in the right place, whatever anyone might say. She tried to catch his eye, but he was about the only person not looking at her.

"So, you are the girl," murmured the man Andreas had approached. His figure was spidery and fragile-looking, and he was the oldest in the room by quite some margin. "I must say, you've caused us some troubles already. What is it this time?"

"The girl," Andreas said, "has somehow acquired these." He flung the bangles into the centre of the table and stepped back.

The old man looked straight up at Eleanor, his blue eyes fixed her with a piercing stare. "What is the meaning of this?"

"They're the name-bangles of the people who would've been last year's students, if they hadn't been killed in Taraska," Eleanor replied.

"She was wearing them as a belt," Andreas said. "It's horrific! How can anyone so casually make jewellery out of the identities of his – sorry, *her* – colleagues?"

"Baht ravh!" Eleanor said hotly, unable to restrain herself. The words were out of her mouth before she realised she'd sworn in Magrad; she'd learnt curses from the pirates though she'd no idea what the actual words meant. "There was nothing casual about it! And nothing to do with jewellery. We went to a lot of trouble to–"

She was interrupted by a loud thump on the table: Laban had slammed his fist into the wood. "Silence!" he barked. It was the first time Eleanor had heard him speak in almost three years and she hadn't imagined that his first words to her, after so long a time, would have such a fierce tone. "You will speak only when you're spoken to."

She was about to open her mouth in protest, but he shot her a warning look so clear and so urgent that she silenced her appeal before she began. She wondered how things had become so serious so quickly, but Laban looked scared, and that was something she'd never seen before.

"Andreas, you will also remain silent until we ask you to speak. If you can keep your voice level, girl," Laban continued, "you may tell us how you come to have these bangles in your possession."

Eleanor took a deep breath, and tried to keep all of her raging emotions from her voice when she spoke. "I was in Taraska last year," she said, thinking it best to start at the beginning. "I was captured – it's a long story – and imprisoned along with a Venncastle student called Raf."

A few of the men exchanged glances, but none of them spoke so Eleanor continued her story.

"After we'd escaped we went back to get our bangles, and we found all these other ones at the same time. The others were dead. Raf said we should bring the bangles back here, so, here they are."

"Where is he?" asked a young, dark-haired man. He looked hardly older than Raf, and very like him.

"I don't know." She turned her eyes to the floor, overwhelmed again by feelings of guilt. "He was too weak to sail, so I came back to the Empire without him."

"And how did you get back?" the old man asked.

"What does that have to do with–"

He tapped his fingers impatiently on the table. "Just answer the question, girl."

"I sailed on a Magrad ship to the edge of Imperial waters, and then a smuggler's boat into Dashfort."

"The pirates aren't famed for their charity. How did you persuade them to carry you?"

Eleanor didn't like the tone that the questions were taking, or the way that they were straying further and further from the original subject, but she didn't dare to make a challenge. The look in Laban's eyes had made her sure of that; she'd never seen him scared before, and the sight had shaken her. She raised her eyes to meet the old man's gaze as steadily as she could. "I worked for my passage," she said.

"So it was just luck that you were the only survivor?" The old man had menace in his voice now. "It was pure blind luck that you – the one person we weren't expecting – managed to survive, and escape from a Tarasanka jail, and somehow buy yourself safe passage across the sea?"

Eleanor looked to Laban for support, but he gave her only a near-imperceptible shake of his head. She was on her own. She could feel her heart beating furiously in her chest; she understood what the old man was accusing her of, but she could see no easy way out.

"What exactly are you suggesting?" she asked, realising that Laban had at least given her one clue – she had to keep her voice calm and level; she couldn't afford to give anything away. And she could answer their charges more easily if she could force them to move from unpleasant implications to direct accusations.

The old man tapped at the table again. "You're asking us to believe in a lot of coincidences," he said. "There are versions of the story which seem more likely. At best, you were a captive who happened to meet some of our aspirant students, and happened to find out from them enough information to complete our tests when you returned. At worst, you were put in there by the Tarasanka lords for that very purpose, and your job here and now is to report back to them."

Eleanor held herself as still as she could manage, forcing herself not to react to the allegations – but she found herself mentally readying for a fight, assessing the shape and structure of the room while reminding herself where she'd stowed her various weapons beneath her clothes. She'd only once bested Laban in a fair fight while he'd been training her, so she knew she stood no chance against this many fully-trained men, but if they were going to condemn her out of hand then she'd take down as many as she could before they got to her.

"What do you have to say for yourself?" the old man prompted when she failed to respond.

"Does it matter what I say?" she asked. "If I were some kind of spy, do you think I'd admit it just because you asked me?"

"We'd like to hear your story in your own words."

"Very well." She took a deep breath, then launched into rapid speech: "I was born in the Charanthe Empire some eighteen years ago and grew up at Mersioc Regional School for Girls, near Port Just. I received my assignment last summer, when I was given a post well beneath my abilities, which I rejected with the aim of seeking out this place like so many before me. I completed the puzzle chamber in Dashfort, but I ended up sailing to Taraska La'on with a smuggling vessel, and some of the crew decided I was more valuable to them as a trinket to sell to the Tarasanka authorities. I was imprisoned and tortured for weeks, along with Raf, and once we were sure we'd kept them busy beyond the equinox we eventually managed to escape. We went back in to get our bangles, and also collected those of the dead boys. Raf was badly injured, and I came back here." She paused, and looked defiantly around the room. "That's my life story in short form. I'm no Tarasanka spy."

"These facts can be checked," Laban said, still avoiding looking at her. As if he had any reason to disbelieve her story!

"Then check them," she said fiercely. "I've nothing to hide. Besides, the Tarasanka lords may be brutal but they're not stupid – certainly not stupid enough to send a spy who stands out as much as I do."

The old man studied her carefully. "And you claim you made your way through the puzzle chamber at Dashfort on your own, before you met the others?" he asked.

"Yes."

"So you won't mind telling us what the number was last year."

"Forty-seven," she said without hesitation, thankful that she was blessed with a good memory.

He nodded. "We'll need time to consider this matter," he said. "Andreas, take the girl back to her room for now – she's no threat."

Andreas led Eleanor in silence back through the corridors, and to the sleeping quarters.

There were two common rooms set aside for the new students, each having five small bedrooms arrayed around it. Jorge, Frederick, Paul, Mack, and Charles had occupied the first set, and the second was for Daniel, Sebastien, Mikhail, and Eleanor, with one spare room. Andreas had his own small suite of rooms at the end of the corridor where the students could find him if they needed him – "If you stay," he added pointedly – and there was also a communal washing area. A chalk board in the corridor set out details of the timetable to which their lives would run, arranged around an eight-day cycle.

Eleanor had one of the corner bedrooms, with a narrow window overlooking the gardens. The room had a bed along one wall and a small desk and chair crammed in alongside. She tucked her bag inside the wooden chest at the foot of the bed, ignoring the closet.

She went to sit in the common room, and Sebastien came to join her a moment later – she wondered how long the others would take.

"You didn't unpack," he said. It wasn't a question. "Why not?"

"I don't have much." She didn't add that she also wanted to be able to move quickly if the council decided against her.

"Well, you can order more clothes tomorrow."

She nodded. It would be nice to have something new; the outfit she'd bought in Taraska was getting worn out but she'd been borrowing Gisele's dresses since she'd reached Almont, too preoccupied to think about replacing her own. But would the tailor really make new things for her if she was in danger of being thrown out?

They fell into an awkward silence, two people with no idea what they might have in common. Eleanor began to wish she'd stayed in her room, but it would've seemed rude to leave again so soon after sitting down.

After an uncomfortably long moment, Sebastien pulled a thin silver pipe from his pocket and began to pick out an old folk melody. Relieved of the need to make conversation, Eleanor took a moment to study the room. Aside from the five chairs, there was a small stove with a kettle hanging over it, and a low table which had a bowl of fruit and a small vase of flowers, a strange touch of frivolity in this otherwise-functional environment. A target board hung on one wall, just far enough from any of the bedroom doors to be a safe practice area, so she took out a knife and made her aim. For all that he appeared to be absorbed in his music, she was sure Sebastien would be assessing her performance, so she took extra care to look casual about it.

"Nice blade," he said as she tossed it towards the target. "That's no school knife."

"No," she agreed. "I picked it up in Taraska." She walked across to measure just how far from the centre it had stuck. The shot had been good; not perfect, but good. The point had missed the bullseye by only a finger's breadth.

Mikhail was the next to emerge from his room, and he flopped carelessly into the chair next to Sebastien. "You've had an interesting year, then, Ellie," he said with a grin.

Later she would blame the rawness of her emotions so soon after finding that Raf hadn't made it to the academy; hearing the diminutive of her name, that only he had ever called her in earnest, triggered something in Eleanor that was beyond her control.

"DON'T EVER CALL ME ELLIE!" she yelled, pulling her knife from the target board and turning the blade towards Mikhail.

He and Sebastien just stared back at her, speechless in their shock.

Daniel's door swung open. "What is happening?" he asked calmly, continuing to fold the shirt he was holding.

Eleanor looked up at him, then back at Mikhail and Sebastien. "Sorry," she said, blushing as she slipped the knife away. "I overreacted. But please don't call me that."

"You are lucky," Daniel said. "If you overreact like that near the Venncastle boys, I would be surprised if you live."

"Why?"

He'd already turned back to his trunk, so Eleanor moved across to the doorway of his room and repeated her question.

"Why do you say that?"

"Venncastle is not like your school, or mine." He picked up a pair of trousers and shook them out before folding them again and placing them on a shelf in his closet. "They think themselves very special. They think the laws of the Empire were not made for them. All very arrogant."

"You saw how they took to you," Mikhail added. "Not sure how long you'd've lasted without everyone else around."

Eleanor didn't know what to say. She wanted to tell them that Raf hadn't been like that, that Raf had been friendly and loyal and strong – but there seemed little point in making herself a target for their animosity when Raf wasn't even here to benefit from her defence. Instead, she just said, "I don't know who would've come off worse if they'd made me fight."

"Two against one?" Mikhail checked. "I know which way I'd bet. Besides, you're tiny!"

"You're not so big yourself," Eleanor said. "And they're fresh out of school. Venncastle may be odd, but they can't have had much experience of real, life-or-death fighting."

"And you?" There was a note of incredulity in Sebastien's voice that she didn't much care for.

A stream of memories flooded through her mind, but she really didn't want to have to explain. They'd probably already decided she was slightly mad. Would they really want to share their living space with someone who'd already killed? They'd all have to lose that kind of sensitivity if they were going to make any progress. "I've got a year on them," she said. "And you."

She caught the glance which passed between Sebastien and Mikhail but decided to let it pass; she didn't want to alienate them any further. Besides, they were right that the boys from Venncastle had been ready to fight her just for turning up – at least Daniel had taken a stand to protect her, whether or not she'd needed it. That made him the closest thing she had to a friend right now.

Feeling more lonely than at any time since she'd left Raf in Taraska, she turned without another word and shut herself back in her bedroom. It was easier to be alone. She heard the conversation in the common room resume as soon as she clicked the door shut, and wondered what the boys were saying about her now she was out of earshot. The pendant Raf had chosen for her felt heavy around her neck, reminding her of the time they'd spent together. With tears welling up in her eyes, she sank down on the bed and wished herself back in Taraska. *I should have stayed.* She brushed the first teardrops from her cheeks, but there was no stemming the flow. *He must be dead. I shouldn't have left him.*

She clung desperately to her pillow, trying to stifle her sobs; she didn't want to be overheard. She didn't want to have to explain.

She'd hated so much about Taraska, hated their slavery and

their taxes, hated the way that absolutely everything in the country had been for sale, and yet in a way the days she'd spent there with Raf after their escape – planning their next steps and wandering invisibly in their counterfeit robes, sparring together and learning from one another – had been the happiest she'd felt all year. She hadn't realised just how much she'd been counting on seeing him again.

And now even Laban was pretending not to know her.

She lay on the bed, staring at the ceiling beams and drifting between dreams and memories, until a quiet knock at the door finally disturbed her reverie.

"It is time for dinner," Daniel said, pushing the door open a fraction. "If you would like any."

Eleanor got unsteadily to her feet and followed the others back to the dining hall without a word. Again the Venncastle alumni sat together, and Eleanor found herself sat next to Mikhail on the end of the row; they ate in uncomfortable silence, and she was relieved once she'd finished and could return to the solitude of her room.

Chapter 17

Eleanor woke the next morning to the sound of birdsong, and a quick glance through the window told her that it was barely dawn. She dressed quickly and hid her pendant under the mattress – there would be few chances to wear jewellery here – before heading down to the dining hall to see about breakfast.

She'd hoped she'd be the earliest riser, as she'd always been at school, but to her annoyance she found Daniel at the breakfast table, munching at a sandwich while apparently absorbed in a book which lay open beside his plate.

"Morning," she said quietly as she took a seat opposite him, and helped herself to a roll from the platter in the middle of the table. The bread was still warm, and filled generously with crisp slices of bacon and gooey melted cheese.

Daniel glanced up at her, then turned the page of his book and continued reading without a word. She was a little irritated by his rudeness, though they hadn't had the best start.

"I'm sorry I was jumpy yesterday," she began. "I'm still adjusting to everything."

He closed the book with a heavy thud; the cover said it was *Finer Details of Apothecary*.

"I was not ignoring you," he said. "I was studying."

She blushed a little. "I just wanted to explain."

"It is new for all of us."

She tried again to pin down the details of his accent as he spoke; it was nothing like any of the voices she'd heard in Taraska or among the Magra, let alone in the Empire, and he appeared unable to use normal speech contractions.

"But we will learn – of each other, and this place, and our needed skills. You must be patient."

"Sorry for interrupting you," Eleanor apologised again, indicating the book. "I don't mind you reading."

He took another mouthful of his breakfast and flipped the book open again in silence, staring intently at the page.

Eleanor wondered how – or indeed whether – he'd managed to find the right place on his first attempt. Maybe looking at a random page was still preferable to talking to her. She didn't really care; she hadn't wanted to see anyone either. For a moment she'd been willing to tell him a little about Raf and her experiences over the last year, hoping to give some explanation for her behaviour, but that moment had passed. She got up and left the room quietly so as not to disturb him further, taking her roll with her to eat as she walked.

She was just chewing on her last crust when she reached the common room again, and was relieved to see no sign that Sebastien or Mikhail had stirred.

She let herself back into her room and went to look out of the window. It was a perfectly still, overcast day; perfect for a little outdoor practice. She pulled out the knife Laban had given her, which was still her favourite despite the way her Tarasanka interrogator had sliced open her face with it. As she turned it over in her fingers, she wondered why Laban had failed to stand up for her in the council yesterday. There was something frightening about the way he'd pretended not to know her, and she'd never seen fear in his eyes before; she wished she could ask him about it, but she wasn't going to try and find him before she knew her way around.

She wanted to get outside, to get moving and shake the worries from her mind, but uncertainty kept her in her room so she satisfied herself with doing headstands beside the bed.

She was disturbed a little later by a knock at the door, and went down with the other students to be fitted for their new clothes. The measurements were being taken in a small room near the dining hall, and they formed a disorderly queue outside.

The tailor was visibly taken aback when Eleanor presented herself but he quickly recovered his composure.

"I'll make you all the usual work clothes," he said as he passed the tape around her waist. "And I'll pass your measurements across to the tannery for your leathers. But what would you like for finery?"

Now it was Eleanor's turn to be surprised. "What will I

need?" She'd left all her best clothes at school for a reason: she'd assumed she wouldn't have any use for them. It had proved true enough over the last year. She thought back to some of her favourite dresses which she'd left in her trunk and wondered whether this tailor – accustomed to dressing only the men of the Association – would make such beautiful clothes as the school's seamstresses. If not, she supposed she could always go back for them; she wouldn't be seen if she snuck through the forest.

"I can make you a selection," the tailor offered. "What are your favourite colours?"

"I like black," she said, then fearing that would be rather boring, added, "Or green. Whatever you think would suit me."

He nodded. "I'll see what I can do for you. Next!"

Eleanor left the room and found Daniel and Sebastien waiting in the corridor.

"Coming to the smithy?" Sebastien asked. "Or have you got enough fancy knives already?"

"I'll come," she said, not sure if she minded the tease in his voice. But certainly she'd never turn down the chance of a shiny new blade to add to her growing collection. "Do you know where it is?"

"Just across the courtyard, I think. It can't be hard to find."

"We are just waiting for Mikhail," Daniel said, and the three fell into an uneasy silence. They were relieved when Mikhail emerged a moment later, and they headed down to the courtyard together.

Even with its double doors thrown wide open to the air, the furnaces made the smithy uncomfortably hot. They were met by a short, bare-chested man with wiry grey hair who introduced himself as Harold; his blond-haired colleague was hammering away at the back of the workshop. Neither of them could have been younger than fifty, and Eleanor wondered if this was a retirement job for members of the Association who survived to enjoy any kind of retirement.

"So, what can I do for you?" Harold asked. "Do you know what you need?"

Mikhail grinned broadly. "Everything!"

218

Eleanor suspected she was the only one who already had truly professional weapons, and even she couldn't wait to get her hands on new ones which were to be wrought especially for her.

Harold smiled at Mikhail's obvious enthusiasm. "Show me what you've got."

Mikhail pulled out his school-issue practice weapons, which amounted to a couple of buckled throwing knives and a standard dagger.

"I'll take those for melting down if you like," Harold said. "You won't be needing them. Now, unless you've any special requests, I'll start you off with a pair of daggers – straight and curved – a basic thrower, and a hunting knife. Here, let me measure your hand."

He had a notched measuring stick, and directed Mikhail to grip it in his fist as he would hold a dagger hilt while Harold scribbled numbers on a chalk board.

"Now, your feet." He placed a board on the floor, and motioned for Mikhail to step onto it.

Mikhail watched in fascination as he made chalk marks around the edges of both boots. "Why're you measuring my feet?"

"You'll need spikes for your shoes." He stood up once he'd finished drawing the outlines and, satisfied, turned from Mikhail to the others. "Are you all in the same boat? Any more of those crappy school knives for me to recycle?"

Sebastien shot a pointed look at Eleanor as he and Daniel laid their school knives on the workbench.

"I don't have anything to melt down," she said quietly.

Harold looked straight at her, and though she took that moment to examine his face closely she saw no distaste or even surprise in his expression. For once, someone wasn't treating her like an alien. "Did you leave them in your room?" he asked. "You can bring them down later."

She shook her head. "I don't have any school knives. Only these ones." From their sheaths at her hips she brought forward the two matched throwing knives she'd bought in Taraska, then the stiletto blade and the short, straight-bladed dagger which completed the set. For reasons she couldn't quite explain, she kept Laban's knife safely in its wrist sheath; something in his expression yesterday had spooked her. If he was too scared to acknowledge her then she didn't want to risk exposing their association.

Harold raised an eyebrow. "Impressive." He picked up one of the throwing knives and turned it in his hand. "Where did you pick up this little lot?"

"I bought them from a market stall in Taraska," she said. Then, because she thought he might appreciate it, added, "It was all I could do to stop myself buying a longsword."

He cocked his head and considered her seriously for a moment. "You'd never be efficient with a full size longsword at your height, even if you could lift it," he said. "But if you ever need a weapon like that, we can easily scale one for you. Anyway, you're generally well equipped – do you have spikes?"

"No spikes."

"Well, then. We'll make you some spikes, and a curved blade, and a little hunting knife to complement your set. If you leave one of yours here, we can match them up."

"Oh, thank you." She picked up her dagger, stiletto, and one of the throwing knives, leaving the other on the bench. "And I was wondering, if it's not too cheeky – I'd quite like a double-ended throwing spike to play with."

"Really?" He looked genuinely shocked.

"You did ask about special requests." She looked at him with wide eyes and gave her sweetest smile; perhaps being a woman had some advantages after all.

"Well, yes, but you've already mastered a far more subtle method." He lifted her throwing knife and held it so the sapphires sparkled in the light of the furnaces. "Why would you want a weapon so lacking in artistry?"

She thought back to some of the year's tougher fights – particularly aboard the *Canny Rose*, where the boat's pitching had defeated her aim. "Sometimes, there isn't that much time for artistry."

His face betrayed his curiosity, but he nodded. "Alright, then.

Now, let's get a measure of you."

She stepped onto the board so that he could draw her feet – the outline fitted completely within that of Mikhail's boots – and then he handed her the measuring rod. She was alarmed to find that, holding it naturally, her fingers didn't reach the first notch – but Harold just smiled, made a couple of new notches, and noted the position of her fingers against them.

He turned next to measuring Daniel and Sebastien's hands and feet, and was just finishing his notes as Jorge, Fred and Charles arrived at the door.

"We should go," Daniel said. "We have been here quite long enough."

"Thanks again," Eleanor said as they left.

"It must be time for lunch," Daniel continued once they were outside. "If we are quick, we could miss the Venncastle set completely."

"You'll have to get used to them," Sebastien said. "They're not going anywhere."

"I do not have to like them." Daniel slammed open the door to the school's accommodation building, and stomped his way up the stairs. Sebastien, Eleanor and Mikhail followed in amused silence, secretly wondering if there was any real reason for his venom.

After they'd enjoyed a substantial lunch, Sebastien suggested they could spend the rest of the afternoon doing a little sparring practice.

Mikhail looked out of the window. "It's raining – we could use the hall for a bit."

"There is more space outside," Daniel said. "A little rain does not hurt."

Eleanor's eyes narrowed. "Are you still just trying to avoid Fred and Jorge? I don't see what you've got against them."

"No, you would not."

He turned and strode out into the rain, leaving Eleanor, Sebastien and Mikhail to exchange exasperated glances and then, because there was no way he could do effective combat practice on his own, to follow after him.

They'd hardly begun when Eleanor was summoned; the

messenger was a young man who, it turned out, was another of Venncastle's ex-students who'd graduated from the academy the year before. They chatted aimlessly as they walked through the corridors; Eleanor thought it might be rude to express her surprise at the number of Venncastle's students who seemed to find the academy, but she couldn't help wondering how they managed to be inherently better than other schools at producing this particular type of student. The idea went against every principle of the Imperial schooling system – but maybe it was simply, as Jorge had noted, that they weren't afraid to guide their boys in the right direction. The young man steered Eleanor through a couple of different corridors, knocked sharply on a smart oak door, and then left her alone to wait.

"Come!" a voice barked from inside.

She pushed the door cautiously and took two light steps into the room. It was a large, empty-feeling room with high vaulted ceilings and its stone walls lined with tapestries. One long sofa and a low table was all the furniture there was, though a couple of target boards and a practice dummy in one corner, and a trapeze and ropes attached to the ceiling beams, suggested that the room's expanse of space was sometimes used for more interesting things. She clicked the door closed behind her.

A moment later, Laban emerged from a connecting door. "Welcome to my humble home," he said with a gentle smile.

"So this is where you live, is it, when you're not camping in a cave in the provinces?" After the way he'd ignored her yesterday, she needed to force him to acknowledge their shared history however she could.

"Something like that. Come, sit down. I've made tea."

She perched at one end of the sofa, and he handed her a mug of steaming tea. The familiar scent of the ironwort brew reminded her of home; she reached for the pot of honey to add a little sweetness, knowing the drink would comfort her just as it always had as a child.

"Are you going to tell me what all this is about?" she asked as she swirled honey into her tea.

"Well, officially I've been checking out your story, which of course is all in order." He gave a conspiratorial wink as he sat alongside her. "Really, I've been wondering how in all the Empire you ended up getting so lost."

"But none of it makes any sense!" As soon as she let herself start, the whole of her confusion flooded out in one breathless tirade. "First they say no-one was expecting me, then I get hauled up before the council just for having those bangles – and then I know I'm in the right place because you're there, but something stops you telling them it's okay, and you just act like you don't even know me! What's going on?!"

"Ahhh." He took a slow mouthful of his tea. "The thing is, you're female."

"I don't understand."

"There's long been some, ahh, disagreement" – he enunciated the word carefully – "in the council about whether we should start to admit women. Some of us believe the current stance is outdated and frankly silly, but there are others who feel just as strongly that a woman could never do this. I'm afraid it's your job to prove the abilities of your sex, but it would never work if they thought you had help."

"You tricked me!" She could feel indignant fury rising in her chest. She'd been ready to forgive yesterday's betrayal only because of the fear she'd seen in his eyes, but if he was playing games – with her, with everyone – then she wasn't about to let it go.

"I did nothing of the sort. I trained you, that's all. You had to make your own decision, as do all our students."

She glared at him. "You knew what I'd do – what you wanted me to do. And you must've known exactly how they'd take it. And what about the other girl? Was she another experiment? Have there been others? Are you just playing with our lives until someone succeeds?"

"To the best of my knowledge, that young lady made the attempt without encouragement. She was unlucky that some of the young men who came up the same year were rather, umm, over-enthusiastic."

"How did you know that wouldn't happen to me?"

"You could have handled it. Everything was under control – but I couldn't have predicted yesterday's little bangle incident.

How did that happen, Eleanor?"

She sipped at her rapidly-cooling tea. His chiding tone made her feel thirteen again, even though he was the one in the wrong this time. "Do I really have to tell the whole story again?"

"You told far from the whole story yesterday. If you didn't fall into the code tower trap along with the rest of our postulants, how did you end up in Taraska La'on?"

She gave a quick account of how she'd caught a chill walking from Port Just to Arche, and how the couple who'd taken her in and tended her fever had offered her the chance to join their smuggling operation in exchange for their continued protection. She skipped over the details of their trip, except to mention the call at Dashfort, and went on to explain how a couple of the crew had spotted a quick profit to be made by selling her to the Tarasanka authorities.

"What did they want with you?"

"Oh, that's where it gets complicated. The harbour master in Port Just – you knew him, right?"

"Myran? I know him, more's the pity."

"He caught me picking pockets in the Port. Just enough so I could eat!" she added hurriedly when she saw the hard look in his eye. "Anyway, I panicked and pulled a knife on him, and somehow he recognised it as your knife. I ran for it, and he put about rumours that there was a red-haired assassin girl in the area."

"Curse that meddler," Laban muttered. "He never could stand being bettered."

"So I gathered," she said, but she neglected to mention her later encounter with Myran in Dashfort. It would only complicate matters. "Anyway, an Imperial assassin apparently fetches a good price over there. I was locked up for months."

"Which is how you came to link up with a Venncastle lad and escape with all those bangles?"

She nodded and swallowed the last mouthful of her tea, preferring not to say more than she had to about her time under torture – the memories still haunted her nightmares but she hoped she'd never have to talk about what she'd been through. Again she wished Raf was here to understand how she felt, and again the feelings of guilt washed over her.

"Besides, you don't work for the Empire, and you're not an assassin," Laban said, interrupting her thoughts.

"That's what Andreas said. I didn't really understand it."

"You will."

She looked questioningly at him, hoping he might offer some further explanation but he just poured himself another cup of tea and offered the pot to her. "And why me, anyway?"

He gave a short laugh. "It's all questions, isn't it? You'll have to learn some patience."

She bit back a sharp retort, and just asked, "But everything is okay with the council now?"

"Oh, yes, for now. But they'll be watching you."

She didn't like the ominous tone in his voice, but she didn't know what to say. He'd brought her into this, it was his responsibility and yet if she ever tried to claim his protection she could see now that he'd set it up perfectly to make sure he could deny everything. The only time she could've called him out was before the council yesterday; she'd trusted him at that critical moment and that chance had now gone forever.

"More tea?" he asked casually.

She shook her head and got to her feet.

"Stay for another cup," he insisted. "We've a lot of catching up to do, and I'm still not sure you've told me the whole story of what you've been doing this last year."

"I've told you quite enough," she said shortly. "And you've certainly given me plenty to think about."

"Have patience," he said. "You'll come to understand in time."

She turned on her heel and strode towards the door.

"Drop round any time you feel like a practice session," he called after her, his tone still irritatingly casual.

"Drop round any time you feel like acknowledging me," she muttered crossly to herself as she closed the door behind her.

Chapter 18

Their first class was athletics, taught by a young man called Karl who had them running circuits outside for almost the whole morning. He was constantly shouting at them to go faster, interrupting their sprints only to order them to do a hundred squat-thrusts in the mud or fifty chin-ups on a handy tree branch.

Eleanor caught him watching her a few times, and wondered vaguely whether he was for or against her presence. It was a strange feeling, to think some people opposed her simply for her gender. She'd experienced something similar among the Magra but that was different – everyone knew foreigners did things differently. This was home.

She didn't have time to dwell on it, though, as Karl pushed them harder and harder. By the time the lunch bell rang out to tell them it was time to break off, they were all exhausted but exhilarated, and more than ready for food.

"You've had it easy today," Karl said, briefly delaying them from going inside, "but I think you get the idea. We're going to be training together every four days, and if you don't want to fall behind then you'll need to put in some extra work in your own time."

"What do you think?" Daniel asked as he walked with Eleanor, Sebastien and Mikhail back to their rooms. "Will it be enough to run five miles each day? Or must we do more?"

"Enough?" Mikhail laughed. "That sounds more than enough to me!"

Daniel glanced around to make sure the others were out of earshot before saying, "We cannot let them win."

"You're taking this all a bit seriously," Sebastien said. "We're not really competing."

"Not yet," Daniel agreed. "But we will, and they must not win."

They all needed to wash themselves clean of mud and sweat

before they went to eat, and Eleanor was glad to get a moment alone with her thoughts as she locked herself in her cubicle. She turned on the tap, thankful to be back in a place where they had the staff and the facilities to keep a boiler constantly refuelled and hot water piped around the building. She filled the basin, stripped off her clothes and scrubbed herself clean. The waste water ran to a drain at the edge of the room in a system much like the one her school had employed – except that there, they hadn't had the luxury of separate cubicles. Surrounded by men this time, she was very glad of the extra privacy.

By the time she'd finished washing her hair and fastened it into a damp plait, the others had gone down to lunch without her. She glanced at the timetable on her way out; the afternoon's lesson was mysteriously titled 'Craft'.

"What do you think it means?" she asked Sebastien after she'd settled beside him and helped herself to fish and potatoes from the huge serving dishes in the middle of the table. Mikhail and Daniel had already gone off somewhere, and the others were huddled close together, deep in hushed conversation at the far end of the table.

He shrugged. "Everything that doesn't fit in anywhere else? Anyway, we'll find out soon enough."

"I suppose so." She'd been hoping for a better answer, but of course he was right. "Do you know what's going on with Daniel?"

Sebastien glanced sideways towards the others before saying, "The rivalry between Venncastle and Hess is pretty old. I don't see why everyone else should have to be caught up in it, though."

"No," she agreed. "We're all in this together."

They finished eating and headed to the classroom just in time for the start of the next lesson. There could hardly have been a sharper contrast from the morning's mindless exertion as the teacher – a middle-aged, bearded man called Robert – gave them a quick succession of puzzles to solve and codes to break. Eleanor was starting to feel that the afternoon was a waste of perfectly good practice time. It was all very well doing athletics and puzzles, but she wanted to get on with learning the skills she'd come here for.

At the end of the lesson, however, Robert gave them an overview of his plan for the year which backed up Sebastien's guess: the class would take in a variety of topics. There would be introductory language sessions; classes on disguises and constructing aliases; picking locks and setting traps; tips on negotiation and diplomacy... it sounded like an intriguing combination. Eleanor only wished they hadn't started with number puzzles that she'd struggled to solve; she was painfully conscious that the council could decide to eject her from the academy at any moment, and fearful of leaving a bad impression on any of the teachers.

The next morning was scheduled as hand-to-hand combat, and since it was pouring with rain the students were directed to the practice hall after breakfast.

"Bloody stupid if you ask me," Jorge muttered as they all settled themselves on the mats to wait for their instructor. "What's the use if you can't fight in a bit of rain?"

The man who eventually arrived to teach them was tall and lithe, stringy muscles well toned though he was white-haired and battle-scarred. The students started getting to their feet as he entered, but he waved at them to sit down again.

"Patience," he said. "My name is Bill, I'll be your teacher for this year. We'll get moving soon enough, but before we start I need to make one thing perfectly clear. This is not the military."

He paused to give the students time to think about his words, causing a number of puzzled expressions as everyone waited to find out why he was stating the obvious.

"I suspect some of you were hoping for top-flight military assignments," he continued. "So you need to change the way you think. I'm going to teach you to fight far better than any soldier, but for you, if you end up in a fight then something's already gone wrong."

Eleanor caught herself nodding slightly – it made sense – but some of the others looked more skeptical.

"And you'd better believe I know what I'm talking about," Bill said, looking straight at Jorge, whose expression still reflected mild distaste that they'd been forced to come inside. "I've been doing this job since before you were born. Now, pair up, and come and get a practice knife each."

They got to their feet and formed pairs around the circle; Eleanor ended up with Daniel, and Paul was left as the odd one out. Bill moved across to his bag and they were stunned to watch him unpack a dozen wooden daggers.

"Wooden knives?" Eleanor whispered to Daniel. "At school we had blunted iron blades by the time we were eight, and sharpened ones at fourteen."

Daniel nodded his agreement, but unfortunately Bill had also overheard her comments.

"Do you have a problem, girl? I'm very happy for you to practise with a real dagger, but I guarantee you'll kill yourself within the month." After a brief pause, he added, "I'm yet to be convinced that would be a great loss. Besides, you don't even have your leathers yet."

She was tempted to take up the challenge inherent in his words but Daniel, seeing her muscles tense, cleared his throat quietly and brought her back to her senses. She had to hold her pride in check; it was possible Bill was right, and she didn't want to throw her life away for such a trivial thing.

"You!" Bill signalled Paul to join him at the front of the class. "What's your name?"

"Paul."

"Looks like you're working with me today."

The first couple of strikes that Bill made them practise were very simple techniques, though that didn't stop him criticizing the way everyone else executed the moves. "Sloppy!" seemed to be his favourite word, accompanied by a slap from the flat of his blade on the offending arm; Paul bore the brunt of it as he was called upon to demonstrate every time, giving everyone else at least a chance to avoid repeating his mistakes.

After he was satisfied with the way they were performing basic thrusts and slices on both sides, Bill showed them a quick way to flick the knife from one hand to the other halfway through the attack, a sleight of hand designed to fool the opponent into blocking the wrong arm.

"That's more like it!" Eleanor cried happily as she managed to get her knife past Daniel's guard for the first time of the morning.

"I will learn to block that, too," he said and redoubled his efforts on the defence, although as Eleanor got faster and more fluid at the swap he had more difficulty keeping track of which hand held the knife.

When their roles were reversed, Daniel's height advantage meant that she was constantly having to extend herself to block his thrusts even when he didn't use the switch, making it much harder to find an effective angle for a riposte.

"You're not making full use of your weight," Bill chastised her after one particularly clumsy dodge.

She looked round in surprise. "I'm not heavy."

"No, you're the lightest person in this room – that should make you the most agile, but you're not using it. If you're going to survive the next two years, you need to take advantage of what you've got rather than worrying about the ways you don't match up."

His words stayed with her as she and Daniel continued sparring, but she wasn't sure how to put the theory into practice. In a hand-to-hand context like this, being small didn't feel like an advantage.

After a quick lunch she made her way back to the practice hall, hoping to have some time alone to reinforce the morning's new techniques for her mind and her muscles – but the room wasn't empty when she arrived.

She recognised the young man from the council at once; the one who looked so very much like Raf. She hesitated on the threshold, studying his profile in the light from the high windows as he sat on the floor sharpening a set of simple throwing knives. He looked up and smiled at her and she blushed, embarrassed to have been caught staring.

"You're early," he said. "I was just setting up."

"I'm sorry – I can come back later." It felt like talking to a ghost; the face was so familiar, but this man was a stranger. She had to keep reminding herself that she didn't know him.

"Oh no, don't worry, come in! I'm Ivan."

230

"Eleanor," she said instinctively. "But you knew that."

"Well, we sort of met earlier, right? Come on, you can help." He handed her a stack of small target boards. "I want these around the walls at that end of the room, various heights – just make sure you mix up the order."

She looked down to see what he meant, and found a number painted neatly in the middle of each target.

"New boards," she said, half to herself, as she followed his directions to the far end of the room. Not a single hole punctured the paintwork.

"They're just temps – we'll destroy them all by the end of today's session."

"Really?" She reached up to hang the first board on one of the many nails in the wall. The wood was a little thin, perhaps, but they looked like they should have more than an afternoon's life in them.

"You've got Bill for hand-to-hand, with his wooden toys, haven't you? Let's just say this is going to be a bit different."

Once he'd finished with the knives, Ivan followed her across the hall and adjusted the placement of a couple of boards, lifting them to higher spots that Eleanor couldn't have reached without climbing.

"Do you want to show me what you can do?" he asked as she straightened the last board on its nail.

She turned to see him waiting, an encouraging smile on his face, and found herself thrown again into confusing and painful memories. He was not Raf; Raf was dead.

She pulled out her Tarasanka throwing knife, wishing she'd kept the pair together and chosen a different blade to leave in the smithy. There was a limit to how impressive she could be with one knife, and for some reason it felt important to impress him. Without turning to check her aim, she threw the knife back towards the last board she'd hung; a satisfying thunk told her she'd found her target.

"Very nice. And a beautiful blade – I take it that's one of the ones you brought back from your adventures in the North?" She was about to ask how he knew, but he pre-empted her question: "Word gets around, you know. Especially here. And the rumour is you're not bad with a thrower."

"I've got a pair," she said as she went to retrieve it from the board. "But the other one's with Harold in the smithy. He's making me some new ones to match."

"Interesting." He studied her intently for a moment, then his face relaxed into a smile again. "You're hardly going to need your graduation set at this rate."

"Graduation set?"

He slid a silver knife from his wrist sheath and handed it to her. It was a heavier design than she was used to but had a perfect balance, and the handle was engraved with intricate whorls and set with a number of small amethysts.

"Normally, you'd get a set of depressingly boring knives to use while you're at the academy," he explained. "Then you design yourself a special set for your graduation. Everyone has his own design... and it looks obvious what yours is going to be, even if you've come to it a bit early."

Eleanor held his knife next to hers, comparing the workmanship of the blades more than the aesthetics of the designs.

"Close your eyes," Ivan said suddenly, interrupting her thoughts; the instruction came as such a surprise that she obeyed before she had chance to think about it.

"Why?" she asked, but kept her eyes shut.

He didn't answer, but put his hands on her shoulders and turned her on the spot until she started to feel dizzy. "Now," he said, "keep them closed, and see if you can hit three and seven for me."

She felt a slight panic constrict her chest. What kind of test was this? She was disoriented and dizzy, with a pair of unmatched knives, and she hadn't been paying much attention to the numbers as she'd placed the boards.

He hadn't changed his position, though. As he'd spun her she hadn't felt him move, hadn't heard a single footstep to suggest he'd stepped away. From his voice, he was now behind her left shoulder; it wasn't much, but it was an anchor she could work from. Though it felt a painfully slow process, she began to slot things in to place in her mind: she'd been facing him... and facing the number nine over his shoulder, she could recall that much, while behind her the board she'd pierced with her first throw was number two. With increasing confidence she began to map out the sequence in her mind, thinking how she'd hung each board in turn as she'd moved around the room. Suddenly, she lunged to her left and flicked both knives into parallel flight through the air; only once she'd heard them both land did she dare to look.

Her own knife was wedged firmly near the centre of the seven; Ivan's heavier blade wobbled precariously, just hooked into the outer ring of board three. He stepped across to claim it back before it fell.

She watched him nervously, wondering whether her performance had been above or below his expectation. It had been a poor shot, by her normal standards, but he'd caught her off-guard and the circumstances had been difficult.

"You didn't cheat," he said as he handed her knife back to her.

It wasn't a question but she nodded anyway, her throat dry, not sure she was off the hook. Would there be more tests?

"You easily could've," he went on. "You knew I couldn't see your eyes. If you'd given me a perfect shot, how could I ever have proved it wasn't genuine?"

"It would still have been cheating."

"So? Out there..." – he gestured towards the window – "if you see an opportunity, you take it."

"Yes, of course." Several moments came to mind when she'd done just that. "But that's different – that's real. We should be able to trust each other here."

He said nothing, just turned from her and sent his knife sailing in an exaggerated arc towards a nearby board.

"Was that the real test, then?" she asked. "Not whether I could do it, but whether I'd cheat?"

"You did do it, and you didn't cheat," he said, still with his back to her. "Those facts are both interesting to me."

Her heart was still hammering, unsure whether she'd performed to his satisfaction. "Is that what you're going to report back?"

"Report?" He turned sharply to face her. "Who said anything about reporting anything?"

"Well, I just assumed, the council..."

He shook his head. "You'll waste a lot of time if you assume every teacher who's also on the council is somehow spying on you. Plenty of us teach from time to time, but we're busy enough without monitoring you especially. No, you'll sink or swim on your own merits now."

She would have pressed him further but just then the door swung open and they both turned to see Fred and Jorge come in.

"Hey Ivan! Jon said you were teaching this year." Fred waved across the hall, then caught sight of Eleanor. "Are we interrupting something?"

"Not at all." Ivan beckoned them further into the room. "We were just warming up. You can start with some stretches while we wait for the others to get here."

One by one the remaining students trickled into the hall and joined the warm-up.

"Do you have your knives yet?" Ivan asked once they were all assembled. Aside from Eleanor, they all shook their heads; he caught her eye and smiled. "Never mind, we've plenty of spares. Form a line against that wall – come on, hurry up, you can listen and walk at the same time can't you? You'll come up one at a time, I'll give you twelve knives, there are twelve boards – you know what to do! Numerical order, of course. Right, who's first? You – what's your name?"

"Daniel."

"Great, Daniel, you're first."

Daniel took the dozen blades, walked to the centre of the practice area and paused, searching for the number 1. His aim was deliberate, but the shot was clean and accurate. He turned to find the second target and continued methodically, sending competent but inartistic shots towards each board in turn.

"Good!" Ivan encouraged him. "Maybe a bit faster next time."

Charles was next and, though he tried to be faster than Daniel, he missed nearly half of the boards; then it was

Eleanor's turn.

She stepped up confidently; she'd learnt the placing of the numbers from watching the previous attempts, and fired out her twelve blades in quick succession. Every one found its mark.

"Very nice," Ivan said. "Right, who's next?"

Chapter 19

The first batch of their new clothes was delivered while they were out at their poisons class the next morning, in time for the afternoon's combat session: a set of simple practice wear, along with some light leather armour from the tannery. But it wasn't until her smarter outfits arrived two days later that Eleanor fully understood why the Association retained its own tailor.

The most beautiful dress in her new collection was a green silk ballgown which skimmed the floor at her feet, and easily rivalled any of her old party dresses for its cut and quality. She pulled the laces tight across her chest, noting with a smile the two stiletto sheathes discretely built into the boning of the bodice, and the loops on the hem which would allow her to hitch up the skirt to a shorter length for running or climbing. She ran her hands down the folds of the fabric and then, because it seemed appropriate, she spun and threw out a cautious back-kick over her bed.

The dress was cut to perfection. As she tested further, she found herself able to move freely in every direction she might want. Yes, she realised, the tailor was as much a specialist as any of them.

She reluctantly placed the dress away in her closet, not sure when she'd have an opportunity to wear something so beautiful, and changed into loose trousers and a short tunic ready for class.

After another exhausting morning of athletics – their circuits interspersed, this time, with intervals of swimming fully clothed in the cold water of the academy's lake – Eleanor was looking forward to the afternoon's climbing class as a chance to show off one of her strongest skills. On her way outside after lunch, however, she caught sight of the schedule for the following afternoon.

Interrogation.

The word gnawed at her. Surely that could only mean one

thing, and she wasn't sure she was ready to face her memories yet. Back in Taraska she'd cursed the gap in her education: why had she never been taught to resist under torture? But now the lesson was imminent she dreaded it and all the old wounds – physical as well as mental – that waited to be reopened.

She tried to push the idea out of her mind, but repeated flashbacks from the previous year denied her any chance of success; she made it only a few steps along the corridor before nausea overcame her. Fortunately she managed to rush to the basin before she was sick, but washing the bitter taste from her mouth and cleaning the flecks of vomit from her hair still made her late for class.

The group had moved outside without her, and her fellow students were attempting to demonstrate their levels of climbing ability by scaling the walls of the academy buildings. She was mortified to see that Laban was taking the class; maybe that was better than making a poor first impression on someone she'd never met before, but the withering look he gave her made her wish the ground would swallow her whole.

"So you've decided to join us after all, Eleanor."

"Sorry I'm late – what have I missed?" she asked, somewhat unnecessarily since she could see perfectly well what everybody else was doing.

"I'm just giving everyone a chance to show me their style. You'll generally have to deal with more walls and rooves than trees or cliffs in this line of work, so we've plenty of scope to practise before we have to leave the grounds... do you want to show me what you can do?"

The stones of the dormitory building were irregular sizes but it was basically an easy climb, although she struggled to focus and made some elementary mistakes, slipping a couple of times and straining her old shoulder injury in the process. Eventually she managed to pull herself up the wall to the top of the bell tower, scrambled up the roof, and stopped just short of Mack who was sitting with one leg either side of the weather vane.

"I hope you're not scared of heights, are you?" he asked, peering down to where Laban was waiting.

"Not a bit," she said, wondering if she still looked queasy.

"I've been climbing as long as I can remember – trees to begin with, of course, but then mostly cliffs."

"We didn't have so many cliffs where me and Seb were at school. It's flat out in the forest."

She was almost shocked at the reminder that Mack and Sebastien had grown up together; however much she disliked Daniel's segregationist attitude, it seemed natural that everyone was spending the majority of their time with the others from the same common room. "You got up here fast enough."

"Well, we had buildings to practise on – it's Daniel I feel sorry for."

Eleanor looked down to where he was pointing. Daniel was still only a few feet from the ground, and looked distinctly uncomfortable about his position on the wall.

"He should have an advantage, being so tall," she said. "He's got better reach."

"That won't help him if he's only climbed ropes before."

They watched for a while as Laban went across to where Daniel was struggling and called out instructions on where to find plausible hand-holds, before summoning everyone back to ground level again to give out general advice based on what he'd observed.

At the end of the lesson, Eleanor was about to go back inside when Laban called her name. The sound of his voice stopped her in her tracks, and she turned to face him.

"A word, if I may."

"Okay." She didn't think refusal was an option.

He waited for the others to disperse before speaking. "Are you taking this entirely seriously, Eleanor?"

The question stunned her. "What? Of course I am!"

"No need to sound so affronted. You came down late, and even then you weren't performing anywhere near your best. I *know* you can do much better than what you showed me today. I hope you have an explanation."

"I was sick," she admitted, though even saying the words made her feel like a failure. "That's why I was late, and I still don't feel right."

"Do you have a fever? You mustn't work if you're ill, child, that's putting yourself in unnecessary danger."

"I don't want to let you down," she said. She couldn't bring herself to explain that she knew precisely what was causing her to be sick; that would only make her seem more pathetic.

"It isn't your fault if you're ill. There are some here who'd say you can work as long as you can stand up, but skirting up bell towers when you're off-colour is only going to end badly."

"Sorry."

"No harm done, this time. But run along to the lab on your way to dinner and get the herbalist to find something to settle your stomach."

She nodded; it was probably a good idea if she wanted to get any sleep.

"And Eleanor?"

"Yes?"

"Come and see me once you're feeling well again. I want to know how you're getting along."

The herbalist gave her a thick, foul-smelling potion to drink, and she skipped dinner and went straight to her room where she spent most of the night retching into the chamber pot.

Barely rested, she rose early even by her standards – before the sun had quite broken the horizon – and helped herself to an apple from the fruit bowl in the common room. It was just about all she could face for breakfast, and she swallowed each mouthful only with difficulty.

Needing to fill the time before their morning class, she headed down to the lake for a swim, hoping to take her mind off thoughts of the afternoon. It didn't work. The water, not yet warmed by the sun, was icy against her skin as she waded into the shallows, but even as the cold numbed her skin it still failed to distract her from her worries. After only half a dozen lengths to and from the small rocky island they'd used as a marker in athletics, she gave up and dried off, frustrated with herself for letting her feelings get the better of her.

She headed back to the dining hall to force herself to eat something. She was bleary-eyed at the breakfast table, fumbling as she reached for a slice of bread and dropping a crust into her tea. She blushed as every head turned to see what had caused the splash.

"Is something wrong?" Daniel asked, studying her closely as she retrieved the soggy crust.

"I slept badly," she said, fishing more crumbs from her drink. It was true enough but she had no wish to go into the reasons.

"You cannot afford to be clumsy in class," he said. "We have to fight this morning."

"It's unarmed – what's the worst that could happen?" Mikhail winked at her, and she managed a weak smile in return, but the morning class didn't worry her so much as what the afternoon might hold.

It was a bright, dry morning so the lesson took place outside on the lawns, the grass providing a soft surface to fall on as they practised leg sweeps and shoulder throws.

"Come on, get up!" their teacher snapped at Eleanor as she lay on her back after one particularly heavy landing. "You're not here to laze around."

"Sorry." She sat up, her head spinning from the blow. "I'm not feeling well this morning."

"Good! Lesson one: the world isn't going to wait for you to feel better again."

He extended a hand to help her to her feet, but as soon as she was upright he twisted her arm and slammed her back to the ground again.

"You have to be prepared to defend yourself however you feel," he said, then left her to get up on her own this time.

She glared at his back; she'd hoped for just a little more sympathy. "I suppose he's right," she muttered to Mikhail, who was partnering her for the morning. "But he didn't have to be like that about it."

The rest of the morning passed slowly and painfully, and she was glad when the bell rang to signal the lunch break, even though it meant the dreaded interrogation lesson was closer.

Though she went with the others to the dining hall, Eleanor managed to eat only a couple of mouthfuls.

"You really are ill, aren't you? Are you sure you're up to this afternoon?" Mikhail asked.

She took a sip of water. The temptation to say 'no' was overwhelming, but she knew she'd only be delaying the inevitable: in another eight days the class would come round again, and with all that time to think about it her nerves would only get worse.

"I'll be fine," she said. Better to get it over with today.

After lunch they went back to the classroom where they'd had their poisons lesson earlier in the week, and before long they were joined by a youthful, blond-haired man.

"My name is David," he said quietly. "I'm here to teach you something about interrogation."

He looked around the room, and after studying each of the students in turn his gaze settled on Eleanor.

"You're nervous," he said. "Why?"

Something in his piercing look told her she wouldn't get away with claiming illness this time, but she didn't know how to explain everything she was feeling.

"I'm fine," she said weakly, though in her heart she knew she couldn't deflect the question.

"Maybe I can tell you," he said. "You told the council you'd been tortured in Taraska. These things leave their marks on a person."

She nodded, aware that everyone was watching her. She'd carefully avoided mentioning the torture episode to her classmates, not ready to face their questions, but there would be no escaping that now.

"Fear is a very appropriate response," he said. "But it will be months before this class considers torture, and we'll put pressure on you only to show you the strength and manner of your own reactions... and in this you have an advantage over your colleagues. Does that go some way towards allaying your fears?"

She nodded again, still not quite daring to open her mouth for fear of the emotions that could flood from her if she let her guard down.

"Like every other discipline you'll study at the academy, we'll be looking at attack and defence together," David continued, turning his attention from Eleanor back to the rest of the group again. "We'll begin with appropriate questioning. To stand any chance of getting the information you want, you'll need to frame appropriate, unambiguous questions. You must give your adversary no opportunity to mislead you unless he chooses to lie – lies can be spotted more easily than misdirection."

He continued in this vein for some time before asking the students to share their ideas on what methods they could use to ensure their questions were sufficiently precise, and moving on to discuss ways of trapping a liar.

Eleanor kept quiet throughout, still reeling from the flood of memories, and no-one pressed her to contribute. At the end of the lesson she almost ran to her room, determined to avoid the others for as long as possible, but it was only delaying the inevitable.

"You were tortured?" Daniel asked her as they sat down for dinner.

"Yes."

Fred leaned across the table towards them. "I suppose you think that makes you special."

She shook her head, but had no chance to think of an appropriate response before Daniel intervened: "Leave her alone. Eleanor, we will talk about this later."

"I don't want to talk about it at all," she protested, but she was glad of the momentary deflection, and finished her meal in silence.

Once she'd eaten she hurried back to her room, but the others weren't far behind. There were no locks or bolts on the bedroom doors, and though Daniel knocked at her door before opening it he seemed to give no regard to her privacy.

"Get out! You can't just walk in here like that."

She waved at him to leave but he stayed in the doorway, a motionless silhouette against the light of the common room lanterns. Sebastien and Mikhail hovered behind him.

"Seriously, Daniel, get out of my room."

"You cannot hide forever."

"I can try."

"You must tell us what happened," Daniel insisted. "If this is something which affects how you behave and makes you ill, we are entitled to know."

"Entitled?" She thought with dismay how much this was just like school all over again – trapped with a group of people who thought they owned some portion of her life just because she happened to share their living quarters. "I don't think so."

"You said we're all in this together," Sebastien added. "We need to know when something's troubling you this much."

She sighed and got to her feet. "If I try to answer your questions, will you let me sleep? It's been a long day."

"So what happened?" Mikhail asked as they all sat down in the common room.

"I'm not sure what you want to know. I was in Taraska, I was locked up and then they tortured us... I'm not going to talk you through every way they hurt us."

"But why you?"

"They wanted to know more about the Association and how to get into the academy – it wasn't just me, it was everyone they could get their hands on. All of last year's students except Jon and Victor."

"Venncastle scum," Daniel muttered.

With Raf in her thoughts more than usual, Eleanor wasn't prepared to let his comments slide. "Can't you leave your school rivalries out of this? We're all on the same side now."

He shook his head. "Not them. Venncastle have loyalty only to Venncastle."

"We're not at school any more!" She looked to the others for support but somehow they both managed to avoid her gaze, Mikhail adjusting his shirt and Sebastien suddenly very interested in his fingernails. "Look, I'd never have got out of there alive if it wasn't for Raf, so I don't really care what you think."

"I would not expect you to understand."

"No?" She got to her feet. "Well I don't expect you to understand what we went through in Taraska, either, so we're having a pointless conversation."

"We have not finished, Eleanor," Daniel called after her, but no-one followed her into her room this time.

She fished out her emerald pendant from under the mattress and sat with it clutched tightly in her fingers, eyes squeezed shut against the tears which threatened to flow, forcing herself to concentrate only on the way the sharp corners of the metal dug into her skin.

She woke when the first rays of sunlight filtered through her window, surprised to find herself still sitting on the edge of the bed, a crick in her neck from the awkward way she'd slept. She tucked the pendant safely out of sight and eased into a few gentle stretches to warm up her stiff muscles.

She wondered whether there would be more awkward questions this morning, but she saw no-one at breakfast, and when the bell rang to summon them outside they were faced with a sight which demanded their attention completely.

Ivan was waiting in the middle of the lawn, surrounded by such a vast array of weaponry that it seemed he must have laid out the entire contents of the Association's armoury.

"I brought you a few things to play with," he said as the students gathered round, grinning at their awed expressions. "This is a practice session, not a lesson, so you're free to ignore me – but I wanted you to have chance to try your hand at a few different styles. Help yourselves. And those of you who aren't already wearing your leathers might want to reconsider."

Eleanor picked up a light, elegantly curved sword from the grass near her feet, and made a couple of experimental slices through the air.

"Of course you don't need to be perfect at everything," Ivan went on. "But don't limit yourself to your favourites, either – if something ever goes wrong, you need to be competent with whatever you can lay your hands on."

Sebastien had chosen a rapier, and Eleanor found herself sparring with him, falling into an easy rhythm of block-and-riposte until Ivan interrupted them.

"You're too comfortable with those," he said, taking the swords from their hands. "You'll have to make mistakes sooner or later, and now is safer than later."

He handed Eleanor a triplet and gave Sebastien a short hook-blade. Eleanor's grip tightened as she considered her next move; there was no chance of scoring an easy point with such close-combat weapons. She wasn't even confident of getting the best out of the triplet, with its three stubby blades extending from evenly-spaced points around the central wooden handle, but she knew Ivan was right – it was better to try unfamilar weapons in this safe environment. And at least the leather armour would protect her from scratches.

Fortunately Sebastien proved to be just as uncomfortable with the sharp curve of the hook-blade, never quite able to position the sharp inner edge where he wanted it, and eventually she managed to trip him and bring one point of the triplet to rest against his throat.

By the end of the session she'd tried out a butterfly knife and a small axe as well as practising with the triplet, and was happily exhausted.

After the exhilaration of fighting the idea of a quiet afternoon studying tracking and stealth felt like a bit of a disappointment, and Eleanor wasn't encouraged to see that their instructor, a lean young man with a shaved head, had an uneven gait which made him appear anything but stealthy as he first approached them.

"We're going to play a game," he announced before even introducing himself. "You must have played hide-and-seek as children?"

The students all nodded, wondering what a childhood game could possibly contribute to their current education.

"This is similar... we call it hunter. Everyone will hide, except for–" He scanned their faces, and pointed sharply at Mack. "You. You'll be the first hunter. And once you find someone, they'll become the next hunter while you find a new hiding place."

He threw a small jar towards Mack, who caught it smartly.

"That's how you'll keep score," he continued. "When you catch someone, you'll use that paste to mark their arm. Obviously, when we finish, the people who've done best will be the ones with fewest marks. The only other rule is that you can't catch whoever's just found you... besides that, do what you can, run away if you can. You have until the count of fifty to find your first hiding place."

Mack closed his eyes and began to count under his breath while the others all scattered, running in different directions, conditioned by the way they'd played as children to pay more attention to finding a good hiding place than to covering their tracks.

Eleanor spied a crack in a dead tree trunk, just wide enough for her to slip inside, but found she arrived there at the same moment as Fred skidded across from the other side of the path. They eyed one another for a moment, then he waved her towards the opening and sprinted away. Surprised by his generosity, she squeezed through the gap and into the hollow of the trunk where the dead wood had rotted away to leave a comfortable amount of space. A damp, musty smell filled her nostrils, a familiar scent that reminded her of the woods where she'd spent so much time as a child. She held herself still, listening for any sound in the forest to indicate the 'hunter' was on the move, sure that Mack must have reached the end of his count by now.

It was a long wait before anyone came close, and she allowed herself to relax until she heard movement just outside her tree. She held her breath, determined not to give herself away. Maybe he'd move on without spotting her hiding place. Moments later, though, a hand came towards her through the crack in the trunk.

She tried to climb clear of her pursuer but the soft, rotten wood dissolved as she tried to pull herself up and she could find no way to support her weight. Thin fingers closed around her wrist and he daubed a thick line of red paste onto her arm.

She slid out of the tree and was surprised to see who it was who'd found her.

"But you knew where I was!"

Fred looked thoroughly unconcerned. "So?"

"That's cheating."

"It's not cheating, it's winning. Not my fault you couldn't be bothered to find anywhere else."

He threw the small pot of paste towards her, and ran off

before she could object. She considered chasing after him but there seemed little point wasting her energy in following him just to continue the argument, particularly since the rules prohibited her from catching him.

With the whole of the academy's grounds to search, Eleanor began to understand why tracking would be an essential skill to succeed at this game – well, unless you cheated by already knowing where someone else was hiding. And in contrast to when she'd played with the other girls at school, she couldn't rely on noisy mistakes to give her a clue.

She returned to the clearing where they'd all started, and followed an easy trail of freshly-disturbed leaves where one of the others had sprinted carelessly between the trees. The tracks ended abruptly and Eleanor looked up, scanning the branches above her head for any sign of movement; there was nothing obvious, but one of the trees nearby was clearly an easy climb so she scrambled up to take a look.

Charles had flattened himself against one of the thicker branches; he was hidden from the ground, but up here there was nowhere to hide and he had nowhere to run to, and he accepted his loss with good grace.

Eleanor followed him down, not wanting to stay where the same clear tracks would give away her position, and moved carefully through the trees until she found another suitable tree – a trunk which was by no means an obvious climb, but well within her abilities, and with several places to hide in the canopy. She sat astride a high branch and waited, listening for any sounds of movement below, and it seemed almost no time before the end of the lesson. When the students gathered to compare their scores she found herself in the middle of the field; Daniel and Paul had avoided capture completely, while Charles had been discovered twice.

Eleanor was half way through her dinner when she remembered she'd been supposed to go and see Laban. She finished her meal quickly, made her excuses to the others, and retraced her earlier steps to find her way to his rooms.

He opened the door with a dagger in each hand, flushed with exertion, but smiled when he saw her. "Ah, Eleanor, at last.

Tea?"

She accepted, and perched herself on the sofa to wait as he tidied away his weapons and added some tea-leaves to a pan of water bubbling on the stove.

"Talk to me," he said, fetching a couple of mugs. "Tell me how everything's going."

"Fine, I think." She wondered what he wanted her to say. "Aside from people not wanting me here... but I can't do much about that. What's the council said?"

"Oh, no-one's mentioned you since you arrived. I think they're waiting to see if you'll get yourself killed." He brought her tea across to her, and settled himself cross-legged on the floor. "Which, naturally, you won't."

"I hope not."

"You'll be fine. Just don't do anything stupid."

"Stupid like throwing in a perfectly respectable job to come here and get myself killed, you mean?"

He looked sternly at her, and she blushed and sipped at her tea. The words had slipped out of her without a second thought, but she told herself she didn't really mean it. Not *really*.

"You know it was the right decision," he said. "You'd have been bored to death as some inconsequential servant of the Empire."

"I suppose so."

"Anyway, I take it you've had no problems with your lessons? They usually start off gently, but it'll pick up – nothing you can't handle, though." He pulled a dagger from his belt and offered it to her. "Show me what you've got, then."

"I'd rather use my own knife."

"As you please. I wasn't sure you'd have yours yet."

"Well, we haven't got our new kit from the smithy, but I've a nice dagger I picked up in Taraska." She unsheathed it as she spoke and got to her feet, dropping into a relaxed and ready stance. "What do you want me to demonstrate?"

"Show me what they've been teaching you." He motioned her towards the stuffed practice dummy, a vaguely human shape with red dots painted at critical strike points.

She thought for a moment then launched herself towards the

248

dummy, focusing her attention on one target spot at its throat, and sliding her knife from right hand to left mid-thrust as they'd practised. The tip of the dagger punctured the dummy's fabric.

"Not bad," he said. "Now see if you can get past me."

She turned towards him and made an attempt, with a double switch to try and confound him, but he blocked her confidently and twisted the dagger from her hand.

"What should I have done differently?" she asked as he returned her knife to her.

"It's not that you did it wrong. But watch."

He lunged towards her and she moved her dagger to parry, slicing into empty air as he flicked his knife across to the other side. He stopped the blade a hair's breadth from her skin, then stepped back.

"Let's do that again," he said. "Only this time, make sure you really watch the knife."

She did as he instructed and found the switch easy to spot when she was concentrating; she turned to block the new angle of attack and was satisfied to hear the clink of metal on metal this time.

"Look round."

She obeyed, and found he suddenly had a second blade in the 'empty' hand, a hair's breadth from her skin.

"Wrist sheath," she muttered as she realised what he'd done. "One more try?"

"No." He sat down and put his feet up on the table. "You'll get onto that in a week or two."

"Why show me, then?"

"So you don't think it's too easy. There's always another trick – or ten – beyond the one you've thought of."

Chapter 20

"Okay, pair up – wait! You've been practising in the same pairs for weeks, let's mix you up a bit." Bill gestured with his knife as he spoke. "Daniel and Charles, Fred and Sebastien, Mikhail and Paul, Jorge and Eleanor – and Mack over here with me, for now. Come on, quickly, we don't have all day."

The way Daniel had steered their group clear of the Venncastle students meant that Eleanor had hardly exchanged two words with Jorge since their first day, and after the way he'd reacted to her then, she hadn't particularly wanted to get to know him. She took a deep breath and stepped across to where he was waiting, determined not to show any nerves though he was easily twice her size.

"Ready?" he asked, flipping the practice knife slowly from hand to hand, somehow managing to make even the wooden blade look threatening. He didn't wait for an answer, but lunged the moment she moved within range. She ducked sideways, surprised by his sudden assault, and almost lost her footing as she turned to block his second thrust.

She stepped back, temporarily out of his reach, and ran through the new technique again in her mind. *Twist, feint, switch, strike.* She imagined her muscles turning into each movement, but Jorge's attacks bore little resemblance to the elegant sequence Bill had demonstrated; he came straight towards her again and though she blocked his knife-thrust he ploughed on, knocking her to the ground with the weight of his body.

"You're not even trying to practise what we've been taught, are you?" she asked as she got to her feet.

He shrugged. "Don't know what you think you're doing, but I'm practising winning. Ready to go again?"

She didn't have chance to reply before he moved towards her, lifting his knife like a club above his head. She raised her own dagger to block him, but misjudged her angle and the wood struck heavily against the bone of her wrist.

The pain shot along her arm and she glared at him. It was a meaningless exercise if they weren't even trying to learn anything, but there was no way she was going to let him win: he was enjoying this too much. Her mind skipped across everything she'd studied since arriving at the academy. She analysed the shifting of his weight and the way he gripped the hilt of his dagger, and recalled endless patterns of attacks and counters. There had to be something in there to help her defeat him.

A twitch in his bicep gave her warning of his next movement and she dodged behind him, taking the opportunity to slam her foot into the small of his back before he had chance to turn.

He growled as he spun to face her and launched himself forwards, letting his wooden dagger clatter to the floor as he opened both hands to grab her. He wrapped his fingers around her throat and lifted her clear off the ground; the whole class had stopped to watch them, but despite Bill's disapproving expression it was too late to do anything except fight on.

Struggling to breathe as Jorge tightened his grip on her neck, she pounded her knee into his groin and brought her hands up to tug at his fingers, all formal techniques forgotten in a wave of pure anger that was only compounded by the urgent need to free herself before he throttled her.

Eventually she twisted his fingers back far enough to force him to drop her. She rolled as she hit the ground then pushed herself to her feet and swung a punch up into his face. He reeled backwards, blood gushing from his nose.

"Enough?" she asked, still gasping for breath.

His face twitched with anger. "I'll get you for this, Eleanor."

"That didn't look much like what I asked you to practise," Bill said coolly, as Jorge began to mop the blood from his face. "So I take it you're both already perfect. Would you care to demonstrate, Eleanor?"

"I didn't start it!" she said, but she could hear the whine in her own voice as she spoke and knew it had been a mistake to say anything.

Bill just glared at her, and beckoned her forwards.

Twist, feint, switch, strike. She rehearsed the sequence in her mind again as she moved forwards, then tried to force her tired limbs to comply as she reached him.

She was in the middle of the switch when Bill stepped suddenly forwards, forced her arms apart with a double block, then slammed into her chest with both palms, sending her flying backwards. She landed with a painful bump and swore under her breath. After a moment's recovery she got to her feet feeling sore and humiliated, wishing the whole class hadn't been watching.

"Not so perfect, then?" Bill asked as she straightened her shirt. "Maybe next time you'll practise what you've been told to."

She struggled not to snap back at him, wanting to object that what he'd done hadn't been part of the set piece, either; he'd simply been determined to spite her. But she was in enough trouble already, so she bit her tongue and kept quiet for the rest of the lesson.

"So what actually happened?" Mikhail asked as they sat down to lunch. "By the time we noticed what was going on, he had his hands round your neck, and I've no idea how you got there from *that* sequence."

Eleanor glanced across to where Jorge was sitting. He looked preoccupied, laughing at whatever Paul had just said, but she lowered her voice anyway.

"He just wouldn't play fair," she said. "He was determined to 'win,' irrespective of actually learning anything, and I wasn't going to let him."

"Do you start to see what I mean about them?" Daniel asked. "They are all the same."

"And I don't see why Bill singled me out," she went on, spearing a carrot with unnecessary force, imagining Jorge's broad nose under her fork. "I *wanted* to practise what he was teaching us, but you can't do paired practice on your own, can you?"

They had a throwing lesson after lunch, though, and after an exhausting, enjoyable session of aiming backwards over her shoulder Eleanor had finally worked off most of her frustration.

Jorge, on the other hand, was still looking daggers at her every time their paths crossed.

The next morning was free for their own training, and Eleanor went out with Mikhail and Daniel to experiment on the practice frame, a wooden construction designed to allow them to perfect their balance while sparring. It was comprised of various fixed and rotating beams set at various heights above a sandy surface. Any misstep would probably be followed by falling headlong into the sand, and the rotating beams in particular meant that they had to pay as much attention to their footing as to their knife-work, adding an extra dimension to the fight.

"Eleanor."

She was on the least stable of the rotating beams when she heard her name, so she skipped along to the end where she could stop in safety before turning to see who'd spoken. Jorge was standing a few feet away, daggers in both hands.

"Time for a rematch," he said, scraping his knives together so the metal screeched.

"Actually, I'm already busy," she said, indicating Mikhail and Daniel, who had stopped their sparring to watch her. "Maybe some other time."

"Now. You and me, right now, no rules."

"No thanks." She turned back to the others, but he wasn't put off.

"You can't run away, Eleanor. You caught me by surprise once, but you won't do it again." He marched across and grabbed her leg, pulling her down into the sand. "I won't let you get away with it."

"Get away with what?" she asked as she scrambled to her feet. "You're just sore that I won, but you're the one who decided to change the rules."

"No rules this time. Come on, girl – if you really think you belong here, come on and show me what you've got when it's real weapons with real blades."

"I don't have to prove anything to you," she said, but even as she spoke she knew it was futile. He was too angry, and it made him doggedly persistent. She knew she'd faced far more troublesome opponents in the past, but maybe she'd have to do something drastic to get him to shut up.

"Stop making excuses," he growled.

"Fine. No rules, you said?"

"No rules."

She slid her throwing knife from its sheath and as he lunged at her she launched it straight towards his ear, then rolled out of his way. As he gripped the side of his head, letting out a low cry of pain, she scrambled back up onto the frame.

"Are you really sure you want to play this game?" she asked, second thrower poised and ready in her hand. "Because next time, I don't think I'll aim for your ear."

"That's not fair."

"Really? You said no rules. So, do you want to do this or not?"

He muttered something under his breath, sheathed his daggers, and stomped away. Eleanor breathed a sigh of relief and went to retrieve her knife from the ground, wiping the blood off on the grass before she slipped it back into its sheath. She hadn't really wanted to kill him – that would have been tricky to explain.

"Where were we?" Eleanor asked, turning back to the others. They were both staring at her like she was some creature that'd just crawled out of the lake; any progress she'd made in persuading them she wasn't crazy had evidently been wiped away with one easy stroke.

In the following days Jorge went back to ignoring Eleanor completely, and the other students were strangely quiet around her, though she suspected they were talking behind her back. She told herself it was better that way. If they didn't really want her to be there in the first place, she'd prefer them to leave her to her own devices. It simply meant she spent more of her spare time jogging or practising complicated throwing sequences rather than sparring with the others.

It was a couple of weeks later when she woke one morning feeling oddly stiff, her arms twisted awkwardly beneath her body. It took her a moment to realise that part of her discomfort was because she wasn't in her own bed, but lying on a hard surface. The floor? She wondered if she could've fallen out of bed, though she hadn't done that since she was an infant, but when she opened her eyes to look she discovered she was blindfolded.

Something very strange was going on.

Her arms and legs were bound and she felt groggy and stupid, her head pounding and making it difficult to concentrate. She needed to work out where she was, that much was obvious, but her mind refused to co-operate. Her first thought was Jorge – had he crept into her room in the night to take his revenge? But she would've expected to wake in time to put up some kind of fight.

She could see nothing, not even light, through the thick fabric of the blindfold. She could tell only that she must be indoors – the room was quiet, there was no movement in the air, and the surface beneath her cheek was a smooth and polished floor.

With some difficulty she managed to roll herself into a sitting position, but she couldn't work her hands free of the ropes which lashed her wrists together. She'd gone to bed with a small stiletto in her wrist sheath, as usual, but now the sheath was empty.

"Eleanor."

"Where am I?" she asked, wondering who the voice belonged to, and how he knew her name. She hadn't worn her identity bangle since reaching the academy, but the speaker certainly wasn't anyone she knew.

"Don't try to struggle." He spoke quietly with a flat Almont accent.

She turned her head towards the sound of his voice. "Tell me how I got here."

"You were drugged. No, don't try to move, you'll only hurt yourself."

Drugged? Well, that made sense of the fuzzy, achey feeling behind her eyes. She wished she knew which drug so she could at least guess how long it would take for all the side-effects to wear off.

"Where am I?" she repeated. "Who are you?"

"Think of me as your friend."

It was all she could do not to laugh.

"I can keep you from the people who'd like to hurt you," he continued. "But only if you trust me."

"That's a lot to ask, after all the drugging and the kidnapping."

"I'm not sure you have very much choice."

She tried again to dislodge her blindfold, pushing at the fabric with her shoulder, but it was tied securely and there was little she could do with her hands bound behind her back.

"Can I have some water?" she asked. If he was going to claim to be her friend, he could hardly deny her such a simple request.

He didn't answer but she heard him walk away, and he returned a few moments later to press a glass against her lips. As he leant across her she could feel the hilt of his dagger pressing into her leg; so close and yet so far beyond her reach. She gulped mouthfuls of cold water and emptied the glass easily, suddenly realising just how thirsty she felt. Maybe that was another effect of the drug.

"So why am I here?" she asked. If she'd learnt one thing from her experiences in Taraska, it was that she couldn't bear being tortured for information she didn't have. "What do you want from me?"

"You're going to help me."

"I don't think that's very likely."

"I don't think you have much choice. You don't want to make me involve my colleagues, believe me."

"Tell me what you want," she said, leaning towards the sound of his voice. "And I'll tell you whether you stand a chance or if you're just going to have to kill me."

"I wouldn't like it to come to that."

"Just tell me what you want."

She heard him stand up. "I'll see you tomorrow, Eleanor. Maybe by then you will have had chance to think things through."

She stuck her tongue out at his back as she listened to his

footsteps retreating. Being drugged and snatched from her bed hadn't done much for her mood, and she was even less impressed with her captor's reticence. This was threatening to be Taraska all over again.

It was a long, headache-filled day before the man returned. Eleanor slept fitfully, unable to judge night and day from under her blindfold. At least the room was comfortably warm, and there were few distractions.

This time he brought water without her having to ask, and a hunk of bread.

"Are you going to tell me what you want from me?" she asked once she'd finished eating.

"We need your help with the Association."

"You came in and took me from my bed. What help can you possibly need?"

"Oh, we know where you're based," There was a hint of laughter in his tone which seemed quite out of place. "That was almost too easy. But we need to know how things work. I need you to tell me about the structures, the people, the traditions."

"Why?"

"Ah, Eleanor, if only you could understand. But the Association is very old, and you are very new."

"Why me, then? If I'm too new to understand anything, how can I possibly be any value to you?"

"You know enough. And you're the Association's first woman. That must put you in a very difficult position, surrounded by all those men. If you help us, we can help you."

"I don't need your help."

"It can't be easy for you, being so alone."

Eleanor found herself merely irritated by his pathetic attempts at sympathy. "It's not all that easy talking to someone I can't see," she said. "Why don't you take off this blindfold, and maybe we can talk."

"I want to help you, Eleanor, truly, but you must know I can't trust you. Not yet."

"What exactly do you think I'm going to do? I can't move – I just want to see who I'm talking to."

"Sorry. That's simply impossible. Maybe once you've proved

yourself to me, I'll consider it. But so far you've given me nothing."

"You haven't asked me for anything that means anything." The frustration crept into her voice again. "You can't expect me to just guess what you want."

"I want your knowledge, Eleanor. Only you know what you can offer me." He moved away. "I'll be back tomorrow."

She still had a dull headache, and was starting to wonder if it was ever going to wear off. Whatever they'd given her, the effects were unpleasant. As she lay there, trying to sleep, she fiddled with the ropes around her wrists. She didn't expect to achieve anything, but it made her feel better that she was at least trying to escape. If she could just get her hands free, she'd have options.

Suddenly, she realised she'd actually managed to free one strand of the rope. She hadn't been anticipating even that much progress. Spurred on by the unexpected success, she continued working at the knot. Gradually, the fibres were moving.

It took her two days, and two more visits from the softly-spoken stranger, before she finally managed to loosen the knots to the stage where she could slip her hands out from between the ropes. She continued to express frustration over his oblique questions, but there was thankfully no sign of a torture chamber here, and she was secretly glad of the delay which gave her the time to work herself free.

Once she finally had the use of her hands, she made much faster progress. She loosed the knots around her feet and twisted the rope around so that, until she moved, it would still look like her ankles were bound. She wanted to look around, but though she shuffled the fabric of the blindfold up as far as she could, it was only enough to see a glimmer of light. She played with the knots at the back of her head for a while, but couldn't find a way to loosen them without removing the blindfold entirely, and if she took off the blindfold he'd know something was wrong. She needed him to come close enough for the rest of her plan to work, so she'd just have to work by sound. She tucked her hands behind her back and held the rope out of sight.

The man arrived with a glass of water as usual. While he was holding the glass to her lips, she swung her arm around to pull the dagger from his sheath.

He jumped up in surprise and she flung the dagger towards him. She leapt to her feet, hearing the clang of metal on metal as he blocked her throw, then the clatter of the knife bouncing to the floor; her aim must've been good enough to worry him, then. She wished Ivan could see her now, with a moving target and a full blindfold. This was a step beyond even what he'd asked her to do.

"Eleanor! Stop!"

She rolled towards where the knife had fallen, sliding her hands along the floor until she regained her weapon. Only then did she take the time to pull the blindfold from her eyes, blinking as she adjusted to the light again.

"Look around you," he said. "You're still at the academy."

She glanced around without dropping her guard. The room was similar enough to plenty of the academy's smaller halls, but she wasn't ready to trust her life to that resemblance.

"So who are you?"

He was a short, blond-haired man, whose appearance was as unfamiliar as his voice had been. He held his knife sideways in front of his body, no more willing than she was to disarm.

"My name's Gerald. I was given the task of testing the students this year."

She wasn't quite sure what to say, still not certain whether to believe him. "Who gave you that job, then? And why?"

"The council wanted to find someone the students hadn't met," he said. "They didn't want you to recognise my voice."

"Have I passed your test, then?" she asked. "And if I'm still at the academy, are you going to put that knife down and let me get a proper meal now? I'm hungry."

"I don't know whether you passed. You weren't supposed to escape."

"What?"

"Those were good knots, and you'd had a lot of locksure. There's no way you should've been able to move, let alone fight."

Locksure. A potent drug to paralyse the muscles, and one whose preparation Eleanor had never quite mastered, though she knew the theory of it. That explained the groggy, achey feelings all too well. She wondered how much they'd given her.

"So what, exactly, was the point of the exercise?"

"To teach you – but it seems you have no wish to learn." He looked disappointed.

"I'm very interested in learning how to escape," she said. "But no, I'm not very interested in learning how to lie still and helpless. And I can't think why you'd want me to acquire that skill. Now, if you don't mind, I'm going home."

She strode past him, watching to see whether he'd move towards her, but although he kept his knife up he let her pass. She found herself in a familiar corridor – so she was indeed in the academy. She went first to the kitchens to get something to eat, and then back to her room.

It was two days before any of the other students returned. As there were no lessons to go to, Eleanor occupied her time with running and target practice, and ever-increasing indignation. She planned the complaints they'd take to the council once the others were back, objecting to such a meaningless setup and insisting that *no* challenge should be set without a real possibility of success.

She was resting in the common room when Daniel and Sebastien eventually arrived back.

"What happened to you?" Sebastien asked, sitting down across from her. "Andreas said you'd been causing trouble again."

"Is that what he said? I only escaped."

"Escaped?"

"Yes – which I would've thought any one of us would've tried, in that situation. And then they had the nerve to suggest that I was the one doing something wrong. It's ridiculous, isn't it? I thought, as soon as you all got back, we should really go and complain about the whole setup."

"Complain about what?" Daniel asked.

"The whole idea! A test you're not expected to pass. Setting up a situation you're not supposed to get out of. It's crazy!

Stupid!"

"Do you think you may be overreacting?"

"No." She looked up at him. "Do you?"

"Perhaps. It was only another lesson – a different format, but still a lesson."

"But what's it supposed to teach? Futility? The art of giving up? It's nonsense!" She flung a knife hard towards the target board to punctuate her point. "Nonsense."

"Maybe it was to teach patience."

"What, so it's impatient to try and get yourself out of a difficult situation? How was I supposed to know it was a silly game to wait out? For all I knew, they were going to kill me."

"I'm surprised you were able to move, let alone fight your way out, with the amount of drugs they kept feeding us," Sebastien said. "What did you say it was called, Daniel?"

"I believe it was locksure."

"It was."

"How do you know?" Daniel looked surprised. "You have never been good at identifying poisons."

"They told me," she snapped, irritated by his comment despite the truth of it. "I really shouldn't have been able to move, by all accounts, but apparently locksure doesn't have such a strong effect on me, after all."

"How can that be?"

"You tell me – you're the expert. Maybe it doesn't work on women."

"Impossible."

"Well, you'd better work it out before you ever come to rely on it. Whatever went wrong, it surprised them, too."

Chapter 21

The students were given two further days for recovery, time to allow all the drug's effects to wear off before they had to start classes again. Then, although the next day was technically one of their free days, they were woken early and informed that they would be taking part in a small competition.

"Think of this as a small practice for the contests next year," Andreas said once he'd gathered all the students down in the practice hall. "Although, unlike next year, today you'll be competing in three teams of three."

He divided them according to where they were sitting, which put Eleanor, Daniel and Sebastien together, Mikhail with Paul and Mack, and Jorge, Fred and Charles in the third team.

"You'll each have a ribbon tied around your wrist," Andreas continued. "Your goal is to keep your own ties safe while attempting to gather as many as possible from the other teams. If you lose your ribbon, you'll have to come straight back to me to collect another one, but you'll only have three lives each. Anyone who loses all three of their ribbons is out of the game, and must come back here without delay, and three points will be deducted for carelessness. You'll score one point for every life you have left and every ribbon you've stolen. We'll play until midday."

He handed out three loops of red ribbon to each team.

"These are tied with quick-release knots, so they'll come off easily if you pull the long end – no, don't try it now – and I'll take a very dim view of your abilities if I find anyone resorts to re-tying the knots. Once you've captured an opponent's ribbon, you're advised to hide it well, somewhere about your person, because we'll have no other way to verify the scores at the end."

Eleanor slipped the loop of ribbon onto her wrist, adjusting it so it wouldn't fall off as she ran.

"I'll send you out one team at a time, and you'll have until the count of fifty until the next team comes out. Jorge's team first, then Sebastien's, then Mack's. Are you all clear on the rules?"

Everyone nodded their agreement.

"Good. Jorge, Fred, Charles – go!"

Once the three of them had left the hall, Andreas started a slow count-down from fifty. He looked across to Sebastien, Daniel and Eleanor as he neared the end of the count, and they got to their feet in readiness.

"Four... three... two... one... – go!"

The students ran for the door.

"We will need to make a plan," Daniel said as they jogged towards the forest.

"Let's concentrate on getting out of sight, first," Sebastien said.

"But what if we plan to track the others?"

"What if they plan to ambush us?" Eleanor said. "I'm with Sebastien, let's hide ourselves somewhere out of the way before we start doing too much thinking."

They made their way between the trees, and down to a bend in the river where they could hide in a dip beside the bank while knowing their backs were moderately well protected by the fast-flowing water.

"We could just stay here," Sebastien said. "It's a good spot to defend."

"What if no-one comes looking?" Eleanor asked. "We can't just opt out and hide – that virtually guarantees us second place."

"We have three lives each," Daniel said. "We should split up, but each come back here to hide once we are on the last life."

As much as she wanted to, Eleanor couldn't think of a better plan to put forward as an alternative.

Neither, apparently, could Sebastien. "Back here when you get down to one life, then, or meet at the practice hall just after midday if you're lucky enough not to get to that stage."

"Okay."

"Okay."

Eleanor's first instinct was to climb; in the dense parts of the forest she knew she could make her way from tree to tree easily enough, and most of her fellow students wouldn't think of looking up when they had plenty of potential threats to keep them occupied at ground level.

She saw Jorge, Fred, and Charles first, but they were moving in one tight formation and she didn't think she could get all three without losing a life of her own. Maybe they'd split up later. She waited for them to pass out of her sight, then continued to make her way between the trees.

She came upon Paul next; he was walking alone, taking each step slowly and purposefully, studying the ground for tracks. She waited until he'd passed beneath her, then dropped down behind him and grabbed his ribbon before he had chance to even react to the sound of her landing.

She tucked the ribbon safely out of the way and started to walk. She was picking her way through some particularly thorny undergrowth when she rounded one large trunk and came upon Mikhail. They both reached out at the same time, and pulled the ribbons away simultaneously.

"Well, that'll teach us," Mikhail laughed as he tucked Eleanor's ribbon into his breast pocket. "Shall we go back and get another one?"

"Sure." She turned to walk alongside him. "We have to go back to the practice hall, don't we?"

"Is this the first life you've lost? You're doing well, then. How many have you caught?"

"Yours is my second. You?"

"Same, but I've lost two."

"Truce till the count of ten once we get new ribbons?" Eleanor suggested as they approached the academy buildings. "Otherwise this could be over quite quickly."

"Truce," he agreed. "Good plan."

Her truce, however, applied only to Mikhail; as they left the practice hall she saw Mack coming in, and found the perfect spot at the edge of the forest where she could wait to pounce on him when he emerged.

After that coup she spent a long while up in the treetops again, moving occasionally between branches and looking for opportunities, but the forest was large and the students had spread widely.

Jorge and Fred were walking back-to-back when she next saw them, having apparently lost Charles somewhere along the way. She was getting bored of waiting, and the challenge appealed; two was surely possible.

Once she was confident that their position was as vulnerable as it would get, she dropped to the ground and seized Jorge's ribbon as she landed, turning immediately to launch herself towards Fred before he could target her.

As she reached out she felt a tug at her own wrist, and the fabric slithered away from her wrist as her fingers closed around Fred's ribbon. Only after she'd recovered her balance did she look to see who her assailant had been, and saw the back of Paul's head as he sprinted off.

She was onto her last life, then.

She ran back to the practice hall, and once she'd got her final ribbon, made her way much more carefully back to the riverside. Daniel and Sebastien were already crouched in the hollow when she reached it.

"How many do you have?" Daniel asked as she sat beside him.

"Five, I think." She searched under her shirt and pulled out all the ribbons. "Yes, five."

"Then we have ten altogether. With our three lives preserved, that should be enough."

Sebastien glanced at the sun's position overhead. "It's nearly time, anyway. We just have to keep out of sight."

They settled back against the bank, and Sebastien stuck a twig in the ground to measure the sun's progress towards its zenith.

The flash of red between the trees caught Eleanor's eye; it was Mikhail running across the path just a few yards further into the forest. He clearly hadn't seen them.

She sprang to her feet.

"What are you doing?" Daniel hissed as she sprinted away, but she didn't turn back to give an answer. There wasn't time.

Mikhail heard her coming, but by the time he turned, she'd launched herself past him and grabbed the end of the ribbon. She hit the ground and rolled, keeping her fingers firmly clenched around the thin strip of fabric.

She ran back to her teammates with the ribbon held aloft, triumphant. "Eleven," she said. "And Mikhail's out."

"We did not need eleven," Daniel said quietly. "Come, it is time to go back."

They were the last ones to reach the practice hall.

"Time to work out the scores," Andreas said. "Please count up your ribbons."

He gave them a few moments to make their tallies, while he pulled the remaining ribbons from their wrists.

"Jorge, your team had two lives left, one man down, and how many ribbons captured?"

"Six," Jorge said, holding them up.

"And Sebastien, with three lives left and everyone still standing, how many ribbons?"

"Eleven."

"Mack. One life left and two men down, and...?"

" Four ribbons."

"Well, we have a very clear winning team, I don't think we need to bother with the detail of the scores." He held out his hand to collect the lengths of ribbon. "Well done. And now I'm sure you're all ready for lunch."

Eleanor and Sebastien congratulated one another as they walked across to the dining hall, and most of the others came across to comment on the comprehensive nature of their victory; only Daniel held himself a little apart, aloof from the celebrations, and he sat quietly throughout the meal.

After lunch, as Eleanor made her way upstairs, she felt a hand on her shoulder. Turning swiftly, she found herself face to face with Daniel.

"That was an unacceptable risk," he said. "You gave away our position, and if you had failed, we could have all been forfeit."

"It worked." She turned to walk away, but he gripped her arm and refused to let her go. She stared at him in astonishment. They'd won, hadn't they?

"It was unnecessary. We had already won."

"So? We didn't lose anything, and it was his last life. I had to

266

go for it."

"You did not 'have' to. You risked your own last life, and ours. You should not have taken such a risk, and most certainly not without permission."

"Permission? What is this, school?" She yanked her arm sharply away from him. "You don't get to give me 'permission' for anything."

She ran up the stairs before he had chance to say another word, and nearly crashed into Sebastien as he came out of the common room.

"Eleanor? Are you okay?"

"Fine," she assured him. "It's just Daniel being an idiot. He's a sore loser."

Sebastien looked puzzled. "But we won."

"Yeah, he's going on about what I did being too risky, even though – as I told him – it worked. I'm sure he's just down about it because he didn't get as many as me."

"Well, it was a big risk."

"Oh, not you as well!"

"Seriously, though, in the real world we're not going to be playing games – it'll be life or death. That's a dangerous time to take risks."

"Which is something I'm perfectly capable of working out for myself."

"But how will you know when it's worth risking your life?"

"That's the thing about risk, isn't it? It's a gamble. You can try to weigh up how likely you are to succeed and what you'll lose if you fail, but you can't really know if it'll work. You just have to decide."

"Sometimes it is not your decision." She hadn't realised Daniel had come up behind her while they were talking. "It was not your decision today, when we were supposed to be a team. You should have at least consulted with us."

She sighed. "I saw a chance, I took it, and it worked. Get over it."

She shut herself in her room and lay on the bed, staring at the ceiling. Nothing seemed right. It seemed that whatever she did recently, someone had a problem with it. It was getting to the stage where she'd stopped enjoying herself.

Why am I putting myself through this?

Hard as she tried, she couldn't find an answer which satisfied her. She'd expected the academy to have its challenges, of course, but she'd never thought it would be this hard. She'd expected to enjoy the development of her skills, not to live in a state of permanent frustration. It simply wasn't worth it.

She had a lump in her throat as she made her way to Laban's rooms, but now she'd made a decision she wanted to get this out of the way as soon as possible. She knocked once but didn't wait for an answer before trying the door – when the handle turned easily, she let herself in. Laban was hanging upside-down from his trapeze, his head a full six feet above the floor, though he somersaulted down as soon as he saw her enter, landing lightly on his feet.

"Tea?" he asked, straightening.

"Thank you." She sat down on the sofa to wait for him, and shortly he returned with two steaming mugs.

"This is a pleasant surprise," he said as he joined her. "What can I do for you?"

She stirred honey into her tea and wondered how she could possibly soften the blow, but there seemed to be no way – and if she couldn't make it any easier for him, she could at least simplify matters for herself by getting this over with quickly.

"I'm leaving," she said quietly.

"Leaving?"

"Yes. I'm going to leave the academy."

He snorted. "Don't be ridiculous."

"I mean it – I don't belong here. I don't want to be part of your experiment any more."

He took a careful sip of his tea. "Are you listening to what you're saying?" he asked. "You don't just leave the academy. Besides, where would you go? You can't waltz back into the Imperial system and expect them to put a roof over your head and food in your mouth."

"Why not? I could tell them you tricked me."

He shook his head. "No-one would be interested, believe me. Well, except maybe for Myran, I'm sure he'd still like to get his hands on you – he always did bear a grudge."

Eleanor swallowed and looked at the floor, her guilty secret weighing heavily on her mind. Laban seemed to take her silence as capitulation.

"You see? However hard you might think things are here, it could be a lot worse. You've got food on the table, a warm bed at night, and good people on your side. The Association looks after its own, always has done."

"But the Association doesn't want a woman!"

"The Association wants good people – and that's all. I know there are some who are a bit old-fashioned, I warned you as much, but most people are on your side. Especially after how well you're doing."

"Well, they're not showing it."

"I know you're angry–"

"Of course I am!" She slammed her mug onto the table, splashing hot liquid across her fingers. "You manipulated me, you're still trying to use me to prove a point, and I'm sick of it."

"Perhaps I did use you." He sipped his drink, looking pensive, as if he'd only just thought of it. "Perhaps I did. But it was only for your own good, only the same as how the whole assignment system makes sure that the Empire uses *everyone* to their best advantage. You belong here."

"I don't. I can't do anything right. They say I shouldn't be here to start with, and I shouldn't try too hard to win, and I certainly shouldn't try to escape from their stupid fake-kidnap, or be upset at the idea of something being unwinnable... How can you say I belong here when everything I do comes out wrong?"

Tears of frustration rolled down her cheeks, and Laban passed her his handkerchief as he spoke.

"You just do things differently to what they're expecting. They're not used to you, yet."

"Why me?" She dried her eyes and took another mouthful of her tea, willing the honeyed taste to soothe her as it always had in her childhood. "If I'm so out of place here, why did you pick me?"

"You have all the right skills. You might do things

differently, but you're doing well."

"Not well enough."

"Ivan says you're one of the most natural throwers he's seen – though he's young, of course. But you're one of the best in your year. And think of the principles at stake here. If our first woman walks out on us, what are the chances for other girls?"

"I don't want to be a principle!"

"Fine. But if you won't think of their future, at least think of your own. Where could you possibly go?"

She avoided meeting his eyes. "There are smugglers who live just as nicely as we do."

"Will you listen to yourself! You're not a criminal."

"I could be."

"Eleanor, Eleanor." He sighed heavily. "I'm bored of hearing this from you. This is just what you always do. You'd have left school if you'd been able to think of any alternative. And here you have about as much freedom as you could ever wish for and you *still* want to give up, just because you think some people don't like you."

"It's not about people liking me."

"Why did you come here?"

"What?" The question surprised her. 'To the academy, or up here?"

"To see me, today."

"To tell you I'm leaving. I just told you that."

"Did you really come to tell me of a firm decision? Or are you expecting me to talk you out of it, like I always told you to stay at school?"

"No! No, absolutely not. I just didn't want to leave without saying goodbye."

"Good, because I'm not going to tell you what to do this time. You're an adult, Eleanor, you have to make your own decisions. But think carefully, because if you can't be happy here, I struggle to believe you'll be any happier somewhere else."

She put her mug down on the table, tea half finished. "I have to go and pack," she said. "I want to be away by first light."

"Stay and finish your drink," Laban said, but she got to her feet and walked to the door without another word. "Good luck finding your happiness," he called after her. "I hope you can find it inside yourself."

As she wrapped her things neatly into a small parcel, his words echoed in her head. Could he possibly be right? Was she just condemned to feel out of place *anywhere*?

She shook her head, trying to shake out such troublesome thoughts, and reached under her mattress for her identity bangle and the pendant Raf had given her. Of course she could be happy – just as soon as she found whatever it was that she really wanted. She clipped the bangle onto her wrist and hung the pendant around her neck. She'd known as soon as she'd seen it that her assignment wasn't the answer, and she'd pinned her hopes on the academy... but this was just another setback. Somewhere out there, she'd find it. She looked hopefully towards the window but it was dark, and she saw only a few drops of rain against the glass.

Once she'd packed up everything that could possibly be useful she went to bed; there was nothing to be gained by sleeping out in the rain, and it was too late to find anywhere to stay in the city. Besides, she had no money, so unless she was willing to pawn her knives she'd have to rob someone to pay for a room. The thought didn't appeal; it had been easy enough to justify petty thieving when the only alternative had been to starve, but this time she was walking out of a safe, warm place where good food was put on the table every day.

All because some people didn't like her, Laban had said. Was that really all that was driving her away?

She gripped the emerald pendant. Raf would never have given up like this... but if Raf had made it, she probably wouldn't be leaving. Again, she caught herself staring longingly into the darkness outside the window. Was this all about her grief? She'd clung to the thought that he might turn up at any moment, but as the days turned into weeks and months, her hopes were fading.

But running away from the academy wasn't going to bring him back.

She got up a little later than usual the next morning, washed her hair, then returned to her room to unpack her clothes back into the closet. She threw herself into athletics with even more than her characteristic abandon, turning frustration into movement as she'd always done as a girl.

She wasn't looking forwards to that afternoon's climbing lesson, dreading facing up to Laban and admitting that, in fact, she hadn't left. She could imagine his smug expression all too well. As it happened, though, he didn't mention her change of heart during the class, and she went to dinner feeling that she'd got away more lightly than she could ever have hoped.

When she got back to her room, though, she found a short note on her pillow inviting her to visit his rooms 'at her convenience.' She crumpled the paper and tossed it across the room, taking a quiet satisfaction in ignoring the request. She'd go eventually, of course, but she didn't want to talk about it yet. She hadn't worked out what had kept her here, yet.

Chapter 22

Eleanor had spent weeks arriving early at the practice hall before every projectiles class, hoping to engineer another chance to talk to Ivan, but it had proved harder than she'd expected. Though he was usually in the hall some time before the bell rang to mark the start of the lesson, several of the other students had also fallen into a pattern of going down to practise in their lunchbreaks. As the seasons shifted it wasn't uncommon for the academy's entire student population to congregate in the hall each day; there was no privacy, and there were some subjects she just couldn't broach in front of the others, so she'd eventually given up any hope of talking to him beyond the light-hearted exchange of classroom banter.

Laban's words, though, gave her a fresh confidence. She'd watched Ivan constantly during their classes, wondering whether he was still testing her, but he'd never again set her such a tricky and unexpected challenge as he had that first day. But if he was telling other people she was doing well, maybe she'd passed his first test after all.

After the next projectiles lesson she decided to try a more direct approach, and cornered him as he was about to leave. "Ivan, can I ask you something?"

"Of course." He turned expectantly to face her. "What's troubling you?"

She'd rehearsed this conversation in her head more times than she could count, guessing at his responses, and she started with the most innocuous question – one to which she was fairly certain she already knew the answer.

"Were you at Venncastle?"

"Yes, that's right."

"With Raf."

He nodded, still no change in his expression. If he was surprised at this turn of questioning, so long a time after their first meeting, he did a good job of concealing it.

"Did you know him well?"

"Fairly well, yes." He watched her as she tried to compose her next question, waiting in silence for her to form the words.

What eventually came out of her mouth was a simple statement which summed up all of her confusion: "You look like him."

She stared him, wide eyes brimming with tears, silently pleading for him to answer the questions she couldn't quite bring herself to ask. Raf would have known, she told herself in the long silence that followed. Raf would've answered her without making her force out impossible words.

"Officially, we shared a school and that was all," he said at last. "But we weren't blind. You haven't missed the resemblance and neither did we – and of course there are plenty of people at Venncastle who share a father, you expect that."

"What? How can you know that?" She struggled to make any kind of sense out of his words. "Surely that's illegal. How can you have families within a school?"

"No families. I don't know who my parents are, any more than you do – but I know they were *good enough*, which narrows it down."

She stared at him blankly. "What?"

"Oh, I forget how new you are – of course you wouldn't understand. A quick history lesson, then, sit down or... would you like to talk over dinner?"

She glanced towards the dining hall, her heart suddenly racing at the idea of having to have the rest of this conversation in public.

"Is something wrong?" Ivan asked.

"I was just hoping to have some privacy," she said. "But we can talk some other time, if you're hungry."

"Oh, we don't have to eat with everyone else. Come on, we'll go via the kitchen and get something sent up to my rooms."

She followed him round to a door at the back of the kitchen, where he left her waiting in the corridor while he went to negotiate with the chef. She leant against the wall, hoping none of her fellow students would come past and ask what she was doing there; she didn't want to explain, but if she'd learnt one

274

thing from their studies in interrogation it was that she was a terrible liar. She could pull off the big deceptions, slipping into another persona without too much trouble, but she had to make herself believe in it – anything less, and she was utterly transparent.

It was only a moment, though, before Ivan emerged again.

"All sorted," he said. "They're doing roast chicken, apparently, and I've asked them to send us some pudding as well."

He led her through the courtyard, round the back of the practice hall, and into a building she hadn't been to before. A couple of corridors and a flight of stairs later, they reached his quarters. The room they came into had a sizeable fireplace, soft chairs, and a small table; it was a smaller space than Laban's high-roofed hall but felt much more welcoming, more like a home than a functional space, though there were tools and small weapons cluttering every surface. Three other doors, closed, led off in different directions.

"Sit down," Ivan suggested, waving her towards a a chair near the fire. He went to put some fresh logs into the grate, and she sat and watched in silence as he stoked up the glowing embers until the fire was roaring.

"So what do you know about Venncastle?" he asked, taking the seat next to her.

"Almost nothing, except it was Raf's school," she said, wondering if she could trust him with the strange story of her visit to the castle. But it was probably safer to keep quiet and let him tell his history.

"Well, in the days before the Empire, Venncastle used to be a real castle," he began, a nostalgic lilt to his voice. "Home to the best army in all the known lands. Do you know how it came to be called Flying Rock Island?"

She shook her head.

"Catapults and trebuchets," he said. "A technology we worked out generations before anyone else in the archipelago, meaning hostile ships would never dare enter our waters for fear of the flying rocks. Backed up by our garrison of elite young men, who'd soon see off trouble if anyone *did* get too close."

"It must have been a quiet life, compared to everyone else," she said, thinking back to the stories of pirates and warring factions that she'd heard when learning about how terrible life had been before the Empire.

"Indeed. We had everything Charan wanted on his side when he was looking to found the Empire, but no reason to join him unless we got something in return. So the army at Flying Rock made a deal: we'd start a school in the old castle, but unlike other schools we'd be permitted to choose which boys to take in. That was the price of our support."

"Why?" Eleanor asked, trying and failing to think of any reason why a school would find it useful to choose between babies.

"We didn't want to lose our edge as the region's elite." Ivan leaned forward and prodded the fire as he spoke. "In the early days there was some doubt over whether the Empire would survive beyond Charan's death, but with the foundation of the school we could make sure we always had a loyal body of men, ready to re-form our own army if we ever needed it. And though that doesn't look likely, it's still a useful resource – Venncastle loyalty is famous across the Empire."

"But how can it help to choose the children? How can you make any judgements on babies, and who they're going to turn out to be?"

"Oh, we make decisions based on the parents. The school is very selective about acceptable fathers, not even all of our ex-students are approved, and then there's some consideration over who the mother is, though we often won't know as much about her. And it works – Venncastle's boys often come here, as you've seen, or they take top positions in the Imperial army, or stay at Flying Rock to train the next generation."

"You make it sound so simple – just like breeding horses."

He let out a brief, snorting laugh. "Sort of, except with horses you can control the pairings, whereas humans like to make their own choices – however badly they might choose. But I know what you mean. Anyway, some of the men bring more children than others, sometimes by more than one woman, so it's not that

276

unusual for boys to share a father, though normally you wouldn't know it. I think it's rare, though, for two kids to look as alike as Raf and I did, even five years apart."

"So you think, you and Raf..." Still she couldn't quite say the words. The idea was simply too strange, and it still felt like treachery even to think about such things.

"Were probably brothers, yes." He leaned back in his chair and let out a pained sigh. "That's what we guessed, though we hardly spoke about it. Even at Venncastle, there are things better not discussed."

"I'm sorry – did you mind my asking?"

"No, I understand. You knew him, and then you met me – how could you not wonder? Especially in ignorance of how our school works. And..." He hesitated for a moment, studying her face. "Well, it's good you should learn these things. If you ever have a son, it's something you should consider."

"Me?"

"Absolutely." He rested his hand on her arm and looked straight into her eyes. "You could choose any of the Association's men, and coupled with your strengths, any boy from such valuable stock would be accepted without question. Venncastle would be the best place for him to grow up with suitable encouragement, with his natural talents nurtured – that way your son would have every possible chance of following in your footsteps."

"Oh." She hadn't really thought about when she'd get around to her child-bearing duty; she'd seen pregnant women and the idea of such drastic changes to her body terrified her. She didn't want to have her movements compromised like that, and she'd always vaguely hoped that following a military career would mean she didn't have to, when there were plenty of other women to do the baby-making.

"But of course you've plenty of other things on your mind at the moment. Just remember you have that option, when the time comes for you to provide children to the Empire."

"Um, thanks." She wasn't really sure what else to say, but it was starting to make sense that so many boys from Venncastle passed through the academy. It was a strange throwback to the way the world must've been before the Empire, when children were expected to follow their parents' careers. "So... you knew Raf better than I did," she said, trying to steer the conversation back to more familiar ground. "There's no chance he could've changed his mind, is there?"

Ivan shook his head. "This is all he's ever wanted to do. Some of the lads go through phases of rebellion – times when they think they'd rather aim for something different – but not Raf."

"That's what I thought." She swallowed, struggling to fight the tears. "That means he's dead, doesn't it? If there was any way he could've been here, he definitely would be."

Ivan drew a deep breath, eyes glistening in the firelight. "I've struggled to think of another explanation," he said. "Without success."

She stifled a sob, and sank forwards to rest her head on her knees as the tears flowed. But she allowed herself only a moment of grief before wiping her eyes and straightening up again; she'd have plenty of time to cry once she was alone. "Sorry."

"Don't be – I understand." Ivan passed her a handkerchief, and she dabbed her eyes some more. "I miss him too. Would it help you to talk about the time you spent with him? You can't have had much chance."

"I'm not sure I can." She bit her lip and closed her eyes, wishing the tears would stop welling up behind her eyelids. "I'm not sure I can talk about it yet."

"Well, that's okay too."

They fell into silence for a moment, watching as the flames licked around the new logs, which fizzed a little as dampness bubbled out of the wood. Ivan picked up a twig from the kindling pile and flicked it towards the fire.

"Can I get you anything to drink?" he asked as the stick blackened in the flames. "I've got some good wine."

"Oh, I'd be fine with just water, thank you."

He disappeared through the nearest door, and Eleanor took the opportunity to pick up a tiny blow-pipe from the table; she was examining it when Ivan came back, a few moments later, with a jug of cloudy liquid.

"Apple juice," he explained. "If you're sure you don't want any wine?"

"I've never really had wine," she said, suddenly feeling a little embarassed. "But apple juice would be lovely."

"Be careful with that," he said, pouring two glasses of juice. "It's loaded. Not with anything fatal, mind you, but probably strong enough that you'd miss dinner."

"Is this another of your specialities?" she asked, lifting the pipe to her lips but resisting the urge to blow.

"That's my favourite weapon," he said. "We'll get on to pipes in class in a few weeks, but you're welcome to have a go now. Just don't aim it at me."

She angled the pipe towards the log pile and expelled one sharp puff of air; the dart bounced off the wood and onto the hearth.

"Good shot."

She dropped to her knees and picked up the fallen dart, being careful not to prick her fingers with the poisoned tip, but the end was crumpled.

"You may as well put it in the fire; it won't fly straight again after that bounce," Ivan said, and passed her a pouch full of new darts. "Here, these ones aren't drugged. Try aiming at something softer, then you won't damage the tip, and if you can get it to stick you'll be able to see precisely how well you've done."

She pushed a new dart into the pipe, and this time she aimed at one of the spare chairs; the dart sank a small way into the corner of a cushion, where it quivered gently.

"I knew you'd be good with a pipe." Ivan reached across to retrieve the dart, and handed it back to her. "It's not hard, if you've a good eye, but you can sneak one of those into places where you'd struggle to carry a knife. Can you hit the seam?"

She wasn't confident in her accuracy, but at least the seam in question was a roughly vertical line, meaning she could concentrate on her horizontal aim. She was preparing to attempt it when a knock at the door disturbed them.

"Oh, that'll be dinner – you can play more later."

Ivan went to answer the knock and Eleanor, disappointed at the break in her concentration, lined up the pipe with the seam and blew. It was close, but she missed her target by a finger's width, and was a couple of inches above where she'd actually aimed.

The servant who came in was struggling under the weight of a very large tray, and Ivan quickly led him on through another door, calling for Eleanor to follow them. She picked up her half-finished apple juice, plucked the dart from the cushion and went through, finding herself in a compact dining room. The table could have comfortably seated eight, but didn't feel uncomfortably large with just the two of them; the cosy space made a nice change from the echoing academy hall. The servant offloaded a whole roast chicken and platters of carrots, potatoes, and cabbage, then a small pie for dessert, with a jug of sweet cream.

"We'll never get through all this," Eleanor said. "This could feed half the academy."

"Don't worry, they'll think of something to make with the leftovers." He carved almost half of the chicken before selecting a couple of thick slices from the breast to put onto her plate. "You'll get chicken casserole tomorrow, I suspect."

"I missed that seam," she said as she helped herself to vegetables. "Carrots?"

"You were distracted."

"No, just inaccurate. It's not something I've done before." She took a forkful of chicken, and was pleasantly surprised by the rich mixture of herbs and mushrooms that made up the stuffing. The Association's chefs never failed to produce solid, satisfying meals, but this was a more delicate flavour than usual.

"It won't take you long, I promise, once we start studying it properly. You're such a natural thrower, and the blowpipe requires much less skill."

"Do you really think I'm a natural?" She was glad he'd used the word before she'd given in to temptation and asked about what Laban had said.

"Absolutely. Though you've clearly had practice, too – you

arrived here with more skill than a lot of our students have when they graduate."

"Well, I used to train all the time in the woods near my school, any time I could get away."

"Like I said, you're a natural. It's just as well you found us, you'd have been wasted anywhere else."

She wanted to say something about Laban's guidance – it felt all wrong to accept the compliments as if she'd done it all by herself – but she'd always promised to keep quiet and this seemed the wrong time to break her silence. Though, of course, she'd already told Raf.

"And of course in Taraska we had plenty of reasons to practise," she said, thinking back. "I taught Raf to throw stars, you know..." She smiled a little at the memory, despite the way her voice cracked as she told it. "He had terrible trouble getting them to catch."

"He always was stronger in close combat – your opposite in that respect."

"It made us a good team. We taught each other so many things, it was..." She stopped herself, and thought for a moment before continuing. "Look, I know this sounds awful, but we had fun. Not being imprisoned – but the escape, the planning, the learning. We did it all together, and until the very end we were enjoying it. Does that sound dreadful?"

"We wouldn't be in this business if we didn't enjoy the danger," Ivan said. "And the challenge. Otherwise we'd still be bored to death in some corner of the Imperial system."

"It seems wrong, though, that I can look back on it when Raf... can't..."

"You mustn't blame yourself. The risks come with the territory. It's not your fault you were lucky this time."

Eleanor turned her attention to her meal, and as she picked at her vegetables she remembered all the strange foods they'd eaten in Taraska; suddenly, it seemed, her mind was flooded with memories from around that time.

"Have you ever had to fight on a boat?" she asked, thinking back to the inconvenient pitching of the *Rose*. Those were safer memories, with less chance she'd suddenly start crying.

"Not yet."

"It feels like stars should be easier, if there's a lot of movement, because you don't have to be so precise – but I haven't had chance to test it. I just wondered whether you knew."

"Well." He paused for a moment's thought, fork frozen half-way to his mouth. "You could replicate it, sort of, with a balance board."

"What's that?"

"You know, where you put a plank on a log," – he rested his fork across his finger to illustrate his point – "and you have to keep your balance by shifting your weight around. Hmm... maybe we'll try that next week. Give the others chance to find out what you mean about knives being tricky – though I wouldn't guarantee stars would be easier."

"Don't tell them it's my fault if you do," she said, trying to sound like she was joking.

"I won't blame you! But it'll be fun, anyway. It's always good to have a challenge or two."

"So what else is on the plan for this year?"

"Well, you've quite a bit more to do with knives. Then darts and pipes, and then we'll do some preliminary work with the stars, though we won't get serious with those till next winter. And there'll be more knife-work next year, too."

Once they'd made the biggest dent they could manage in the chicken and vegetables, Ivan cut a couple of generous slices of the pie – which turned out to have a pear and walnut filling – and rang for someone to collect the leftovers.

"We only get pudding on our days off, usually," Eleanor said, pouring a small lake of cream into her bowl. "Not that I'm complaining."

"I had to ask for it," he said. "But maybe that's the advantage of graduating. Overnight, this place suddenly stops feeling like school – and you realise you can just ask for whatever you want."

"Are you coming down to combat practice tomorrow? Because you'll have to go easy on me after all this."

"I wasn't planning on it, but I will if you think you need an extra push." He winked at her, and she was caught off guard again by just how very much like Raf he was.

"Oh, I didn't... I mean..." She blushed, and tried again: "We get on fine without you, I just like all the extra toys you bring down."

He grinned. "Then I'll be sure to be there, with plenty of toys."

"You're the only one who lets us borrow your weapons to try out, you know."

"Well, I'm the only person who has half of these things," he said between mouthfuls of pie. "It's useful to have a few surprises up your sleeve, but as with any good idea, not everyone sees the benefit. Besides, you're only using my research collection. I wouldn't let the whole class loose on my personal weaponry."

"I'm sorry if I spoiled your evening," Eleanor said, getting to her feet to add her empty bowl to the stack of used dishes. "I just... well, there were some things I needed to understand. Anyway, I'll leave you to whatever your plans were... thank you for your time..."

"You haven't spoiled anything." He stood up, blocking her route to the door. "And you don't have to rush off – I can give you some more tips with that pipe, if you like."

"Are you sure? I don't want to trouble you more than I already have."

"It's no trouble. Honestly. Come on, let's see how quickly you get the hang of this."

"You weren't at dinner," Mikhail said as Eleanor sat down for breakfast the next morning. "Are you okay?"

"I'm fine." She helped herself to a couple of sausages. "Why wouldn't I be?"

Mikhail shrugged. "You've been acting odd lately."

"Maybe I just am odd." She certainly wasn't going to deny that it had been a strange few weeks. "But I'm okay."

"So where were you last night?" Sebastien asked.

"Just practising." It was almost true. "I got carried away."

"But you must eat," Daniel said, pushing the plate of

sausages towards her.

She rolled her eyes and let out an exaggerated sigh. "It's not your job to tell me what I 'must' do, thanks. I'm an adult, I can do whatever I want."

As he'd promised, Ivan had laid out his collection of unusual weapons in the practice hall, though he was nowhere to be seen when the students arrived after breakfast. As she tightened the straps of her leather armour, Eleanor wondered if he'd felt as sleepy as she did this morning, after they'd talked and trained late into the night.

"I need some more practice with that hook-blade," Sebastien said, eyes scanning the floor until he spotted a similar, slightly shorter version. "Though I really don't understand why anyone would choose such an awkward primary."

"I'll take you on," Mikhail offered, hefting a small battle-axe.

Eleanor glanced at Daniel. "I suppose that leaves us, then. What're you going to try?"

"I do not see the point of this," he said, gesturing towards the spread of weapons. "I will use my usual daggers. I am not yet perfect with these basics, so why would I move to something else?"

"Suit yourself. I'm going to look for something more exciting."

"I do not understand your obsession with excitement," Daniel said, but he didn't try to stop her.

She picked her way between the different knives and axes and cudgels, waiting for something to grab her attention. After a few moments, a twin-bladed dagger caught her eye; she picked it up and gripped it as she imagined it was supposed to be held, as if the longer blade was the blade of a normal dagger. The shorter blade then pointed down from the base of the handle. Yes, she could think of times when that would be useful for a backwards thrust or an unusual counter. She spun the handle a couple of times between her fingers, wondering if the construction was balanced enough to double as a heavy kind of throwing spike.

"Have you chosen?" Daniel asked.

"Don't be so impatient, I'm coming."

He waited with his weapons held in a high guard, his long dagger in his right hand, the shorter blade in his left. Eleanor's grip tightened on her weapon as she tried to work out how she should use it to best effect. It was like having primary and secondary in one hand; there were advantages, certainly, but her empty hand felt vulnerable.

They edged around one another for a while, making occasional feints but both stopping short of a committed attack. Eleanor couldn't imagine what was holding Daniel back, but she was glad of it; for her own part, the unfamiliarity of the weapon made her hesitate.

And then, as if by some unspoken agreement, they both lunged forwards at once. Their blades locked together, then Eleanor had to twist her arm away in time to use her shorter blade to block his second thrust. Using the one weapon for twice the work felt rushed and wrong at first, but after a couple more exchanges she was beginning to get the hang of it, and the movements finally started to flow. The key, she realised, was not to stop. If she overcommitted to any given direction then she was in trouble, losing valuable time to recover herself, but so long as she kept the twin blades moving smoothly from side to side, she could easily counter both of his knives.

Now, she just had to find a way to turn her parries into a successful counter-attack.

She was sure she was missing something. Daniel was certainly working harder than she was, and there had to be some way to turn it to her advantage, but she couldn't work out how to change her smooth defensive motions into anything that would get past his guard.

What she eventually did felt almost like cheating, using her dual blades to lift Daniel's knives above her head before ducking beneath his arm and tapping him with the stiletto from her wrist-sheath. Even as she relished the victory, she wondered if there was some way she could have done it without resorting to a separate knife.

"May I interrupt?" Ivan's voice disturbed them as they untangled themselves. They looked round in surprise; he must have arrived while they were both fully engrossed in the fight.

"Daniel, I think it's time you tried something a bit less familiar."

Daniel shook his head. "I do not see the point."

"You need to experiment," Ivan said. "I've always said you should try to move outside your comfort zone before you're forced to."

"You have always said we could ignore you," Daniel said. "And I am doing my best, but you make it difficult."

"Okay, as you please." Ivan made no attempt to hide the exasperation in his voice. "Eleanor, I thought you might like to try this."

He held out what looked to be a pair of leather straps, with a very small knife attached.

"What is it?"

"Your new second. Give me your spare hand."

She held out her left hand, still puzzled, and watched as he pulled the straps taut across her palm, causing the flat of the blade to press hard against her skin.

"It's a palm-blade," he explained, still holding her fingers. "It won't get in your way, but when you move like this..."

He raised her arm, then twisted her hand as he brought it down again, causing the knife to slide sideways.

"I like that!"

"I thought you might. And it's perfect backup to a weapon like that harping knife you've got there which, as you've spotted, is only half-useful on its own."

She went to push the palm-blade back into its home position, but Ivan stopped her.

"No, you'll cut your fingers doing that. You just need to flick your wrist." He demonstrated with his own left hand and she copied the movement; the blade slid neatly back into place.

"Have you almost finished?" Daniel asked. "We are wasting time."

Eleanor smiled apologetically at Ivan, and turned back to Daniel. "Ready when you are," she said, and in contrast to their previous bout, she really felt ready this time.

With every exchange of blows she grew more confident with the harping knife, and even managed to touch Daniel with a couple of strikes from the primary blade, though she was pleased with the extra options which the palm-blade gave her for close-range attack.

While everyone else dumped their weapons and disappeared for lunch, Eleanor sat cross-legged on the floor, placed the harping knife by her side, and began to loosen the straps of the palm-blade.

Ivan strolled across and crouched beside her. "How did you get on with that?"

"Fantastic." She slid the straps from her fingers and held it up to him. "Next time I have to ask the smithy for something, I'm getting one of those made, too."

"Keep that one for practice, if you like."

"Really?"

"Sure," he said, pushing it back into her hand. "Well, at least until you get your own."

She smiled, wrapped the straps around the blade, and slipped it into her pocket.

"It certainly suits your style," he said. "And you were getting pretty good with that harping knife, too."

"I can't decide whether I liked it or not," she admitted, picking it up and studying it again. "There are some neat tricks, I suppose, but I think I'd rather have a normal dagger."

"Well, it's all about what you're used to – at least you're not afraid to try a few things out. But look, if you're not rushing off, let me show you how I'd use it."

"I'm not rushing anywhere." She handed him the harping knife and pulled out her own twin daggers.

Suddenly facing the harping knife from the other side, she saw what a very good defensive wall it made, and struggled to find a plausible angle of attack. Maybe that was what had slowed Daniel, even when she'd been unsure how to wield it properly. After she risked her first feint, however, she fell easily into an alternating rhythm, attacking from one side and then the other, constantly trying to slip past before Ivan could swing the next blade across to block her.

Then, he did something she hadn't anticipated.

With one fluid movement he blocked her latest thrust, spun

the harping knife in a fast circle to knock her other dagger clear out of the way before she even started to move towards her next attack, and brought the short blade up beneath her chin before she could recover herself from the surprise.

"And now, I have something else to learn," she said, replaying his movements in her mind. She wondered how quickly she'd be able to replicate that sequence, and whether she could block it if she knew what was coming. "I knew there had to be some good attacks with that thing."

"The thing about hand-to-hand," Ivan said as he stepped back and started to gather up the assorted weapons from the floor, "is that whatever you're holding, you have to treat it as an extension of your body. You have to understand every way you can move your blade, with just the same confidence as you know every way you can move your wrist or your foot."

"That's what makes it so much fun trying different weapons. They don't always do what you expect."

"Just make sure you never lose that attitude," he said. "As long as you're enjoying yourself, you'll always be ahead of those who fight because they have to."

She picked up the harping knife and tried to copy the set of movements he'd performed, but it didn't feel quite right. "What am I doing wrong?" she asked, trying the sequence for a second time.

"Here, it might be easier with an actual opponent." He armed himself with a pair of short daggers and stepped across so she could try the moves against him.

"I'm still not getting it right."

"Looks pretty good to me. You just need to practise a few times."

"No." She shook her head. "It's feeling awkward. I'm copying exactly what you did – or I thought I was – but something's not quite right."

"Maybe that's where you're going wrong. You don't want to copy me too carefully."

At first she thought he was joking, but there was no laughter in his face. "What do you mean?" she asked.

"Everyone has to find their own style, but especially since

you're a woman. Your body's a different shape, you shouldn't expect your joints to work exactly the same as mine. Take my ideas, by all means, but you'll have to find your own execution."

Chapter 23

It was the shortest night of the year when the students were woken by doors banging and raised voices. Eleanor rolled out of bed and grabbed her dagger, then stepped outside to see what was happening; Daniel, Sebastien and Mikhail had evidently had the same thought. It was dark in the common room aside from a glint of moonlight but it was enough to see that, despite their varying degrees of undress, they'd all reached for their weapons.

"Any idea what's going on?" Eleanor asked.

"It sounds like it's coming from upstairs," Mikhail said. "But the second years are meant to be out tonight. Shall we go and look?"

Sebastien opened the door to the corridor, and they fell instinctively into a close formation behind him, with Mikhail walking backwards to watch their backs.

They were about to start up the stairs when Fred came down, bare-chested and tousle-haired, having evidently been roused from his own bed not long before.

"Go back to sleep," he said, waving them away. "You can't possibly be any help."

"What's going on?" Sebastien asked.

"It's nothing you need to be up for, just a bit of an argument over this latest contest. Jon and Victor just got back, and... well, you'll hear soon enough. Nothing to keep you awake."

"It sounded like something," Mikhail said. "It sounded like a riot – or maybe a herd of cattle."

"Just tempers running a bit high, but I think it's calmed down now, for tonight at least. Go back to bed," Fred insisted. "That's where I'm going. You'll hear all about it in the morning, no doubt."

They exchanged puzzled glances but no-one was really in the mood for an argument. At least if it was just some internal upset, there probably wasn't that much reason to lose sleep over it.

"What do you think it could be?" Mikhail asked as they got back to their common room.

"Fighting over who won this contest, by the sound of it," Sebastien said. "Must've been close."

"I do not care for their petty arguments," Daniel muttered. "They should not make so much noise when we are sleeping."

Sebastien lifted the kettle onto the stove. "Well, since we're wide awake now, who wants a drink before we go back to bed?"

They sipped tea and debated what all the fuss could have been about, but without anything on which to hang their speculations, the conversation soon petered out. Daniel was glad of the excuse to mutter about his mistrust of anything to do with Venncastle and its ex-students; the others, tired and somewhat bored, listened in silence. Eventually they reached the end of their drinks, the excitement of being woken had worn off, and they were ready to go back to bed.

Neither Jon nor Victor appeared in the dining hall the next morning, though Eleanor and Mikhail, curious to find out what had happened during the night, arrived early and managed to spin out their breakfast until the bell rang for the morning's unarmed combat session.

As they practised their throws and locks together, they discussed their theories as to what might have happened, and joked about how messy it could be if two of the academy's graduating students got into a serious fight.

At lunch, however, their curiosity was finally satisfied.

"The council can't reach an agreement," Jon was explaining as they arrived in the dining hall. He was sitting with Victor, Fred and Jorge at one end of the table, but his irate tones carried easily across the room. "They're being so bloody slow."

"They can't be seriously suggesting neither of you should get it." Fred sounded upset. "That's ridiculous."

"They're discussing it," Victor said. "They won't rule anything out, and meanwhile we're just left hanging."

"And we're supposed to come to this dinner and act like nothing's wrong," Jon added. "Without knowing if either of us is even going to get on the council. I don't even care which of us they choose, I just think it's stupid that they're taking so long over it."

The graduation dinner would be held in the Association's main banquet hall, and the first years had all been invited along to join the evening's celebrations. After the events of the previous night, however, they were starting to wonder what exactly they'd be celebrating. Tonight was supposed to mark Jon and Victor's transition from academy students into fully-fledged members of the Association, but if the council still hadn't made a decision on their fates, it was going to be a very strange kind of graduation.

They were let out of interrogation early, and advised to change into their formal clothes.

Eleanor went to her room and unfolded her emerald gown. This was the first opportunity she'd had to smarten herself up, and she was looking forwards to dressing like a girl for once; she hadn't worn a skirt since she'd left Gisele's. She tied her hair back and, after only a moment's hesitation, reached under the mattress for her pendant and fastened it around her neck. The gems matched the colour of the dress perfectly, and she wished Raf could be here to see her wear it. She had to wipe away a tear before she ventured out to face the others.

It was a long walk to the Association's main hall, and the first years – with the exception of Fred and Jorge – all traipsed through the woods together, still gossiping about the night's disturbances and whether the council would have made their decision in time for the meal.

A single table in one corner of the capacious banqueting hall was set aside for the students, and they were ushered to their seats past a sea of faces they mostly didn't recognise. At the far end of the hall, the council had a long table to themselves.

There was no sign of Jon or Victor, and Fred and Jorge were also missing.

"Some Venncastle thing is happening," Daniel said. "I do not know what they will do, but they are plotting something."

For once, Eleanor didn't think she could tell him to stop being melodramatic. This precise set of absentees couldn't be a coincidence.

They waited, not wanting to start eating without the guests of honour, and wondered where the Venncastle students could possibly have got to. Mack confirmed that Jorge and Fred hadn't been back to their common room after that afternoon's lesson; no-one had seen Jon or Victor since lunch. The food was kept warm in heated tureens, but eventually someone at the council table got to his feet and announced that they would start the meal regardless, "not wishing to waste this splendid feast by allowing it to spoil, after all the effort our chefs have put into preparing it."

"It's not like Jorge to miss a meal," Eleanor said as she lifted the lid from one of the tureens, releasing a cloud of steam into the air.

"I tell you, they are plotting something," Daniel said.

"More for us," Mikhail added, helping himself to extra bread. "But I'm sure they'll turn up eventually, and then we'll find out if they have been up to anything."

"It is what, not if," Daniel said stubbornly.

The food was, as usual, delicious. They were on to second servings of dessert before Jon and Victor burst in, with Fred and Jorge a few steps behind. Though they weren't obviously armed, they marched like a very small army.

They ignored the student table and strode straight up to where the council were sitting. The room fell silent, waiting.

"We want a decision," Jon said. "Now."

"This is highly irregular," Ragal said softly. The students had to strain to make out his words. "The council is not in session."

"You can't leave us hanging like this."

"The council will not be rushed. There are hard decisions to make, and any decision has implications."

"You can't expect us to just lie down and take this," Victor said. "We can't sit down to dinner and pretend everything's normal."

"We'd rather assumed you weren't going to bother to grace us with your presence at all," Bill said.

"We just want an answer."

"We will not do this lightly," Ragal said. "You will simply

293

have to have patience."

Jorge moved suddenly, pulling his dagger from its sheath and moving to hold it against Ragal's throat. The old man turned at lightning speed, knocking his chair to the floor, then threw Jorge over his shoulder onto the table, pinning him under his own blade.

"You fool," Ragal said, shaking his head. "You're still wet behind the ears, and you really think you can be any threat to someone of my experience? Really? I may be getting old, but I'm not dead yet."

He turned back to the room, and this time projected his voice so everyone could hear him clearly: "I think tonight's celebrations are over."

The first-years didn't need any encouragement to leave, though Jorge and Fred were still at the far end of the room. They walked back to their rooms in stunned silence.

They'd been given a free morning the next day so they could recover from the excesses of the graduation dinner, and after breakfast Eleanor made her way to Ivan's apartment. He opened the door with a whittling knife in one hand and a half-fashioned blowpipe in the other.

"Oh, hi Eleanor, come in," he said, stepping back to let her past. "What can I do for you?"

"Are you busy?"

"Not in a way that matters – I can talk and sculpt at the same time."

"Wouldn't you rather get someone else to make your weapons for you? It must take a very long time."

"Well, I have Harold do my metalwork, but I enjoy the process of making little things now and then. It gives me chance to invent, and I'm sure it keeps me careful with my weapons."

"It would do!"

"Anyway, take a seat... how can I help?"

"If you're sure you have the time, I was just wondering if you could explain what's happening with Jon and Victor. Last night was quite a scene."

"Haven't you heard?"

"Only fragments and rumours. It's very confusing. Everyone's guessing – even them – but you're on the council, so I thought you'd know the truth."

"Well, I can tell you what's happened so far, though the story's far from over." He sat down, and continued to shave slivers of wood from the end of the pipe as he spoke. "In the shortest possible form, neither Jon or Victor succeeded at the task which was set for them, and it was decided that, in these unusual circumstances, neither of them had really earned a seat in the council."

"I get the impression that's quite unusual," Eleanor said, picking her words carefully.

"Unprecedented," Ivan agreed. "And, between you and me, it wasn't a terribly obvious decision. It certainly wasn't unanimous."

"So what's going to happen next? Will there be a fourth contest?"

"At the moment, it seems unlikely, but you never can tell. Right now, it looks most likely that we simply won't co-opt anyone onto the council this year." He set his knife down on the table, and picked up a tiny drill which he began to work into the end of the pipe. "This sets a worrying precedent, and it opens up all sorts of questions. People are asking whether the mission we set was simply too hard, but we shouldn't have to hold back when we're dealing with our graduating students. The final contest is always a task that actually needs doing – we shouldn't have to compromise on that, even if it means that sometimes, no-one succeeds. So you can see why it's a bit fraught."

"Of course."

"It shouldn't have any implications for your year – not yet, anyway. There's always a slight danger of some fool carrying a majority along with the idea that the third contest should be made more structured, but I don't think it's all that likely. There's a long tradition of the summer contest being real. I suspect we're just going to have to put this year down to a bad experience."

"Wouldn't it make more sense to just re-run the contest?"

"That would be my choice, but there are those who'd rather

see the seat empty than let another Venncastle man on the council, and because of that they'll block anything that gives Jon and Victor a second chance. You remember what I told you about the school – and there are plenty who resent us for the ways in which we're unique."

"Like Daniel."

Ivan nodded. "He's not alone. There are plenty who feel we're taking over, even while they recognise the benefits our men bring to the Association."

"And are you? Taking over?"

"Not in the slightest. It seems popular to believe that Venncastle is trying to reform the Association into the image of its old army – but if we'd wanted to maintain our army, we could've simply refused the Empire in the first place. I think the current setup works for everyone, except those here who feel threatened by our numbers."

"It's good for us to have a school that guarantees to send a couple of good candidates each year," Eleanor said. "It must be."

"Not least because we know they'll turn up," Ivan said. "The Association loses good people every year, just because we don't tell them we're expecting them."

"I thought that was the whole point. You have to be determined enough to turn down your assignment."

"If you screen the students well enough, you can find kids who you know are going to be fine. At Venncastle, we're not afraid to point those boys in the right direction." He blew the loose wood shavings from his pipe, and began to work his drill into the next hole. "You don't want to leave too much to chance."

"Don't you think that's sort of cheating?"

"Perhaps it technically is. But the school at Venncastle is as old as the Empire, and the Association is much older – I see it as an echo of the past. Before the Assessors invented all these complex metrics for schools to evaluate every facet of every child's life, the Association just went and picked out the boys they wanted."

"But it does give ammunition to those who worry that you're

making your own rules."

"I suppose so, yes." He watched her for a moment. "The thing is, Eleanor, making your own rules is part of this game. Anyone who says otherwise is living in a dream – and might not be living at all for much longer, if they let their ideals cloud their judgement. Please don't let them fool you into copying their mistakes."

She laughed. "I think I can make enough mistakes all on my own."

"Well, that's how you learn. Make them early and often, and there's less to go wrong when it matters. But there's a world of difference between the occasional missed opportunity and a completely flawed perspective. I just don't want you to be sucked in by their dangerous idealism."

Chapter 24

Eleanor had forgotten what day it was until Sebastien reminded her, as they finished their morning combat session, that she'd better get cleaned up quickly – it was the day after the equinox, this year's new students would already have arrived, and they were expected to introduce themselves over lunch. Eleanor washed as fast as she was able and ran down to the dining hall with her hair still dripping, but despite her best efforts she was last to the table and had to settle for a seat with her back to the door.

She was looking forward to seeing the new faces, hoping their awe and excitement would remind her how she'd felt a year ago. Things were starting to feel serious for the academy's older students, with contests looming just over the horizon and the shadow of Jon and Victor's failure still hanging over them. A little fresh enthusiasm might help her to stop worrying about the challenges ahead, at least for a while.

The door clicked open almost silently, and several sets of footsteps came to a halt. "And here we have the second years," said a voice which Eleanor recognised as Victor's. She wondered how different it must feel for the new intake, coming into a room *full* of older students compared to only two when she'd arrived.

"I'd recognise that hair anywhere," said a second, equally familiar voice, and Eleanor felt a hand rest lightly on her shoulder.

She turned, her eyes widening in recognition.

"Raf!" she cried, jumping to her feet. "You're alive!" Instinctively she threw her arms around his neck, but withdrew quickly and awkwardly when she realised everyone was watching them. She felt the heat rise in her cheeks, and saw he was also blushing. "Sorry," she muttered.

"Don't be," he said, suddenly beaming at her. "I'm alive. Better than that – look at me, I'm doing great!"

Obediently, she studied him. He had the same dark features, the same choppy black hair, and he was still stick-thin though he'd grown even taller in the last year. And he looked much better, naturally, now that he wasn't bruised and bleeding and starving. Only a couple of thin scars, snaking across his cheek and along his jaw, remained to show the pain they'd been through together.

She wanted to reach out and run her finger along the scars, remembering the way she'd tended those wounds, remembering the feel of his skin under her hands. But she was already conscious of the way the others were staring.

She beckoned him to sit beside her, but he shook his head.

"I have to catch up with Victor – and little Jorgie and Freddie were only kids last time I saw them." Seeing the look of disappointment on her face, he winked at her and added, "Better for us to talk later, privately."

She found herself blushing again as he went to take a seat with Jorge, Fred, Victor, and a couple of other newcomers. All through the decadent five-course meal she found herself watching him out of the corner of her eye, leaving Mikhail and Sebastien to carry the conversation with the new students who sat beside her.

He's alive!

As she played half-heartedly with her food, listening to the jocular exchanges between the Venncastle boys, she told herself she was just relieved that he was okay – that her burning desire to talk to him was mere curiosity about what he'd been up to over the intervening months. But that would have to wait.

Eleanor hadn't even caught the names of all the new students by the time they got up to go to the afternoon's poisons lesson. They had a new instructor for the second year, a towering, broad-shouldered man, his copper hair flecked with grey, who introduced himself as Albert.

Eleanor struggled to pay attention to the class, and he got very frustrated with her lack of focus, but somehow she just couldn't bring herself to concentrate on slow-acting venoms.

She was relieved when the end of the lesson finally arrived. Remembering the structure of their own introductory day the previous year, Eleanor guessed that Raf would be free until dinner – hoping he'd be using the time to settle in and unpack, she set off to find him. There weren't many student rooms at the academy, so she tried one common room at random, where puzzled first-years pointed her along the corridor to the next suite. She felt sick with nerves as she pushed the door open.

"Hey! It's Raf's girl!" The lad who called out was one of those who'd sat with the Venncastle group at lunch; from his confidence, Eleanor wondered if he was also from the same school. "Come in, we'll fetch your boyfriend."

He didn't need to do anything, though – hearing the commotion, Raf emerged from his room.

"What are you kids up to?" he asked, then caught sight of Eleanor hovering by the door. "Ellie! Come in! They haven't been bothering you, have they?"

"No, it's fine," she said, but she shot a fierce glare at the younger lad as she followed Raf into his room.

He steered her into the only chair, grabbed a bottle and two glasses from his shelf, and settled himself on the bed. "Sorry about earlier," he said, pouring out two helpings of bright red juice. "Here, try this, you'll love it. Venncastle's famous spring nectar."

She took a mouthful, then coughed as the drink caught her throat unexpectedly; it was not merely juice, and the alcohol burned.

"Didn't mean to brush you off," he continued. "But the Venncastle crowd are a bit of an institution here, you'd probably noticed – two new kids this year as well as me. So I thought I'd best get that bit out of the way first, and we can talk better here."

"You guessed I'd come and find you?"

"I'd have tracked you down if you hadn't come – I'm not scared of venturing into second year rooms! Do you like the drink?"

"It's strong," she said, sipping at it again.

"Oh, that's just because you're not used to it. I've been drinking this at school since I was ten – I finally managed to find a stall in town that sells it."

"So..." Eleanor took another cautious mouthful of the drink. "So how are you?" It was the question she'd wanted to ask all day, but she was scared of what the answer might be. She'd never quite stopped feeling guilty for leaving him in Taraska.

"Oh, I'm fine. Seriously," he said when he caught her worried expression, "I've been absolutely great. Got back to the Empire, nipped round all the clues again to get the new numbers, and I've been living in Almont for half a year just waiting for that blasted door to open."

"I thought you were dead!" she cried, half-sobbing. "When you weren't here – I thought they must've found you. I thought... horrible things. Too horrible."

He moved to put a comforting arm around her shoulder as she dissolved into tears. She clasped desperately at his collar, wondering why everything she'd felt over the last couple of years had to come flooding out now, after she'd managed to hold herself together for so long. It should have been a happy reunion, but she couldn't stem the tears.

"It's okay," he said, stroking her hair. "I've been worried about you, too – there was no easy way to find out if you'd made it through, from out there."

Even as her tears subsided she clung to him, nestling comfortably against his chest, his arms resting reassuringly across her back. She could feel the throb of his heart against her ear, a tangible proof that he was still very much alive, and she didn't want to let go. She didn't know how long they sat there but eventually he prised her away from him, noting that they'd probably already missed dinner.

"I'm sorry," she said, swallowing down the last of her juice in one gulp and wiping her eyes on her sleeve. "I didn't mean to cry on you."

"It's okay. Really. But you see why it's better to catch up on our own."

She nodded, blushing, ashamed to imagine what her classmates would have thought if she'd cried like this over lunch. "Let's go and see if the kitchen has any leftovers," she suggested.

They found a pot of soup bubbling gently. Eleanor filled

bowls for both of them, lit a candle from the embers of the fire, and led Raf to sit in the deserted dining hall. It felt even bigger than usual as the flickering candlelight magnified the shadows.

They ate in silence, both delighted to know the other was alive, but neither of them wanting to spoil the evening by starting the only conversation they really needed to have. The painful stories could wait.

"Tomorrow's free," Eleanor said as they were finishing their soup. "We could do something – maybe a walk? I could show you round."

"Well, I have to see the smith and the tailor, I think, but otherwise..." He smiled broadly at her. "Yes, that'd be nice."

They washed out their bowls and walked back to the sleeping quarters together.

"Come and find me tomorrow?" Eleanor suggested, trying to sound more relaxed than she felt. "Just as soon as you're done with the fittings."

"I'll do that."

He gave her a brief hug before they went their separate ways for the night, and she almost skipped back to her room. Considering how long she'd spent simply crying, the evening hadn't turned out too badly. Raf was alive, he didn't hate her for leaving him in that state, and he was going to spend the next day with her... yes, it could have been much worse.

The next morning she got up for breakfast as early as usual, but a combination of eating slowly and going back for second and third helpings enabled her to loiter in the dining hall for much longer than she normally did, hoping she'd happen to run into Raf. By the time everyone else had been and gone, however, she had to accept that maybe he wasn't actually going to bother with breakfast. Feeling a little disappointed, she headed back to her room.

"You're running a bit late this morning," Mikhail teased when she finally reached the common room. "Do you want to get outside and do some target practice?"

"Not today," she said, though she would have loved to experiment with her throwing stars after the latest techniques Ivan had demonstrated. She'd already decided that she'd have to settle for the practice board in the common room this morning, and hopefully Raf would be along soon enough.

"You are being strange," Daniel said, staring at her. "Are you ill?"

"No, I'm fine." She was reluctant to explain; somehow she didn't think they'd understand. For the first time since she'd left school, Eleanor caught herself wishing for some female company. The girls would have known how she was feeling with barely a word of explanation necessary.

Once the others had gone outside she combed her hair, and stained her lips with a few berries from the fruit bowl in the common room – a trick she'd learnt at school, though she'd never had much use for it before.

She spent the morning flinging stars carelessly at the target board, quickly growing bored with the limited options of indoor practice. She tried to entertain herself by taking shots under her leg, backwards over her shoulder, or with her eyes closed, but her heart wasn't really in it. She looked towards the door at every sound, waiting, but Raf hadn't appeared by the time the others came in for lunch and she felt silly as she joined them in the dining hall. She'd missed a whole morning's practice, and for what?

"Did you have a good morning?" Daniel asked, looking intently at her.

"Very productive," she lied. "I've been catching up on poisons."

"Do you need some help this afternoon?"

She realised she'd picked the wrong lie to tell; Daniel wouldn't want to miss the opportunity to show off.

"No, thanks," she said. "I think I'm getting there, and I'll understand it better if I manage it on my own."

"Are you sure?"

"Certain," she said shortly. Poisons might not be her strongest subject, but she didn't want to give him any more reasons to be smug.

They sat in awkward silence through lunch, then Eleanor returned to the common room while the others headed outside again. After her thoughtless lie she was going to be under a lot of pressure in the next poisons class, so she sat down to flick through her notes. Why did Daniel have to be so outstandingly brilliant at her worst subject? She wouldn't have cared if it was anyone else, but he'd been insufferable lately.

She flicked first to the list of common natural venoms, which she'd copied out alongside their antivenoms where any existed. Those with no known antidote had always struck her as the most interesting, but there was also less to learn: know the effects, handle with caution, and administer with subtlety. Knowledge of antivenoms and their interactions, on the other hand, could be handy in a tight spot – though Eleanor maintained a silent conviction that it was better to avoid being poisoned in the first place.

She'd read nearly all the notes she'd ever made – and it was almost time for dinner – by the time Raf finally let himself into her common room.

"I'm so sorry," he said as he closed the door behind him. "I feel awful, I've wasted your day. I just got caught up in practice." He held up a shiny throwing knife by way of an explanation. "I wasn't expecting to actually get a new knife today. I'm really sorry."

She gave him a reluctant smile; she did understand, she'd have felt the same with a new blade. She went over to examine the knife. Unsurprisingly for one of Harold's, it was well made: very solid and well-balanced, though it was boringly plain in its design.

"Nice," she agreed. Though not as pretty as the ones they'd bought in Taraska; she wondered if he still had those weapons.

"Shall we have that walk before dinner?" He opened the door to let her pass.

"You must be hungry," she said, looking up at him as they started down the corridor. "You missed breakfast and lunch."

"I just got carried away. Besides, we know what hunger really means, and 'only' one hot meal today doesn't qualify."

It was true; she realised with a pang of guilt that she'd become spoilt since moving into the academy. In some ways it was just like being at school again, with three meals cooked for them each day and all their laundry and cleaning taken care of.

She knew she was getting lazy and pampered here, despite the rigorous training schedule.

They walked twice round the outside of the academy buildings, mostly in silence, just enjoying one another's company.

"Tell me what happened," Eleanor said as they began their third circuit.

"It's not much of a story."

"Tell me anyway."

"Well." He hooked his arm through hers as they walked. "You know the state I was in when you left me."

"Sorry," she murmured.

He shook his head, and squeezed her arm. "No need to apologise. We did exactly what we needed to do. I passed out after you left – I'd lost a lot of blood. The landlord fixed me up, and he bought me some herbs that were *very* good for the pain, but not so good for my mind. I must have spent a few months stupefied by whatever it was, before the money ran out and supply, unsurprisingly, dried up."

"That's why you missed the equinox? You were drugged?"

"It was good stuff," he said. "Couldn't feel a thing... made it very hard to tell when I was better, and no-one else was bothering to tell me, so long as they could keep taking my money. Bloody Tarasanka profit-mongers!"

"So how did you get back, if you'd run out of money?"

"Oh, just stowed away. Not that hard, really – loads of space on those smuggler ships, there's always some gap ready for the next haul, they just took a somewhat roundabout route home. Now come on," he interrupted himself as they reached the door of their living quarters again. "We'd better go inside or we'll miss dinner."

When they reached the dining hall, they found that most of the others had already been and gone; they sat with one of Raf's Venncastle colleagues, the younger lad who'd teased Eleanor the previous day, who turned out to be called Greg.

"So when did the academy start taking girls?" he asked almost as soon as they sat down with steaming bowls of sausage casserole. "Or are you just an exception because you're

Raf's girl? Where did you pick up a girl like that from anyway, Raf?"

Raf and Eleanor looked at each other, exchanging raised eyebrows and amused smiles.

"We met on the other side of the world," Raf said. "Where we had a thoroughly enjoyable time being tortured."

Greg looked at Eleanor and she nodded her confirmation, enjoying the astonishment in his eyes as he realised it wasn't a joke.

"But still," he blustered, trying to recover himself. "Girls at the academy? When did that happen?"

"When I arrived and let myself in."

His expression froze. "So it really is just you?"

"Just me."

He considered this for a moment, then broke into a broad grin. "Raf, you're a jammy sod! Well done!"

Raf laughed, and Eleanor wondered if he was ever planning to correct the assumption that she was his girlfriend. Maybe he wanted it to be true? She wasn't even sure how anyone knew whether they were going to be girlfriend and boyfriend – though she was fairly sure that Raf was the closest she'd ever come to it. But being locked in a cell together had hardly been a matter of choice for either of them.

"Well, I'll leave you to it," Greg said with a wink as he got up from the table.

Once Eleanor and Raf had both eaten their fill of the casserole – to her amusement, he went back for second and third helpings – they started back towards their sleeping quarters.

"Was that true?" he asked as they climbed the stairs. "Or were you just teasing Greg?"

"What?"

"That they only started accepting girls because you arrived."

"Oh, I'm sure that's true," she said. "They weren't expecting me."

"Well done!" He clapped his hand onto her shoulder. "I'm impressed."

"Why?" It was a silly thing to be impressed by. "You knew I

was coming here. And you've seen me hold my own in a fight."

"I'm not surprised you got in! But I warned you they might be a bit old-fashioned here – and they've let you stay, and by all accounts you're doing great."

"Not everyone likes it." She didn't want to say that it seemed to be some of his old schoolmates who were the most hostile towards her, particularly Jorge – and she certainly wasn't going to mention her earlier crisis of confidence.

"Well, you just have to win the contests, don't you? Once you've got that council seat, there's nothing anyone can do."

She couldn't help smiling; it was sweet of him to so blithely assume that she could win.

"So I've told you what I've been up to – when do I get to hear the rest of your story?" he asked, pausing as they reached the end of his corridor.

"You're going to be so busy for the next few days – like this morning but worse!" She'd felt lonely while she was waiting, but now she could joke about it without any bad feeling – and his rueful smile said he understood.

"I don't even have my timetable yet."

"So why don't you just drop in next time you happen to have a free evening?"

He nodded his agreement, and she gave him a quick hug before running up the next flight of stairs to the second year rooms. She knew her slight breathlessness as she reached the common room wasn't down to the exertion of climbing the steps.

"Eleanor!" Daniel called out to her before she could let herself into her bedroom. She turned to face him, annoyed to have her thoughts interrupted. "You have been talking to that Raf again?"

"Yes."

"You should be careful."

"Of what?" she asked, beginning to wish she'd just ignored him.

"He is one of them," Daniel said. "Venncastle. They are not to be trusted."

"Raf and I faced death together in Taraska."

She moved to leave the conversation but he stepped across in front of her, blocking her way.

"Nevertheless..."

"I trust him. Okay?"

"It is not okay, Eleanor, he is..."

"You can't tell me who my friends are!" she interrupted, furious now.

"I try only to protect you."

"Well, don't!" She glared at him, silently daring him to tell her that she needed protecting. Just because she was the only girl at the academy – did he really think she was so weak? He'd never have tried to 'protect' the others.

He gave a casual shrug. "You do as you wish," he said, then turned and strode from the room before she had chance to respond.

"I will," she muttered, glowering after him as he walked away.

Mikhail's door opened, and he peered out into the common room. "You okay?" he asked Eleanor.

"He needs to stop interfering."

Mikhail grinned broadly. "Aw, he only does it 'cause he likes you."

"Really?" Eleanor's voice was icy. She didn't even want it to be true. "Well, he needs to learn to show it!" She turned and walked purposefully into her room, slamming the door behind her.

Chapter 25

Only a few days after the new first years had arrived, the older students were summoned after dinner one evening to have the rules of the upcoming contest explained to them. A spidery, silver-haired man was waiting for them – Eleanor recognised him as the same man who had presided over the council the first time she'd been called into this room. He was alone in the council chamber when they arrived.

"Sit," he said, indicating the empty seats around the table. "This will be the first and last time most of you will take a seat in this room, so make the most of it."

He waited for the students to sit, and an expectant silence fell over the room.

"My name is Ragal. This is our council chamber, and in a little under a year, one of you will take up a seat here. You are here today so that I may explain this process." He stopped and turned sharply to the two Venncastle youths, who were whispering together. "Do you have something to say?"

Fred shook his head, but Jorge said, "What about Jon and Victor?"

"What about them?"

"One of *them* should've got a seat. Don't know how we can trust you if you can change the rules like that."

"Last year was a special case, and we will not discuss it. Two students is not a large pool to choose from."

"But–"

"That is the end of the matter," Ragal said firmly. "We will not discuss it. You are here so that I may explain the rules which will govern your lives for the next nine months."

He waited until he was sure the interruptions were over before continuing.

"There will be three contests, spaced across the year on the next three festivals. Much like the three tests you completed before you could enter here, the contests will each have a different emphasis, requiring a particular quality or skill. However, the style is different. Each of the admission tests demanded one particular solution of you. In the challenges to come, you will be free to choose your own approach."

The students listened silently; even Jorge was too absorbed to pursue his objections.

"In the winter contest, to be held on the shortest day, there will be three points awarded to whoever comes first, two points for second place, and one point for third. The spring contest will be harder, but the top three students will earn four, three, and two points respectively. The summer contest will be different. In the summer, only the top three students will compete, and there will be only one winner who will take up his seat in this chamber."

"What if there's a tie?" Fred asked.

"A tie in the final contest would be decided by points from the earlier rounds, but it has never happened. Now, you may wish to know the nature of the winter contest, since you have less than three months to prepare."

They all nodded.

"On the day of the solstice there will be a tournament. As there are nine of you, you'll be divided into three groups of three, and each of you will fight against the other two within your group. The three winners will progress to a final round to fight for the available points. Questions?"

Paul raised his hand. "What kind of fighting?"

"Normal hand-to-hand rules. Full leather armour, two weapons of your choice, but no throwing or projectiles."

To decide the groups for the first round, all their names were inscribed on small wooden blocks and shuffled in an old cloth bag.

"The first group," Ragal said, giving the bag an extra shake before dipping his hand in, "will be... Charles... Jorge... and Mikhail."

He passed across the blocks to show he hadn't fixed the draw, then proceeded to pick the next three names. Eleanor was drawn against Sebastien and Paul, and the final group consisted of Mack, Fred and Daniel. The students looked around the room, viewing their new competitors in a different light now.

Eleanor fell into step with Mikhail as they walked back to their rooms. "I don't stand a chance," she said. "No throwing... that's a harsh rule."

"They don't want you to kill us all." Mikhail laughed as he spoke. "I wouldn't want to be up against you if you were allowed to throw knives at me, those things can do some serious damage."

She shrugged. "You're not in my group anyway."

"No, I've got Jorge – that's worse!"

Daniel turned sharply to face them. "Do not expect he will play fair."

"No." Eleanor thought back to the first time she'd faced Jorge in the ring. "He's not subtle, though, is he? You'll be able to see what's coming. Who're you most worried about, Daniel?"

He paused for a moment, thinking. "Maybe you."

"I meant in your group! I don't even think I'll get to the final."

"You are better than you think," he said. "You are unpredictable – and you have an easy group in the first round, so you will have more energy for later."

Sebastien twisted his face into an expression of mock indignation and Eleanor had to clap one hand to her mouth to keep from laughing out loud, but if Daniel even noticed he showed no sign of it.

"I'm going to wind down with a little target practice," Eleanor said once they got back to the common room. "Develop some of these skills I'm not allowed to use. Anyone else?"

Daniel and Sebastien made their excuses and went straight to bed.

"Oh, why not?" Mikhail went to set up the target board while Eleanor unsheathed her knives.

They were taking turns to flick knives at the board when Raf threw the door open.

"Ellie – put that knife down! We're going out. Are you coming?"

She shuffled uncomfortably. "I have to practise. And sleep."

"You're not at school any more. Come on – it'll be fun."

"Where are you going?" she said, thinking it couldn't hurt to ask.

"Fred knows a tavern that sells the spring nectar – that's the drink I gave you, that we used to have at school. So we thought we might start there."

"I really shouldn't..."

"Come on," he interrupted her. "It's a free day tomorrow, and we'll get you back in time for bed."

Mikhail looked on with amusement as Raf scooped Eleanor up in his arms and carried her into the corridor. She kicked half-heartedly against him but allowed him to carry her down to where the others were waiting, where he lowered her to the ground.

"Bringing your girlfriend, Raf?" Greg asked.

Raf glowered down at him. "Is there a problem?"

"No problem," he said quickly.

Jorge looked darkly at Eleanor but said nothing, Fred mumbled a brief hello, and the other youth introduced himself as Nate, the third Venncastle student in the new intake. They all headed out into the darkness, and Eleanor matched her pace to Raf's long strides. They walked a little way behind the others and she hoped they wouldn't be too resentful of her tagging along.

"How are we going to get out of the academy?" she asked as they walked across the lawns; she'd assumed they would have left by the passage she'd arrived through, but of course the door was supposed to be locked except on the equinox.

"Haven't you been out?" he asked, astonished. "In a whole year?"

"No – I've been studying, I've been busy..." As she spoke she realised how pathetic she must sound to him.

"You've languished in your room all year? Honestly, what's happened to you?"

She thought back to how she'd met him in Taraska; of course she must have seemed quite adventurous to have ended up there, but didn't he realise it had just been a string of particularly strange co-incidences?

"So which way are we going?" she asked, hoping to change

the subject. "Where's this tavern?"

"It's over at the east side of town."

She thought back to the time she'd spent in Almont. "Near the cattle market?"

"That's right."

Raf slipped his arm around her waist as they walked and she edged gradually closer, enjoying the warmth of his body next to hers on the chilly autumn evening. They cut through the forest, and had to hike across a couple of fields before they came to the southern outskirts of the city. They cut briefly across a corner of the Marble Quarter, which almost glowed in the moonlight, then into the scruffier lanes of the east side.

The inn was tucked away down a narrow side-street, but despite the improbable location it was heaving with customers, and a few youths drinking from large tankards also leaned against the walls outside.

Raf held the door open and ushered Eleanor inside. A few low benches provided seating at the edges of the room, but most of the clientele were standing with their drinks.

"Did you say you've been here before?" he asked Fred once they'd caught up with the others, who were already collecting drinks from the bar.

"Just once," Fred replied, passing across two large glasses of the bright red juice. "But we had to come back."

"Of course," Raf agreed. "Do they have links to school, then?"

"We didn't find out. More likely someone just sold the recipe, isn't it?"

"I found a little stall that sells it by the bottle, too," Raf said. "I'll show you if we come out on market day, but I've got stocks in my room."

"We'll all be coming to your room, then," Nate laughed.

Eleanor took a cautious mouthful, determined not to let the burning sensation catch her by surprise this time.

"Ellie's not used to the alcohol – are you?" Raf said when he noticed how carefully she was sipping the drink.

She blushed, hoping no-one would notice in the dim light of the tavern, and shook her head.

"I heard you threatened to kill anyone who calls you 'Ellie'," Fred said thoughtfully.

"Did you?" Raf looked at her in surprise.

"I don't think I quite said that! Probably what you heard is that I overreacted once, which is certainly true, but I was a bit worked up already. I'm not generally homicidal."

Fred shrugged and turned back to pick up his drink from the bar, but Raf wasn't prepared to let the subject drop so easily.

"Would you prefer me to call you something else?" he asked, moving her a few steps away from the others.

"No!" She realised she'd almost cried out her response, and forced her voice back to a more reasonable level before she continued. "Honestly, no. It's just that you're the only person who's ever really called me that, and then Mikhail used it just when I'd found out you weren't here and I thought you were dead... It wasn't a good day."

"But you don't mind? I can call you 'Eleanor' if you prefer."

"No, I like it when you say it, that's..." She struggled for an appropriate word. "It's what I'm used to."

"If you're sure."

She nodded. He put his arm around her shoulders and steered her round to where the others were chatting about the upcoming contest.

"I've got an easy first round," Fred was saying. "Daniel's more of a theorist, and we know Mack's weaknesses. So I expect I'll see you in the final, right Jorge?"

"Should think so," Jorge agreed.

"Who do you think's going to win your group, Eleanor?" Fred asked her.

"I'm not sure."

Raf squeezed her shoulder. "No need for false modesty, Ellie. We're all friends here."

"I don't really know how Paul fights," she said. "I can take out Sebastien on a good day, but you know I'm stronger over distance."

"Oh, come on! You had those Tarasanka bastards over a barrel – you can handle a couple of students."

"Was that when you were tortured?" Nate asked, his eyes

314

glinting with eager curiousity. "What was it like?"

Eleanor gripped Raf's hand and thought how much she prefered it when people decided she was scary or maybe slightly insane – in any case, not worth pestering with questions. These young Venncastle lads were a bit too familiar and much too inquisitive.

"I don't think we want to spoil our evening talking about that kind of thing," Raf said.

"You won, didn't you?" Jorge asked. "What's the problem?"

"Maybe if I sliced your face open," Raf said, and reached out to trace a mirror of his own scar across Jorge's cheek as he spoke, "we could see how you like it. Or," – he lightened his tone – "we could just enjoy our drinks and not think about that sort of thing."

"No need to be like that about it." Jorge took a large swig of his drink, and the group fell into awkward silence.

"Who wants to find somewhere with music?" Raf asked as they started getting towards the end of their drinks. He looked straight at Eleanor. "I know you can dance."

She blushed, remembering that night in Taraska when she'd danced as though her life depended on it. She'd forgotten he'd been watching her then, and she felt a little embarrassed that he'd seen her make such a public display of herself.

"I'll come wherever you like," she said.

"Anyone else?"

"You two should go ahead – wouldn't want to crowd you," Greg said, giving Eleanor a meaningful look which made the colour rise to her cheeks again. "We might catch you later."

She swallowed the rest of her drink and allowed Raf to lead her through the moonlit streets to another, larger tavern. A cheery number from the string quartet drifted out through the windows, someone was singing, and inside a number of couples were twirling on the dancefloor.

Still outside in the moonlight, Raf linked his hands behind her head and she held his shoulders to steady herself as she felt the effects of the alcohol in her blood, moving gently to a rhythm far less frenetic than the ones she'd danced to in Taraska. A light breeze ruffled her shirt and she shivered.

"You mustn't let them bother you," he said, stroking her hair as they swayed in time to the music. "They're just kids. They don't get it."

"I know." She moved a little closer and leaned her head on his shoulder. "I really don't want to talk about it."

"So long as you know it's not personal. And you will be in that final at the tournament. You know you can always come and find me if you need someone to practise with."

"Thanks."

They danced outside for a couple of songs, then went inside to get something to drink. The others never joined them but they danced and drank, drank and danced until the music stopped, and they realised with some surprise that they were the last customers left in the tavern.

Dawn was breaking by the time they stumbled back to the academy, and as Eleanor fell into bed she wondered how long it would be before her roommates woke her ready for another day of training.

By the time she crawled out of bed, though, the sun was high in the sky and the others had gone out without her; going down to the dining hall, she found she was early for lunch rather than late for breakfast, and sat down alone to eat.

"Where have you been?" Daniel asked her when he and Mikhail came in, sweaty and tired-looking, from a morning of sparring in the woods.

"I was resting." She didn't like the accusatory tone in his voice. She could hardly deny that she'd been a bit lazy, but he had no right to call her on it.

"You must've stayed out very late." Mikhail winked at her. She tried to signal him to shut up, but it was too late. "I didn't hear you come in."

"Were you out last night?" Daniel asked. "Where did you go?"

"Into town. But I don't really see how that's any of your business." She looked down at her food and rammed her fork fiercely into a sausage.

"You cannot think only of yourself."

"I need a break sometimes – not that you'd understand that.

316

We're not all as obsessive as you."

"And to be fair," Mikhail added, "we were training right up until he actually carried her out of the room."

"Who did?"

Eleanor shot a furious glance at Mikhail but immediately regretted it. It wasn't his fault that Daniel was such an intolerable jerk.

"Raf," she said flatly. Keeping the evening's events secret was clearly not going to work, so she'd have to take a more pre-emptive tack. "I went out with Raf and his friends from Venncastle last night, we had a great time, and it has absolutely nothing to do with you."

Daniel shook his head. "It concerns everyone if you are socialising with the enemy."

"The *enemy*?" There was no way she could hide her incredulity. "Enemy? Really?! You don't even know what that means."

"Even with our first contest on the horizon, you still are so naïve. You will never be one of them, you know. They may use you but they will never accept you."

She got to her feet. "You've been spouting rubbish like this all year, but Raf stood back-to-back with me against a real enemy, so you'll have to forgive me I don't actually care what you've got to say about it."

She turned on her heel and stormed from the room, leaving her meal unfinished on the table.

Raf was standing in the lake when she managed to track him down, splashing around in the shallows with a few of his classmates and generally making the most of a pleasant afternoon.

He waved when he spotted her. "Hey Ellie! Are you coming in?"

She shook her head, but slipped off her shoes and walked across the damp shale to talk to him. "I wanted to take you up on your offer, if you meant it."

"What, a bit of practice?" He waded towards her as he spoke. "Any time, no problem."

"Any time, as in now?"

"Why don't you come in for a swim first?"

"Oh, I didn't bring anything to change into."

He reached up and pulled hard on her arm, causing her to fall with a heavy splash; she could hear the others laughing as she got to her feet again.

"Now you're already wet," Raf said, a broad grin on his face. "You might as well stay in for a bit."

She couldn't help smiling back. "Race you to the island, then," she said, starting to swim before she even finished the sentence.

He dived after her, but she thought she was getting away until she felt his hand close around her ankle and he pulled her back, stopping her in the water until he could move up beside her.

"Cheat!" she cried, spluttering as her mouth filled with water.

He laughed, released her leg, and pushed himself through the water again. She watched as he sped on with powerful strokes, then sculled across to join him on the rocks.

"Are you okay?" he asked, extending his hand to help her up.

"I'm fine."

"You looked like you had something on your mind."

"Oh, it's just Daniel. He's being an absolute nightmare since you turned up," she said, scrambling out of the water. The wet clothes clung to her skin and her hair was dripping down her back. "He's got a thing about Venncastle. He's always been funny around Fred and Jorge, but he really can't deal with the fact that you're my friend."

"He's from Hess, right?"

"That's right."

Raf nodded. "They hate us, it goes way back. They're just bitter that while they rolled over and agreed to Charan's every idea from the first, the garrison of Flying Rock negotiated a few concessions in exchange for their support. Speaking of school – did you go last year, before you came here?"

"Yes, though I had to break in before anyone would listen to me."

"You did what?" He allowed himself to fall backwards into

the lake, laughing so hard she was almost afraid he might drown. "Oh, Ellie, you really are quite something!"

She waited for him to recover himself before saying, "Well, they wouldn't let me in, what was I supposed to do?"

"Couldn't you just leave a message with the guards?" He pulled himself back up onto the rocks. "That's all I was suggesting."

"They weren't taking me seriously. Honestly, the guards at your school are about the most awkward, intransigent people I've ever met – so I went up the cliff instead."

"That's priceless. I don't know if anyone's ever broken into the school before – wait till I tell the others!"

She shook her head. "Please don't."

"Why not? It's a fantastic story!"

"Really, I'd just rather you didn't give anyone any more reasons to be suspicious of me."

He shrugged. "Well, if you like. You have to tell me everything though."

"Later. You promised me some practice."

"Come on, then." He dived into the water and started back towards the shore. "What weapons are you going to use for the tournament?"

She kicked hard to keep up with him. "I haven't decided."

"Well, from what I know of your style you'll want your stiletto or maybe your palm-blade as second... what else are you carrying today?"

"A couple of throwers – that's no use – and a hunting knife." She made a quick check of her pockets as they reached the shallows. "That's all."

"Well, you can try with that, though you'll probably want a longer primary for the tournament. Still, shall we have a play?" He strode across to his clothes, dried himself quickly and tossed the towel to Eleanor.

"What am I up against?"

"Oh, I'll use a pair of daggers," he said, voice slightly muffled as he pulled his shirt over his head. "You'll see a lot of people choosing that, and it's a solid combination, though personally I think it's a bit boring."

Eleanor squeezed as much water as she could from her hair and her clothes, glad that she'd picked out a lightweight tunic that morning, and spread Raf's towel across a large rock where it could dry in the sun. She armed herself with the hunting knife in her right hand and her stiletto in her left, and turned to find Raf already waiting for her a few feet away from the shore.

He dropped into a low stance as she approached, and blocked her first couple of strikes much too easily.

"Bill hasn't got you practising with wooden daggers, then?" she asked as she made a third attempt to get past his guard.

"Oh, he has! But that's only in that one class. It'd be silly to lose the feel of a real knife in your hand."

He stepped to her left and flicked his dagger sideways, forcing her to twist out of his way as she blocked, but she ducked under his arm and came up beside him, her body pressed against his chest and her stiletto against his neck.

"Or the feel of a real blade against your throat, for that matter," he laughed, giving her a quick hug before she lowered the knife. "Though it's still very different when you trust the hand that holds the knife."

"I don't think I could ever forget what that feels like for real," she said. "Just like I'll never forget what it's like to have someone *really* want to kill me, even though it's been over a year."

"No," he agreed. "And it's not something they can teach, is it? However hard they try."

Chapter 26

Eleanor added a little powdered charcoal to her beaker, but it just formed lumps floating in the liquid, which was almost certainly not what was meant to happen. She cursed under her breath, and promised herself that once she'd graduated she'd get someone else to prepare her poisons for her. It was all very well that they needed to learn how to use the different mixtures, but if she had to make them herself she'd just be condemned to perpetually amateur results.

Daniel, to her left, was too engrossed in his own perfect concoction to pay attention to her troubles. She scanned the room and caught Fred's eye, the only other person who didn't have his head bent over the desk in quiet concentration. He mimed falling asleep, and she had to bite her lip to stop herself laughing.

With an exaggerated sigh, she turned back to breaking up the little black clumps floating in her beaker. By the end of the class she had something resembling a paste, though it was still lumpy, and looked nothing like Daniel's smooth mixture. She wondered briefly whether she could salvage it, but she didn't want to waste time trying if it was irrecoverable, so she tipped it away when Albert wasn't looking.

"Are you coming out with us again tonight?" Fred asked as they left the classroom.

"Maybe." Raf hadn't mentioned it, but then he hadn't given her much notice last time.

"Well, we'll be meeting downstairs after dinner, same as usual if you fancy it."

"Thanks." Well, it wasn't as if she'd had any other plans.

She made her way to the hall after dinner, where Fred, Greg and Nate were already waiting when she arrived. A moment later Raf sprinted down the stairs.

"Ellie, there you are! You weren't in your room."

"You must've just missed me."

"Well, you've got the hang of this, obviously... same every time we've got a day off, so I probably don't need to fetch you anyway." He turned to Fred. "I suggested Ivan should come out, so we should wait a while at least. Where's Jorge this evening?"

"He's getting crazy about this contest," Fred said. "He'll do anything to win, and right now that seems to mean conning Charles into practice sessions any time he can."

Ivan came round the corner at that moment, and clapped his hand onto Fred's shoulder. "But we're expecting you to win – you're way ahead of him."

Fred rolled his eyes. "I wouldn't say that to him unless you want an earful. He's getting pretty wound up about it."

"So, are we expecting anyone else?" Ivan asked, looking round the group. His eyes rested briefly on Eleanor but he didn't say anything to acknowledge her.

"Maybe Jon," Greg said. "I heard he's just got back from wherever-it-was."

"Are the council really determined not to fix that bloody mess over the summer contest?" Fred asked, directing his question mostly to Ivan.

"The decision was made."

"But it's not too late. Couldn't they have a re-run or something?"

"We can talk about it later," Ivan said, as Jon rounded the corner. "Not tonight."

"What are we not talking about tonight?" Jon asked.

"Nothing. Come on, let's go."

They went to the tavern where Raf and Eleanor had danced, though it was still early and the music hadn't started yet.

"So how was your trip?" Nate asked Jon as they settled down with their drinks. "Anything exciting?"

"Easy enough," he said. "Nice to be back, though. I hope Vic's looking after you lot alright, is he? He said he wouldn't come out this year 'cause of all his responsibilities."

"I'm glad someone's setting a good example for our new students," Ivan said. "I do wonder if I should really be encouraging you lot."

"We don't need much encouragement," Greg said.

"Oh, I know that, but even so. It probably doesn't look good."

"It's great to see you again, though," Raf said. "It's been too long."

"Two years too long, kid. You got very lost."

"Not how I would've chosen to spend my time either." He glanced at Eleanor and she squeezed his hand. "I would've much rather been here."

"At least you made it," Eleanor said. "We'd all but given up."

"And I never thought you'd fall back into my year," Nate said, laughing. "Never thought we'd catch you up – did we, Greg?"

"I think you'll find you've nowhere near caught me," Raf said. "I've had two years in the real world while you were still at school. You kids have a long way to go to catch up."

Eleanor yawned; it had been a long day, and she was feeling decidedly sleepy.

"Tired?" Raf asked.

"A little, yeah. I might not stay out that long."

"Do you want to go now?" He drained the last drops from his drink. "I'll walk you back."

"I can take care of myself, you know, if you want to stay out. I don't need a minder."

"A girl out on her own, this late and in this part of town? Who knows what kind of trouble you might get into? I wouldn't want you having to explain to some Imperial jailer why you killed a man in some dark alleyway."

She rolled her eyes but she was secretly glad of the company; the walk would feel even longer if she was alone. They walked in comfortable silence through the city's dark streets, until they turned to cut across the Grand Square and were surprised to run into a crowd who were mostly dressed in their nightclothes. They stood in small groups, huddling together against the cold of the night, whispering and muttering.

Raf lifted Eleanor onto his shoulders so she could see above their heads.

"Looks like a fire," she said. Orange flames flickered in the darkness. "It might even be the palace."

"Rebels, then." Raf lowered her to the ground again. "Come on, we'll be better off going round."

She nodded, eyes flickering across the crowd. "We don't want to get caught up in anything."

"Oh, this lot are harmless – they must be the palace staff. But you're right, trouble's never far away from rebels."

"Do you think it's getting worse?" Eleanor asked as they turned into a quieter street. "We never used to hear of things like this."

"They're getting bolder," Raf said. "And maybe more organised. But there've been rebels causing trouble since the Empire was formed."

"I don't get it. I thought I hated the system when I was at school, but I just wanted to run away – I don't see the point of setting fires and starting fights."

"There is no point," Raf said. "It's just stupid."

They fell into silence again as they made their way back across the fields and into the academy's grounds. They were about to part ways to go to their respective rooms, but Eleanor put her hand on Raf's arm to stop him.

"I asked Ivan about you, you know," she said when he turned to see what she wanted. "Last year."

"What did he say?"

"He said you might be his brother." She looked steadily into his eyes as she spoke, waiting for a reaction, but his face betrayed nothing. "Is that what you think?"

"What would you think, if you grew up at school with someone who mirrored your features so closely?"

"I'm not sure. We're not supposed to ask that kind of question... I doubt I'd even have thought of it. It's been three generations since anyone was allowed to think things like that."

"Did Ivan explain how the school selects its children?"

She nodded. "Briefly."

"Then you'll understand that you're not supposed to wonder if one of the teachers is your father, either, but for everyone at Venncastle it's an unspoken question. You go through a phase where you think it might matter."

"Doesn't it?"

"No. You spend a while monitoring how every one of the teachers treats you and your classmates, and eventually you realise there are no clues. No-one gets special treatment. Your first loyalty is to the school, and so is theirs. It's as if *everyone* who's been through the school before you is your father... or your older brother. Why worry about blood?"

"He's fond of you, though." She thought back to her conversations with Ivan, and the way his eyes had moistened whenever they'd talked about Raf, the only affectionate emotion she'd really seen since arriving at the academy. "For whatever reason."

"Are we going to get some practice in tomorrow?"

The change of subject caught her by surprise, and it took her a moment to work out what had happened. "Probably. I'm supposed to be doing some running with Mikhail, but I could come round after that."

"Do that, then. And if you really want to talk about families, we can talk more tomorrow."

Her run with Mikhail ended up using up the whole of the following day, a thirty-mile circuit through the forest and around the lake, with intervals of climbing and swimming, and it was dark by the time they returned to the academy.

Eleanor knocked lightly at Raf's door and let herself in, wondering if she was too late to talk him into some sparring, and no sooner was she through the door than he put a large glass of spring nectar into her hands.

"Drink this."

She looked suspiciously at the drink. "I thought we were going to practise."

"We are."

"I don't understand."

"One of the things you need to practise is keeping your balance after a couple of drinks. Drink up!"

She wasn't entirely convinced, but she couldn't think of any good arguments against him so she emptied the glass in two large gulps. "Aren't you having any?"

He shook his head, but refilled her glass. "I've had plenty of practice with that stuff already."

He led her out into the darkness, across to the practice frame, and hopped up onto one of the beams before offering his hand to help her up. Once she was on her feet he backed away from her and she wobbled uncertainly, toes gripping the edges of the beam as she shuffled towards him.

"This isn't very fair," she said, pulling out her dagger and pointing it towards him. "You've made me all dizzy, everything's spinning, and now you expect me to fight up here."

"No, put the knife away."

She tilted her head to look at him, puzzled, and almost lost her balance, recovering herself into a crouching position on the beam.

"Seriously, Ellie, put it away. I don't want you hurting yourself."

It took her three attempts to get the blade back into its sheath. "Remind me again what we're doing? I thought we were going to practise."

"This is practice." He stepped away from her again and climbed onto the next-highest beam. "Not everything has to be about fighting. You're going to have enough trouble with your balance, but see if you can keep up with me."

She pushed herself to her feet again, standing with her feet across the beam, and edged sideways towards him. As soon as she got almost close enough to reach out and touch him he moved away, leaving her to negotiate the climb to the next beam on her own as he scrambled up to higher levels of the frame.

Her legs wobbling with every step, she hurried to try and match his pace, but whenever she thought she was getting close, he simply moved to somewhere harder to reach. She was trying to swing herself up to a much higher beam when she lost her balance and toppled onto the sand below, crying out with surprise as she hit the ground.

"Oh, Ellie!" Raf somersaulted down, scattering sand across her belly as he landed beside her, and offered his hand to help her up. "That was pretty good, though."

"It was awful."

"No, it would've been awful if you were sober, but you're not. That's the whole point. Come on, let's try again."

"I don't want to."

"C'mon, Ellie, don't get upset. I'm just trying to teach you a new skill."

"But this is silly," she pouted. "I wanted to practise for the contest."

"Tomorrow, I promise. Just humour me this evening." He gripped her wrist and pulled her up, though her legs wobbled beneath her as she tried to stand. "One more time, okay?"

"Okay, just once."

He helped her onto the first beam again, and again he left her balancing uncertainly while he retreated into further and higher places, although he was kind enough to avoid the rotating beams.

After she fell into the sand again he tried to persuade her to have a third attempt, but she was determined she'd had enough.

"I've fallen over twice now, isn't that enough for you?"

He offered his hand to help her up, but she pulled him down onto the sand beside her.

"Don't you want to go in?" he asked.

"It's a nice evening." She lay back, and shuffled her body until the sand was supporting her comfortably. "Look, there's almost no clouds. Look at all the stars."

He rested next to her, but she was conscious he was watching her rather than the sky.

"What do you think about harping knife and palm-blade?" she asked. "For the contest, I mean."

"It's not about what I think, Ellie, it's what you're happy with."

"I know that. But you're stronger on hand-to-hand than I am." She picked up a handful of sand and let it trickle through her fingers, scattering grains across her stomach. "You know I'd never get within ten yards of a fight in the real world, if I could just end it from a distance, but of course they won't let me fight my way. So I'd like to hear your thoughts."

"Well, it's a strong combination if you're confident with it.

And like anything interesting, if you're not confident, it could go horribly wrong – so again it comes back to what you're happy with."

"Can we practise tomorrow? I want to know what you'd do against it, because Ivan can still get past me, but so far as I can tell he was born with a harping knife in his hand."

"And a pipe between his teeth. Yep, that sounds like Ivan." He tilted her face so she was looking straight into his eyes. "You shouldn't assume you're not good at something just because you're not quite at his standard, you know."

"That sounds like the voice of experience. Something you learnt at school?"

"Something like that." He took a deep, slow breath. "Look, I can't really explain what it was like, growing up with Ivan always a few steps ahead of me. I don't even understand it myself. But mostly, it felt like looking into a mirror and seeing a slightly better version of myself. A reflection I could never quite live up to. I can only imagine what he must've thought about me."

"Do you think that's what it was like in the old days? Before the Empire, I mean – before children went to school."

"It must've been very strange. Can you imagine knowing your parents, and maybe even their parents, and having who-knows-how-many brothers or sisters? How would you know who you were supposed to be, with all those people expecting you to be like them? It was hard enough with one!"

"I always thought it sounded quite nice. But then, I never knew who I wanted to be anyway."

"It's better to have a choice. Even if you end up choosing the same thing... because I don't think I could've been happy anywhere but here, but at least I knew there were other possibilities, however remote."

"Really? I wanted to be a dancer, when I was much younger, and then I had my heart set on the Specials."

"I've always wanted this."

"But you were lucky. In most of the Empire, this place is just a legend. A fairytale – like Hess, we didn't believe in them either. It was only when I saw my assignment that I started to wonder."

"Ah, of course – the Association has never worried about what the girls' schools might think. If we're not expecting you, it doesn't matter if you think it's real or not."

"It might be time to put that right, once I get my council seat." She sat up and brushed the sand from her hair. "So can we do some proper training tomorrow?"

"You don't think this was proper? It'll serve you well."

"It wasn't what I was expecting to practise. Anyway, I want to try out the harping knife with you – I don't want to give up the element of surprise by using it too much against the others. No-one's going to expect me to pick that combination for the contest, they'll expect me to be using something a bit more... well... normal. So if I go for it, I want it to be a surprise."

The days leading up to the first contest passed in a haze of training and nerves, and Eleanor found the days were generally vanishing much more quickly now she was spending so much time with Raf and his friends. Whether they were studiously training or relaxing with a few drinks, it was certainly more fun than sitting alone in her room.

On the morning of the winter solstice they assembled after breakfast in the practice hall, which had been transformed into a compact arena for the contest. A thick rope was strung out to mark the limits of the fighting area, and benches had been arranged around the outside for everyone who wanted to watch: an assortment of first years, academy instructors, and other, unfamiliar faces had come along for the spectacle. The most notable absence was Bill; the rumour was that their hand-to-hand instructor objected to the rules under which the contest fights were held, but this was how it had always been done, and he stood no chance of getting it changed to disallow the swords, axes, and cudgels which he considered "far too military" for the Association's needs.

Ragal was officiating, with a shrill whistle between his teeth for whenever he needed to draw their attention, and a blackboard propped on a large A-frame laid out the running order, with space for the finalists' deciding bouts to be chalked in underneath.

The first fight saw Mack pitted against Fred. As they warmed up, Eleanor recalled Fred's confident words in the tavern, just after they'd found out who they were each facing in the first round. He certainly didn't look ruffled by being up first, whereas Mack looked a little nervous; once the fight started, it became clear that his nerves were getting the better of him, and he made a string of silly mistakes which allowed Fred to get a dagger under his chin.

Charles and Jorge were next, and after the amount they'd been practising together they each knew the other's style intimately. The familiarity showed in every block and counter. Charles was hardly bothering to follow through on thrusts he knew would be parried. It was starting to look like it could be a very long fight until Jorge, with characteristic bluntness, forced his way forwards and knocked Charles to the ground where he could pin his opponent down for a convincing, if sudden, victory.

Eleanor's first fight of the morning was against Sebastien. As she adjusted the straps of her leathers and followed him into the ring, she thought about the hundred times they'd practised together. With everyone watching, and something real to play for, this was going to be very different to casual sparring.

She held the harping knife diagonally in front of her chest, guarding her body, with her palm-blade ready to protect her left hand. Sebastien was fighting with a curved sword and a short dagger, a combination he'd become very comfortable with over the previous year, though Eleanor could usually slip her stiletto past his guard. In a fleeting moment of panic she wondered if she'd made a mistake going for a more unusual combination, but she loved the defensive wall that the harping knife gave her. And Sebastien certainly looked surprised when he first saw what she'd chosen, which could only work in her favour.

She flicked away his first few strikes without effort, but though it seemed easy, something was missing. She thought back to every time she'd fought for something that mattered – it all felt so different when winning meant survival, and the alternative was death. She needed to recapture that sense of urgency if she was to stand any chance at all of putting meaning into her movements.

After her next parry she stepped back, giving herself a moment to breathe and think before she launched herself back into the fight. Sebastien always opted for a sword, liking to put some distance between himself and his opponent, and she realised she had to get his blade out of the way if she was going to get close enough to make a winning strike. Otherwise they'd spend all day exchanging casual fencing which would only, eventually, tire them both.

With this in mind, when Sebastien next thrust his sword towards her she caught the hilt with the long blade of her harping knife, and instead of just blocking his attack she forced his arm down towards the floor and held it, using her palm-blade to block the secondary attack of his dagger, then darted forwards and brought the harping knife up against his chest. Ragal blew his whistle and Eleanor stepped back, then offered her hand for him to shake.

After the second round of fights, in which Daniel beat Mack, Jorge flattened Mikhail, and Sebastien narrowly defeated Paul, they broke off for lunch.

"Enjoying yourself?" Raf asked Eleanor as they walked across to the dining hall. "You had a good first fight."

"I was thinking of all the times we fought to survive," she said. "But it's much harder to really mean it in such a fake environment."

"This is a kind of survival, though."

"What do you mean?"

"You're fighting to stay in the set of people who can win. It might not be life or death, but it is important, Ellie. You mustn't forget that."

"I suppose so."

"Looking forward to this afternoon?" Jorge asked, as he and Fred caught them up. "You going to be joining me in the finals, El?"

"I'll do my best," she said. "You're lucky to have got yours out of the way."

"It was easy," Jorge said. "Only got you standing between

331

me and the top slot this afternoon, eh Fred?"

"You haven't seen Eleanor at her best yet," Raf said, squeezing her shoulder. "Don't rule her out."

"If you say so." Jorge shrugged, but he didn't look convinced.

Eleanor was secretly pleased he was being so dismissive: if he didn't class her as a threat, he wouldn't be paying much attention to her style. That could only help her if she did end up facing him in the finals.

Fred excused himself from the table after only a couple of mouthfuls to go and warm up for his next fight.

"Thought you weren't worried about Daniel," Nate said.

"Didn't say I was worried," Fred replied. "But I don't want to be fighting on a full stomach, so I might as well keep my muscles warm."

As it happened, Daniel and Fred were both doing stretches in the ring when the others returned from lunch. They cast occasional glances at one another but each was maintaining a determined pretence of being more interested in his personal exercises than in the imminent competition.

When Ragal blew his whistle and instructed them to arm themselves, however, a predatory look came over Daniel's features. Eleanor was taken aback by the transformation; she'd never before seen Daniel look anything but bored with a fight, but this time he looked positively restless, itching to get started. As usual, he was fighting with one long and one short dagger, which he held tip-to-tip in front of his body until Ragal's next whistle blast signalled the beginning of the fight.

Daniel's style was always a cautious one, and despite the change that had come over him he still kept his daggers in a close guard and his weight well over his back foot.

Fred made a couple of over-confident attacks in the first few moments, which were easily knocked back, and then he too realised that Daniel was fighting in a fundamentally different mode today. After his next, more considered approaches were parried with equally effortless movements, he was starting to look slightly disconcerted.

Daniel, on the other hand, was evidently enjoying himself.

He made several quick strikes, fell back for a moment, then launched himself back into the fight. Precisely what happened next was unclear even to those involved, but it ended with Fred's knives flying across the room – Greg had to move his feet quickly out of the way as one of the blades spun towards him – and Daniel flat out on his stomach on the floor. He pushed himself into a kneeling position and twisted up, thrusting his dagger against Fred's stomach, and Ragal blew his whistle to stop the fight. Fred went to collect his knives with a sour look on his face.

Since neither of them could win after Jorge's earlier victories, Mikhail and Charles agreed to skip their fight, meaning the next – and last – of the qualifying fights saw Eleanor come up against Paul.

As she adjusted the straps of her palm-blade, in the back of her mind she wondered what the tie-breaker would be if she lost, leaving them on one victory each. But she couldn't afford to waste energy on that kind of thought. Far better to focus on winning now and make sure the question didn't arise.

She swung the harping knife as she waited for Ragal's signal to begin, getting into a comfortable rhythm. After the whistle, though she edged forwards, she continued to wait for Paul to attack. She'd been watching him in their hand-to-hand classes ever since they'd been drawn against one another, but they'd seldom been paired together, and she was unfamiliar with his style. Given the defensive strength of the harping knife, she had time to wait and see what he brought against her.

What he presented was a series of short, jabbing thrusts with his left arm, while he kept his right blade in a defensive position. They were attacks she could parry without difficulty, though he kept them coming with a speed that kept her on her toes, and with an unusually high proportion of feints. Indeed, she soon realised that every third attack he made involved a similar misdirection, though she tried not to give any clues that she'd spotted a pattern and continued to follow his feints before switching back to block his secondary attacks. While he thought he was surprising her, he had no reason to change his tactics. Eventually the moment she'd been waiting for presented itself and she blocked his feint with a strong sideways blow, spun the harping knife to deflect his right arm, and ducked around to bring her palm-blade up behind his ear for a winning attack.

They moved straight into the finals, and Ragal decreed that Daniel and Jorge should be the first pair to contest their places, since Eleanor had just fought. They readied themselves as Eleanor sat on the sidelines and sipped from her flask.

Again, Daniel was eager to get started, and Jorge eyed him suspiciously. He'd been so sure that Fred would be his first opponent in the finals, and Daniel was an unknown quantity. He'd never bothered to pay much attention to the quiet theorist – but the quiet theorist had just disarmed Fred with apparent ease, and that was worrisome.

Jorge was fighting with two long daggers, one straight-edged and one serrated, which he held in an inverted V in front of his chest while he waited. At the sound of the whistle, before Ragal had even taken a breath, he charged forwards with both blades swinging.

Daniel stood perfectly still, daggers held in the textbook position which he always adopted, and waited for the storm to reach him. He moved only when he had to, deflecting Jorge's blows with the minimum of effort, and making no attempt to counter until, after a dozen quick parries, he saw his chance to strike. Taken by surprise, Jorge tried to block but opened his right side in the process, and Daniel's second attack sealed his victory.

Daniel stayed in the ring for the next fight, and Eleanor wondered whether she'd see the same predatory look in his eyes as when he'd faced Fred and Jorge, but apparently that look was reserved only for Venncastle opponents.

He was breathing heavily from his previous exertions, but shook his head impatiently when Ragal suggested taking a short break.

"I see you have gone for the 'exciting' option again," he said to Eleanor as they faced each other, waiting for the whistle.

"I'd prefer to say interesting," she said, giving the harping knife a quick twirl. "We don't want too much excitement, do we?"

"Are you confident you have now learnt how to wield it?"

Ragal blew his whistle.

"I'm in the final, aren't I?" she said. "I'd say I've probably got the hang of it by now."

"We shall see."

They circled one other with a few feet between them, both reluctant to make the first attack, both having got this far with a mostly defensive strategy.

"It seems we could be here for a very long time," Daniel said.

Eleanor wondered why he was talking so much. He was hardly the Empire's most talkative person, generally, and he hadn't been like this in his earlier fights. Maybe he just knew how much it would irritate her.

She resolved to ignore him completely, but it was harder than she anticipated.

"Do you not wish to show me what you can do?" he asked, beckoning her forwards.

"You go ahead," she said, spreading her arms wide to give him an easy line. He didn't take the bait. "Come on, I'm giving you an open target, what more do you need?"

"I am waiting for the same as you."

"Really? Well, if you drop your guard I'll have a go, how's that sound?"

He took two steps backwards and lowered his arms, pointing both daggers towards the floor. "Done."

Eleanor wished she was allowed to use her best skills; if she threw the harping knife there was no way he could move in time to block it. But that wasn't an option, and she'd promised to make some attack, so she skipped forwards and thrust the harping knife towards his chest.

She was expecting the parry from his long blade, and he brought his second dagger round in a predictable counter which she blocked with her palm-blade. What she failed to anticipate was that he would drop his short dagger to catch hold of her wrist, move too close for her harping knife to be effective, and flick his remaining dagger under her arm to press against her throat. No, that wasn't like Daniel at all.

She felt a little bit cheated. Facing someone like Ivan or Raf, she would have expected the unexpected, and she might have had chance to react. Against Daniel, the surprise caught her, and she only realised exactly what had happened when she heard the whistle.

Jorge came into the ring before Daniel had even left, but Eleanor ignored him and ducked under the rope to get a drink of water from her flask, determined to have at least a short rest before the next round.

She was about to go back into the ring when it hit her.

"Wait... I want to change my blades."

"Are you crazy?" Mikhail asked as she thrust the flask back into his hands. "How can you change at such a late stage?"

"Different opponent, different style," she said, trying to sound mysterious. She winked at him, then turned and jogged across to where the first-years were watching the spectacle, leaving her harping knife on the floor by her seat. "Raf, can I borrow your stiletto?"

"What? What's happened to yours?"

"Nothing – I just want to borrow yours." She unfastened her palm-blade and offered it to him. "I want to swap."

"Ellie, that's crazy. You've been practising with those for ages."

"I know," she said, leaning across to take the stiletto from the sheath at his waist. She held it up alongside her own. "These make a good pair, don't they? I thought they'd be well matched."

"What are you doing?" Raf dropped his voice to a troubled whisper. "You can't take two stilettos into a knife-fight."

She grinned. "You've got Bill for hand-to-hand, haven't you?"

"Yes – why?"

"Did he give you that silly speech about how, if you end up using what he's teaching, you've already made a mistake?"

Raf nodded, still looking puzzled.

"Think about it, and if it doesn't make sense I'll explain later," she said. "Just lend me your knife. And look after this for me." She pressed the palm-blade into his hand, then turned back to where Jorge was waiting.

"Ready now?" he asked, a faint note of amusement in his voice, as she returned to the middle of the arena.

She nodded.

Ragal gave a sharp blast of his whistle to signal the fight to begin, and Jorge lunged immediately as she'd guessed he would; by the time he'd followed through to where she'd been she was out of the way, over to his left. Another lunge, and this time she rolled and came up behind him, slightly too slow to make a clear strike of her own before he turned.

She ducked easily away from his next few attempts, watching his frustration mount. It was going precisely as she'd hoped; now she simply had to wait for the inevitable mistake.

Every time he aimed a strike at where she had been, half a moment later she'd moved to somewhere else, leaving him to stab at empty air. For all his growls of frustration, he couldn't get close.

And then, suddenly, the moment came.

She ducked, he turned, and he got it wrong – leaving her with a clear line to his back. She wasted no time in darting towards him, sandwiching his neck between her twin blades for an undeniable victory. And just like that, without a single blow exchanged, the fight was over.

"Well, whatever that was about, it seemed to work – but what in all the Empire were you thinking?" Mikhail asked when she went back to pick up her flask.

"I was going to lose." She took a long mouthful of water, aware that everyone was suddenly listening to her, and she hadn't given nearly enough of an answer. "I know how Jorge fights, and he's twice my size – if I'd tried to tackle him the way I fought the others, I wouldn't have stood a chance. He would've just crushed me."

"But – two stilettos?" Sebastien asked.

"It felt all wrong with two different knives. I know all the theories, I've practised for months, but it just felt... unbalanced. I know how strange it sounds, but for what I had to do, I needed symmetry."

She glanced across the faces of the other students. Jorge had stormed off after the whistle, and was nowhere to be seen, but everyone else was still watching her. With the exception of Raf, who caught her eye and smiled, they all looked thoroughly bemused. She smiled to herself. For all that she'd worried about not fitting in, maybe being the wildcard could work to her advantage – and no-one was going to tell her she didn't belong here now she'd scored second place.

After everyone dispersed, she went up to Raf's room to give his knife back.

"Thanks for the loan," she said, taking a seat at the end of his bed. "I hope you didn't mind – I knew yours was about the same size and weight as mine."

"Of course I don't mind. Jorge, on the other hand, is going to be hopping mad," he said, laughing. "You should've seen the look on his face when you kept dodging him."

"I can imagine."

"But it really worked for you. I'll admit I was confused at the beginning, but once I saw what you were doing... wow."

"You're the only person who didn't look confused afterwards. I think most of them are still trying to work out what I actually did."

"Ah, they're all kids. Anyway, do you want a drink before dinner? You look like you could use it."

"Thanks."

He poured two tall glasses of spring nectar, apparently the only drink he kept in his room. "Cheers."

"Cheers." She took a large mouthful. "So, what did you make of today's sport? I'm sure you were paying more attention than I was."

"I doubt it – if I know you at all, you were constantly watching for mistakes and angles."

"That's different to just watching. I could only see it through my fighting eyes. What did it look like from the outside?"

"Well, you did brilliantly, of course. But you've got the points to prove that, you don't need me to tell you about it. Other than that, a few good fights, bit of a disappointing show from Venncastle, but it was a fun day. Can't wait for next year."

338

"You'll have to watch out for that Venncastle trap, though."

He looked puzzled. "What trap?"

"The overconfidence, I mean. It got Fred and Jorge today – I wouldn't want to see that happen to you."

"And you said I was paying more attention!" He laughed and took a gulp of his drink. "You'll tell me if I start to get lazy, though, won't you?"

"Definitely. And I'll come down to watch you compete, of course – it must be a fun day off."

"Oh, it was entertaining. But I can understand why Bill boycotts it – it's not the most realistic test."

"No. I did get there, though, with the urgency. By the end it almost felt real."

Chapter 27

After a morning of vigorous circuits, when they were all more than ready for bathing and lunch, Karl told them that they couldn't go straight back to their rooms. He'd had a message from Harold asking the students to gather by the smithy straight after the class.

"Sorry to keep you from your food," Harold said once they'd all assembled in the courtyard. "This won't take long. As you've probably heard, you need to design your graduation knives some time in the next few weeks. Now, it'll take me a while to make all these up, and I'd like you to be able to use them for the final contest in the summer, so we've got a bit of a deadline and I thought I'd better talk you through what you need to be doing."

He brought out a couple of his own knives and handed them out, passing one to each end of the line of students.

"These are mine, which is about as complex as you can get with pure metalwork, but I was showing off. I'd thank you if you kept yours a bit more simple, but that gives you an idea what's possible."

He hefted a large jar onto the worktop in front of him, and pulled out a handful of gemstones.

"Now, you'll probably want some colour in there, so we've got amethysts, turquoise, sapphires, emeralds, rubies..." He paused, and shuffled through the gems with one stubby finger. "A few opals, loads of citrine – not that you should let that influence your choices, we can always get more. That's why you need to give me plenty of time."

"So what do we actually need to do?" Jorge asked. "I'm hungry."

"You need to come up with a design, some combination of engraving and gemstones, to identify your weapons," Harold said, looking slightly flustered at having his flow interrupted. "I really need you all to have finished your designs by the equinox, but don't be shy if you've got something to show me earlier than that. I'll need to check your ideas against the record of existing designs, anyway, so it's worth your while to come early."

"Alright." Jorge turned from the group. "C'mon, Fred, let's go. I'm just gonna write my name."

"It would help," Harold said, raising his voice as Jorge walked away. "If you designed something that could fit nicely inside a square or circle – you'll need lots of those – and that could also be stretched along a knife hilt."

Jorge didn't stop, although no-one went with him.

"As I was saying," Harold continued once he'd disappeared into the dining hall. "We've got plenty of colours for you to choose from, you can mix and match if you like, and you'll need to sketch out the arrangement you want. Then I'll check it against everyone else's designs, make sure you've got something unique, and start forging your weapons. Any questions about any of that?"

"How are we supposed to know what's been done before?" Charles asked. "It'd be really annoying to design something and then find out it's already been taken."

"It doesn't happen often," Harold said. "Unless you really want something extremely simple, in which case, come and talk to me first."

Eleanor traced imaginary designs in the air with the point of her knife during the afternoon's lesson, while Robert's words about the secrets of plausible disguise drifted over her. But whatever she came up with, she was struggling to picture anything she'd like more than the beautiful knives she was already using.

The following afternoon, while they were supposed to be practising new techniques with throwing stars, she wandered across to where Ivan was sitting to watch.

"Problem, Eleanor?" he asked as she sat beside him.

"Not exactly. I wanted to ask you about graduation designs."

"Oh?"

"You probably don't remember, but there was something you said when you first saw my practice knives."

"Don't underestimate my memory." He spoke with a serious tone, but there was a glint in his eye. "What did I say?"

"About the graduation set, and how I might've come to my design a bit early."

"Ah, yes. I was right, wasn't I?"

"That's what I'm trying to work out. The thing is, they're beautiful knives, but I've no proof they're unique."

"Well, it's Harold who makes the rules. But you bought them in Taraska, didn't you? That should be enough distance to reassure him."

"Do you think so?"

"That's my guess – but you'd have to ask him to be sure. Anyway, let's see where you're up to with these stars."

She got to her feet and fired two stars towards the nearest target; Ivan nodded his satisfaction, and left her to practise while he went to see what the others were up to.

After a quick dinner, she went up to see Raf.

"Raf – your girlfriend's here again!" Greg called out when she came into their common room, before opening the door to Raf's room and pushing her lightly through the doorway.

Raf looked up with a smile from where he was sitting, cross-legged on the floor, sharpening his knives.

"Welcome back," he said. "Make yourself comfortable, I won't be long."

"Why do you let them call me your girlfriend?" she asked as she perched on the edge of his bed. The question had been troubling her ever since Greg had first started using the term.

"You know how these things go," he replied, without looking up from his knife this time. "If you deny that kind of thing, they'll only get more insistent. I'm sure they'll get bored of it eventually."

Her heart sank a little; that wasn't really the answer she'd hoped for, in the moments when she'd let herself have any thoughts about what he might say.

"Anyway, I came to talk about graduation knives," she said, changing the subject as swiftly as she could. "I can't decide what to do about mine."

"What's troubling you?"

"Well, I've got all these lovely ones from Taraska, and all the others Harold's already made to match, but there's no guarantee there aren't more in Taraska with the same design. So I don't know if they'll let me carry on with these ones, and it might be fun to come up with something new anyway... I'm torn."

"Why don't you do a new design, and then you can decide which to use? That way you'd have a backup if they say you can't use the Tarasanka ones."

"I suppose so."

He sheathed the newly sharpened dagger, and moved on to his stiletto. "You don't sound convinced."

"Well, I'm not keen on wasting time."

"Then why don't you just ask someone whether it's okay to use your ones? Then if they say no, you can get on with your new design."

"You're right, of course. I'm sure I'm being silly, because I do love these ones, I just keep worrying about whether they're really unique. Anyway, enough of that – are we going out tomorrow?"

"I hadn't decided, but I certainly will if you're going to come."

She nodded. "I'd like that."

He got up, sheathed his various knives, and dropped his sharpening block onto the desk.

"What's this code?" she asked, sliding a sheet of paper out from under where the sharpening block had landed. "I can't make it out."

"Oh, that's just school notes." He sat beside her on the bed, and took the paper from her hand. "Yeah, really boring stuff."

"You coded your school notes?"

"They made us use it for most of our work, for practice."

"Will you teach me?"

"I'm not sure I should." He folded the paper before putting it back on the desk. "It's a Venncastle code."

"Well, at least let me try to break it. I need a bit of a break from thinking about this next contest."

"How can you think about it when you don't even know what the rules are going to be?"

"That's what I'm thinking about! It's hard to prepare for something so unknown."

"Just assume they'll test everything," Raf said. "Even if they don't, it'll put you in a good position for the third contest, because that really could be anything."

"That's if I even get through to the last one."

"Ellie! Of course you will. You've already got two points, and I'm sure you'll do great next month."

"Thanks, but I'd rather be realistic."

"I am being realistic, you've got a great chance. Besides, I want you to win."

"Really? Why?"

"Aside from wanting the best person to get the job? Well, there's the selfish angle – I'm fully expecting to win my year, and if I'm on the council I'd quite like you to be there. And if I somehow don't win my seat, I'll need you to watch my back in there!"

"You're not going to have a problem, are you?"

"I like to hope not."

It was in the middle of a climbing lesson three days later, when she was hanging by two fingers from the guttering of the bell tower, that Eleanor realised what she wanted to do about her graduation knives. If Harold would let her. She didn't know enough about metalwork to be sure whether her idea was plausible, but it would be her preferred solution.

She went across to the smithy before dinner, and found Harold busily beating the edge of a curved sword. She waited by the door and watched as he finished hammering and plunged the blade into cold water.

As the hissing died away, she spoke up: "Have you got a moment?"

"Of course. What can I do for you?"

"It's about the graduation designs."

"Oh, have you done it already?" He came across the room towards her, wiping his hands on his trousers. "Let's have a look then."

"No, I haven't finished, I was just thinking and... well, I

wanted to check the rules. You've got a record of everyone's designs, haven't you?"

"Indeed."

"And I'm sure you can tell me what's possible."

"I should certainly hope so."

"The thing is, I've got really nice weapons already, you know that," – she pulled one of her throwers from its sheath – "And I don't want to have to get rid of them. But, of course, there's no guarantee the weaponsmith in Taraska didn't make more of this design."

"Well, I won't stop you on that account." He took her knife and examined it. "It's a risk, but it's your decision. I've already got that design on file for you, and you're right, it's a beauty."

"Actually, I wondered if I could draw some kind of variant on the current design – if you'd be able to change them."

"Depends what you come up with." He walked across to a cupboard at the back of the smithy and started sorting through a pile of metal sheets. "Adding stuff is easier than taking bits out, but I'm sure I can have a go. Might be hard to work between those gems, mind you, they're quite close-set."

He came back to her with a square sheet of metal, around six inches across, that had her identity number inscribed in one corner and an enlarged copy of her design taking up most of the space in the middle. The sapphires were drawn in outline, the blue ones each marked with a little cross in the middle, and the white ones with a circle.

"This is yours so far," he said, handing it across to her. "Of course if you start from scratch, I'll throw this on the scrap heap, but it's yours if you want to work from it."

"Thanks. Can I borrow it for a couple of days?"

"By all means – that's why I dug it out for you. Just try not to lose it."

She took the design back to her room and copied it onto a slate, then experimented with adding a few extra scrolls and circles around groups of gems. She made several attempts, erasing her additions each time and restoring the original design before trying again.

Eventually, she settled on a simple outline that she thought she was happy with, and went to see if Raf was around to give her a second opinion.

"Hey, Ellie," he smiled as he opened the door. "What's up?"

"I had an idea about the knives," she said, holding the slate behind her back. "And I wanted to see what you think before I take it back down to Harold."

"If you're happy, that's all that matters. I'm sure it'll look fantastic, whatever you've done."

"The thing is, I thought I could just *slightly* change the ones I've got, so even if someone else has brought some back to the Empire with the same design, they wouldn't be the same any more. Then I can keep my knives."

"Sounds like a great idea. Show me?"

She held out the slate and waited, still standing in the doorway.

"Looks good." He handed it back. "Nice and simple."

"Thanks. I think I'm going to take it down to Harold in the morning."

"Why not now?"

"I don't know. I wanted to sleep on it, make sure I'm still happy tomorrow."

"Go now." He pressed the slate back into her hand. "You'll sleep better once you've got a resolution."

She knew he was right, and Harold would probably still be working, so she went straight down to the smithy. As she'd suspected, the fires were still hot.

"Got an idea?" Harold asked when he caught sight of her.

She handed him the metal sheet with her current design, and the slate on which she'd sketched her new idea. "What do you think?"

"Looks fine to me." He held the two side by side. "Can't see any problems with that. And no-one else has brought me a design yet, so I can get straight on with yours."

"So what now? Do I have to leave all my knives here so you can change them?"

"I wouldn't, if I were you. We'll do them a couple at a time. It should be fairly quick, compared to forging a whole new set of blades – but is there anything else you want me to make, while

I'm at it?"

"Well..." She thought for a moment. "I haven't got my own harping knife yet, and I could always do with more stars."

"I can do that. Leave me a couple of your daggers, then, and I'll make a start tomorrow."

Chapter 28

All of the academy's students were up before the sun on the morning of the spring equinox. They assembled in the practice hall, whispering in groups of three or four, shivering in the chilly air of the early morning; the second years because they had to be, the first years simply curious, although they were herded out of the way before anything interesting happened.

The second years knew this was going to be harder, or at least more complicated, than the simple knock-out fights of the winter contest – but anything beyond that was guesswork. By all accounts, the rules changed every year, but that didn't stop them from speculating about what they might be in for.

After what seemed like an inordinate wait, Ragal came in to the hall, and clapped his hands to get their attention. The students fell silent.

"This contest will begin at sunrise," he said. "So we don't have much time, but thankfully the rules are simple. I have here a list of challenges for you." He held a large roll of parchment above his head. "The tasks fall under four distinct themes, and each theme contains seven challenges, of increasing difficulty. As you move on to each harder challenge, you'll need information from the previous challenge in that theme in order to complete it, and to make your lives a little more interesting, the challenges are physically spread around the Association's grounds."

He extracted a large map from the roll of papers, and pinned it to the wall. The map covered most of the grounds around the academy, an area of several square miles. There were various numbers dotted around, mostly in the forests, though one digit in the middle of the lake immediately caught Eleanor's interest, and a small number were clustered near the buildings.

"Each number represents the location of one challenge, with different colours for different themes. Remember that challenges from any given theme must be completed *in order*.

You won't be able to start with the higher scores, so you'll need to plan your route carefully.

"You will be ranked on both depth and breadth. Each challenge has a points value, with the points increasing as the challenges get harder. Only your highest-scoring result from each theme will be counted, and for any theme in which you don't complete even stage one, you'll lose one point. To succeed you'll need a solid strategy, and you mustn't neglect your timing, because if you're not back in this hall before the sun dips beneath the horizon you will be disqualified, irrespective of how many points you may have gathered."

He glanced up at the windows, where pink sunlight was now beginning to filter into the hall. "And now, you may begin."

He unrolled the list of challenges and pinned it beside the map, before stepping clear to let the students read.

Eleanor scanned the information. The individual challenges all had cryptic names, but she wasn't going to waste time second-guessing what each might stand for when that was probably irrelevant – what mattered were the themes. Projectiles, that was her most obvious strength, she'd be fine with Tracking, and Locks was also a possibility, she'd always been reasonable with a set of picks. Poisons was the one she needed to avoid. There was nothing that sounded like fighting, presumably because their hand-to-hand skills had been tested already. It was nice not to have to think about the others for once.

There was a scoring chart alongside the list of challenges, giving details of the points for each stage. One point for stage one, three points for stage two, six points for stage three... all the way up to twenty-eight points for stage seven, if the day was long enough for anyone to get that far.

She turned her attention next to the map. The spacing of the tasks across the grounds seemed to be a key element if she wanted to avoid wasting too much time running around, but the tasks from different themes were all mixed up, as were the different stages. Whatever strategy she went for, there was no way to avoid going back over the same ground, but somehow she needed to decide whether it would be better to complete the harder tasks in her favourite themes or do more of the easier ones. She wondered how they were supposed to judge the relative complexity of the different tasks and different stages before even seeing them. But perhaps that was part of the challenge.

Before she'd even finished reading the list she'd heard a couple of students already jogging out of the hall. By the time she'd memorised the position of every number on the map and decided on a starting strategy, only Daniel was apparently still thinking.

"Good luck," she said, then made her way outside without waiting for a response, and sat down to fasten her spikes to her shoes.

She jogged first to the first-stage challenge in the Projectiles theme; that was an obvious place to start, she was so confident that it would be her strongest area. Also, it was a long way from any of the others, and the second-stage Projectiles was near to the start of the first Tracking task. By the time she'd done those three, she reasoned, she'd have a good feel for how the day was going to work out, and since she didn't know where the Tracking route would take her, it would be hard to plan further ahead.

The ground was soft from recent rainfall, and her feet slipped a little even with the spikes. She saw none of the others as she made her way into the forest.

The first Projectiles task was a very simple setup: a metal box was suspended high in the air by a number of chains stretched tightly between the trees, and there were eight identical targets irregularly placed around the sides of the cube. There were no explicit instructions, but Eleanor guessed she had to hit them all. Certainly there was nothing to choose between them.

She tried with a blowpipe first, worried about damaging her knives on the metal; the dart caught on the fabric of the target and hung there, but nothing seemed to happen. Maybe it needed more force.

She stepped back, pulled her throwing knives from their sheaths, and flicked one of them up towards the target. It hit hard and bounced off, but this time something had changed: the target had popped out by over a finger's width. She threw another knife, causing the second target to pop out in a similar fashion, before going to retrieve both knives from the grass.

She was lining up her third shot when she noticed the low clicking sound coming from the box. A few moments later, two loud pops disturbed her. She looked back at the targets she'd so recently hit; but now, there was no sign she'd achieved anything.

Clearly, time was of the essence.

She pulled out six more knives and tucked them into her belt, lining them up ready for use. She took a deep breath and started firing knives at targets, running in a large circle around the clearing to take aim at the different sides of the box.

As soon as her final knife hit the eighth target, something fell from the bottom of the box, and all the targets clicked back into their original positions. She caught her knife as it fell, then went to see what had dropped to the ground.

It turned out to be a wooden token, about the size of her palm, with *Projectiles 1* inscribed on one side, and three mysterious words on the other: *CHOOSE THE SQUARES*. Presumably that would make more sense once she got to the second task. She pocketed the token, collected up her knives, and started running between the trees.

At the second Projectiles station, a fast-flowing stream prevented her getting closer than about fifty paces from the target board, and would also stop her retrieving any knives or stars she might use to hit the targets. It would have to be darts, then – assuming these targets would respond to so light a touch. There were around fifty small targets spread across the board, with shapes divided roughly equally between circles, squares, triangles, and diamonds.

She pulled out her pipe and aimed at the most central of the square targets.

As with the first task, the target popped out by a small amount once she'd hit it, and she wondered whether she was working against the same sort of timer. If so, that would account for what made this task harder, since there were twice as many targets to hit before the time elapsed.

She soon found her answer.

The first time she missed a target and caught the board to its side, a loud pop resulted as the three targets she'd previously hit clicked back to their starting positions.

It wasn't time that mattered, then. It was precision. Or possibly, precision *and* timing.

And she needed to successfully reach all of the targets before she ran out of darts, or she'd have to waste a ridiculous amount of time going back to restock.

She managed to reset the board twice more before she finally succeeded in hitting all the targets without any mistakes. The second token was catapulted across the stream towards the ground at her feet, and she caught it just before it rolled into the water. She pocketed it without bothering to read the clue, and sprinted to the start of the first Tracking challenge, just a few yards further into the forest.

She got to the clearing where the task had been marked on the map, and stopped short. Whereas the Projectiles challenges had been obvious, here there was nothing. Her first thought was to wonder whether one of the others had been here before her and hidden the whole setup to stop anyone else competing in the theme, but she quickly realised the truth was a lot more subtle. This was a test of Tracking. She needed to find the tracks.

She dropped to her knees and began to examine the ground, looking for anything out of place. They'd have to have done something more durable than simple footprints, given the number of students running around all day in the forest, but she wasn't really sure what she was looking for. She just hoped she'd recognise it when she saw it.

She worked outwards in small circles from the middle of the clearing, feeling the ground with her hands while looking for anything out of the ordinary. It didn't take her that long to find it; a trail of small glass beads led between the trees.

At the end of the trail, the tokens were tucked within the hollow of a rotten tree trunk. She pulled one out and read the reverse before stowing it safely in the pouch at her waist:

FOLLOW THE BLUE PATH. At least the instructions were all proving quite straightforward; nothing cryptic yet.

The trail of beads had taken her to the edge of the forest and along the lake; now she had to decide what to do next. Comparing the second Projectiles task to the first, she felt confident that she'd get more points by pushing up through the levels rather than trying to cover everything, even with the minus points. It would also mean she had fewer choices at the end of each task, so less chance of getting bogged down with planning – that could only be good for speed.

The third Projectiles task was close, too.

When she reached it, she found it consisted of a set of moving targets, each of which was attached to a long iron rod which sometimes swung like a pendulum, and sometimes slid from side to side or up and down. The clue she'd picked up from the second task read simply *WAIT FOR THE PATTERN.*

Eleanor watched the movement of the targets. It looked random at first – she wouldn't have suspected there was any pattern if she hadn't been told to look. Eventually, however, she realised the targets were all following the same extended sequence of movements, although at different speeds.

But to wait for it? She didn't know what that meant. Wait for it to do what?

She pulled out a knife and aimed at one of the targets. When she hit it, its movement abruptly stopped. So far, so good – probably. She shrugged to herself, and flicked another knife at another target. It too came to a juddering halt... then a moment later, both targets began to move again.

She chewed on the hilt of her knife and watched the targets carving their swirling paths through the air. What was she supposed to do? She stopped the first target again, and waited, wondering whether it would start again on its own. Apparently not.

She threw another knife; this wasn't like the previous task, she could get her weapons back, so it was better to be doing something and see if she happened upon something that worked. This time, the second target stopped and didn't restart. The two static targets taunted her, a pair of parallel bars sticking out while the others continued to move.

Suddenly it struck her: they were parallel. Of course! That was what was different this time. Quite by chance, she'd stopped them both at the same point in the pattern. And they'd stayed stopped.

She picked off the targets one by one, after that, waiting until each one was approaching the same position before she released her knife. She found she had to watch each target through a couple of cycles before she could tune in to the speed of its movements – an essential prerequisite to catching it at the right point in the cycle.

Once she'd managed to stop all the targets, the Projectiles 3 token dropped from somewhere above her head, before – one by one – the targets started to move again. The clue for the next task said *MIND YOUR HEAD*.

She was only about a mile from the second stage Tracking task, while the fourth Projectiles was on the far side of the lake, so she ran to the start of the Tracking route.

It took her a while to find the right path to follow; she found a few red fibres caught on a bramble, and some white ones in the grass, but the start of the blue path was concealed in the bark of a tree. Once she'd found it, though, following the trail of blue fibres took her up a particularly gnarled tree trunk, and on to a tricky climb through the canopy, where she eventually came to a stack of tokens in an abandoned bird's nest.

The back of the token read *DON'T FORGET TO LOOK UP*.

She dropped out of the tree and ran straight to the third task in the Tracking theme, which had been marked as starting right in the middle of the academy courtyard. With the words of the clue in her mind, she started by scanning the rooftops, but there was nothing obvious up there, so she knelt to examine the floor as usual.

It felt strangely exposed in the middle of the courtyard, after all the previous tasks under cover of the trees, and she couldn't shake the feeling that someone might be watching from one of the windows.

What she found was a loose cobblestone, and then another four stones further out. Continuing in the same direction she found that she could wobble the stones with her feet to find the path. When she ran out of trail near the wall of the practice hall, she tried lifting the cobble to look for tokens, but there was nothing except earth underneath it.

Remembering the clue, she looked again at the roof above her head, but she couldn't see anything. When she started climbing to get a better look, though, she almost fell as she trusted her weight to a brick which moved beneath her. A little more exploration and she found another wobbly brick a little further up, and then another. The path led her up, and then across the roof-tiles which were also loose in places. Eventually she found the next token inside the chimney stack; it read *START 50 YARDS NORTH OF THE 4*.

It could only be referring to the 4 on the map which marked the supposed beginning of that task. But before she could do that she had to complete the fourth Projectiles task, which was apparently taking place inside a nearby barn.

She opened the door cautiously, wondering what traps might have been sprung, but nothing seemed to happen as she stepped inside. The target board was suspended from the ceiling, with five small targets arranged in a cross formation. The board itself was suspended and rotating gently on the end of a chain.

It made sense to have to mind her head; to get a good shot she'd need to be underneath the target, and that meant every knife she threw would be falling back towards her.

She flicked the first knife and stepped back, then heard a click from one of the haystacks to her right. She ducked only just in time to avoid the circular blade which came flying towards her at eye-level. On any of the lads, it would've been at the height of their throat.

By the time she'd got back to her feet, the timer on the board had expired, and the target had reset. She drew a long dagger for her left hand, lined up five throwing knives, and started to throw. For each target she hit, one of the circular blades came towards her, and she had to deflect them to avoid having her face sliced open. But to reach all the targets in time, she couldn't afford to stop throwing.

The token was fired towards her after she hit the fifth target;

she knocked it away with her dagger before she realised what she'd done, and had to go and scrabble in the hay to retrieve it.

Then she made her way back to the edge of the woods, to the fourth challenge in the Tracking theme which featured a trail of tiny arrows chalked on trees. The trail led her deep into the forest, and she wondered whether she should be heading for stage five Tracking next if she finished in time. It wasn't much further away, and these challenges didn't seem to be getting harder at quite the same rate as the Projectiles ones.

As she jogged through a sparse area of the forest, looking ahead to see if she could spot the next marker, she felt something brush against her leg. Before she even had chance to look what it might have been, she was upside down, hoisted into the air by a rope around her ankle. She cursed herself for being so careless.

The trap had lifted her high off the ground, but not high enough that she could reach the branches above. She reached up to grip the rope above her leg and pulled herself up, climbing the rope which held her, until she reached the top. She cut the rope away from her ankle and climbed down to the ground again.

Evidently she was going to have to be more careful than she'd thought.

As she continued onwards she looked, now, not only for the next marker on the trail but also for any signs of hidden rope traps. She'd got away lightly this time, but there was no telling what else they might've set up, and it might not always be so easy to get down.

The path looped and doubled back, taking her on an inconveniently lengthy trail, and she was starting to wonder, somewhat impatiently, if she was nearing the end yet when the ground disappeared from under her feet. She gave an involuntary yelp as she fell through what had appeared to be solid ground, but turned out to be a thin layer of sticks, moss, and leaves. Soil and leaves trickled down on to her head as she sat in the bottom of the pit.

With the spikes on her shoes, and a couple of knives to generate hand-holds, it wasn't too difficult to climb out, though the earth at the sides of the hole was crumbly and she slipped back a couple of times.

She reached the end of the trail without further complications, retrieved the token from beneath a pile of leaves, and considered her options. It was too early to go back... she should just about have time to complete one of the stage five tasks before sunset – but which one? If there were going to be hidden traps, maybe Tracking wasn't as easy as she'd thought... plus, Projectiles stage five was nearer, and probably more likely that she could rush it if necessary.

She was just about to jog across to see what the fifth task was, when she caught sight of a familiar mop of blond hair moving through the trees. Daniel. She wondered where he was up to, replaying the map in her head... but of course, the stage three Poisons task was set up just around the corner. As she was about to run off, she hesitated; something was troubling her.

It took her a moment to identify the cause of her concern: if Daniel was only just about to start the third Poisons task, when that was clearly his strongest subject, he must have gone for a much broader strategy.

If he was doing two themes at stage 4 then he was just progressing quite slowly, and she'd beat him if she got her stage five. But it seemed unlikely he would have needed to spend so much time planning for such a comparatively simple strategy. On the other hand, if he'd gone for all four themes up to stage three... She added up both sets of scores in her head. It was close, but she was definitely on the wrong side, even if she managed to complete stage five Projectiles before the sun dipped below the horizon. Those bloody minus points. But the first stage tasks for Poisons and Locks were both miles away, there was absolutely no way she'd have time to reach either of them after completing one of the stage five tasks.

But she couldn't afford to finish behind Daniel, of all people, when he'd beaten her in the first contest. She couldn't let him increase his lead.

She'd started to creep forwards before she really understood what she was doing, the idea dawned so slowly, but the more she thought about it the more certain she became that this was the only way to guarantee coming in ahead of him. When she thought she'd gone about far enough, and then a few paces extra for luck, she scrambled up the nearest big tree. Still taking care not to make any sounds that might give away her presence, she began to crawl along the thickest branch that would take her in the right direction.

They were in a dense area of the forest, and she'd been right to assume she could make her way forward in the canopy; with only a couple of false starts, she managed to find herself a position with an unobstructed view of where Daniel was working.

There was a set of vials in front of him, and as she watched he poured one into another, turning the liquid green, and then a few drops from that into the next. The contents of the third vial turned orange, and he set it to one side before turning to grind a few grains and powders with the pestle and mortar. He emptied the contents into a beaker and heated it over a small burner, until it formed a fine white powder.

There was a large metal box to the side of the workbench, with a wheel on the front and two small funnels sticking out of the top. Daniel poured a few drops of the orange liquid into one of the funnels, shook about half of the powder into the other, then turned the wheel.

Eleanor wondered what he was doing, but a moment later the box ejected a wooden token from its base. Whatever it was, he'd clearly succeeded.

Daniel picked up the token and she squinted to try and read the words, a task made harder because he didn't bother taking the time to read them himself. *FIRST MAKE THE ANTIDOTE* was what she made out before he pocketed the token and jogged away, but it looked like there might have been more words beneath his fingers. She could only hope that would be enough to get her going.

She had some difficulty remembering where the stage four Poisons task was located; it wasn't one she'd ever have dreamed of needing. But although her recollection was hazy, she was confident that Daniel wasn't going in even vaguely that direction. That confirmed her suspicions, then. He must have opted for breadth in his strategy, and that meant she needed to complete stage four Poisons herself to beat him.

Even as she ran across the forest, she wondered if she was being stupid to think she stood any chance of succeeding, but she had to try. It was the only way she could possibly come in ahead of Daniel, and if she didn't do this she'd just be letting him increase his lead. If she could get one point ahead of him from this contest, they'd be level going in to the third and final stage.

She slowed down once she reached what she thought was the right area, towards the northern shore of the lake, and started looking around for anything that could be the challenge station. It didn't take her long to find it, though it was tucked away in a dip in the ground.

FIRST MAKE THE ANTIDOTE. But the antidote to what? She wished she'd been able to see the whole message.

There was a low work surface set up with a number of jars and bottles, mostly unlabelled, and she sat cross-legged on the ground to examine the task. There were no obvious instructions, but there was a metal box similar to the one she'd watched Daniel open... judging from what she'd seen, they were fitted with some special kind of lock that would only open once the right mixtures were poured into the funnels. She needed to work out what would trigger the mechanism of this box.

Her contemplation was disturbed by a sting at her neck; she batted at what she thought was a fly, but instead found a tiny dart caught in her skin.

She pulled it out and examined it, wondering what she'd been stung with. Presumably something that would impair her performance if she didn't deal with it. She looked at the various bottles and jars, recognising amongst the contents whispernut seeds, powders of hemlock and barren-root, and spelwood essence. Two empty beakers were labelled 'Sourfire' and 'Heart-Freeze', so presumably she had to make those mixtures to unlock the box. Thankfully, those were both things she'd succeeded with in the past. Unfortunately, though, both could also be used as an antidote – they each counteracted a different class of poison, and she didn't know what had been on that dart.

She was sure Daniel would know some clever test to find out – but she couldn't waste her time thinking about how much better he'd be at this task. He was off doing something else. She only hoped she could be lucky here to stand a chance of exceeding his score.

That thought brought her focus straight back to the task at hand. There was no time to lose.

Had the dart been doped with some kind of sedative or paralytic, in which case she needed to make the sourfire first, or was it more likely to be a stimulant, in which case she'd need the heart-freeze? If she took the wrong one, she'd make herself a lot worse. And how long did she have before the effects of the drug really kicked in and affected her performance?

Her head was already starting to ache as she measured out a small quantity of vespin powder into the 'Sourfire' jar, but that told her nothing useful. And unless the symptoms quickly gave her a clue one way or the other, she'd simply have to make them both, and wait until she was sufficiently afflicted by the poison to be able to identify it. She added six drops of merrilwort to the beaker and started to stir it in, then started working through the other ingredients in turn.

The clue worried her, though. If she, with her limited skill, would have time to make them both before she passed out, why would anyone need the clue at all?

She stopped mixing, took a few deep breaths, and put her fingers to her wrist to measure her heartbeat. As she'd thought: her pulse was racing. It wasn't entirely conclusive – it could just be her nerves getting the better of her – but perhaps it was enough to suggest she should focus on the heart-freeze first. She'd have to start again with the sourfire, though, if she stopped in the middle of making it.

She hesitated for a moment, then opened the hemlock. A tiny dose should be enough; if she was right about what she was experiencing, this would alleviate the symptoms for a while, and if she was wrong, it would only make it slightly worse.

She sprinkled a small quantity of the powder on to her tongue, swallowed, and continued with preparing the sourfire. She wasn't sure if it was the hemlock or her imagination that caused her headache to ease; she knew she could talk herself out of feeling pain, sometimes.

Once she'd finished mixing up the sourfire, and put it to one side to settle, she picked out what she thought were the right ingredients for heart-freeze. It had been such a long time since she'd made it, and she could only hope her memories were accurate. There were plenty of ingredients on the bench which she wasn't going to use at all, but presumably that was just designed to make sure she knew what she was doing.

She mixed the ingredients together, heated it briefly, and studied the result with a critical eye. It looked awful, nothing like the smooth paste she was hoping for, but no amount of stirring and heating was making any difference. And the sun was getting worryingly low.

She took up one of the measuring spoons, forced herself to swallow a mouthful of the lumpy mixture, and then turned her attention to the metal box. There were no markings by the funnels, so presumably it didn't matter which was which. She poured most of the sourfire into the left-hand funnel, upended the botched heart-freeze into the right-hand side, and closed her eyes before turning the wheel which would mix them, not even wanting to think what might happen if she got it wrong.

A few low clicking noises came from the box, and then it ejected the token. She seized it and leapt to her feet, knocking the jar of vespin to the ground, but didn't bother to stop and set it straight – it was too late for anyone else to have a chance, anyway. She turned and ran, sprinting as fast as she could around the lake, trying not to let herself think about how close the sun was getting to the horizon. The last thing she needed was an extra distraction. Her head was pounding, she was dripping with sweat, and panting with overpowering thirst. She longed to stop and scoop up water from the lake, but there wasn't time.

She sprinted through the double doors of the practice hall and brought herself to an abrupt halt in the middle of the room, wondering if she was too late. She glanced at Ragal, and he waved her towards the end of the hall, where a board was set up with a list of the students' names, each of which had a wooden ledge alongside it with and a set of four small notches for holding one token from each theme.

Eleanor looked at the numbers already displayed, and was about to reach for her own tokens when she was suddenly overcome with dizziness and nausea. She sank to her knees and struggled to stop herself vomiting.

"Are you okay?" Mikhail asked.

"I will be," she said, forcing a smile. "Just got poisoned – nothing serious."

He helped her to her feet, and she turned her attention back to the board. As she'd predicted, Daniel had stage three across all four themes. Mikhail had two at stage three and two at stage two, Jorge had stage six in Tracking and a couple of others at stage one, Mack had Locks 5 and the others at stage one, and Paul and Charles had a couple each at stage four.

Only Sebastien and Fred had managed to disqualify themselves by failing to make it back before sunset. Their rows were empty, as was hers... but it was time to do something about that.

She pulled the stack of tokens from her pocket and placed the three important ones onto the board: *Tracking 4*; *Projectiles 4*; *Poisons 4*. Unless she'd seriously misunderstood the scoring, that guaranteed her victory.

"As you may have noticed, the sun has set," Ragal said, walking across to the board as Eleanor stepped away. "Your colleagues will evidently not be joining us. Has anyone here yet to put his claim on the board?"

The assembled students were silent, waiting.

"The final scores, then. It appears that third place goes to Jorge for his admirable progress in Tracking, with a final score of twenty-two points."

Everyone clapped politely, although Jorge looked far from happy with the result.

"Second place goes to Daniel for his comprehensive achievement across the stage three challenges, scoring twenty-four points in total."

They clapped some more.

"And first place today, for an impressive three categories at stage four, goes to Eleanor, who scores twenty-nine points."

She felt a silly grin creeping across her face as the applause continued. She'd done it. First place! She'd actually done it.

"As you know, the winner of today's contest gets four points towards the council race," Ragal continued. "Second place is worth three, and third is worth two. Combined with the scores from the winter contest, that leaves Eleanor and Daniel jointly leading on six points each, with Jorge just behind on three. The three of you will progress to the summer contest."

Eleanor didn't hear the rest of his speech, if there was more; she was overcome with dizziness again, and woke up in the herbalist's lab, only to be told there was no way she was allowed to go for dinner. Celebrations would have to come later.

Chapter 29

"You sure you're okay?" Mikhail asked Eleanor when she returned to the common room.

"Yeah, definitely. They've given me some nasty stuff to drink any time I start feeling sick again."

"How is three at stage four even possible?" he asked. "Did the higher stages really not take that much longer than the early ones?"

"They took longer, I just..." She hesitated, wondering whether she could afford to come clean. Would they take her victory away from her, just because she'd taken an opportunity when it presented itself? She took a deep breath. "I didn't do quite all of the earlier ones, that's all."

"You what?"

"You heard me. I skipped a couple of the earlier ones."

Sebastien and Daniel came in from dinner just as she finished speaking, and Daniel took a seat opposite her.

"I do not understand at all," he said, looking thoroughly perplexed. "You are not really good with apothecary, I do not understand why you would choose Poisons over Locks."

"I was lucky." She didn't want to mention the shape her luck had taken, afraid he might take it personally. "It just fell into place."

"She didn't do all the lower stages," Mikhail said, and she smiled a little at his incredulity. "I didn't think that was possible."

"It is not," Daniel said. "Certainly it was not possible in Poisons. What did you mean, Eleanor?"

She studied her dirt-encrusted fingernails for a moment, trying to think of a suitable way to phrase her answer.

"I might have happened to find the clue from Poisons stage three," she said, feeling a faint blush rising in her cheeks. "And I might have happened to be very, very lucky with the stage four task."

364

There was a long silence. Eleanor shuffled uncomfortably in her chair, wishing she'd managed to postpone this conversation for long enough to think of a good explanation, and wondering if her oblique words would be enough to satisfy their curiosity.

"I am the only person who had Poisons at stage three," Daniel said, very slowly. "And after I had got that token, I came straight back to the hall. Your story does not make sense."

"Okay." Eleanor sighed. There was clearly no escaping from the whole truth. "Okay, look, I read it over your shoulder. I'm sorry. But I saw the chance and I had to take it."

"You read the clue from stage three when I completed it?"

"Yes."

"Then you did not really win."

"What? How can you say that?"

"You have not played fairly."

"Who said anything about fair? What happened to 'we need to beat the evil Venncastle'?"

"If you act this way, you are no better. It is not a real victory."

"Four points." She held up her fingers to emphasise the point. "That's the only kind of victory there is!"

She looked to Sebastien for support but he shook his head. "If you're going to justify cheating, maybe you should go and play with your Venncastle friends," he said. "They seem to appreciate that kind of logic."

Mikhail said nothing but wouldn't meet her gaze, and she realised it would be a while before they forgave her for this, if they ever did. She could cope with Daniel being a bad loser, he'd been like that all year – but if the others also thought she'd done something wrong then she needed to think it over.

She got up and left without a word, and walked straight into Raf's room without sparing even a sideways glance for the other lads in his common room, who called out their congratulations as she passed.

He wasn't there so she lay on his bed with her arms tucked behind her head, staring up at the ceiling and wondering whether she'd really blown it this time.

She was dozing off by the time Raf came in and sat on the

bed beside her.

"Are you okay, Ellie?"

"I need to know what you think," she said, looking up at him. "They're saying I cheated."

"Who's saying that?"

'It doesn't matter who. Daniel, Sebastien... everyone. But I need to know what you think – have I gone too far this time?"

"Okay, relax. Take a deep breath, and tell me what happened."

"Well, I'd done stage four in both Tracking and Projectiles, and it was getting quite late. I was about to go off in search of a stage five, and then I passed Daniel on his way to Poisons stage three, and I realised what he was doing and that he was going to beat me, so I..." She shook her head, fighting back tears that she couldn't explain. "I watched him, you see, and I read the clue from his stage three token, so I could do stage four Poisons. That's how I won. Do you think that's cheating?"

"You won, didn't you?" He squeezed her hand. "And the alternative was to lose. Faced with that choice, you just did what you needed to do."

"Is it really that simple?"

"Unless you want to make it more complicated. Come on, get up." He pulled her into a sitting position. "Let's go out and celebrate your victory."

"I'm not sure I want to go out."

"You're coming. You'll enjoy yourself once we're there, and you can't claim you need to work right now. Besides, it's spring carnival."

"We could go tomorrow," she suggested, but he shook his head.

"We're going now. Besides, you've got your banquet tomorrow – you won, remember? Come on."

"Do I have time to get changed?" she asked, but he shook his head and pulled her out of the room and down the stairs.

They could hear the distant sounds of the carnival as soon as they got outside, even before they left the academy's grounds, and by the time they made their way to the Marble Quarter they were surrounded by a party in full swing, to the sound of numerous drummers pounding their overlapping rhythms, working together to fill the city with a lively beat. The streets were heaving, not just with visiting revellers but with brightly-dressed dancers gyrating, acrobats balancing in human towers, and jugglers exchanging fire-sticks above the heads of the crowd.

The kind of food stalls usually hidden away in the city's markets and poorer quarters now lined both sides of the road, tucked between the marble columns along with stalls selling all manner of toys and souvenirs. Apparently the city's fanatical cleaners were taking a break for a couple of days. Eleanor took a deep breath, savouring the rich variety of smells as smoke from steamed sausages and grilled fish intermingled with the sweet scents of candied nuts and boiled fruits.

"Wasn't this worth coming out for?" Raf asked.

She nodded, still soaking up the atmosphere, amazed by the transformation which had overtaken the city.

They allowed themselves to be swept along in the sea of people, and Raf disappeared from her sights as the crowds surged forwards. She was skirting up a nearby drainpipe to look for him when he reappeared balancing two overflowing flagons of ale and large bags of deep-fried chicken pieces, char-grilled shrimps, and roasted almonds.

"What are you doing up there?" he asked when he spotted her.

"Looking for you!" She jumped down and helped herself to a handful of nuts. They were still warm from the brazier, and sticky with half-melted sugar which clung to her fingers.

He passed her one of the flagons. "Sometimes I think you should've been an acrobat."

"It'd be fun for about a month," she said, looking up at the nearest human tower, a stack of six young men, each one sitting on the shoulders of the man below. "But I'd get bored of having to do the same thing over and over. At least we get plenty of variety in our training."

They wandered through the streets, allowing the crowds to steer their movement, and rounded the corner into the Grand Square – though they probably wouldn't have recognised it if they hadn't known where they were. The curved steps leading up to the palace gates had been turned into the seats of an amphitheatre, with a temporary stage set up around – and in the case of the highwire, above – the fountain. A large wooden frame built high above the stage supported ropes, rings, and a pair of swinging trapeze bars.

Eleanor and Raf squeezed through the crowd and found space to sit down just as the bells rang out to mark the start of a new show.

The first performers to take to the stage were two young women on four-foot stilts, dressed in skimpy tasselled outfits, teetering along with spinning plates balanced along their arms.

"They must be cold," Eleanor whispered, shivering at the thought: for all that they were celebrating spring, it was barely past winter, and she wouldn't have wanted to be out without a thick jumper.

Then the music started, and a troupe of brightly-coloured entertainers streamed across the platform, shinning up ropes and posing on the high-wire, jumping from the trapeze and doing cartwheels along the beams, with others stamping or clapping in time to the beat.

Raf and Eleanor leaned forwards to watch, sipping at their drinks as the dancers and acrobats moved across the stage. When the show finished, they got to their feet and cheered along with the rest of the crowd.

As they made their way back into the streets, their attention was caught by a human pyramid.

"Ten dollars if you can get up here!" cried the young acrobat who stood atop nine of his colleagues. "Ten dollars if you can top the pyramid! Only one dollar to try!"

A young man in military dress stopped to take up the challenge, so the acrobat who'd been calling out somersaulted to the ground to take his dollar. The soldier didn't even manage to make it to the second layer of the pyramid, though, as the acrobats jogged and jostled to unsteady him.

"I could do that," Eleanor muttered. "Easy."

"Of course you could," Raf agreed.

"Have you got a dollar?"

"I might have, but you don't need to go up there. You've got nothing to prove."

"That guy's in the Specials – that's where I thought I'd end up." Eleanor tugged at Raf's arm, pulling him towards the acrobats. "I can't believe he *fell off*."

"Yeah, but he's drunk. And, now I think of it, so are you."

"I want to have a go. It'll be fun – carnivals are all about having some fun! And ten dollars would be nice, I'll buy you another drink when I win..." She slipped one hand into his pocket while she spoke, fishing for change, and came out with a dollar held proudly aloft. "Thank you!"

She heard him sigh, but he didn't try to stop her. She handed the coin to the acrobat, and started her ascent. The acrobats who made up the lower layers of the pyramid were clearly determined to make it as difficult as they could, moving to try and destabilize her, but she dug her fingers into their slippery skin and hauled herself up, finding toe-holds on reluctant hips and shoulders. Eventually, she managed to pull herself to kneel across the shoulders of the pair of acrobats at the top of the stack.

"You see!" she called down to Raf. It looked a *very* long way down. "I don't need a lousy uniform, do I? Look! I told you I could do it!"

Raf rolled his eyes at her, and beckoned her to come down.

"Now, where's my ten dollars?" she demanded of the acrobat to her left. He pointed down to the young man who'd taken her dollar in the first place. "Where's my ten dollars?" she yelled down, cupping her hands to make sure he heard her.

"You have to stand up, miss," he shouted back. "No money if you can't stand up."

Annoyed that the rules seemed to be changing in front of her eyes, she struggled to her feet, not sure whether the unsteadiness she felt was more a consequence of the alcohol or the constantly-moving tower she was trying to balance on.

"Done! You can pay him." She pointed down at Raf, but the acrobat shook his head.

"You'll have to let go first. You're not standing up properly."

"If you don't give me my money," she said, "I'm going to

stand here all night and yell about how it's all a fraud, and you don't want *anyone* to win."

Her fingers clasped around the hilt of her dagger, but Raf saw her and began to scramble up the pyramid, to the indignant cries of the acrobats.

"Hey! You haven't paid! You need to pay your dollar if you want a turn, mister!"

"I don't want a turn," he said, pulling himself up until his face was level with Eleanor's feet. "I'm just taking my friend home. Come on, Ellie."

"I want my ten dollars!"

"Forget the money. It's time we got you home."

He reached up and took her hand, pulling her downwards until she eventually realised it would be easier to keep her balance if she climbed down by herself. Once her feet were safely back on solid ground, however, she was determined to claim her prize. She marched up to the acrobat who'd taken her dollar, who was still trying to drum up further business.

"I want my ten dollars. You can't say I didn't win."

"Too late now, isn't it? You can't prove you did it."

She lunged forwards but Raf caught her round the waist before she could reach for her knife, and pulled her out of the way.

"Come on, Ellie. It's not worth it."

"I want my money." She struggled against his arms. "I *won*."

"On the scale of things you've won today, ten dollars is nothing. Come on, let's go home."

"No."

He sighed. "If I let go of you, will you promise to stay still?"

"Why?"

"Just don't go attacking anyone, okay? And I'll get your money."

"Okay."

"Promise?" he asked, still holding her tightly.

"I promise."

"Good." He let go of her waist, turned to the acrobat – who was watching in some amazement – and picked him up by the collar. "Now, are you going to give this young lady her winnings, or am I going to have to report you? I know the city guards really didn't want any trouble tonight, they're busy enough worrying about rebels."

The acrobat paled and reached inside his coat, producing two five-dollar coins. "Didn't mean any offence, sir," he mumbled as he handed them to Eleanor. "Don't want any trouble."

"If you want us to go away quietly, you'd best make it fifteen," Raf said. "Otherwise I'm sure the girl can make good on her promise to drive all your custom away."

The acrobat handed across another five dollars, and Raf let go of his collar before turning back to Eleanor. "Are you ready to go home now?"

"I promised to buy you something."

"Another time." He put his arm around her shoulder and steered her back towards the academy, and she leaned into him for support.

"Are we coming back tomorrow? I think I like the carnival."

"You've got your banquet tomorrow. You won, remember?"

"Oh, that's not going to be fun." She stumbled on a wonky cobblestone, and grabbed hold of him to steady herself. "Dinner with a load of old men who wish I wasn't even here."

"Most people don't feel like that."

"Most of them *do*."

"If that's true, it's even more important for you to go. Force it home to them how well you're doing."

"But I'd much rather come out with you."

"You'll be fine. Wish I could come, but I'll get Ivan to look after you."

"I don't need looking after!" She pouted her lips in an exaggerated sulk. "I just don't think it's going to be much fun."

"If you think like that, it won't be. Much better to decide to enjoy yourself in spite of anyone who's not on your side – then they'll know they can't touch you."

The celebratory dinner was to be held in the Association's main banquet hall, and Eleanor was determined not to be late. She pulled her favourite emerald gown out of her closet, slipped her stilettos into the bodice sheathes, and stepped into the skirt.

371

She'd just finished tightening the laces of the corset when a knock at the door disturbed her.

"Who is it?" she called, reaching for her comb. "I'm a bit busy!"

"Your escort for the evening," came the reply. "Don't hurry yourself, I'll make myself comfortable out here."

By the time she opened the door, he'd already settled himself in one of the common room chairs.

"Ivan! What are you doing here?"

"I'm going to escort you to your banquet, when you're ready."

"Did Raf send you? Because I'm going to kill him, I told him I didn't need any kind of special treatment, I'm fine. I'm just doing my hair."

"No special treatment," Ivan said. "I'm just going to walk you across. And no, Raf didn't 'send' me, I don't know where you've got that from."

"Okay, never mind. I won't be long."

She closed the door again and leaned against the wall, trying to decide whether she believed him. What were the chances he'd come of his own volition, only a day after Raf had threatened to make him look after her? It didn't seem all that likely. Still, there was nothing she could do about it now.

She ran the comb through her hair, stained her lips, and straightened her skirt. Once she was sure she looked presentable, she went out to where Ivan was waiting.

"Ready?" he checked.

"Ready."

It was over a mile to the banquet hall from the student accommodation block where Eleanor had her room, and she had to hitch up her skirt to stop it trailing in the mud as they walked.

"So who's going to be there tonight?" she asked.

"Everyone who's in town," Ivan said. "Well, apart from the other students, of course. But all the academy's instructors, most of the council, and everyone else in the Association who isn't working on something away from Almont."

"And yet you really expect me to believe, out of all those people, you just came to fetch me because you felt like it?"

372

He hesitated for a moment. "Do you want me to be honest with you?"

"Always."

"You mustn't blame Raf, though – this has nothing to do with him."

"Okay." She'd reserve judgement on whether she believed him until after she'd heard his story.

"The thing is, this is going to be an uncomfortable evening for some people, and I'd prefer it not to be uncomfortable for you when you should be celebrating. Some of my colleagues don't appreciate that a woman might be doing as well as you've done. I hope I can insulate you from a part of that."

"Well, that's sweet of you, but I really don't need insulating. They're all going to have to get used to me sooner or later. I do intend to win, you know."

"And of course everyone will come round, given time, but these things are slow to change. I can do small things that may help, even if it's just to make sure you sit with people who'll be friendly, this one evening. Let the dissenters see you from a distance this time. You'll have plenty of chances to get to know them later."

"And you're sure Raf didn't put you up to this?"

"He didn't have to. Besides, I know the lay of the land in these parts better than he does, and I know you shouldn't be worrying about it tonight. This one's for you to enjoy. The politics can wait."

They walked on in silence for a little longer before Eleanor asked, "Did you hear anything about what happened in the contest?"

"Aside from your impressive score, you mean?"

"Did you hear how I got that score?" She wasn't sure if Daniel had made any official complaints.

"Three themes at stage four, wasn't it? Which is very good going, Eleanor. Very good indeed. I helped set up the Projectiles tasks, of course, and I did wonder if you'd go right to the end – you would've loved the seventh challenge, it was beautiful."

"You said something to me once about making our own

rules," she said. "I think I might have redefined the contest rules, just a little."

"How so?"

"You're not supposed to be able to do the higher levels without completing the the level below, right?"

"That's right."

She wondered if she was making a mistake to trust him, but Raf had almost convinced her it was fine. She just wanted a second opinion before sitting down to celebrate her victory.

"But that's not actually what's enforced. What you actually need is to read the clue from the lower level."

"It's the same thing. Getting the token – the clue – is completing the task. There's no other definition. If you find an easy way to get one of them, that's just skill."

"Even if you read the clue over someone else's shoulder?"

He paused in the middle of the path, silent. She stood a few feet away and watched him, waiting for the words that could exonerate or condemn her, hoping she'd judged him correctly.

"I saw the chance and I took it," she said when the silence had gone on too long.

"How many people know this?" he asked, quietly.

"That's partly what I wanted to find out. Not many, it seems. Daniel, Mikhail, Sebastien, Raf... and now you."

"I'd keep it that way, if you can. Speaking personally, I'm nothing but impressed, but there are some who'd take it less well."

"Albert will know there's something wrong, though. There was no way I could've done four Poisons tasks, it would've taken me months."

"But you did stage four?"

"Yes."

"That's not a trivial achievement – especially since it's your least favourite subject. You've every right to feel proud of yourself. And I doubt it would even occur to Albert to wonder whether you really did all the tasks. You had the token, therefore you did it."

"Do you think I'll be in trouble, then? If word gets round?"

"In trouble? No. I just think you'll be unpopular in some

circles."

"I already am."

"Different circles. Trust me, the same people think very poorly of me. I'm probably being silly, though – these things always get out. It would just be better for you if it didn't get out until later." He put his arm around her shoulders. "Come on, let's put the whole thing out of our minds – we've got some serious celebrating to do."

The banqueting hall was as vast as she'd remembered it, but it was laid out differently tonight. Unlike at Jon and Victor's graduation dinner, there was no student table this evening, and no separate table for the council. Instead, the tables were arranged in one huge rectangular formation around the room. Ivan steered Eleanor to her designated seat next to Ragal, and took the chair to her left for himself.

"Congratulations," he said, pouring a generous amount of wine into her tumbler. "You've earned it."

"Have I?"

"Even more than you could imagine."

Chapter 30

"Curses!" Eleanor cried, stopping abruptly in the middle of the stairs. "I forgot my stars. I'll catch you up."

"Can't you get them later?" She'd been walking back from their projectiles lesson with Fred, since her own room-mates still weren't talking to her, and they were half way back to their rooms when she realised her mistake. And the class had already run late.

"No, I'll go now, before someone else picks them up. They're not marked."

"Well, see you at dinner," Fred said, slipping past her.

She sprinted back down to the practice hall, and was about to push the door open when she heard Jorge's unmistakable voice protest from the room beyond: "But I *am* trying!"

"Not hard enough." That sounded like Ivan. She wondered if Jorge's basic, soulless throwing technique had finally got him in trouble.

"But..."

"No buts. We need you to win this; after last year's fiasco we can't afford to lose any more influence."

Eleanor froze, hand still resting on the doorknob. They could only be talking about the contest. She wasn't supposed to be hearing this, and common sense told her to make a silent exit, but curiosity held her by the door.

"I know that, but that blasted girl's a cheat and–"

Ivan cut him off. "Do you like being bested by a woman?"

"No." Jorge's voice was suddenly quiet, ashamed; Ivan had known the right nerve to strike, and it hit Eleanor too like a kick to the stomach. Ivan was one of the few who'd never treated her like an imposter. Almost unable to believe what she was hearing, she bent and pressed her eye to the keyhole.

"That's why you have to make up excuses about cheating," Ivan continued. It was definitely him. "Or her extra year of experience, or the idea that people are soft on her because she's a girl. None of that has anything to do with why you keep failing!"

"I'll train more," Jorge promised. "I'll make sure I do better this time."

Ivan slammed his fist against the table. "You're completely missing the point! You won't win this by being stronger, of course you're stronger than her, and than Daniel. It isn't enough! Do you have any idea why you're currently third?"

There was an uncomfortably long silence; Eleanor watched them, looking for any indication that they might be about to move, ready to run if she had to.

"I thought not," Ivan said at last. "So let me tell you what Daniel and Eleanor have got that you, somehow, seem to be incapable of grasping. Instinct. His instincts are subtle and meticulous, hers are fast and by all accounts deadly, but at the end of the day they both listen to the ancient voices in their heads."

"Instinct?" Jorge sounded skeptical, but Eleanor knew Ivan was right. Most of her finest moments had been instinctive reactions – there wasn't time to think in the tightest of corners. Though she wasn't sure about Daniel, who tended to over-think everything.

"Instinct," Ivan repeated. "And in an ideal world, between now and the next challenge you'd learn to start listening to yours, assuming you've got some. The only certainty is, one way or another, Venncastle needs you to win."

"I'll try."

"Have you heard anything I've said? Trying isn't good enough."

"What more can I do?"

"You owe it to the school to do better than just 'trying'. Fred's out of the running, so you're our only hope – failure is not an option. So it's time you pulled yourself together and start acting like you might be worthy of your heritage!"

"Will you help me?"

"What in all the Empire do you think I'm trying to do? I'll help you any way I can, but you have to do some of the work yourself."

Eleanor stood up and edged quietly away from the door, feeling sick to her stomach at the conspiracy she'd apparently unearthed. Of course she knew there was some anger amongst the Venncastle contingent over Jon and Victor's combined failure – that would've been hard to miss – but this was something different. She'd never thought Ivan, of all people, would have turned against her. Venncastle loyalty was legendary, he'd told her that much, but he'd always given the impression that the Association mattered to him, too.

She wondered if she should take it all as a rather oblique compliment – at least she was being considered a threat rather than a joke. But she really wanted to win, that was the only way she could guarantee her future position, and she was troubled by the idea of Jorge's strength being directed by Ivan's brain.

And she couldn't assume it was just Ivan – who knew how many others might be involved? Venncastle certainly had the numbers.

She walked straight back to her room and barricaded herself inside, no longer interested in food or even getting a wash. There was too much to think about.

She sat on her bed and poured the last dregs out of a bottle of spring nectar that Raf had given her. She wished she could go and talk to him about what she'd heard, but for the first time she'd found something she didn't dare mention to him – not given that it was Ivan, and Jorge, and maybe the whole of his school that was implicated.

She wondered briefly if there was anyone else she could talk to, but there was no-one she felt close enough to trust, when she didn't want Ivan to find out she'd been listening. She even considered approaching Daniel, the one person guaranteed to sympathise with anti-Venncastle sentiments, but even if he was prepared to talk to her he'd only think she was being weak or, worse, he'd want to rush her into doing something about it. And she wasn't sure she could bear him smugly pointing out that he'd been right all along to be paranoid.

She gulped down the drink, wishing she'd had more than half a glass left; the lightheaded, careless feeling appealed to her more than it ever had before. As she sat and stared out of the window, watching the sky gradually darken, she thought about what to do next, turning over each possibility in her mind.

She could try to report what she'd witnessed to the council, but then she'd have to admit to listening, and she'd have trouble proving anything since – so far as she could tell – no-one had actually done anything yet. Jorge and Ivan would deny any wrongdoing, it was unlikely the council would take any action based on her word against theirs, but Ivan would be warned. And he was far from stupid, he'd almost certainly just take more care in any future plans. Besides, there were enough Venncastle graduates around to make her life extremely uncomfortable.

She could ignore it and try to carry on exactly as before, but she didn't know if she could make herself forget what she'd heard. She'd have particular trouble talking to people like Ivan and, especially, Raf... indeed, all the students from Venncastle whom she'd spent so much time with over the last few months. She was starting to wish she'd listened to Daniel's advice and avoided them all, if this was how they'd look to repay her friendship.

No use going to the council, then, and doing nothing wasn't an option.

Only one course of action seemed to remain: she'd have to take matters into her own hands. She'd keep tabs on Jorge until the summer contest, investigate Ivan's every move, and make absolutely sure they didn't have chance to cheat.

She started her surveillance the next morning, arriving early for breakfast and spinning out her meal until Jorge had finished his, then walking a couple of paces behind him until he disappeared back into his room. She went to pick up her own weapons ready for class. She couldn't stake out the corridor to see if he went out again, that would be too conspicuous, but they had combat practice next, and from the wooden practice frame in the grounds she'd have a clear view of the entrance to Ivan's building.

She jogged downstairs. Unsurprisingly, considering the drizzly weather, no-one else had yet come to practise outside. She climbed up onto the frame and amused herself doing hand-stands and somersaults along one of the rotating beams. If anyone saw her, they'd just assume she wanted to work on her balance.

The morning passed without incident, Jorge was present as expected at lunch, and he wouldn't have dared to miss the afternoon's poisons class. Albert gave them a detailed lecture on making complex tinctures to mimic the effects of common natural venoms, with the goal of tricking the victim into taking a supposed remedy which would actually speed their demise. Eleanor found this much more interesting than most of what they studied in poisons – at least it was clever – but her focus was on Jorge. When Fred let slip that Ivan would be going out that evening, however, she finally allowed herself a moment of relaxation. There was nothing Jorge could do on his own.

The next day was free, and after an early breakfast Eleanor took up her position on the practice frame again. It was raining even harder than the previous morning, and she was fairly sure she'd have the place to herself.

The one thing she'd forgotten to plan for, however, was what to do if she saw anything.

She was hanging upside-down from one of the higher beams, flicking knives and stars towards a nearby tree, when she spotted Jorge running across the yard, cloak wrapped tightly around his shoulders.

Once he'd ducked inside Ivan's building she dropped to the ground, recovered her weapons, and ran after him. The second she stepped into the vestibule she knew she'd made one crucial mistake: she was dripping wet, and her tracks would be obvious in the corridors.

She stripped off her outer clothes and shoes, wrapped them into a tight bundle, and tucked the whole package out of sight behind a pillar. If she ran into anyone she might have trouble explaining why she was wandering around barefoot in her vest and shorts, but at least she stood a chance of getting there without leaving conspicuous trails of water.

She followed Jorge's damp footsteps to Ivan's door and pressed her eye to the keyhole. This was where her plans ran out. She couldn't just burst in and disturb them, and even if she brought someone else along as a witness, there was no way to prove they were conspiring. No, the only way forward was to try and find out *what* they were planning so she could catch them out later, when they tried to put their plans into action.

"What is it you want me to do?" Jorge said. "You don't seem to believe I'm doing my best."

"Are you?" Ivan sounded angry. "Because if this is all you're capable of, maybe you should take a good look in the mirror and think about whether you're really cut out for this. Did our assessors make a mistake putting you forwards?"

"No, sir."

"Then you'll have to give me more than this."

"What is it you want?"

Eleanor missed his reply because she heard footsteps approaching in the distance and, with nowhere else to go in the dead end of the corridor, she braced one hand against each wall and pulled herself up, flattening her body against the ceiling. The footsteps turned out to be a servant, bringing a tray of sandwiches for Ivan and Jorge's lunch. It took her a moment to spot the opportunity: with both of them out of the way in the dining room, she could let herself into the sitting room and find somewhere to hide. That way she'd stand more chance of hearing everything. Once the servant had come out and disappeared around the corner, she dropped lightly to the floor and slipped inside the room.

"Did you hear something?" Ivan asked.

Eleanor panicked, threw herself to the ground, and rolled under the sofa, trying to keep as quiet as she could.

"What?"

"Oh, never mind. Probably just the wind."

They chatted harmlessly about the unseasonally stormy weather as they ate their lunch, then came back through to the sitting room. Jorge sat directly above Eleanor's head, and she could feel the fabric brush against her cheek.

"On your feet, then," Ivan said sharply. "If you're serious about getting this then you don't have time to waste sitting down."

"Show me one more time."

"No, no, you're missing the point. This isn't about copying

me. Put the blindfold back on."

There was a moment's shuffling, and then Jorge stood up.

"Now turn around three times and throw."

Eleanor watched Jorge's feet as he turned on the spot, remembering acutely how she'd felt when Ivan had spun her and then asked her to take aim. She'd had it harder, too, with all the different numbers on the boards.

She was brought out of her reverie by a series of loud crashes as Jorge's inaccuracy brought half a shelf of tools down onto the floor. A stick of chalk rolled under the sofa and came to rest against Eleanor's arm, and she willed Ivan not to bother to look for it.

She heard a crack as Ivan slammed his hand against something wooden; probably the door. "Get out of here," he growled. "Go and practise somewhere where there's less to break. And don't come back until you can do it without thinking."

Eleanor heard the door click open and then closed, and Ivan sat down with a heavy sigh. From the little cutting sounds, and the offcuts of wood and leather landing on the floor near her face, she guessed he must be making one of his weapons.

He stayed there for what felt like an eternity, and it wasn't until he snuffed out the lanterns and went to bed that Eleanor felt she could risk moving. As she crept out and went to retrieve her clothes from the vestibule, she felt a little dispirited. She'd wasted a whole day to keep an eye on Jorge, but she hadn't witnessed anything worse than a little extra help with his throwing. After all the times she'd gone to Ivan for guidance, she couldn't begrudge him that.

She threw herself into her lessons over the next few days, trying to put the whole business out of her mind, but she kept wondering whether that was really all there was to it. If Ivan really wanted to guarantee Jorge winning the contest, he was going to have to do more than teach him a couple of knife tricks.

It was after their craft lecture the following week that she next noticed Jorge branch off in the direction of Ivan's building. She stopped to adjust her boot laces, waited for the others to disappear from sight around the corner, and doubled back to follow him.

"Why can't you tell me what it's going to be?" Jorge was asking as she put her ear to the door. She was getting worryingly familiar with this position.

"Because I don't know. You're so bloody impatient! I can't give you information that hasn't even been decided yet."

"But you will, once you know, won't you?"

"Once the council have decided, you'll all find out within a day or two. Meanwhile, pay attention to your case studies, and if you still think you need my help once it's been announced, you know where to find me. But only if you've mastered the blindfold."

Fearing Ivan's impatience would bring the conversation to an abrupt end, Eleanor turned and ran, not stopping until she reached the dining hall.

Raf and Greg came in just before she'd finished her dinner; she crammed the remains of her roll into her mouth and got up to leave the room.

"Ellie!" Raf came running after her and caught her arm. "Are you avoiding me?"

"No," she lied, spitting crumbs everywhere. "Just very busy – there's a lot riding on this last contest, you know."

"I'm sorry." He rested his hand on her shoulder. "It was a stupid question. I know you've got a lot on your mind, it just seems such a long time since we really had time to talk... you've seemed a bit distant, and then rushing off like that with barely a 'hello'."

"I'm just working hard," she assured him. She didn't know how she could possibly explain why she didn't want to see him right now; it wasn't even his fault. But he'd never believe what she'd learnt about his school's conspiracy unless – worse – he already knew. Yet if they got talking, and particularly if he got her drinking, she wasn't sure she could avoid spilling out everything that was on her mind. "Look, I need to get on, but we'll catch up once all this nonsense is over."

"Promise?"

She nodded.

He gave her a brief hug. "Good luck, Ellie. I'm rooting for you."

She made her way back to her room in a daze and pulled her emerald necklace out from beneath the matress. She sat on the edge of the bed, clasping the pendant tightly in both hands and trying to fill her mind with happy memories from the moment Raf had given it to her. She wanted so badly to believe that he wasn't involved in Ivan's plot. She desperately needed to believe his words of support were genuine. Yet if there was any chance his Venncastle loyalty would colour his judgement, then she couldn't risk exposing what little she already knew. She needed to keep an eye on Jorge without any risk he might notice her, and that meant not trusting anyone.

After projectiles the next day, Ivan called her back just as she was about to leave the hall.

"Yes?" She turned to face him, heart pounding. Had he seen her running away from his room? Had he worked out what she'd heard?

"Do you have a moment?"

"Of course." She hoped she'd managed to force her voice into a natural timbre, but she felt frozen inside.

"Sit down." He waved her across to the low benches at the side of the hall, and once the other students had all gone, he went to join her there.

"Is there a problem?" she asked. "I know I'm not getting the hang of multiple stars as quickly as you might expect, but I am getting there."

"This isn't about your performance – you're making fine progress on a difficult skill. Nothing to complain about there. This is, well, personal."

She waited for him to elaborate without looking at him, hoping he couldn't hear the way her heart was hammering, painfully conscious of every beat.

"The thing is," he went on, "young Raf's a bit worried he might've done something to upset you, and I wondered if there was anything I could do to mediate."

"He hasn't upset me at all."

"Really?"

384

"I've just been so busy lately. You're working us hard!"

"Well, you mustn't spend all your time working, it's not healthy. You need some breaks, and you need to spend some time with your friends, so I'll expect you to go along tomorrow night – and you can consider that an order."

"But I–"

"No excuses, Eleanor. I'll tell Raf he's to fetch you if you don't turn up at the usual time."

She didn't know what to say; she certainly couldn't explain why she didn't want to go out with them, so she kept quiet. Maybe she could hide somewhere the following evening, or pretend to be out, though she couldn't expect any help from her roommates.

"I'm glad that's settled, then," Ivan said, getting to his feet. "You know you can always come and see me if you need anything, don't you?"

"Thanks," she said, though he was the last person who could help her with her current problems.

When she got back to her room after dinner, still thinking about everything Ivan had said, she started to wonder whether she should invent something to go and talk to him about. She knew the way he left things scattered around his room, so if he was working on anything to help Jorge, there might be evidence lying around.

But first, she had to get through an evening of pretending to be sociable with some indeterminate number of Venncastle students.

She spent as long as she reasonably could over her dinner the following evening, then went to her room to get changed, hoping against the odds that they might have left without her, but when she eventually made her way down the stairs she met Raf on his way up.

"You are coming out then, Ellie?" he said, turning to fall into step beside her. "I was just about to come and look for you, I thought you might've changed your mind."

"Ivan told me I had to," she said. "He thinks I'm working too hard."

"Well, I'm glad to see you – it's been far too long."

"Yeah, it has." She looked at his earnest expression and wished she didn't have to work so hard to avoid him, then reminded herself sternly that that was precisely why he was a danger to her. Her instinct was to trust him, but for once she couldn't afford to risk following her instincts.

They reached the bottom of the stairs where Fred, Nate and Greg were waiting.

"Shouldn't you be training?" Fred asked when he caught sight of Eleanor. "Jorge hasn't been out in weeks."

"I'm sure it'll do me good to have a break," she said. "No-one can work constantly, can they?"

"He's having a good try," Fred said. "And knowing you, I'd have thought you'd want to put in just as much time."

"Ivan's told Ellie she's to stop being such a workaholic," Raf said. "Don't put her off now she's agreed to come out!"

"Is Ivan coming?" Eleanor asked. She didn't like the thought of what he and Jorge might be getting up to together while she was out of the way.

"Not tonight."

"I think you should go and get him, after all the fuss he made about me working too much. Make him come for one drink, at least."

"Oh, he's much worse than you for getting caught up in work – always has been. But you won't change his mind if he thinks he's got too much on."

Eleanor was wary of what the others might think if she tried too hard to persuade them, so she satisfied herself with the thought that she'd visit Ivan tomorrow and see what she could find in his rooms. Meanwhile, she simply had to stay on her guard and make sure *she* didn't give anything away.

They went to a tavern that Eleanor didn't recognise, somewhere on the north side of town, where Raf bought tankards of beer for everyone.

"So, you won't be coming out so often after the solstice," Nate said, looking between Fred and Eleanor. "Who d'you think's likely to be coming from school this year?"

"Definitely Hal," Fred said. "And maybe Robbie or Sam?"

"Not Robbie," Raf said. "He's good, technically, but he hasn't got the spirit for it. He'd be much better off in some corner of the army."

"I think Kit would be okay, too," Nate said. "Though maybe he's a bit military."

"I think they want him to stay and teach," Fred said. "He's the best swordsman we've had in years."

Raf put his arm around Eleanor's shoulder. "Sorry, Ellie, this can't be much interest to you."

"It's fine, don't worry." She'd been quietly glad of a topic where she could reasonably keep her mouth shut.

"There are some murmurings that the Empire might be losing patience with us, since all our best students tend to be opt-outs," Raf went on, turning back to the others. "And Ivan said something about them wanting to bring the Association into line, too, so it's not just school stuff."

"The Empress is getting grumpy in her old age," Fred said. "But she won't last long if she tries to make too many changes."

"I heard she's planning to expand the Empire," Greg said. "Try again to take the southern mountains. Though if a couple of Flying Rock's best men couldn't even get back alive, I don't see the chances."

Fred laughed. "What's the odds we'll get that mission next year, then? What d'you think, El, you up for a trip to the mountains?"

"If that's what we have to do, why not?"

"But it's impossible," Greg said. "The mountain men are vicious – they've destroyed whole legions. No-one comes back from the mountains."

Eleanor smiled. "Definitely one for us, then. Nobody's infallible."

She let it get to mid-afternoon the next day before she decided to go and call on Ivan. He waved her into his sitting room and offered her a drink before asking why she was visiting.

"You said I could come if I needed to talk," she said, taking a seat by the fireplace although the grate was cold.

"Of course."

"I'm a bit concerned about this final contest," she said, fiddling with a star she'd had in her pocket. "It's hard to prepare for something so important, when we don't know what it is."

"I'm afraid I can't give you any hints," Ivan said, sitting beside her. "No-one knows what it's going to be, yet. It won't be decided until a few days beforehand – it just depends on what needs to be done."

"I wasn't expecting you to tell me, even if you knew... I mean, I wouldn't want to cheat." She paused momentarily for emphasis. "I just thought you might have some general advice."

"All I can suggest is that you don't worry about training 'for the contest.' Forget about the contest, and focus on becoming the best that you can be – that'll serve you best in the long run. And this won't be like the last rounds: no staged fights, no carefully designed challenges to stretch you in particular directions, just a job that needs doing."

"It really could be absolutely anything?"

"Anything. So pay attention to all the missions you're taught about – case studies can give you a lot of clues. And whatever it is, you'll approach it in whatever way suits your style, so the most important thing is to be comfortable with yourself. That isn't an area where you have trouble. You just need to make sure you're in your best possible condition, and everything will fall into place on the night."

Even though she'd asked the question without any real interest in his answer, she had to keep reminding herself not to take his words at face value; if he was helping Jorge, anything he said to her was unlikely to be good advice. But it didn't help that, aside from the part about forgetting the contest – which was plainly impossible – it all sounded very reasonable and sensible. There was nothing that stood out as being designed to steer her in the wrong direction.

"Anyway, did you have a good time last night?" he asked. "I did check with Raf that you'd made it."

"I'm sure it was good for me to get out. It's a shame you couldn't come yourself – I'm sure it's not good for you to get overworked, either."

"Maybe next time, but things are busy in the real world at the moment. There's a lot of council stuff to do."

"And students always pestering you for help," she said, thinking of Jorge more than herself.

"Not so much of that, thankfully," he said, too quickly.

"Well, I won't keep you long. I think I just needed reassuring."

"Please don't think I'm rushing you, Eleanor. You're always welcome to take up some of my time."

"Well, if you did have time while I'm here, I wondered if you'd take a quick look at my stars technique. I'm sure there's something not quite right."

"Of course, of course. Let's have a quick play before dinner."

"If you ordered some food, I could eat with you." She gave him what she hoped was her sweetest smile. "Then we'd have loads of time to practise."

"I can do that. It's probably getting late already – let me go and have a word with the kitchen now, and then we'll have a look at those stars of yours."

"Will you ask them for dessert?" she asked as he reached the door.

"You should always have dessert if you want it. Wait here, then; I won't be long."

She counted to ten after he'd left the room, just to be sure he'd really gone, and then started her search. They'd be going into the dining room once the food arrived, so she went to try the other doors first. She had to move quickly before he got back.

The leftmost door opened into a small bedroom with a pallet on the floor, and shelves along the walls full of all kinds of bits and pieces. Eleanor's heart sank when she saw just how cluttered the space was but she walked the length of the room quickly, scanning every surface for anything that looked out of place. It was hard to define the norm for this room, though; there were parts of broken weapons and half-finished pipes, whittling knives and wood shavings, assorted darts and pellets, various unmarked bottles and jars, scraps of parchment and reels of wire. Any of it or none of it could have been part of some project to help Jorge defeat her.

The next door turned out to be a store cupboard, filled with weapons and larger tools. Nothing of interest stood out, though Eleanor caught herself admiring the size of his private armoury, every hilt marked with some variant of the same amethyst design he'd showed her on their first meeting.

She pushed the door closed and went back to examining the shelves and table-tops in the sitting room. She was shuffling through tools on the shelf by the window when Ivan came back; she froze as she heard the door open. She'd assumed she would have heard him in the corridor, giving herself enough time to get back to her seat and pretend she hadn't moved, but now she'd just have to brazen it out.

"Looking for something?" Ivan asked. He sounded more amused than angry.

"Just wondering if you had any more interesting weapons lying around," she said, hoping she'd managed to sound sufficiently casual about it. Nothing would be worse than acting guilty. "After all, I'm in love with that palm-blade, and I know you enjoy making stuff... I just wondered if you had anything else exciting lurking in here."

"Well, if you're after something really fun, I can show you a little design I've been working on." He went through to his bedroom and came out holding something that looked like a glove.

"What's that?"

He slipped his hand into the glove, and now Eleanor could see that the design left his fingers open, and there was some additional structure built in across the back of his hand. He made a small movement with his thumb and something tiny fired across the room, lodging in the back of a chair.

"Recognise it?" he asked.

She shook her head, but went to pull the missile from where it had stuck. It was a small metal bolt, only about the length of her smallest finger, but it had easily sunk into the wood of the chair.

"It's a portable version of the mechanism from the Puzzle Chamber – and of course, we used a version of it in the stage four Projectiles task. It's taken me about two years to get it working at this size, but I think I've cracked it now. Can you imagine having this much force in your pocket?"

"Incredible." She could only hope that Ivan's plan didn't involve arming Jorge with one of these. "How soon will you be able to equip everyone?"

He shook his head. "Never. This is just too powerful – we can't risk the design falling into enemy hands. No, we can only make a few of them, and we can only use them when we know we're fully in control."

"Could you block it?" she asked. "If you knew it was coming, I mean."

"Probably, but it'll be tough to deflect something that small, and that fast."

Their dinner arrived while Eleanor was still examining the new invention, and she carried it through to the dining room with her. She had a quick look around the room whilst Ivan served the food, but again she saw nothing amongst the clutter that stood out as important.

As she ate, her eyes flicked between Ivan's new creation and the cluttered shelves behind him.

"Now, shall we have a look at your stars?" Ivan asked once they'd finished.

He went across to his armoury closet and brought out a target board, which he hung on the wall, and four stars, which he passed to Eleanor.

"Now, what is it that was giving you trouble?"

"It's the aiming," she said. She held two stars ready in each hand, then flicked her left wrist to send one pair sailing neatly towards the target. "So that was fine. I'm okay as long as I want them to go parallel. But if I want to spread them..."

She released the stars from her right hand to demonstrate, trying to send them to opposite edges of the board, but although they spun off in roughly the right directions they'd both started to wobble before they reached the target. They bounced without catching and fell to the floor, ineffectual.

"See?"

"Curious." He picked up the stars and handed two of them back to her, keeping the others for himself. "Most people have more trouble getting them to fly straight. Show me again."

She tried again, and the same thing happened.

"Ah, I think I see what you're doing. You're trying to use your hand movement to steer them, but you can't do two things at once that way. You need to start off with the stars angled as you want them" – he held up his own hand to demonstrate – "and then just throw them as if they were going to go straight. They'll spread on their own."

He flicked his wrist towards the target, and the stars flew out in two smooth arcs towards the edges of the board.

Eleanor adjusted her grip, took a deep breath, and tried again. It wasn't perfect, and only one of the stars caught properly in the target, but it was a definite improvement. She started to wonder, not for the first time, what was going on: Ivan wasn't acting like he was out to sabotage her. Yet she knew what she'd heard, and she couldn't afford to relax her guard for even an instant.

Chapter 31

Only Eleanor, Daniel and Jorge were summoned from their dinner. That could mean only one thing: it was time for them to learn what the task for their final contest would be. The messenger led them to the council chamber where Ragal was waiting, alone.

"I'm sure you know why you're here," he said. "The three of you are our remaining candidates for the council. This final contest could place any one of you into this year's seat. Seven days from now, on the shortest night of the year, you will settle this competition. Tonight, the council has finished defining the third and final contest."

The students looked at one another. For once, Jorge's typical arrogance looked dented; whether Ivan's words had sunk in, or simply his succession of third places had affected him, for the first time in the year he didn't look certain that he would win.

"The site for your mission will be the house of the ambassador from Taraska," Ragal continued. Eleanor felt the blood drain from her face. "The current ambassador here is the second son of the king, and we have reason to believe that the king is sending across plans for the new citadel being erected in Taraska La'on. Your challenge will be to bring back those plans. You will have from sunset to sunrise, if you need it, but you'll be racing one another more than the sun. The first candidate to return with the plans will be the winner, and will be co-opted onto the council with immediate effect. Good luck."

Daniel headed back towards the dining hall, but Eleanor was more interested in where Jorge was going. She slowed down, dropping a few steps behind him, but on this occasion he went straight back to his room. She was sure it wouldn't be long, though, before he went to ask Ivan's advice.

In fact, it was three days later that Jorge was mysteriously missing from the tracking lesson. As soon as the class split up to follow some trails, Eleanor crept off to see if she he was, indeed, visiting Ivan.

She walked up to Ivan's room, trying to look innocent as she passed Albert in the hall, and pressed her ear to the door.

"You might want to ask Raf about Taraska," Ivan was saying. "He's been there, so I'm sure he can tell you the sort of people they are."

"Raf's not on our side," Jorge said.

"What do you mean?"

"Raf wants *Ellie* to win."

"I suspect he just realises that she's in a much better position than you are – and between her and Daniel, I know who I'd choose."

"It's not about the current ranks." As usual, Jorge sounded put out. "He's been helping her since before the first contest."

"Well, worse things than Eleanor have happened to the council."

"But she's a girl!"

"She's a very competent woman."

"Why are you defending her?"

Eleanor found it very strange to listen to them talking about her. She wondered if Jorge's animosity towards her was still grounded in their earliest confrontations; he'd done a good job of ignoring her for most of the last two years.

"Because you continue to underestimate her. And until you acknowledge her strengths, you stand no chance of defeating her."

"But I thought you wanted me to win."

"That's the plan. Why do you think you're here right now? But, since you haven't yet convinced me you can pull this off, Eleanor is my fall-back."

"Are you helping her, too?"

"She doesn't need any help – which is why, if you forced me to make a bet, I'd put money on her. You've a hard job ahead of you."

Despite the strange circumstances of the compliment, Eleanor blushed. But what did he mean, she was his fall-back? Fall-back what? She tiptoed away from the door, head spinning.

What did it all mean? She'd been planning to go back to class, but somehow she didn't think she could face it. They'd barely miss her, and she'd learn more by taking a scouting trip into the city.

She locked herself in her room for two full days before the summer solstice, having first stocked her closet with bread, fruit and cheese. She knew she should be training, but although she made some half-hearted efforts at stretches and sit-ups, she found it hard to force herself to any meaningful exertion. Mostly she stared out of the window, and tried to talk herself into believing that the embassy guards wouldn't be as sadistic as the men who'd tortured her in the Tarasanka cells. *No*, said the voice in the back of her mind, *they'll probably just kill you if they catch you.* The thought wasn't terribly reassuring.

Not for the first time, she wished she could talk to Raf about her fears. He was the one person guaranteed to understand... but once she started to express her feelings, how could she guarantee that she wouldn't spill out her thoughts about Jorge and Ivan? She'd had enough trouble keeping quiet when she'd talked to him about normal things. No, it was safer not to talk to anyone until it was all over.

Eventually, the designated evening arrived.

As the sun began to dip she dressed in her favourite black work-clothes, scraped her hair back into a tight bun, and wrapped a dark scarf around her hair. Then she smeared dirt into her skin; if she needed to fade into the shadows, she couldn't afford to let her pale complexion give her away.

Once she was satisfied with her appearance, it was time to arm herself, more thoroughly than she'd ever done before: two stilettos in her wrist sheathes, throwing knives and daggers at both hips, a harping knife across her back, palm-blade strapped tightly in place, blowpipe tucked behind her ear, and a poisoned dagger sheathed safely out of the way inside her boot. Then there were the other tools. She prepared a small pack with throwing stars, lock picks, climbing spikes, a spool of fine wire, and vials of fast-acting poison, anaesthetic, and oil. She wrapped everything tightly in strips of fabric so her pockets wouldn't rattle. Finally, she looped a few yards of rope as a belt around her waist. Whatever challenges the night presented, she wanted to make sure she was properly equipped.

Unlike the previous contests, this time there was no-one officiating. There would be no grand send-off. Although she was sure Jorge and Daniel would be similarly preparing themselves as the sun dropped below the horizon, she wasn't even expecting to see them until they arrived back at the academy – assuming they all made it back safely. Ragal had been more than clear that the risks of the summer contest were the same risks they'd face in daily life in the Association. And given that this mission was linked to Taraska, Eleanor had no difficulty believing that death was one of those risks.

Satisfied that she was as ready as she'd ever be, she stepped out into the common room. Mikhail and Sebastien were playing dice and both studiously ignored her, keeping their eyes fixed on the game board until she'd left the room. She wondered if they'd speak to her again once it was all over. If not, at least she wouldn't be sharing her living space with them for much longer.

She left the Association's grounds by the same route she'd taken so many times with Raf and the others, emerging into a quiet Almont side-street. She glanced around, slightly troubled by the brightness of the moon's light, and as soon as she'd made sure she was alone on the street she pulled herself up the nearest wall and scrambled across the roof tiles towards the Marble Quarter.

She made her way quickly across the rooftops of the city, picking the easiest path between buildings; it wasn't the most direct route to her target, but it was certainly the least likely to raise suspicions, and she had high hopes of reaching the embassy – or at least a neighbouring roof – without detection. If anyone heard her rattle the tiles above their heads, she'd be well on her way before they had chance to rise from their beds, come out into the night, and climb up to look for her.

As she shuffled along one particularly narrow ledge, gripping the tiles for stability, she wondered what strategies Jorge and Daniel had adopted. She probably wouldn't find out until they all got back to compare notes. She had to try and forget about them, to focus her attention on the task at hand without worrying about the competitive element... but it would make hunting for the plans so much more of a challenge when it was impossible to be sure that one of the others hadn't already got them.

She'd taken a casual stroll past the ambassador's house a few days earlier, just to make sure she knew where it was, but everything looked very different from this level. Thankfully, the embassy building was topped with a gold dome just like so many of the towers in Taraska La'on, so it would be hard to mistake it against the typical square silhouettes of the native Charanthe buildings. Eleanor wondered if any builder in the Empire even knew how to make a roof stay up in that shape.

It started to rain just as she reached the edge of the embassy's roof. She shuffled across the tiles on her stomach, taking more care now not to generate any sound that might give her away, and moving more slowly to avoid slipping on the wet slates.

She'd hoped there might be a door in the side of the tower, but although she completed a careful circuit of the dome, there wasn't any sign of an entrance. It wasn't *that* much like the buildings in Taraska, then. She'd have to go down.

She looped the end of her rope around one of the antefixes which decorated the base of the dome and lowered herself off the edge, abseiling slowly until her head reached the level of the highest row of windows. Maybe that could be a way in... but there were bars at the windows which were embedded in the stone of the walls, and the bars certainly weren't set wide enough for her to squeeze between them.

A few feet beneath her, however, her eye was caught by a balcony running along half the length of the wall. That must have a door, there wasn't much point in having a balcony if you couldn't get in and out.

She ran out of rope just above where she needed to be and had to let herself drop onto the balcony, leaving the rope dangling above her, making a mental note to come back for it later.

She wasn't surprised that the doors leading off the balcony were locked; she'd have been disappointed at the lax security if they hadn't been. She pulled her lock picks out of her pack, and it didn't take her long to encourage the lock to open. She oiled the hinges to be sure of a quiet entrance and slipped inside, tucking her picks out of the way in her hair.

She was in a large hall which looked like it was probably some kind of reception room, empty aside from a few chairs, with strange, gaudy paintings on the walls. Paint seemed an odd alternative to tapestries – there was no way the paint would help to keep any warmth in the room – but maybe whoever had set up this place was proving a point about their wealth. Whatever it was, the designs painted along the walls didn't appeal to Eleanor's tastes at all, and she was quite glad to make her way out into the corridor.

It was dark in the halls, where there were no windows for the moonlight to filter through, but she hadn't brought any candles; she couldn't risk anything that might draw attention to her presence.

As she crept along, making sure every step was silent, she wondered where she was going. She'd made no plans beyond getting inside the building, and now she wondered whether she'd secretly doubted getting even this far. After Jon and Victor's failure last year, with her concerns about what Jorge and Ivan were up to, and given her fear and hatred of anything connected with Taraska – she'd certainly had plenty of things to worry about. In retrospect, she suspected her worries had stopped her from doing all she could have done to prepare. This was very different to the staged competitions in the academy, and she'd had a week to get herself ready for it. Most likely there was more she could have done.

She could feel panic beginning to take hold of her, and told herself not to be so silly. She was here; nothing else mattered. Levelling critical thoughts at herself wasn't going to help her stay alive, find the plans, and get out of here in one piece.

She had to work out where they'd keep something so important.

She thought back to the time she and Raf had escaped from the cell in Taraska. They'd found their identity bangles and her knife quite straightforwardly, but they'd been in the same part of the building to start with, and it wasn't clear that the guards thought those were important objects worth guarding.

Plans for a new citadel, though. Those had to be special. Why would anyone have sent them here to start with? That was probably key to where they'd be. Had they been sent for approval or for information, for action or for safekeeping?

Taraska and Charanthe coexisted only in uneasy truce, each prefering most of the time to pretend the other didn't exist, the 'anything goes' attitude of Tarasanka law enforcement contrasting sharply with the Empire's slew of regulations. It would be an odd decision to send the plans for a new citadel into what was almost enemy territory, and whatever the reason, they'd surely want to guard them well.

She tiptoed through the corridors, working her way systematically through the building, up and down stairs, examining the different floors as quietly as she could, always ready to hide if she heard anyone approach.

Eventually she found a door on the ground floor, at the end of a dark corridor, which had easily twice as many locks as any other she'd seen. That was promising. She pulled out her lock picks and went to work.

The locks were a strange design, with cylinders which clicked back into place as soon as she removed her picks; to get all the locks open simultaneously she had to wedge her tension wrenches in place in three of the locks, so she could work on the fourth and finally push the door open. The space beyond was pitch black, and she paused to light a small lantern.

A flight of stone stairs led down into the cellars beneath the house. Eleanor took each step carefully, expecting traps, but only one of the steps seemed to be sprung and she stepped over it easily.

The walls were hewn from the bedrock, and were covered in mossy growth. The air smelled damp and mouldy, and there was a cold draught coming from somewhere above her head as she made her way along the passageway. The path progressed for around a hundred yards before it forked, with branches running left and right. Eleanor dropped to her knees and examined the floor. The moss on the floor to her left was scuffed and slimy, whereas to the right it was undisturbed.

She followed the left-hand path, step by cautious step, wondering whether the ambassador – or at least his guards – were keeping watch on this place. It was hard to imagine they could see anything through the thick darkness of the underground passages. Maybe they really assumed their clever locks would be enough to deter intruders.

She heard the click at the same time as she felt the floor move under her foot; the air moved as something swished through the darkness towards her head, and flattened herself against the wall just in time. It swung back and forth, and when it eventually came to rest she reached out and found an axe hanging from a rope.

She took even more careful steps as she continued through the passage, but she still had to duck quickly out of the way of another two axes before she eventually reached another door.

After three more complex locks, she found herself in a cold, damp vault. The plans were laid out on a mahogany table, weighted down by four smooth rocks at the corners. Though she took a careful look around the room, dagger in her hand, there was no sign that any of the others had been here.

Eleanor glanced across the diagrams, satisfying herself that this did indeed appear to be what she was after, then she moved the rocks, folded the papers, and slipped them into her deepest pocket. She was about to make her way out of the vault when she heard a muffled footstep to her left. She recognised him even by his silhouette. Daniel. He stepped towards her into the light.

"Don't move," she hissed. She already had a dagger in her right hand and she poised it ready for throwing. There was no way he could get to her first.

"Eleanor," he breathed, sounding almost relieved.

"I mean it," she said. "One more step and I'll kill you. I haven't come this far to have you take it all away from me."

Then she heard another movement behind her and she spun quickly on her heel, stepping backwards towards Daniel, preferring to have her back to the opponent she knew rather than the approaching stranger.

Two more steps and her assailant was visible: Jorge was rushing towards her, dagger held high, murder in his eyes. In the next few moments, everything seemed to happen at once. Eleanor raised her throwing arm, but Daniel moved faster and before she could release the weapon he was past her, forcing her arm down, deflecting her blade and pushing her off-balance. As she steadied herself, she saw Daniel's hand plunge down towards Jorge's shoulder and watched as he fell heavily to the ground, clearly unconscious.

"I could have handled him!" Eleanor whispered crossly, not daring to raise her voice.

"You would have killed him," Daniel said. "Now, he will just sleep, and when he wakes he will know it is too late."

"What did you do?"

"Not much," he said. "Just a little soporific I have made – it is quick, but it does not last long. It should wear off well before dawn."

Eleanor wanted to ask why – why had he acted to protect her, why did he feel Jorge's life was worth saving, why hadn't he also drugged her as he passed her? – but she knew they didn't have time to get into a protracted discussion. Instead, she held up her knife, said: "That doesn't get you off the hook. I'll still kill you if I have to."

"This is not a competition." Daniel spoke firmly, looking straight back into her eyes, ignoring the blade. "It is not about proving you deserve to be here. It is not about whether you can beat me. It is about getting out of here alive – both of us."

"I got this far," she muttered bitterly. It was bad enough that he was here, without him suggesting that she might actually still be in danger now she had the prize in her grasp.

He paused for a moment, then: "Do you know why we are here?"

"What do you mean?"

"It is not a trick question. Do you know why we are here tonight?"

"To get the citadel plans, or to win this contest, depending on which way you look at it."

"That is only your reason for agreeing to come. Why do you

imagine the Taraskan king would send his secret citadel plans here?"

"Tarasanka."

"What?"

"It's Tarasanka, not Taraskan, that's the way words change in their language when – oh, never mind. I'm not sure why. His son, I suppose."

"His son does not need these plans. There is no good reason to send citadel plans to an enemy state. They would not do it. So why are we here?"

"Because, whether or not there's a good reason for it, the plans are here. And I assume the Association has some use for that information, though I wouldn't expect to know what they're going to do with it."

"On the contrary, I suspect the Association has no use for those plans, because those plans are not real. I believe the reason we are here is because the Taraskan authorities want us to be here. They would not really store important documents here, not even in a vault with such elaborate security."

"Why would they bother to set all this up around some fake documents?"

"To lure us into their trap, of course. Why would anyone store valuables in such an obvious place, when much more easily you could slip them unseen amongst the clutter everyday life? This place is like a signpost: *look, here are the important things you would like to steal*. They have taken every step to make sure it is easy for us."

Eleanor thought of the Code Tower trap which had ensnared Raf and so many of the others. "Do you think they're planning to ship us back to Taraska?"

"I have wondered, but I do not think it is important. We do not wish to find out. We need only to get out of here."

"What about Jorge?" She glanced at the mound of his body, rising and falling with heavy breaths. "We can't leave him here if it's a trap."

"A moment ago you would have killed him."

"He was trying to kill me! But what *they* do to you, that's much worse. Besides, think of the risks if they question him –

we're going to have to carry him."

Jorge had been a solidly built youth when he'd arrived at the academy, and over the past two years he'd only grown broader and more muscular. It took both of them to lift him, Daniel gripping his shoulders and Eleanor holding his legs. They carried him with some difficulty through the narrow passages and up the stairs leading back to the main embassy building. Once they came out through the multiply-locked door and into a normal corridor again, Eleanor paused and looked around, trying to regain her bearings.

"I came in from upstairs, but this looks like the most direct route out," she said, moving towards a nearby door.

"Wait!" Daniel hissed.

She stopped with her hand on the doorknob. "What?"

"That door was well guarded."

"Do you have a better plan? I don't fancy carrying that weight over the rooftops."

"I merely thought you should know. You are welcome to them."

Eleanor dropped Jorge's feet and grabbed a pair of knives. "Okay, here's what we're going to do. You keep him out of the way, and be ready to run when I give the word. You can carry him on your own for a few feet, can't you?"

"Yes."

"Good. But keep something aimed at the door – if any of the guards try to run this way, you'll need to deal with them before they can raise the alarm."

Daniel rolled Jorge's body over his shoulders, crouched against the wall, and pulled out a blowpipe. She didn't ask what he'd loaded in it.

She pushed open the door, flung both knives in parallel, and then two more. Three of the guards fell, one ducked out of the way, and a fifth barreled towards her and carried her back out the way she'd come in. She heard the pop of Daniel's dart, and felt herself falling as her awareness faded.

When she came to, the guard's body was trapping her leg, and Daniel was bent over her head.

"What's going on?" she asked, feeling strangely lightheaded.

She felt a slight pinch at her neck and he held up a dart. "I am sorry, I have caught you by accident. Do not worry, I have administered the antidote – you should feel no ill effects."

She pushed the body away from her. "Did you get the other one?"

He shook his head. "Just him. Come, then. If there were others we must move quickly."

They carried Jorge through the guard room, Eleanor stopping briefly to pick up her knives, and out into the street.

They paused to rest in a narrow alleyway, several streets away from the embassy building. Eleanor released Jorge's feet and stepped back.

"Well, I don't think we need to carry him all the way home. He should be safe enough here till he wakes up, shouldn't he?"

"He should wake soon," Daniel said. "He will be safe."

Chapter 32

Eleanor and Daniel returned to the academy in good spirits, filled with excitement and relief, unable to stop talking through their narrow escape. Dawn was breaking as they reached the academy's courtyard.

"Do you think we're supposed to report to someone?" Eleanor asked. "Or should we try to get some sleep?"

"I will not be sleeping," Daniel said. "There is too much thinking to do. But perhaps we could make a drink before we try too hard to report back."

They went up to the common room and put the kettle on the stove, keeping quiet so as not to disturb the others from their sleep. The water hadn't even boiled, however, before their peace was broken by a loud knocking. Sebastien and Mikhail both emerged half-dressed from their rooms, bleary-eyed, to see what was happening as Eleanor opened the door.

"Eleanor, Daniel," Andreas said. "Follow me. Your colleague has just returned, and he has some very serious allegations."

There was nothing in his tone to allow argument so the two students followed in silence, not daring to ask what allegations he was talking about.

Andreas led them into the council chamber, where a group of stony-faced men sat around a large oak table. Eleanor recognised some of the same faces from the previous time she'd been brought before the council; some were now more familiar from their time in the academy, others she hadn't seen before, and still others were missing. When she managed to catch Laban's eye he sent her a brief smile in greeting but made no open acknowledgement of her, and she wondered if he'd always be too afraid to acknowledge his part in her training. Ivan was carefully avoiding her gaze altogether.

"The students," Andreas said shortly, and gave a small bow before backing off to stand by the door.

"Thank you," Ragal said. He turned to Eleanor and Daniel. "I speak for the council in this matter. Do you know why you are here?"

Eleanor began "Andreas said..." but Daniel cut her off with a sharp "No."

"Your colleague Jorge has just returned from his attempt on the third mission," Ragal said. "He has given us some cause for concern, claiming that the two of you have been working together, and that you drugged him to ensure he could not succeed. What do you have to say in your defence?"

"I administered a soporific," Daniel said, "but Jorge was in no danger of completing the mission first. He was merely about to kill Eleanor."

"Merely?" she cried, and instantly regretted the outburst. Ragal was looking expectantly at her, eyebrows raised, clearly waiting for her version of the story. "Jorge attacked me," she confirmed. "If Daniel hadn't interfered, he wouldn't have made it back here to tell tales."

"I do not see that he can complain," Daniel said. "We even carried him out of the embassy. He was in no danger."

"Self-defence is reasonable, we have precedent for that," Ragal said. "What of the other charge?"

"*What* other charge?" Eleanor asked.

"Collusion."

She glowered at Daniel; this was all his fault. If he hadn't tried to help her, she wouldn't be standing here accused of cheating. But then, she reminded herself, softening, if they hadn't worked together against the guards then maybe neither of them would still be alive. And he was the only one who'd spotted the trap.

"Is it collusion that we both came back?" she demanded, emboldened by the memory. "Is it wrong, in your eyes, that we decided it was better to co-operate and succeed, than to fight each other and fail? Isn't it better that we helped each other?"

"It's unconventional."

"That may be," Daniel said softly, "but how can you say it is wrong?"

"There will be a vote of the council," Ragal decreed. "If you uphold Jorge's complaint, raise your left hand. If you support the defendants, raise your right hand."

Hands went up one by one; it was a close call.

Once he'd counted and re-counted, Ragal turned back to Eleanor and Daniel. "You are cleared," he told them. "I assume you have returned with the plans?"

Eleanor reached under her clothes and pulled out the papers.

"Today's result would appear to be a draw. Since you were each on six points already, with one victory each from the earlier rounds, we have a tie. You may decide between you who will join the council. If you cannot agree, you may fight."

Eleanor glanced at Daniel, their eyes locked briefly, and then both spoke at once.

"I will stand aside," said Daniel, at the same moment as Eleanor said, "We both deserve it."

"Eleanor has done more to earn this," Daniel said. "She has killed three guards to get us out of the embassy, and she was first to reach the plans. I am willing to stand aside."

Eleanor shook her head. "I won't let you do that. But I won't give up my right, either."

"You would prefer to fight?" Laban's voice was filled with cool astonishment.

The familiar sound of his voice reassured her even though he spoke coldly. Her resolve strengthened and she reached for her knife, the one he'd left for her all those years ago. It seemed appropriate. And let the others read what they would into the fact that she carried one knife with Laban's design instead of her own; it was too late for them to decide she didn't belong here.

The blade glinted as it flashed through the air, coming to a juddering halt in the table less than half a finger's width from Laban's resting hands. He looked up in surprise but she thought she caught a hint of approval in his eyes – it had, after all, been a very good shot.

"I will not fight," she said. "The council is being stupid. The fact that we're both here proves that Daniel and I are well-matched. We're both more than capable of inflicting a deadly blow if you demand it. Why would you choose two dead candidates over two live additions to the council? Give us both what we've earned."

"Impossible," Ragal said shortly, but Eleanor could see admiration creeping into the faces of many around the table. There would be another vote, she guessed, and that meant they needed more than half the room to agree.

"You changed the rules after last year's *fiasco*." She stared straight at Ivan as she spoke, selecting her words carefully to echo what he'd said to Jorge. She could never prove any sort of conspiracy, of course, but she hoped she wouldn't have to try. It should be enough to plant the possibility in his mind. "Last year, you decided none of your graduates were up to scratch. Allow yourselves a little common sense and one of us can fill last year's space."

She met Daniel's eyes again and she knew they were both struggling not to smile. It was hard to imagine how the council could argue against her.

Ragal looked down, apparently studying the backs of his hands. "We will vote," he said at last. "Does anyone have any questions first?"

Silence.

"If you agree to the girl's suggestion, raise your left hand. If you do not, raise your right."

Hands went up around the room; it was painfully close. Ivan hesitated, looking around at the others, then slowly lifted his left hand.

Ragal shrugged, not willing or able to contradict the will of the council. "Very well, then. Take your seats."

Eleanor shot a triumphant look at Daniel as they sat in two of the vacant chairs.

"As is traditional," Ragal continued, "your first duty is to nominate one of the new graduates to take care of this year's incoming students."

Eleanor and Daniel both said "Sebastien" at the same time, then looked at each other in surprise.

"He will be a good model for them," Daniel said.

Eleanor nodded. "And he won't scare them too much."

"Very well. You can inform him yourselves. The next issue

is that of your first mission. There is work that needs doing in Faliska. We'd planned that to be the first task for our newest member of the council, but we couldn't have anticipated this outcome. However, I think it's possible that you could travel together, if you were amenable."

They glanced at one another. "Okay."

"Your graduation dinner is tonight, of course, but you should plan to sail with the tide tomorrow evening. First, though, I expect you'll want some food, and probably sleep. You'll be briefed over lunch tomorrow."

With the meeting over they went down to breakfast on a high, jubilant from the day's second victory. Jorge wasn't at the table, though the way the room fell silent when they entered suggested the story might have got around.

Eleanor and Daniel sat together at one end of the table. They felt strangely distant from the rest of the students, more than the one or two empty seats which actually separated them. Something had changed during the night.

"Our last meal in the academy," Eleanor said, suddenly overcome with nostalgia. It felt a little bit like leaving school, but without the uncertainty. This time, they knew exactly what was coming next. "We're all done studying."

"There is always more to learn," Daniel said.

"Of course, but it'll be different now. I don't have to pretend to be competent with apothecary any more, I can just ask you."

"If you must."

She leaned in towards him so the others wouldn't overhear, then whispered, "But when are you going to tell the council what you suspect about those plans? You can't let them act on false information."

"There will be time tomorrow. I did not wish to complicate matters while we had yet to establish the result."

"Don't you think it was all too easy?"

"What do you mean?"

"The embassy."

"It did not seem so easy to me."

"We walked out of there." Eleanor helped herself to another sausage, ravenous after the night's exertions. "If they'd set all that up to trap us, why would they let us leave so easily?"

"You killed three of them. They could not have planned for that."

"Yeah, but if we hadn't needed to carry Jorge, we could've just gone out a different way."

"Tell me what you are thinking."

"Maybe they didn't just want us to go in. Maybe they wanted us to come out, with those papers."

Daniel shrugged. 'We will examine the plans tomorrow."

"But..."

"There is no sense in wasting our time with guesses."

Eleanor turned back to her food. She supposed he was right, but they'd given the plans to the council, and she didn't want to have to wait a whole day to find out if she was right. But it wasn't worth arguing about. She went straight to bed after they'd finished breakfast, with only a brief diversion to scrub the night's camouflage from her face. If she was going to be awake to enjoy the graduation dinner that evening, she needed to force herself to sleep despite the way the night's events kept replaying themselves behind her eyelids.

Daniel also went to his room, though he still claimed he wouldn't be able to rest. Eleanor suspected he might change his mind about that if he'd just get into bed.

She packed her weapons and tools into a travelling case as she undressed, ready for the next day's journey. Then, she slept.

She woke in the mid-afternoon, and there was no sign of any of the others when she peered out into the common room, so she finished her packing and then jogged across to the lake to use up some of the time before dinner.

As she completed her circuit and returned to her room, memories of previous dinners ran through her mind. This time, she was quite sure, Ivan wouldn't come to escort her. Whether or not he'd been involved in Jorge's decision to attack her – something she'd need to find out later – the outcome was exactly the opposite of what he'd wanted. And at some point he'd have questions about her accidental eavesdropping, but that wouldn't be tonight. She remembered his words from before the previous banquet: this night was for her to enjoy, there'd be more than enough time for politics later. The sentiment seemed equally applicable tonight.

She pulled all the fine clothes out of her closet and considered her options. She'd only worn her green dress so far – and as much as she loved it, it felt like time for a change. After a moment's deliberation, she settled on a dramatic black gown with an intricately beaded bodice.

All the students would be going across for the dinner. Eleanor wondered if she could avoid talking to Jorge and his Venncastle friends. She'd spent enough time with the Venncastle lads to know that, collectively, subtlety wasn't their strongest attribute – but she didn't want to spend her graduation dinner defending herself against second-hand allegations. If she could just avoid them tonight and tomorrow then she'd be off to Faliska with Daniel, and they'd have time to lose interest.

She brushed her hair straight and dabbed a little oil so that her lips glistened when she pouted into the mirror. She had to look perfect for her victory celebration. As she studied her face she realised how completely she'd become accustomed to her misshaped nose and her now-fading scars; she couldn't pinpoint the exact moment when her changed features had stopped horrifying her, but now every mark was just a part of her history. And maybe a stranger who'd never known how she used to look would simply assume she was born with that kink in the bridge of her nose.

Daniel and Sebastien were already in the common room when she stepped out; both were dressed in fine tunics of bright embroidered silk, Daniel in blue, Sebastien in red.

"Well, you clean up nicely!" Sebastien said as she came to join them, and she realised he hadn't seen her in a dress since the previous year's graduation night.

"You don't look so bad yourself. Are we waiting for Mikhail?"

"We were waiting for you," Daniel said, rapping sharply on Mikhail's door. "Mikhail is ready."

As they walked across to the banqueting hall they talked about various matters of no importance, carefully avoiding any mention of the fact that it had been months since they'd spoken.

411

Apparently the sequence of events which had pushed her and Daniel into co-operating had also been enough to absolve her. Maybe it was enough, in the eyes of the others, that Daniel seemed to have forgiven her. Well, she wasn't going to spoil the evening by talking about it.

In the hall, Daniel and Eleanor were waved across to where the rest of the council were sitting, while Mikhail and Sebastien were at the student table for the final time. Eleanor found herself seated between Bill, who grunted his congratulations, and a man she'd never met before, who shook her hand and introduced himself as Dek. From a few seats further down, Laban caught her eye and smiled as she took her place. As she helped herself to soup and a large glass of wine, for the first time since the morning's successes she felt herself swelling with pride at her achievement. So many of those around her had doubted she should even be at the academy, in the beginning; now, there could be no question she'd proved her worth.

After six courses and seemingly endless small-talk Eleanor left the table alone, hoping to creep away unnoticed while the others were still engrossed in the evening's celebrations. She'd made her appearance, and now she wanted some time alone to collect her thoughts. But Raf called out to her as she started along the path into the woods; he must've followed her from the hall.

"Ellie!"

She turned. "Oh. Hi."

"You don't sound thrilled." He looked hurt.

"I was preoccupied," she said. "I've had a hard day. I'm tired."

"I'll walk with you," he offered, and she knew there was no way to shake him off without hurting his feelings. "I won't keep you up – I just wanted to hear what happened."

"Didn't Jorge tell you?"

"Well, he told us his version. What – you think I'm automatically going to side with him? Is that what this is about?"

"What *what* is about?" she asked, exasperated. "I already told you, I'm tired."

"You're angry. Do you really think I'd just take his word over yours?"

She stopped walking and looked up at him, trying to read his face. "Venncastle loyalty, right?"

"Ellie! After what we went through together, you've earned just as much of my loyalty as anyone from school! If you don't *know* that..." He shrugged. "I don't know what to say."

"Then don't bother," she snapped, and turned to walk away, but he caught her elbow.

"Don't storm off. I want to hear your side of the story."

"He tried to kill me," she said, her voice little more than a whisper. "What more do you need to know?"

Raf's face shifted instantly into a look of pure rage. "I'll kill him!"

"You'll do nothing of the kind." She rested her hand on his arm. "We'll deal with it in council. I'll make sure he doesn't get off lightly."

He relaxed a little. "At least you got your council seat. How did they resolve the draw?"

"Well, Daniel offered to stand aside, but I wasn't going to let him."

"That's the silliest thing you've ever said," he laughed. "I'm glad you changed your mind."

She glared at him. "I didn't change my mind. I just insisted we should both have seats."

"You did what?"

"You heard me." She turned to start walking again, and this time he matched her pace.

"But – why?"

"Why not? It was the right thing to do."

"You just said he offered to stand aside. Why would you turn that down?"

"It would've been all wrong. He deserves it too."

"If he's stupid enough to offer–"

"Daniel's not stupid," she interrupted.

Raf laughed again, and she found herself wanting to slap him.

"I thought you hated him?"

413

"Well, he's an arrogant jerk." *Like you*, she added silently, still fuming. "But he's not stupid. And he deserves a seat on that council just as much as I do."

"You might both deserve it, but you needed it more. You've got more to prove."

"Because I'm a woman?" she asked, hoping her voice didn't betray the fury bubbling beneath the surface. How could he, of all people, say such a thing?

"Exactly."

"If that's what you think," she said, fighting back tears, "then you can think about it on your own. And if you've got an apology for me by the time I get back, I might just about be ready to hear it!"

She started to run, determined that he wouldn't reach out and stop her this time.

He called after her: "I didn't mean it like that, Ellie, you know I didn't. You know I don't think that! Ellie, wait!"

But she was in no mood for listening. She sprinted to the building and up to her bedroom, slamming the door behind her and jamming the chair under the handle so there was no way he could come in. It wasn't long before he caught up; he pounded at the door and called out to her, but she just buried her head under the pillow and tried to block out the noise.

Eleanor had almost finished packing when the messenger came to summon them. Daniel was already sitting in the common room, his cases stacked neatly by his chair.

"Albert will see you in the council chamber now," the messenger said, then left them without further instructions.

"Raf was here," Daniel said as they started to walk.

"What?"

"He was waiting when we got in last night."

Eleanor rolled her eyes. She'd just assumed he'd gone back to his own room once he'd stopped banging on her door, but evidently not.

"I am amazed he was not afraid to show his face, now we have all seen proof of the treachery of Venncastle."

Eleanor pressed her lips together. It was almost instinctive to jump to Raf's defence whenever Daniel complained about Venncastle, but now she didn't feel like defending him. So what if he hadn't known exactly what Jorge was planning? They were all the same.

"He said he was waiting for you," Daniel continued. "We made him leave. He will not trouble you again."

"Well, he's hardly going to follow us to Faliska."

She knocked at the door of the council chamber, and waited.

"Come in," Albert said. He was poring over a set of maps at one end of the table. "You don't have to wait to be asked, now you've graduated. Get some lunch, and then I'll show you where we need you to go."

Eleanor helped herself to a sandwich and went to look over Albert's shoulder.

"This is Faliska," he said, waving his hand across a huge swathe of the map. "I'm sure you can see why it's important to us."

"Taraska," Eleanor said. The city-state was nestled into a corner of Faliska's coastline.

"Precisely."

"It is a vast country," Daniel said.

"Three or four times the area of the Empire, we think, but most of it is empty desert. Almost every settlement is along this stretch of coast."

Eleanor picked up one of the larger scale maps of the area around Taraska. "But we're going to the capital of Faliska?"

"You'll take the boat to Faliska La'un in the first instance, yes. You'll be travelling with the Charanthe trade delegation, but at some point you'll probably need to break off and go further afield. No-one's quite sure what Taraska is planning, but we've reports of strange activity in the border regions."

"Our cover is to be traders?" Daniel asked. "But what are we to trade?"

"Well, the trade delegation are going out to negotiate new treaties. We set up one space for a weapons envoy, but we'll need a second trade area to account for Eleanor. Something where you know enough to be convincing."

"I could do cloth," Eleanor said. It was the only thing she

remembered the smugglers selling in Taraska.

"That's one of the real ones, I'm afraid."

"What are the others?"

"Gold and medicine."

"Ummm, then what about fish?"

Albert nodded. "That should be fine. Of course, neither of you will have the authority to actually agree any trades, but that shouldn't be a problem."

"And what will be our identities? Do you have new bangles for us?"

"Oh, Faliska's friendly enough. You should be safe to travel under your real names for this one."

Daniel looked unconvinced. "We should not be using our real identities for this kind of work."

"You'll be fine. It's not as if your identities mean anything to them. Now, we've put together a pack of notes for you to read on the boat – you'll have plenty of time. And obviously you'll make sure to lose the papers overboard before you get anywhere near Faliskan waters."

"And what if we encounter pirates?"

"The brief is coded – the pirates wouldn't get anything from it."

"The Magra aren't going to bother about a few scraps of paper anyhow," Eleanor said. "They're only interested in collecting their tax."

Albert stared at her. "Tax?"

"That's how they see it. If you want to pass through their waters, they want their cut. But they don't care what business we've got in Faliska."

"Well, that's all you really need to know. Take as long as you need to study the maps, and the boat will leave with this evening's tide. You need to leave everything tidy – we'll need your rooms for the new students before you get back."

Albert got to his feet to leave, and Eleanor elbowed Daniel so hard that he dropped his plate. He bent to the floor to pick up the pieces, leaving Eleanor to deal with Albert's surprise.

"Before you go, there's a message we'd like to pass to the council," she said, glaring at the top of Daniel's head as he continued to clear the floor meticulously. "Daniel has a theory about those plans we got from the Tarasanka embassy."

"Oh?"

"He thought it was all a bit easy... we wondered whether the plans were some kind of trap."

Daniel got to his feet, hands full of pottery fragments. "Do not act without considering their intentions."

"We'll bear that in mind," Albert said. "Now, if you'll excuse me, I have a class to teach."

"Fish?" Daniel asked as the door swung closed behind him. "How can you be envoy for fish?"

"Well, I spent so long on boats, fishing for my supper–"

"I do not mean that you lack the knowledge. But fish is not traded. It could not be."

"Well, that's what makes it perfect – we're not supposed to agree any trades. That'll make my job easy."

She turned back to the maps and they spent a little longer committing the details to memory, then went to finish packing their things. It was strange to imagine that some other students would be living in their rooms by the time they returned to the Empire.

As their cart trundled towards the port, Eleanor ran through her story again and again in her mind. Fish envoy. Now there was an assignment she never would have imagined for herself.